BED OF NAILS

BED OF NAILS

MICHAEL SLADE

PENGUIN
CANADA

PENGUIN CANADA
Published by the Penguin Group
Penguin Books, a division of Pearson Canada, 10 Alcorn Avenue, Toronto, Ontario,
Canada M4V 3B2
Penguin Books Ltd, 80 Strand, London WC2R 0RL, England
Penguin Putnam Inc., 375 Hudson Street, New York, New York 10014, U.S.A.
Penguin Books Australia Ltd, 250 Camberwell Road, Camberwell, Victoria 3124, Australia
Penguin Books India (P) Ltd, 11, Community Centre, Panchsheel Park,
New Delhi – 110 017, India
Penguin Books (NZ) Ltd, cnr Rosedale and Airborne Roads, Albany, Auckland 1310,
New Zealand
Penguin Books (South Africa) (Pty) Ltd, 24 Sturdee Avenue, Rosebank 2196, South Africa

Penguin Books Ltd, Registered Offices: 80 Strand, London WC2R 0RL, England

First published 2003

1 3 5 7 9 10 8 6 4 2

Copyright © Headhunter Holdings Ltd., 2003

*Publisher's note: This book is a work of fiction. Names, characters, places and incidents
either are the product of the author's imagination or are used fictitiously, and any
resemblance to actual persons living or dead, events, or locales is entirely coincidental.*

Printed and bound in Canada

NATIONAL LIBRARY OF CANADA CATALOGUING IN PUBLICATION

Slade, Michael
Bed of nails / Michael Slade.

ISBN 0-14-301383-1

I. Title.

PS8587.L35B43 2003   C813'.54   C2003-901638-2
PR9199.3.S55115B34 2003

American Library of Congress Cataloguing in Publication Data Available

Visit Penguin Books' website at **www.penguin.ca**

*For the
World Horror Conventioneers—
Seattle, Chicago, Kansas City*

PART I
TIME MACHINE

Two little whores, shivering with fright,
Seek a cozy doorway in the middle of the night.
Jack's knife flashes, then there's but one,
And the last one's the ripest for Jack's idea of fun.

—Anonymous, 1888

RIPPER

As I draw the knife across her neck, the clock strikes one, a single *bong* from St. Mary's Whitechapel, here in the East End. The chime echoes into Dutfield's Yard from Berner Street, where it mingles with the sounds of reverie coming from the International Working Men's Educational Club. Saturday nights are open house at the club, and as a political debate on "The Necessity for Socialism among Jews" has ended, an impromptu singsong is under way. The club is a gathering place for Russian, Polish and German Jews displaced by the pogroms of eastern Europe, and here among close to a million people living in abject filth and squalor in the slums of London, those refugees have found sanctuary. Their sexual urges are serviced by twelve hundred whores who ply their trade in the dingy streets, one of whom I have lured into this pitch-black court, where the blood streaming out of her slashed throat now gushes onto the cobblestones of Dutfield's Yard.

Clop . . . clop . . . clop . . .

Horse's hoofs.

Someone's coming.

Berner Street runs south from Commercial Road. Dutfield's Yard opens west off Berner Street. The yard narrows behind a pair of large wooden gates, which are still angled open so the stragglers singing in the club can exit to the street. The club occupies the right-hand side of the court, facing the terraced cottages of sweat-shop tailors and cigarette-makers. To enter the court, you grope your way for twenty feet through a shroud of darkness that lies between the blind walls just inside the gates. Farther in, lights glimmer from the upper-story windows of the club onto the cottage roofs, but that seems only to intensify the gloom in the rest of the yard.

Clop . . . clop . . . clop . . .

The horse draws nearer. It's pulling a cart down Berner Street from Commercial Road.

Approaching wheels trundle over paving stones.

With no time to rip her, I dart into the angle between the gate and the club's blind wall.

Clop . . . clop . . . clop . . .

The horse turns into the yard.

Through cracks between the boards of the gate, I watch the driver enter on his pony cart. It is lighter out in Berner Street than it is within the court, and though the gas lamps have been extinguished for the night, I recognize the silhouette as that of a Jew who sells cheap jewelry by day and works as steward of the club by night. Suddenly, the pony shies away to the left, almost pitching the hawker forward onto his head. The Jew tries to urge the frightened pony to pull straight, but the reluctant animal balks at obeying the command. The pony is more afraid of me than it is of the bleeding whore.

Still seated on the trap just inside the gates, the hawker jabs at the cobblestones with his long-handled whip, and when he pokes something soft and yielding with its tip, he jumps down from the cart and strikes a match for a closer look.

Knife in hand, I plan to stab him if he looks this way.

Those sulfurous fogs—"London particulars"—don't aid my hunt tonight, but it is wet and windy enough to serve this Jack. I can see what the swag dealer sees by the guttering glow of that match, and it thrills me to wait for wide-eyed horror to twist his face.

The whore's name is Long Liz Stride. Gaunt and scraggy, she's a big, raw-boned woman, wasting away from hunger. Crumpled near the wall, she could be a pile of clothes: a black worsted jacket trimmed with fur over a dress of rusty black sateen. The jacket and bodice beneath are unbuttoned down her breast—as you expect with a common wench—but I had no time to dishevel the garments below. She lies across the yard on her left side, her legs in white stockings drawn up and her feet in spring-side boots against the wall. Her right arm, its hand slick and bloody, is over her stomach. Her left arm extends behind her back, its hand clutching a packet of cashews. Her bare head rests almost in line with the carriageway, and her white crepe bonnet is mired in the mud.

A *fallen* woman.

Ha ha!

Jack's idea of fun.

Perhaps the Jew thinks Liz is drunk. He reaches out to touch her face. The dead don't come any warmer than her, and the flickering flame of the match seems to burnish her with life. Her facial features are sharp and pinched. She looks much older than her forty-odd years. All the teeth are gone from her lower left jaw, a detail exposed by her gaping mouth. The Jew's fingers drop to the silk scarf around her neck, its checked bow tugged tightly to one side from when I cinched it sharply to stifle any cry. The bottom edge got frayed as my knife slit her throat, severing her windpipe and one carotid artery. Abruptly, a puff of wind snuffs the match, but not before the gawking hawker has light enough to see blood hemorrhaging out of the fresh wound.

Up he jumps.

Off he dashes.

That glimpse should send him screaming bloody murder into the club.

I escape up the street. Tonight will have to be a double event. September 30, 1888. A night London will remember for a long time. First came Polly Nichols, on August 31. Then came Annie Chapman, on September 8. Now Elizabeth Stride has fallen to my knife. Who will be next to face Jack the Ripper in this, my autumn of terror?

My cape billows around me as I run west toward Aldgate. Drizzle collects in the brim of my top hat and overflows in my wake. The streets of the East End form an intricate maze, but I'm familiar with their many twists and turns. Rows of rotting houses slip by on my flanks as I weave through the passages and courts with interconnecting alleys that are the crumbling ruins of forgotten slums in this dark metropolis. Only the main roads glow with gaslight, and even there the small lamps glare hundreds of yards apart. The shadows I cast swallow up chunks of their sickly illumination.

Whitechapel is a slag heap of humanity. Smoke begrimes its brick cliffs, which are pockmarked with grubby windows. Crammed cellar to roof behind each sooty facade is a welter of rags, refuse and disease, open sores and bestial faces. Beggars, thieves, fraudulent tricksters and middle-aged drabs pack into vermin-ridden doss-houses for the night, while those who can't afford four pence for a bed are turned out to fend for themselves in the mean streets. Outside, after dark, the East End is one vast brothel in which tired, broken-spirited harlots offer gin-puffed lips and sagging flesh to any man who wants them for a few pennies or a crust of stale bread. They trudge the cobblestones in hobnailed boots, their only homes the garments on their backs and their only possessions the measly items stuffed in their pockets.

Whores ripe for ripping with Jacky's hungry knife.

Come and get it, luv.

Who'll be next?

The smell of blood is in the air of my destination. Also known as Butcher's Row and Blood Alley, Aldgate is home to the slaughter-houses and offal dumps that serve genteel Victorian London. So overloaded with death are the abattoirs that the killing of animals is also carried out in the streets. My nostrils flare and my lungs fill as I close on Mitre Square, for bloodlust fuels my occult quest.

I spot her as I turn up Duke Street from Aldgate. In the pub beside me, tipsy women dance on the sawdust-strewn floor of a raucous, rowdy bar, kicking up their legs to flash their frilly bloomers amid a chorus of appreciative hoots from the soused men. The whore staggers down Duke Street on unsteady feet, so I slow my pace to encounter her at the mouth of Church Passage into Mitre Square. I know this square, and it's a good place for ripping.

The time is just after one-thirty on Sunday morning. Mitre Square is half a mile west of Dutfield's Yard. I met other whores along the way as I detoured from there to here, but they were in the *wrong* place at the right time. If I'm to project myself into the astral plane, if I'm to breach the barricade to the other realm, I must sacrifice life at the final point of the cross.

I must kill here, at the *right* place.

And I must do it quickly, for a police constable patrols through the square every fifteen minutes.

One-thirty saw him pass.

One-forty-five will see him return.

An odor of cheap gin wafts from the tart as we come face to face. Addiction to the bottle has ravaged her. She's in her mid-forties, but she looks sixty to me. I'm several inches taller, so I gaze down on her bonnet of black straw trimmed with black beads and black-and-green velvet. Her black cloth jacket has a fake fur collar and three large metal buttons. The dress beneath is of a dark green print, patterned with Michaelmas daisies and golden lilies.

"'Allo, old cock," she slurs. "A shilling for m' cunny?"

I tip my hat.

I flash a smile. I yearn to flash my knife.

Instead, I hold up a shiny coin to lure her into the passage.

"What's your name?" I inquire.

"Kate," she replies.

Narrow, covered Church Passage runs between a synagogue and a school, from Duke Street to Mitre Square. Separated by another corridor in from King Street, the warehouses of the tea merchants Kearley and Tonge line the two sides of the quadrangle immediately to our right. Across the square, straight ahead, is the broad opening that exits out to Mitre Street beyond. To its left, three unoccupied cottages form a blind corner that's the darkest nook in the empty, lonely square. That's where I lead Kate to transact business.

Here, a high fence seals off a hidden yard. The ground is too dirty to fuck me lying down, so the whore leans back against the planked wall to service me standing up. Reaching down to grab her lower garments by the hems, she hikes up her dress, along with her drab linsey skirt, her dark green alpaca petticoat and her grubby white chemise. I glance down to glare at what she offers me. She wears no drawers or stays above brown ribbed, knee-high stockings and laced men's boots, so I take in the slack flesh of her pale, bare belly.

"M' shilling?" she says.

"From hell," I reply.

That's when I seize her by the neck to squelch any cry. My hands grip her relentlessly until she passes out. Her pockets contain everything she owns in this world, and as she jerks, a thimble and a metal box clatter to the cobblestones. Pushing her to the ground so her head angles left, I draw the knife from beneath my cape with my right hand. Yanking the blade across her, I slice through the vessels on just one side of her neck so the initial spurts of arterial blood are directed away from me and my clothes. The seven-inch slash cuts so deep that I feel the blade scrape across buried bones. Around her neck she wears a ribbon and a piece of old, coarse white apron in place of a scarf. The blood gushing out of her turns the white band ochre.

In a frenzy, I go to work on her face. Light from the warehouse across the square glints off the steel blade as it crisscrosses through her features. It slits both eyelids. It nips off the tip of her nose. It gashes over the nasal bridge and angles down to her jaw. It peels triangular skin flaps from both cheeks. It widens her open mouth in a grisly grin. It clefts her upper lip down to one incisor tooth. It—

Clomp . . . clomp . . .

What's that?

Out in Mitre Street?

Clomp . . . clomp . . .

Nearer!

Approaching the gap to the square.

This time, it's not the *clop, clop* of horse's hoofs.

Instead, it's the *clomp, clomp* of flat feet.

PC Watkins, walking his beat?

Is it one-forty-five already?

My, how time flies when you're having fun.

Again, there's no time to rip her, but rip her I must. She's the right person in the right place at the right time. So, careful to avoid the pool of warm blood creeping across the pavement, I kneel over the dead whore and cleave my knife into her belly just above the pubic bone. Clutching the garments she raised for me with my other hand, I shove them up so they bunch on her chest as the blade begins to rip, shearing up her abdomen like the sound of a torn sheet. To make sure she's open, I stick and rip her several times, the steel angling and cutting upward to her sternum.

Clomp . . . clomp . . .

Faster!

Seconds count!

The constable is entering the square. The rays from his bull's-eye lantern precede him as he turns in from Mitre Street. The footsteps that herald him echo behind my back. Lamplight spilling across the pavement borders the dark nook of the southwest corner, where I'm still ripping the whore.

Out come her intestines.

I heave the slimy entrails across her right shoulder.

My haste in disemboweling her severed loose a two-foot coil that flops with a telltale splat onto the cobblestones between her left arm and her body.

The smell of shit fouls my nostrils as I grip with both hands and pull her apart like curtains.

I know anatomy.

I grope around inside her.

A slice here, a slice there, and out comes her left kidney.

The cop is in the square.

I can tell by the dimming of the lantern's light that the bull's-eye swings away.

A horizontal cut through the membrane over the uterus enables me to yank out her womb.

Yes, that does it!

I've signed the cross in blood.

And through that occult symbol, I've opened the path to the astral plane!

The bull's-eye is turning.

The lamplight now swings this way.

And what its glow reveals to the startled bobby is Jacky's bloody art. The whore lies sprawled on her back, with her head inclined

11

toward her left shoulder. Head to the wall, her feet are to the square. Her bonnet is still tied in place. Her throat yawns open from her right lobe across to behind her left ear. Blood is pooled on the pavement around her left shoulder and upper arm. Blood streams under her neck and flows away with the ground slope. With both palms up, the fingers slightly curled, her arms lie at her sides as if feeling the air for rain. Her left leg extends in line with her body. Her right leg is bent at the thigh and knee. Organs disarrayed, and two of them missing, her belly is ripped open like a pig's in the market.

What the lamplight doesn't reveal to the constable is *me*. Opening the path to the astral plane allows my consciousness to fly through space and time, to intercept vibrations from the occult realm and ritually alter the wavelengths to change the here and now. *Quod superius, sicut inferius.* "As above, so below." That's how reality works. The basic law of Magick.

Watkins blows his whistle.

He is summoning help.

But Jack the Ripper no longer kneels in Mitre Square.

I have dematerialized into the mist that swirls around the body of the whore, around the grimy streets of Whitechapel.

The lamplight catches her.

It doesn't catch me.

For I am streaking along the wormhole that burrows through space and time, heading thousands of miles west from London's East End and more than a century forward from 1888, until once again I am safe in my hideout here at Colony Farm.

I have the kidney.

I have the womb.

And I'm home in time for dinner.

LUNATIC

Port Coquitlam, British Columbia
November 1

The eeriest mile on the West Coast was no longer eerie. It used to be that you would drive inland from Vancouver and turn south off the highway onto sinister Colony Farm Road. The farm was wedged into one crook at the junction of the Coquitlam and Fraser rivers, and the spooky road cut through the foggy flatlands along both flanks to reach what was then the Riverside Unit for the criminally insane. Colony Farm dated from 1905, a period when the principal causes of insanity were thought to be heredity, intemperance, syphilis and masturbation. Work therapy was in vogue as a cure for lunacy, so the government purchased a thousand acres way out here in God's country as a place to work the loonies. Essondale was the name of the asylum built on the slope of Mount Coquitlam to the north; through its bars the locked-up inmates had a river view. Parents who wished to frighten their kids away from "self-abuse" would threaten to send them to Essondale.

Essondale.

Does that not *sound* like a loony bin?

The "work" in "work therapy" was done on the flatlands below. A 450-acre patch was diked and ditched as Colony Farm, and by 1911, the slave labor at Essondale was producing more than seven hundred tons of crops and twenty thousand gallons of milk. Colony Farm was described as having "the best-equipped barns, stables, dairy equipment and yards in Canada, if not the continent."

Befitting that picture-postcard image, a line of elm trees was planted along one side of the road that bisected the farmland.

The Second World War saw major advances in treating the insane. Electro-convulsive shock therapy—ECT—was introduced in 1942. One hundred and thirty-eight Essondale patients were strapped to restraining chairs the following year. With gags wedged between their teeth so they wouldn't bite off their tongues and electrodes taped to their temples to zap in therapeutic juice, their brains were cooked to unscramble their minds. Psycho-surgery arrived in 1945. Disruptive inmates were treated by neurosurgeons who lobotomized them, cutting the bad chunks from their troubled gray matter. Insulin shock was used to plunge others into a chemical coma.

Now do you feel better?

A new facility built at Colony Farm was intended to house veterans injured in the war. The complex, however, was never used for that. Instead, Essondale was revamped in the postwar years. The asylum on the mountain became Riverview, and the war vets' hospital a mile away on the miasmic flats spreading out to the Fraser became the Riverside Unit for the criminally insane. There, only the spookiest psychos were caged at the end of the eeriest mile.

Riverside.

Does that, too, not sound like a madhouse?

The rising moon beamed down on the flats as the black van turned off the highway onto Colony Farm Road. If the Goth had driven across this lonely marsh a few years ago, it would have seemed as if Halloween had summoned its monsters and demons here after last night's festivities. Leaves shedding from the skeletal limbs of the overhanging elms would have tumbled about the windshield for the entire mile. The fleeting form of a werewolf might have lurked in the jerky shadows between the tree trunks, its chilling howl masked by those of local coyotes baying at the full moon. And surely those wisps exhaled by the murky marsh were ghosts haunting the graveyard of some forgotten tribe, for the bank at the end of this road was an Indian reserve.

The farm, however, had not been worked for many years. That neglect had resulted in ditches not being drained, which had resulted in water rotting the roots of the towering elms, and that in turn had brought several crashing down across the road. It was only a matter of time until someone got crushed, so the government had been forced to fell all but a few of the trees. Consequently, the eeriest mile had lost its creepy shadows, and the road the Goth drove tonight was a wide-open space of moonlit grass, thistle and bramble mats.

Gone, too, was the brooding haunted house.

Its back to the dikes along the polluted Fraser River, the Riverside Unit for the criminally insane had exuded an ominous mood. On a full-moon night like tonight, the light of lunacy would shine down upon the three floors of that dual-winged snake pit. Through the crosshatched bars in rows of darkened windows would glare the eyes of freaked-out men trapped inside, accompanied by screams from those with cooked and cut-up brains. Black crows perched along the eaves of the flat roof would caw at cars that ran the gauntlet of the eeriest mile.

But no longer.

For Riverside was rubble.

All that remained of the booby hatch that housed the damned in a not-so-distant past was an empty, overgrown lot behind a chain-link fence. Sixty million dollars—that's what it had cost to construct the new Forensic Psychiatric Hospital at Colony Farm. Built not a stone's throw away from the old asylum, FPH resembled a gated residential enclave in an upscale rural neighborhood. Sixteen buildings set in seven and a half landscaped acres surrounded by fields, like those around the lot out front, where the Goth parked the van.

A walkway approached a gate wrought out of vertical bars and a connecting circle. Beyond the gate stretched green lawns, with Fir Hall located in the center. There, patients went to school and attended chapel. Radiating from the hub of the hall, spoke-like paths joined it to residences ringed around the wheel's rim: the Birch Unit, the Cottonwood Unit, Dogwood House, and such. This side of the gate, the walkway was bordered by the Golden Willow administration building on the left and Central Control in the Birch Unit opposite. Hidden behind Central Control was Ashworth House, where the hospital's high-security psychos were confined. Ash 2 had the wards reserved for the homicidal maniacs of FPH. Ash 2 was the destination of the Goth.

Everything about FPH bored the Goth to death. Just the occultist's luck to be trapped in such an insipid era, when all aspects of dark mystery were bled from life and in their stead was substituted pablum for the mind. Milieu therapy. That's what this snooze of a pleasant, peaceful place had devolved into. A curse upon these banal, mundane times. Gone were those malevolent trees haunting the eeriest mile. Gone were those caws of "Nevermore!" from dark ravens on Poe's House of Usher. Gone were those gibbering screams from brains mutilated in the name of weird science.

Gone, gone, gone . . .

So that's why the Goth was here.

—— • ——

While the Goth was clearing security at Central Control, a nurse named Rudi Lucke was making rounds in Ashworth 2, checking the patient rooms on both ground-floor wards. Five staff worked the three-to-eleven shift, and each knew from past experience that tonight would be more testing than usual. The word "lunatic" had been removed from the Mental Hospitals Act in 1940, but as with later attempts at political correctness, that didn't exterminate lunacy from real life. For whatever reasons—psychological, physiological or a mix of both—patients committed to mental hospitals worldwide got more agitated or psychotic on nights when the lunar disk was full.

Nights like tonight.

Yorick wasn't the real name of the man in A2-5. The name on the card in the holder beside the door was "Burton, Percy." First name last, last name first.

"We call him Yorick," Rudi said, "on account of the skull."

The remark was aimed at the young nurse who accompanied Rudi on rounds. A recent arrival from the outback of Australia,

Jock Ogilvie had been commandeered from Ash 1, the wing responsible for assessing any unstable accused remanded by courts to see if they were fit to stand trial. On full-moon nights, extra muscle was imported into Ash 2, the higher-security ward that treated NCR-MDs, those determined by law to be Not Criminally Responsible on account of Mental Disorder. The Australian bodybuilder dwarfed Rudi and was the perfect muscle for the job.

"Listen," Rudi said, cupping an ear.

A stentorian voice boomed so loudly from A2-5 that there was no need for Jock to amplify.

"Alas, poor Yorick. I knew him, Horatio—a fellow of infinite jest, of most excellent fancy . . ."

"Recognize it?"

"No."

"Shakespeare's *Hamlet?*"

"Sorry," said Jock with a shrug of his gorilla shoulders. "Not my cup of tea."

"*Hamlet.* Act V. The graveyard scene. The prince of Denmark and Horatio are onstage when gravediggers accidentally unearth a skull. The skull is that of Yorick—"

"Is Hamlet the Danish prince?"

Rudi blinked. Were there actually people in this world who didn't know that? "Yes," he said evenly, like he did with the vacuous patients. "Hamlet's the prince."

The Aussie smiled, pleased with himself. Brawn but no brains, Rudi thought.

"Hamlet takes the skull and holds it out in his hand. Peek through the door, Jock. What's Yorick doing?"

The door to room A2-5 was blue. Though the wing was sealed, the doors in this ward were unlocked. FPH was a hospital, not an asylum, so patients were free to leave their rooms at will (under the watchful eyes of the nurses stationed at one end of the hall) to go to the communal toilets, the kitchen and dining room, the TV room, the smoking room and the quiet room for reading. Rounds were made every half-hour to ensure all was well, the procedure being that a nurse would stroll the lengths of both wards to take a surreptitious peek through the judas window in each patient's door.

"Christ," said Jock, peeking in. "Is that skull real?"

"The original was. That's why Yorick's here."

The Aussie bent closer for a better look through the window.

"Yorick was a local actor who couldn't land the role of Hamlet. In Shakespeare's play, Hamlet holds out the skull of the jester who used to entertain the royal court. The prop ignites the prince's thoughts on death and mortality. Yorick convinced himself that a genuine skull would help him master the role, so he rushed to the apartment next door and decapitated his neighbor. He cooked the head in a pot on the stove to boil away the flesh. When police arrived to investigate a complaint about the smell, they found Yorick rehearsing the graveyard scene. Addressing the dripping skull of his headless neighbor, he was delivering the 'Alas, poor Yorick' lines."

"And *this* skull?" Jock asked.

"Plastic," Rudi replied. "We purchased it at a Halloween store. It keeps Yorick happy."

Five inches wide by three feet tall, the window was a vertical slit through the door. Positioned off-center, near the handle, it gave Jock a view of the entire room except for the corner by the hinges. The lights were out and moonbeams slanted in through the opposite window. A thin, naked man stood silhouetted against the lunar glow. He held the plastic skull out at arm's length in one hand so that the skeletal features of the prop faced him. As the thundering thespian recited Hamlet's speech, his other hand was engaged in "self-abuse."

"How abhorred my imagination is!" Yorick hammed with gusto. "My gorge rises at it. Here hung those lips that I have kissed I know not how oft."

Crushing the lipless teeth of the skull against his own slobbering mouth, the patient in A2-5 engaged in passionate French kissing with the prop. The overpowering ecstasy of mastering the bard prompted Yorick to explode in an anticlimactic climax.

"He shoots, he scores," Jock reported.

Sports held no interest for the older nurse. Rudi's self-image was that of a sensitive, artistic, thinking man.

"I can't make out the writing on the wall," Jock said.

"That's where Yorick scrawled his last will and testament."

"He's got stuff to leave?"

"His skull," Rudi explained.

"The plastic prop?"

"No, Jock. The real skull inside his head. He bequeathed it to the playhouse to use in performances after his death. In the end, Yorick will appear onstage in *Hamlet*."

"Humph," Jock grunted. "He's really out of his head. I'll bet he's the most psychotic patient in Ash 2."

"No," said Rudi. "That would be the Ripper."

While the Goth was being led from Central Control in the Birch Unit out front through a series of high-tech security doors to an interview room in Ashworth House, Rudi and Jock rounded the V-angle in Ash 2 to check the other open ward.

"Phew!" Jock recoiled. "What's that stink?"

"The Mud Man," Rudi said, nodding toward room A2-12.

"The *Madman?* You call him that?"

"The *Mud* Man," Rudi repeated, taking more care with his diction the second time.

Jock peeked through the window.

"Oh, I see," he said.

"We'll clean him up later. Once he's through re-sculpting his face with his evening shit."

The way Rudi saw it, this was outer space, these two wards with eleven beds each angled out from the nursing station like a pair of horns. The station was positioned in the crook of the V so its cockpit windows could watch both halls for alien trouble. Twice an hour, one of the nurses left the module for a spacewalk out here among these monsters.

"Room 13," Rudi said, approaching the next door. "That's where the Ripper hides when he's here."

Jock eyed the last and first names on the card in the slot for A2-13. "Why's he called the Ripper?"

"You don't recall the case? It made headlines around the world a few years back."

Jock had been off on he-man junkets in the outback of Australia, crocodile-wrestling atop Ayers Rock or some such acts of derring-do. He'd come to B.C. as a foreign nurse, lured by the government's recent recruitment scheme. The pay was good, and there were new challenges to conquer in a sportsman's paradise.

"I don't read the papers."

"Oh," said Rudi, not surprised. "In that case, I'd better fill you in. It happened on Deadman's Island, miles off the West Coast. You've read Agatha Christie's *And Then There Were None*?"

Jock shook his head.

Rudi shook his too. This hunk with the sun-bleached hair infused with new meaning the term "dumb blond." Were there actually people in this world who hadn't read—or seen—the best whodunit ever written? The story had been filmed at least four times.

"Inspired by that book, the Ripper invited thirteen guests— mostly writers—to a mystery weekend at a secluded hideaway, then he killed them off one by one in gruesome ways so he could precipitate a great occult event."

"What ways?" Jock asked.

"Ingenious booby traps. A good example is the hogger. You know how a deli cuts meat with a slicing machine? Well, the Ripper rigged a corridor with a series of spring-activated knives hidden in horizontal slits along the walls. The floor stepped down several inches every two feet. A guest chased the Ripper into the gallery. On reaching the far end of the hall, the Ripper flipped a switch that turned each terrace into a pressure plate. Stepping on one snapped a razor-sharp sickle from one of the slits in the walls, and because the floor was terraced, each blade whacked off a thicker chunk. Forward momentum hacked the pursuer's legs down to stumps, and when the amputee toppled, his hands and arms were reduced too. Unable to support himself, he pitched onto his face. That was sliced off by the final blade."

"Human salami," Jock said.

"Diabolical, eh?"

"What great occult event did he hope would result?"

"Astral projection."

"Huh?"

"Come on. I'll show you."

Rudi ushered Jock into the Ripper's private room. Stepping across the threshold, the younger nurse flicked on the overhead lights, which were recessed into the ceiling so they couldn't be broken. The space measured six feet across by ten deep. A bed with a brick headboard at one end was bolted to the wall in the far left corner. Beneath the window opposite the door, a plain shelf with no drawers served as a desk. An open cupboard with no hangers stood in the blind corner behind the door. Because no other furnishings were permitted in Ash 2, piles of books were stacked on the bare floor. The books covered subjects as diverse as the history of Jack the Ripper and modern astrophysics. Photos, maps, charts and calculations culled from their pages were arranged in a series of juxtaposed collages that papered the cinder-block walls.

"Weird," Jock said, following the mural from the space beside the headboard around to the facing wall. "It looks like some kind of tunnel from here to there."

"Or from there to here," Rudi added.

"I don't get it."

"See how it's arranged? Those scribbles on the wall beside his pillow are Einstein's theory of relativity and notes from Hawking's *A Brief History of Time*. They lead into the tunnel from this end. The tunnel is a mishmash of occult symbols that spiral across to the other wall. That end of the tunnel is fashioned from a deck of tarot cards. The map feeding into it charts the East End of London in 1888. Marked on the map are the five crime sites where Jack the Ripper's victims were found. The two lines connecting the first four sites intersect to symbolize an inverted cross. The photos arrayed around the map are morgue shots and letters from the Ripper case."

"So what's the tunnel?" Jock asked.

"Do you know what a wormhole is?"

The younger man frowned at such a dumb question. "A wormhole is a hole burrowed in wood by a worm."

The kid was no rocket scientist, that was obvious. Rudi wondered if it was worth the effort it would take to explain wormholes to him. But Jock was already weaving through the maze of books to study the photos around the East End map. Among the shots of Jack's victims snapped at the morgue was the note mailed with a human kidney to the Whitechapel Vigilance Committee on October 16, 1888. It read:

From hell

Mr Lusk
Sor

I send you half the Kidne I took from one women prasarved it for you tother piece I fried and ate it was very nise I may send you the bloody knif that took it out if you only wate a whil longer

signed

Catch me when
You can

"Was Jack the Ripper a cannibal?" Jock asked.

"Our Ripper, too," Rudi replied.

"You mean he thinks he's Jack the Ripper reincarnated?"

"No, he thinks he's Jack the Ripper *himself.*"

"You're right. He's sicker than Yorick. Where's the Ripper now?"

"Time-traveling," Rudi said.

WORMHOLE

"The Ripper has a visitor," Julie advised when Rudi and Jock returned to the nursing station. The Forensic Psychiatric Hospital had a staff of 375 for 242 patients. The nursing crunch had resulted in a shortfall of therapists, so both men and women now worked in all wards of Ashworth House. "I thought it wise, in light of his condition earlier, to have you escort him."

"Okay," Rudi said.

"Okay," Jock echoed.

In Ash 2, there were three wards off the nursing station. The open wards that V'd from the front windows had unlocked doors. However, if a psychotic became troublesome by acting out, he could be locked away in the seclusion ward, the door to which branched off the rear of the nursing station, between the security monitor that spied on those who sought entry to Ash 2 and the meds room that held the drugs dispensed to keep patients calm.

When the Ripper went time-traveling, the staff moved him to the seclusion ward.

Strangely, the door to that ward was kept open for a better view of the corridor. There was no need for Rudi and Jock to buzz the key reader with their fobs—the electronic passes that registered who opened which door at what time in Central Control—so the pair walked straight to the Ripper's locked cell.

"What's he doing?" Jock asked, peeking through the window.

"What does it look like he's doing?"

"Chewing his cud."

"See any food?"

"No."

"Nor do you want to. What the Ripper thinks he's eating is organ meat from his latest victim."

———·•·———

The Ripper sat cross-legged on the floor, enjoying Catharine Eddowes's kidney. Blood dribbled down his chin and dripped from his fingers as he chewed the dark delicacy with relish. Kate was the name she had offered him at the mouth to Mitre Square, but now that he had traveled here by the wormhole through space-time, the hindsight of history informed him that Kate was merely her working name. The seclusion room in which he dined was starker than his sleeping quarters in the unlocked ward: just an oblong cell with a toilet and a sink, and a bed that consisted of a mattress on the floor, wrapped in a strong sheet that wouldn't tear. Kate's uterus lay in the pool of blood congealing between his thighs, tempting him as dessert.

The door swung open.

"You have a visitor," someone said.

The Ripper glanced up at the pair of nurses blocking the threshold. One was Rudi. Wiry, fine-boned, in his mid-forties. The hulk, however, was new to Ash 2. Too big, too blond, he looked dumb as dog shit. No doubt his talent as a nurse was largely in his size.

"I need things from my room."

"We'll stop on the way," said Rudi.

Kate's kidney in one hand, her uterus in the other, the Ripper left seclusion under guard.

———·•·———

The Ripper was dressed in the jogging suit issued to all Ash 2 patients—a dark navy-blue sweatshirt with matching baggy sweatpants—and he wore a pair of Velcro runners on his feet. It looked as if FPH had outfitted him for comfort, but the real reason for the casual attire was that no hangers would be required in his room. As for the nurses, they wore street clothes: plain short-sleeved shirts, blue jeans and loafers. In fact, the relaxed dress code was strictly enforced to fool patients out of viewing them as psychiatric nurses. No ties, so there was nothing to seize, cinch or convert into nooses. No logos or T-shirt prints to set off the unstable.

They walked down a hall lined with peach walls and a peach floor with blue stepping-stone squares. The walls were forged from cement blocks reinforced with steel grating, so beneath the benign facade was a corridor cage. Instead of bars, the windows had horizontal slats. But they, too, were a clever sham, for the glass in them was Lexan—an unbreakable polycarbonate resin—and inside the slats were backup bars that rotated so hacksaw blades could not grab hold. Also, the nurses carried pen alarms for protection. Trigger the beam in any direction and it would bounce off the confining surfaces until it hit a sensor in the ceiling, and that would set off a general alarm to summon the entire staff of Ashworth House to quell trouble in less than thirty seconds.

With patients like the Ripper, security was crucial.

The interview room, however, could not be bugged. Among other uses, this was where Ash 2 patients instructed their lawyers, so solicitor–client privilege dictated the need for privacy. Privacy was also necessary for tonight's meeting, for what brought the Goth and the Ripper together was a plot to commit murder.

"I've thought about it," the Goth said, once they were alone. "I'm willing to pay the price."

"There can be no turning back."

"I understand."

"The sign *must* be drawn in blood."

"No problem," said the Goth.

"In addition, you must shed blood for me."

"I'll do whatever it takes for you to give me the key."

"Whatever?"

"Whatever."

"Then pick a card," said the Ripper.

The interview room in which they conspired was eight feet by ten. The stark furnishings were two chairs and the table between them. Could a room be duller and more antiseptic than this? Where was the gaslight? The wainscoted walls? The carved library table? The high-backed wing chairs? Missing was any sense of art or atmosphere. This sterile box was a metaphor for the outside world, where the Goth—born out of place and out of time—was trapped for life.

Unless . . .

Hopefully . . .

The Goth picked a card.

En route from the seclusion ward to here, the Ripper had fetched three visual aids from his room. The first was a plastic coffee cup with a finger handle. The second was a shatterproof hourglass of the type used to time a boiled egg. The third was the twenty-two-card deck now stacked on the table between them, from which the Goth selected the face-down significator.

"$E = MC^2$," said the Ripper.

"Einstein's theory of relativity," replied the Goth.

"Energy equals mass times the speed of light squared."

"Space and time are relative, not absolute concepts."

"How did Einstein formulate that?"

"Thought," said the Goth.

"What is thought?"

"Energy sparking neurons in our brains."

"How?" asked the Ripper.

"A smidgen of energy lights up a brain neuron and is released as heat."

"Hold that thought," said the florid psychotic.

A foul, metallic smell like rancid goat cheese permeated the room. There's the sweat of work, the sweat of fear, and there's this—the sweat of insanity. The stench oozed out in chemicals dispersed as the Ripper's aura. The Goth was intoxicated.

"The big bang," said the Ripper.

"The birth of the universe."

"The cosmic seed was a featureless point of space-time, speckled with tiny lumps of radiation. Then *bang*"—the Ripper thumped the table—"and the universe grew. The tiny lumps evolved into larger lumps, and eventually into galaxies, stars, *us*. Now back to that thought you're holding. Where'd you store it?"

"In my memory."

"How?"

"The same way a computer stores memory. In it, energy moves an electron within the hard drive. In me, it lights up a neuron in the memory bank of my brain."

"So you remember the past?"

"Yes."

"Why can't you remember the future?"

"Because time runs forward."

"Like this?" the Ripper said. He flipped the hourglass over on the table so the sand began to flow.

The Goth nodded. "From the past to the future."

"So that's the arrow of time?"

"Uh-huh. It points in that direction."

"Why?" asked the Ripper.

"I don't know."

"Because the arrow of time is the arrow of entropy."

"Who says?"

"Hawking. You know who he is?"

"Sure. The astrophysicist. *A Brief History of Time*. Supposedly the brightest scientist since Einstein."

"Entropy is disorder. Start with that. The reason the arrow of time is the arrow of entropy is that the beginning was a low-entropy seed, and after the big bang exploded to expand the universe, what followed was a future of greater disorder. That's why we know a film that shows fragments of shattered porcelain coming together in the shape of a cup is running backwards."

The Ripper tapped the cup on the table.

"Heat—roiling, chaotic heat—increases entropy. As you said, the energy that sparks a neuron in your brain to create a memory is released as heat. Because entropy increases in the same direction as the arrow of time—in other words, from the past to the future— that's *why* memories are made in the past."

"Sounds logical," said the Goth.

"So what about black holes?"

The eyes of the Ripper could be black holes, the Goth thought. So intense was the pull of the psycho's stare that it seemed to suck the flesh of his face into both dark orbs, creasing and crinkling it into the squint of all squints. His upper lip receded like a rising curtain from the lower edge of his teeth, the tips of his canines jutting down like a vampire's fangs. Here was a man, from the Goth's point of view, who gazed at wonders that others couldn't see.

"How do we explain the weirdness of black holes? Collapsed stars so dense that not even light escapes their gravitational pull. Regions out there"—the Ripper's eyes rolled back into his head—"where the density of matter approaches infinity. Black holes"—the eyes returned—"warp space and time in bizarre ways."

"Time warps," said the Goth, hypnotized.

"Black holes slurp up stars, gas and anything else they can. What gets eaten never reappears. Since that matter is lost eternally, we're left with the question, Where did it go?"

"Time warps?" repeated the Goth.

"Consider the topology of this plastic cup." The Ripper picked it up and held the mug out between them.

"What's topology?"

"The mathematics of deformations in geometric constructions. Do you see how the handle is actually a distorted extension of the cup itself? In 1935, Einstein theorized that a super-dense object would curve space-time—the combined mathematical representation of space *and* time—so tightly that it would form a kind of 'throat' linking two different regions of space. The same way a cup distorts into a handle, higher-dimensional space warps into 'handles' too, and those handles allow signals, or matter, to travel along their tunnels as shortcuts between regions distant in space and time."

"To a parallel universe?"

"Through another *dimension*."

"What dimension?"

"The occult realm."

The Ripper switched the cup for the hourglass. The timepiece sat in his palm so the sand continued to flow.

"Ordinary journeys transport us through three dimensions of space and one dimension of time. In effect, we follow the same mathematically curved trajectory across the surface of this planet that a worm follows to crawl around the surface of an apple."

The Ripper's index finger caressed the upper bowl of the hourglass.

"But what if we could access a higher-dimensional shortcut where space-time had warped into a tunnel that pierced the innards of the apple like a wormhole? Not only would travel to a distant point on the surface be greatly shortened, but we would also be able to time-travel within that higher dimension."

"Back *and* forth?" asked the Goth.

"Why not?" said the Ripper. And with that, he turned the hourglass over on his palm so the sand of time reversed its flow from the future to the past.

"A time warp," said the Goth.

"A time warp," agreed the Ripper.

"Can that be done?"

"I've done it many times."

"You found the wormhole through space-time?"

"I found *a* wormhole from there to here. How else do you think I traveled from the East End of London back in 1888 to the future of here and now?"

"Why Vancouver?"

"I don't know. The Magick is in the cards. It must be predestined that I meet *you*."

"To give me the key?"

"If you're chosen."

"How will you know that?"

"The card you just picked. If you're chosen, your significator will be the Hanged Man."

Folie à deux is the form of psychosis in which delusional ideas are shared by two people in close association. Mental illness transfers from one to the other like a sexually transmitted disease. What the Ripper and the Goth were doing tonight was essentially mind-fucking, the smell of rancid madness now oozing from both partners.

"Turn over the card."

The Goth obeyed.

What stared up at them from the table was this:

THE HANGED MAN.

"The Hanged Man," said the Goth.

"You *are* chosen."

"Now will you give me the key to the occult realm?"

"Yes, if you swear in return that you'll shed blood for me."

"Whose blood?"

"Do you swear?"

"I swear," confirmed the Goth.

The Ripper nodded. "I want you to kill a cop."

tHE HANGED MAN

North Vancouver, British Columbia
November 3 (Two days later)

Inspector Zinc Chandler of Special X—the Special External Section of the Royal Canadian Mounted Police—was fishing his regimental badge from his jacket pocket to flash at the uniformed constable standing guard at this end of the hotel corridor, when the young Asian woman said, "I recognize you, sir. You'll find Sergeant Kidd in the room."

There was no need for her to indicate which room. Halfway along this hall on the middle floor of the Lions Gate, those who made murder their business—the coroner and the cleanup crew from the body removal service—kibitzed in front of a doorjamb that had been dusted with fingerprint powder while Ident forensic techs finished combing the crime scene beyond that threshold.

"Chandler," the coroner enthused on spotting Zinc. "A crucifixion is one for the memoirs, eh?"

The coroner was a ruddy-faced boozer in a gravy-stained suit who emitted an aura of strong cologne mixed with wintergreen breath mints used to mask the odor of Scotch. A jolly fellow known for his gallows humor, the coroner was on the cusp of retirement. No doubt the memoirs he mentioned were already in the works, Zinc thought.

"A crucifixion?" Chandler asked.

"So I'm told."

"You've not been in?"

31

"Too cramped. Too many cooks, old boy."

Zinc peeked in through the door frame but couldn't see the corpse. Just the black sergeant and two techs in "bunny suits"—disposable white coveralls with hoods and full foot coverage so that the crime site wouldn't be contaminated—vacuuming for hairs and fibers.

"You're thinking Easter, right?"

"Huh?" said Chandler, turning his attention back to the coroner.

"Easter's more appropriate than Halloween."

"Oh, you mean Jesus on the cross?"

"Right, Easter's the proper time for crucifixion. Unless, of course, the crucifix is upside down."

"Is it?" Chandler asked.

The coroner nodded, licking his lips as if it were time to wet his whistle again.

One of the techs spied Zinc and called out, "Suits are in the bag by the door, Inspector. We're through with that half of the room. No need to use the path of contamination."

Fetching the Ident bag from beside the hinges, Zinc removed a bunny suit and began to pull it on.

"It reminds me of that myth from the trenches in the First World War," the coroner said. "The rumor emerged from the Second Battle of Ypres in 1915. A Canadian sergeant, the story goes, was found nailed to a barn door with German bayonets through his hands and feet. The details changed with each retelling. He was nailed to a house. He was nailed to a tree. He was tied up with rope. He was tied up with wire. Nothing mattered but the image of crucifixion. In a Christian era, what better propaganda? A Hunnish enemy had mocked Christ's agony on the cross. When the rumor spread to New York, Yanks began enlisting even though they weren't in the war. And heaven help the Kraut who fell into our hands. After the crucified soldier, Canucks got a bad rep for abusing POWs."

"I've seen that image," Zinc said.

"*Canada's Golgotha.* A sculptor cast the myth in bronze after the war. In it, the soldier hangs crucified in his great coat as Germans mock him from below like Romans did Christ. The rendition outraged postwar Germans, and they demanded that we prove the atrocity really occurred. When we couldn't, the offending sculpture was crated up and stored away for fifty years."

"It's like that guy in Wyoming," said one of the undertakers from body removal.

"What guy?" the coroner asked, shifting his attention to an anecdote that he could include in his memoirs. Out came pen and notebook to jot the salient details.

"It was in the paper a few years ago. Some rednecks in Wyoming, or one of those cowboy states, abducted a young gay man and drove him out onto the prairies. They pistol-whipped him until his skull caved in, then left him lashed to a fence for eighteen hours to freeze to death. How many murders are there annually in the States? How many gays endure hate crimes every year? Few of those make the news, but that one caused a fuss. Politicians fronting the Christian right had to cope with the martyr image of a gay, who supposedly sinned against God's law, being crucified on a fence."

The coroner smiled as he scribbled notes. "Crucifixion carries baggage."

On that note, Zinc turned and crossed the threshold. A short entry hall with a bathroom on the left expanded into a wide room overlooking the front street. The last words Zinc caught from the coroner were "Find out if this vic was gay."

The trouble with a rumor is that it distorts the facts. Zinc had no idea what crime-scene hearsay had spawned the image of crucifixion in the old boy's mind, but there were problems with bringing this reality into line with that description.

The entrance to Vancouver's harbor is dubbed the Lions Gate. It takes that name from two North Shore mountain peaks, which are called the Lions because they resemble a pair of crouching cats. In pioneer times, lumber equaled money, so a skid road slid logs down the mountainside to the village of Lonsdale on the harborfront, which was basically a few shacks around a rickety dock. The passing years upgraded the skid road into Lonsdale Avenue and transformed the village of Lonsdale into North Vancouver. Befitting its new status as a world-class city, North Van needed a decent hotel, so the Lions Gate was constructed on Lower Lonsdale.

Recently, the heritage hotel had been refurbished to meet the party vices of Hollywood North. Thanks to a worthless Canadian dollar, filming was frantic on the North Shore. High rollers from L.A. would blow into town and head straight to the Lounge Lizard bar on the ground floor of the Lions Gate. There, they could score blow to snort up their addicted snouts, then, should one of the high-class hookers who hung out around the bar catch their fancy, they could rent a room upstairs to get blown or to high-roll around in the hay.

A room like this.

The room was actually two rooms converted into one. The central support was a T-beam from the days when it was common for local mills to churn out timber thirty inches in diameter and seventy feet long without a single knot. Standing alone, the flanking wall gone, it looked like the cross on which Christ was crucified. The beam, however, wasn't upside down, so it didn't qualify as an inverted crucifix. Only the victim hung in reverse, his naked body dangling from the cross-arm of the T by a rope cinched around his right ankle. His left leg was bent so it crossed behind his right thigh, and it had been tied in place to hold it there. Crucifixion requires outstretched arms, but this man's wrists were cuffed together at the small of his back. The only connection with what was done to Christ was the crown of thorns that trickled blood from the victim's brow. But on closer inspection, that too was exposed as a distortion, for what Zinc saw when he squatted beside the body—careful to avoid the blood pooling around the cross—was that the thorns were actually a nimbus of nails hammered into the dead man's skull.

This wasn't a crucifixion.

It was an *occult* symbol.

A symbol just as powerful to those who believe in Magick.

"The Hanged Man," Zinc said.

"Yep," Sergeant Kidd agreed, joining him near the strung-up body.

"The coroner said he was crucified."

"I'm probably to blame. I told him the vic was tied upside down to a T-cross."

"Rumors," scoffed the inspector.

The black Mountie nodded. "I never believe them. As often as not, the best ones turn out to be bogus."

It occurred to Zinc that he had heard a rumor about Rachel Kidd and a cross of another kind. Not about the sergeant herself, but about her father.

Born in Birmingham, Alabama, during the civil rights era, Rachel had been a fetus in her mother's womb on the night that four Klansmen in ghostlike sheets and pointed hoods grabbed her dad. They drove him to a deserted field and lit a burning cross, then, having staked him to the ground at the foot of the fiery symbol, the racists castrated the screaming man with a razor blade. According to the rumor, they passed his severed testicles around in a paper cup so each could raise the hem of his hood to spit on the bloody trophies. The cops who'd investigated were Klansmen too, so that's why the Kidds had moved to the Pacific Northwest, where Rachel eventually donned red serge and became the first black promoted up the Mounted's ranks.

Tall, lithe and lean, the sergeant was currently posted to North Van GIS, the homicide squad of the local detachment. A body found at the foot of the Lions fell within Kidd's jurisdiction, but the hierarchy of command was such that a murder with leads outside the country might be usurped by Special X. Protocol had demanded that Rachel place a courtesy call to Zinc's unit, the Special External Section at RCMP H.Q. across the harbor.

"The vic's from L.A.," she said, crouching beside the inspector.

"Name?"

"Cardoza. Romeo Cardoza."

"You're kidding? Who the hell would name their kid Romeo?"

"Mr. and Mrs. Cardoza?"

"Very funny."

"Mind if I ask a question, sir?" Rachel asked.

"No."

"Who would name their kid Zinc?"

Chandler's natural steel-gray hair had been that color since birth. Its metallic tint gave rise to his name. Six-foot-two and almost two hundred pounds, Zinc had a physique muscled from hard work on the family farm in Saskatchewan during his youth and workouts since. Rugged and sharp-featured, his face was hard and gaunt, his good looks marred by the strain of fighting back from two serious wounds: a bullet to the head while hunting a killer named Cutthroat in Hong Kong, and a knife to the back on Deadman's Island to stop a psychotic who thought he was Jack the Ripper.

"You're sure you want to ask that question, Corporal?"

"Yes," said Rachel.

"You're *quite* sure, Constable?"

"On second thought . . ."

The Mounties shared a laugh, then, all kidding aside, the two got down to work.

"L.A., you said?" Zinc asked.

"Yeah, a movie producer. He flew in yesterday afternoon on Air Canada."

"Staying here?"

"Uh-uh. The Hyatt over town. No one *stays* here. The Lions Gate is where you score . . . in more ways than one."

"Sex? Drugs?"

"Down in the bar. The rock-'n'-roll's up here. Rock in the form of cocaine. Roll in the form of fucking."

"What brought Romeo to Vancouver?"

"Money problems. His studio's shooting a film up here that's way over budget."

"Title?" Zinc asked.

"Bed of Nails."

The beam from which the hanged man hung was halfway across the double room. The techs had finished with the half at the inspector's back and were now searching the half beyond the beam for clues. They had cleared a path of contamination to the queen-size bed against the far wall. There, while Zinc and Rachel squatted near the suspended corpse, Dr. Gillian Macbeth, the forensic pathologist, examined the state of the bedding. *"Bed of Nails,"* Gill echoed, waving Zinc toward her. "Fitting title. Get a look at this."

The room took on a definite chill as both Mounties approached the bed. Sandwiched between the women, Zinc watched his breath condense in imaginary puffs. There was no love lost between Rachel and Gill, and that, more than anything, explained why the coroner was cowering out in the hall. These two had issues, as yet unresolved. Macbeth was an attractive surgeon on the gray side of forty. Having spent her fertile years building a successful career, she'd taken a stab at motherhood as her bio clock ran down. The father-to-be was a corporal with Special X, who Kidd had mistakenly arrested for the murder of his mother. That freed the actual killer to plant a bomb on the cruise ship that sailed the Mounties off into the sunset for their Red Serge Ball. The explosion had hurled Gill into a cruel aborting sea, and—*tick . . . tock . . . tick*—her bio clock ran out. Zinc's girlfriend, Alexis Hunt, wrote a book about the case. In print, Gill had challenged Rachel's competence as a cop, and Kidd was convinced that had damaged her career. It was all the two could do to be outwardly civil to each other, while daggers thrown by their scornful eyes whizzed over Chandler's shoulders.

"Here's where it happened," Gill said, indicating the rumpled bed. "See the hammer? And the extra nails?"

The bloody tools flanked the gore-spattered pillow.

"That wad looks like a gag."

"Likely stuffed in his mouth. To silence him while they hammered the nails into his brain."

"They?" Zinc said.

"Two killers would be my bet. The base of his penis and his anus are both chafed raw."

"A two-on-one?"

"That's how I see it."

"A female in front and a male behind?"

"Or two males, front and back, to form a daisy chain."

"Or two females," Rachel interjected. "One laying him while the other reamed him with a dildo."

"Semen?"

"Just his. On his flaccid penis. They likely used condoms for safe sex and to capture DNA," Gill said.

"Find any safes?"

"No," said Rachel.

"Tidy killers."

"Hip to forensics."

"Short nails," Zinc said, eyeing the pillow spikes.

The pathologist nodded. "The nails are short for a slow death. Just long enough to punch through the skull and pierce his brain. Judging from the blood sprays, they moved around. I think the nails were hammered in while the three had sex."

Zinc conjured up the crime in his mind's eye. High-rolling Romeo flies in from Hollywood. He taxis from the airport to the Hyatt Regency downtown, and later proceeds across the Lions Gate Bridge to the Lions Gate hotel, here on the North Shore. Why? To meet someone connected with the troubled *Bed of Nails?* Or was it to score some action?

"Find any drugs?" he asked.

"Yeah, over here."

The answer came from one of the techs examining a table by the front windows.

"Coke?"

"You got it. Chopped with this."

The man held up a tarot card in a plastic evidence bag.

"The Hanged Man," Zinc said. "A calling card?"

"It was used to chop six lines on this table. You can see traces of powder."

Zinc continued laying out the scenario in his mind. The high roller makes a connection in the bar downstairs. Romeo rents this room for a snort and a fuck. The three do two lines each at the window table, then strip off their clothes and climb into bed. Things turn kinky when Romeo's sex partners cuff his hands together at the small of his back and stuff the gag wad into his mouth. With one working him in front and the other behind, the two get their sexual kicks by adding spurts of blood from Romeo's brain. Nail by nail, they hammer a halo around his skull. The shallow depth keeps him from dying too soon. The one in front gets death-throe pumps from his groin. The one behind enjoys the clenches of his anal sphincter.

Bang . . .

Bang . . .

Bang . . .

Like Maxwell's silver hammer in the Beatles' song.

Until . . .

Clang . . .

Clang . . .

Clang . . .

They're sure he's dead.

After that, they drag his body over to the beam and string him up like the Hanged Man on the coke-cutting card.

"Who found him?" Zinc asked.

"A chambermaid. She came in this morning to make up the room and here he was," said Rachel.

"Anything stolen?"

"The coke and the cash in his wallet. Unless he traveled on plastic without a bill to his name."

"May I see that card?" Chandler asked the tech.

The Ident cop handed him the coke cutter sealed in the plastic bag. Zinc noted the nimbus around the Hanged Man's head. Did that explain the halo of nails hammered into Romeo's brain?

"If you ladies will excuse me, I'm going down to the bar."

"Drinking on duty?" Gill teased.

"Looking for Romeo's Juliet."

Hooker

The world's oldest profession was almost as old as Vancouver itself. Whisky—the basic necessity of any frontier town—arrived on the south shore of Burrard Inlet in 1869, when Gassy Jack Deighton built a saloon to found what is now this city. Sex—an even more basic necessity if there is to be urban growth—arrived with Birdie Stewart in 1873, when she opened the first cathouse in what had become known as Gastown, kitty-corner from the booze and two doors away from the Methodist parsonage. The demographics of the day were bullish for business. Horny men outnumbered loose women twenty to one.

By the turn of the century, Dupont Street was Vancouver's colony of vice. A card game, an opium pipe, pleasures of the flesh—whatever your desire, come down to Chinatown. The red-light district got a boost in 1906, when the San Francisco earthquake shook the booties of a lot of brothel madams north. The Americans—as they are wont—brought their advertising and marketing skills to this den of iniquity, and before long there were scantily clad temptresses on wanton display in bordello windows and harlots in gaudy garments flouncing about on the streets.

Vancouver, back then, had a puritanical streak. Loosely defined, a puritan is a prig who loses sleep knowing that someone, some-where, may be having fun. The shocking revelation that church-goers saw "boys in that vicinity who could not be older than fifteen or twenty" was too much, and it forced the police to crack down with a "no flouncing" order.

The breakup of Chinatown's vice colony spread 112 whore-houses to other parts of the city. The hooker history of Vancouver from then on became one of cops chasing Pearls, Violets and Carmens all over town. Each time the vice squad closed a house of ill repute, the pros found new lodgings at accommodating hotels. B.C.'s Liquor Control Act was such that you couldn't license a bar or pub unless you offered rooms, so the city was inundated with drinking establishments that kept empty cribs on the upper floors. That law was tailor-made to turn every booze can into a knocking shop. A working girl could troll for dates downstairs at the bar, then rent a private room upstairs by the hour.

Ergo, the Lions Gate. In its present form.

Those who make their living on their backs and their knees won a decisive victory in the Penthouse case. For three decades, the Penthouse was the hottest club in town. That's where visiting celebrities like Frank Sinatra and his Rat Pack hung out. With no rooms to let, it was a "bottle joint," unlicensed premises where BYOB was the rule. The club charged dearly for glasses, ice and mix. On any given night, a patron also had his choice of somewhere between 30 and 150 hookers to take elsewhere on his arm. Those were the days before ATMs, so the Penthouse made a killing off credit card advances. For instant cash to pay for prospective athlet-ics, the patron paid the club a 20-percent surcharge. For that, he also got his picture taken by the cops, who surreptitiously photographed each couple leaving the premises.

The Penthouse trial was a *cause célèbre*. The owners were charged with living off the avails of prostitution. "Sure, we took the 20 percent," was their defense, "but it was none of our business what the patrons did with the money." Of the seven hundred photos snapped by the cops, only two hundred were offered by the Crown as evidence. The rest, according to one detective, were a blackmailer's wet dream, for the men caught in the photos were prominent lawyers, doctors, celebrities and politicians from across the colorful spectrum of Vancouver's establishment.

With the Penthouse shut for the two-year duration of the case, the working girls went back to flouncing on the streets, only this time they let it all hang out in the ritzy West End. The public hue and cry deafened city hall, so when that two-million-dollar fiasco at taxpayers' expense resulted in acquittal of the club on all counts, Vancouver was relieved to see the girls retreat into bars.

Today, Sin City is a wide-open town. There's a hooker bar to cater to every demographic. For Hollywood high rollers, the Lounge Lizard at the Lions Gate is the *in* place. Feel free to transact business in the bar. Just don't flounce on the streets.

The Lounge Lizard was slithering with the lunchtime crowd when Zinc entered through the lobby door and made his way to the bar. Because the hotel dated from pioneer days, the decor was British Empire gentlemen's club in style and atmosphere. Dark wood walls with plenty of brass and overstuffed wing chairs around cocktail tables. Folks transacting business tended to congregate at the mirror-backed bar, which spanned the entire length of the off-street wall.

Bar stools were at a premium just after high noon. Luckily for the Mountie, a movie mogul had just negotiated a nooner, so Zinc procured one of the seats vacated by the happy hooker and her john. The other stool fell to an asexual academic whom the cop pegged as a radical feminist here to research her master's thesis in women's studies.

"I don't muff dive," said the blonde hooker on her other side.

"You're a pawn, don't you see?" countered the feminist.

"Oh? How so?" replied the blonde.

"In a patriarchal world, men are ultimately responsible for forcing women into prostitution."

"Really?"

"Really."

"Have you any idea how much money I make? Enough to put both of us through graduate school. If a john wants to flip me a C-note or two to give him a hummer, what fucking business is that of yours, Ms. Holier Than Thou?"

Good question, Chandler thought.

"And come to think of it, honey," said the blonde, "you wouldn't *be* here if some john hadn't blown a load."

The academic huffed.

"In the real world, baby, they're all johns," said the hooker.

On that *coup de grâce,* the inspector cocked an ear to eavesdrop on the conversation on his starboard side.

"What's your name?"

"Stanley."

"Hi, Stan. I'm Mona. Moaning Mona, to my friends. What do you do?"

"I'm a studio accountant."

"Mmm," purred Mona. "Would you like to count my beans?"

"I know a joke," said Stanley, "about a woman like you and a man like me."

"I like jokes." She placed her hand on his thigh.

Stanley looked like . . . well, like an accountant. His bald pate had a comb-over of seven strands plastered in place. Thick Coke-bottle glasses magnified his beady eyes, strained no doubt by too many years of adding up false figures. It was hard to know which was more endearing: the cute little dimple on his chin or his roly-poly belly.

"A woman walks into her accountant's office," he said, "and tells him that she needs to file her taxes."

"Fat chance," Mona said, squeezing his pudge.

"The accountant informs her, 'Before we start, I need to ask some questions.' He gets her name, address and social security number, then he asks her, 'What's your occupation?'"

"The woman replies, 'I'm a hooker.'"

A sharp intake of breath from mock shock almost popped Mona's bountiful breasts out of her bodice. Her free hand rose like Betty Boop's to her luscious mouth. "No!" she gasped, wide-eyed.

Stanley's Adam's apple caught in his dry throat as he struggled to complete the joke.

"The accountant balks and says, 'No, no, no. That won't work. It's much too crass. Let's rephrase it.'

"'Okay,' the woman says. 'I'm a prostitute.'

"'No,' replies the accountant. 'That's still too crude. Try again.'

"The woman thinks for a moment, scratching her head. Then she tells him, 'I'm a chicken farmer.'

"Puzzled, the accountant asks, 'What does chicken farming have to do with being a whore'"—Stanley's voice broke on uttering that word—"'or a prostitute?'

"'Well,' the client replies, 'I raised five thousand cocks last year.'"

Mona laughed the sort of deep throaty laugh that would terrify a mama's boy's mom, and her hand slid toward the beckoning bulge in the fidgeting bean-counter's pants. "Shall we make that five thousand and one?" the hooker asked.

"How much?" Stan croaked.

"An even grand. For the best afternoon of your life."

"Phew. That's expensive."

"You don't think I'm worth it?"

Mona crossed her long legs on the bar stool to expose creamy thighs complemented by garters and nylons, seen through the slit of her tight green dress. Elbow on her knee, chin in her free palm, she leaned toward Stan so he (and Zinc) could gaze down the valley of her awesome cleavage to the mystery beyond. Her quizzical eyes were emeralds the same shade as her clinging sheath and her red hair as wild as licking flames. As a faithful male in a strong relationship with Alexis Hunt, the inspector would keep his wanton lust in check. But he had to acknowledge that Moaning Mona would be cheap at twice the price.

"I don't know," said Stan. "Can't you go lower?"

"An accountant goes into a bar," Mona said, "and sits down beside the sexiest hooker in the place.

"'How much?' he asks.

"'A grand,' she says.

"'Gee, I don't know,' he hems and haws. 'Can't you go lower?'

"'Sure,' says the hooker. 'For less, you get a penguin.'

"'What's a penguin?' the accountant asks.

"'You'll see,' she replies.

"So off they go to one of the upstairs rooms, where the horny guy drops his pants and waits for his 'penguin.' The hooker kneels and gives him the ultimate blow job. Then, just as the accountant's about to come, she stops, gets up and walks away. With his pants around his ankles, the cheapskate waddles after her. 'Hey, wait a minute,' he shouts. 'What's a penguin?'"

Stan was still waiting for the punchline when the eavesdropping Zinc burst out laughing.

Mona winked at him over Stan's sparse pate.

"Hello, handsome. What sharp ears you have. Shall we make that five thousand and two?"

And that's when the barkeep approached Zinc.

"What'll it be, sir?"

"Information."

The Mountie flashed his bison-crested regimental badge.

"Tsk-tsk," Mona clucked. "What a waste."

"Oh no," Stan gulped, and bolted from the bar.

"Our graft's paid up to date, Officer," the barkeep said.

"Where can we talk?"

The young man flicked his wary eyes toward the end of the bar.

As Zinc swung off the bar stool, Mona said, "Did you hear the one about the hooker and the horny cop?"

———— •◦• ————

"I gotta warn you. I'm an actor," the barkeep said. He looked like a snow stud in ads for boarding on Whistler Mountain's usuriously ticketed slopes.

"This your day job?"

"Night job, actually. I'm working double shift to cover a bad case of the flu."

"What's your name?"

"Denny."

"Denny what?"

"Am I in some kind of trouble?"

"Not yet," said the Mountie.

"Denny . . . Dennis Tobin."

"You work last night?"

45

"Yes," said Denny. "What's this about? The guy upstairs? There's nothing I can tell you."

"Why the warning that you're an actor?"

Denny cracked a cautious smirk. "I've seen this scene enacted in a thousand noir films. A cop goes into a bar and leans on the bartender for information. He strong-arms him with"—the young thespian dropped his voice to a growl—"'Is that a hooker I see? Are those two high on drugs? Either you talk, buddy, or we'll be all over this place like a dose of salts. You won't know what hit—'"

"What's a dose of salts?" Zinc asked.

Denny blinked. "Beats me."

"Are you going to blame me for that?"

"For what?"

"Beating you."

Denny's smirk switched to a genuine grin.

"The guy upstairs," Zinc said. "What've you heard?"

"Nothing."

"No? Then how do you know about him?"

"Hey, I work here. I heard the basics. Thelma found him when she did the room this morning. He's naked. He's dead. He's hanging upside down. He's got a halo of nails in his skull. And shit's gonna hit the fan in here when the news breaks."

"Too bad for you."

"Why?"

"You'll be out of work. And all because you kept mum instead of helping me."

"No way."

"Think about it, Denny. Would you haunt a bar to relax when the patrons are being stalked by a psycho like that? This spot will be as dead as the stiff—is 'stiff' a word they use in those noir films?—is upstairs. Will you be able to land another cool job like this? Tending bar at the *in* place for the film industry? I doubt it. Now let's take a look at the flip side of the coin. Instead of playing the sap—you do know what a sap is?—you could be a Hollywood hero, front and center. Say the shit hits the fan when news of this breaks. Word spreads far and wide, to every mover and shaker in the film biz. Then—*presto!*—the psycho is caught before he and/or she can kill again. Why? Because of the sharp eyes and ears of a certain hero who tends the bar in question. I see a movie of the week in the cards. Hell, maybe even a feature film. And who better to play the hero than the hero himself? Hollywood loves that sort of self-congratulatory stuff. Well, Denny? Whaddaya say? Are you a good enough actor to play *yourself*?"

Zinc caught a glint of starlight in the barkeep's eyes.

"Well . . ." drawled Denny.

"Well, what?"

"I might have caught something."

"Something like?"

"The dead guy talking to a hooker last night."

"Now we're getting somewhere."

"A hooker *and* her pimp."

"Somewhere further."

"A pimp who also deals coke."

"Oh, hell, Denny. Forget that feature film. You have a block-buster on your hands."

"You figure?"

"The stiff's an L.A. producer. Work it out. Look what happened to those involved in the O.J. case."

That was enough for Denny. The cameras were already rolling in his mind.

"The hooker and her pimp are new players in town. They followed the money up from L.A. The pair began coming in about a week ago. To be blunt, we want them gone. They're too heavy for the ambience of the bar."

"How so?"

"Rough trade. Black leather and such. She's into discipline. S&M. He's into coke. His own supply."

"What'd you hear?"

"Nothing. The place was packed. Just saw them talking. And I put two and two together."

"From what?"

"Another deal. One I overheard the first night those two came in."

"A week ago?"

"Yeah. The guy upstairs. Was he screwed in the ass?"

"You tell me."

"You're the cop."

"I'm not at liberty to discuss details of a case under investigation."

"A dollar says the stiff was sandwich meat."

"What's that?"

"You know. Between two pieces of bread. Pussy fucked in front. Cock plowed behind."

"And if?"

"It's them. They've done that before."

"How do you know?"

"Big ears," Denny said, tapping both sides of his head. "A patron drinks too much, then talks too loud. He does a coke-and-sex transaction at the bar. The barkeep overhears."

"Overhears what?"

"Remember that director with the gerbil up his ass? It happened in Hollywood a few years back? He had to go to the hospital to get it pulled out. Gerbiling, remember? It was a Tinseltown fad."

"Can't say that I do."

"Hollywood spawns kinks. Anyway," Denny said, "he's in town to shoot a film."

"The gerbil director?"

The barkeep laughed. "I hope they have an animal wrangler on his set. He's a regular in the bar, Mr. Gerbil. He's the one I overheard cut a deal with the pair."

"For a sandwich?"

"Uh-huh."

"For a two-on-one with the same hooker and pimp you saw talking with the dead man in the bar last night?"

Denny went back to his cop voice. "Is that what you guys call an M.O.?"

"The hooker's name?"

"Joey."

"Joey what?"

The barkeep shrugged.

"And the pimp?"

"Gord."

"Just Gord?"

"I think he's her brother. Family resemblance. They might even be twins."

"Know where they live?"

"I know where they hang out."

"Here, you mean?"

"If they didn't blow town after last night, the pair should wander in around ten."

PIMP

"Hello, handsome. I knew you'd be back."

"Hi, Mona," Zinc said, taking the stool beside her at the bar of the Lounge Lizard in the Lions Gate.

"How's tricks?" she asked.

"Shouldn't that be my line? Did Stan the Accountant return to count your beans after I left?"

"Shh," shushed Mona, her index finger bisecting her pouted lips. "That's a secret. I never betray a client."

"Solicitor–client privilege?"

"Tsk-tsk, Big Red. Soliciting is against the law."

A shadow fell across them from the far side of the bar. "What'll it be, sir?" asked Denny the Barkeep.

"A 7 UP."

"Now *that's* a drinking problem."

"And something for the lady."

"The lady wants you," Mona said, leaning forward, neck arched as she crossed her legs. Between her décolletage and the dress slit up to her garters, the swath of green suddenly shrank to the size of a torso-hugging corset.

"Oo-la-la," Zinc said. "But I'm just browsing."

"On duty?"

"You could say."

"I read this book," moaned Mona.

"Which book?"

"Mailer."

"Norman?"

"Tough Guys Don't Fuck," she teased.

The 7 UP hit the bar with too hard a tap for what you would expect from an experienced barkeep. "Heads up," Denny whispered as the cop's attention swung back to him. Though a Wild West gunslinger would not be caught dead in a bar like this for fear of being plugged in the back, the mirror beyond Denny gave Chandler a complete panoramic reflection of the room behind him. Despite his earlier prediction, the bar wasn't devoid of patrons, for those who feared they might fall prey to a psycho stalker were replaced by the curious, drawn to the excitement of hanging out at a murder scene. At six-foot-two and seated on a high bar stool, Zinc could see over the heads of most of the standing-room-only crowd to where a black leather pair stood just inside the door to the street, surveying the pickings for predators at this upscale watering hole for Hollywood's meat on the hoof.

Survival of the fittest.

King of the beasts.

The law of the jungle ruled tonight at the Lions Gate.

The beast at the gate reminded Zinc of U2's Bono. Black hair, cut short like a helmet on his head. Dark wraparound shades, even though it was nighttime and he was indoors. A black leather jacket, designer label, with black leather pants to match. His black boots probably cost Zinc's monthly salary.

The hooker who had slinked in with the pimp was a lithe, beautiful, blatantly sexual, sado-erotic dominatrix. She too was sheathed in black leather, but hers fit as tight as a glove. Her black hair was short, cut like a man's, yet there could be no doubt about this night creature's gender. The tight top, wedged open in a V that plunged almost as deep as her navel, made Chandler want to kick himself for not investing in breast-implant stocks when they first hit the market. As for her pants, they were as hip-hugging as a second skin, and tailored so they subtly outlined her pubic mound. A black belt woven with silver chains hung loosely around her waist. Black boots with spiked heels encased her feet. And encircling her neck was a black choker linked to a silver chain that ran like a leash to the pimp's clenched fist.

Sniff, sniff . . .

Flare, flare . . .

Their nostrils twitched. The pimp and his hooker had coked up to prowl the bar.

"Ooh," said Mona. "So that's your type." She was watching Zinc watch the door in the bar's mirror. "I see you naked on the floor with her spiked heel on your spine, while a cat-o'-nine-tails in her grip stripes and checks your bottom."

"Keep my seat warm."

Zinc swiveled off the stool.

"Mess with her, Big Red, and your seat'll be warm for weeks."

"We don't want a barroom brawl," warned Denny, as the inspector waded into the crowd.

What makes life dangerous is the unexpected. The "oh no" that blindsides you out of the blue. A whammy like the whammy that hit Zinc now.

"Hey, Inshpector," a voice in the bar crowd called out.

It was Stan the Accountant, drunkenly waving to Zinc.

Which caught the attention of both the pimp and his hooker.

"Wha's goin' down? A big drug busht?"

Oh no, Zinc thought.

And that's when the coked-up pimp drew his gun.

When you'd been a cop as long as Zinc had, you learned to read the signs. The pimp's attention focused on him from across this crowded room, and what it expressed was: one, I've been to jail; two, I'm not going back; and three, I'm holding a lot of coke to deal to these hungry snouts tonight.

As the gunman raised the .357 to aim its muzzle at Zinc, the Mountie reached into his plainclothes jacket for the Smith & Wesson holstered at his waist. Pandemonium seized the bar crowd. With the sight of the lethal hardware, all thoughts of heroics died. Patrons were dashing, diving and scrambling every which way to save their skins, when—*bwam!*—one of them took the slug meant for Zinc. Her face was there, and then it wasn't, as she spun into the Mountie. Down they both went as—*bwam! bwam!*—the Python Magnum in the pimp's fist spit again.

Panicked patrons threw themselves flat to get out of the line of fire. The standing-room-only crowd required too much horizontal floor-space, so there was no alternative but to go for a layered effect. Zinc had to bushwhack his way up through a thicket of arms and legs to regain his feet, and by the time the periscope of his head broke the surface of this sea of squirming flesh, the predators were gone.

"Police! Police! Coming through! Get out of the way!" he yelled as he stepped around, over and sometimes on the melee.

The Mountie burst out of the bar onto Lonsdale Avenue. Wouldn't you know it? Not a cop car in sight. Standing at the curb on the east side of the street, he turned his head left toward the harbor, a minute's walk away to the south. Through puffs of fog condensing in the chill night air from his ragged panting, Zinc could see the old ship that used to be the Seven Seas floating restaurant, its lights now snuffed by a financial crisis. Beyond that, the SeaBus chugged across the moon-dappled water toward the distant lights of the port's loading docks.

But no sign of the pair.

Nor was there any trace of them uphill to the north. The neon strip that marked the skid road of yesteryear ran up the mountain-side to hunt the Lions crouched on the ridge. Squinting hard to spot the fugitives if they were fleeing on foot, Zinc caught the rumble of an engine revving in the next-door parking lot. Before he could sprint to intercept it at the exit across the sidewalk, a convertible with its top up came screeching out in a peel of rubber to fishtail up the street.

"Damn!" cursed Chandler.

The lot was full when he'd arrived, so his car was a block away.

At zero to sixty in 6.2 seconds, the car took off in a flash. The rumble-mobile was a 1970 Oldsmobile 442, Indy pace car model. Beneath the hood scoops, a 455-cubic-inch engine and four-barreled carb made it fly. Rebuilt with loving care so "the numbers matched," it was a white beauty with black and red racing stripes. The rumble came from straight pipes that left Zinc eating its dust, and as the two-door automatic roared away from him, the last detail that mooned the Mountie was the ass-end California plate.

Rumble, rumble . . .

What an echo, reverberating behind him.

No, not an echo.

An independent growl.

The Mountie looked back to find a chopper angling off Esplanade onto Lower Lonsdale. With a bushy red beard and long rusty locks flapping in the wind behind his horned Viking helmet, the biker could have been the Norse god Thor of Valhalla, who hurls the thunderbolts in Scandinavian myth, out for a putt on his custom-made machine. Built from the ground up for this leather-clad giant—there was so much leather on view tonight that surely cattle would soon be on the endangered species list—the hog was a fat-tire rigid chopper with a 38-degree raked front end. To transfer power to the road, that was the best style of frame. And power there was in the stage-four, 96-cubic-inch S&S stroker engine, the 3-inch open-belt primary drive Primo to thrust oomph from the motor to the transmission, and the one-of-a-kind Teflon-coated driveline. The rake in front made it a bit difficult for high-speed cornering, but with a crotch rocket like that, all ya really gotta do is grab a fistful of throttle, kick her down and hang on. Baby will always getcha home.

Perfect, thought Zinc.

Hiding the Smith behind his back and fishing his regimental badge from his pocket, the Mountie stepped out into the uphill lane of Lonsdale to stop the chopper. The biker danced a toe-tap tango to gear down, then wrenched the front brake handle and hit the rear brake pedal. Only then—once the hog grunted to a halt—did Zinc realize that Red Beard was all brawn. And twice his size.

"Police," Chandler barked. "Emergency. I'm commandeering your bike."

"Fuck you," Red Beard snarled.

"You're obstructing."

"I'll do more 'n that if ya try t' steal ma hawg."

Zinc flashed the pistol.

"What? Yer gonna shoot me?"

The outlaw's laugh was a blast in a canyon.

"Then start shootin', Cop. Ya want ma hawg, ya gotta pry it from ma cold, dead hands."

The Mountie's glare dropped to the hog. The machine was a work of art. It gleamed from several coats of smoked gunmetal-gray metallic paint and tons of chrome with lots of polished billet aluminum. The seat was a Corbin gunfighter that tapered over the fender. No way would the biker surrender his baby without a fight.

"Okay," Chandler said. "I'm commandeering *you*."

"Yer gonna ride bitch on a rigid?"

"That's the idea."

"Cop, this is a one-man horse that now and then gets a little skank on the back."

"Let's ride."

"It's your ass."

Zinc swung on behind Red Beard.

"Pig on a hawg. Hang on, Cop. Yer really gonna feel it. Ya got just enough padding back there to keep Mama's clam from sticking to the fender."

"Shut up and go."

A squeal of rubber up the hill galvanized Red Beard into action. It wasn't necessary for Zinc to point out their quarry. To avoid the red light at Third, the Olds took the corner at Second in a skid, then disappeared to the east in a haze of dark exhaust.

The howl as the bike shot forward was what you'd get from a werewolf with its balls crushed in a vise. The Mounties patrol on Harleys—the stereotypical bike gang's bike—but this machine was born from an evolved gene pool. So unexpected was the rocket thrust that Zinc was caught off guard. Holstering his pistol to call in the chase, he had his portable radio halfway from his belt to his other hand so that he could switch channels from E Com, the Mounties' central communications network, to North Van detachment's dedicated frequency to summon backup and direct roadblocks. When the g-force of the chopper launching into hot pursuit almost hurled him from the saddle, Zinc was forced to pincer-grip both arms around the barrel chest of the biker and hang on for dear life.

The radio went flying.

The hog took the corner at Second as the Olds careened off that street onto St. Georges a block ahead to zoom north again. Second was wide, so the bike could really open up, and the Cheers bar and the fast-food joints whizzed by in a blur. Then they too were on St. Georges and heading up to Third when the rumble-mobile took a hard right into a long, thin alley. A man taking the garbage out was almost clipped as the fugitives put pedal to metal to shake off the pursuers. Three-story apartment blocks and cars parked, noses in, flashed past the hog as it narrowed the gap. Bursting out the far end to meet a No Exit sign, the Olds—unable to continue straight—almost flipped as it cornered left onto St. Andrews. Red Beard gripped the clutch on one handle and worked the toe shifter to gear down. From the corner of his right eye as they exited from the alley, Zinc caught a glimpse of the B.C. Rail tracks along the harbor and a burned-out boat moored ashore. Then his vision swung north in a dizzying whirl as the biker popped the clutch and cranked the throttle.

It was launch time.

Holy shit!

If Red Beard was trying to impress him, Zinc was impressed. This man rode his hog as if it were an extension of his body. If Red Beard was trying to scare him, Zinc had his heart in his throat. This was like riding a roller coaster with half the tracks missing. St. Andrews Avenue climbed the mountain until there was nowhere to go but into alpine bush. At this speed, every cross street became a ramp that launched motor vehicles into space. Ahead, the undercarriage of the Olds was putting on a light show, throwing off sparks as metal scraped concrete each time it leapfrogged a level. Arms straight, the biker leaned back like a bat out of hell—reminding Zinc of a rock album he had once seen— but no matter how heavy the metal of the chopper was, it wasn't heavy enough to keep them on the ground.

Can pigs fly?

The hog was airborne.

Through Third, through Fourth, through Fifth, through Sixth, the all-out chase continued. A car along any crossroad and they'd be creamed. Headlights would flash a warning, but there would not be enough time to brake. Fancy houses streaked by on both flanks. Bow windows. Peaked roofs. Dormer gables. Tudor boarding. Front porches. Shallow lawns. Some dated from pioneer times, while others were retro constructions. All were going up and down in queasy undulations as the airborne, earthbound, airborne, earthbound hog ascended the mountain.

"Yer gonna ride bitch on a rigid? It's your ass," the biker had said. Only now did Zinc fully understand the content of Red Beard's warning. The tapered seat was wedged in the crack of his butt like a thong bikini. The rigid meant that the bike's frame had no rear suspension. In other words, no shock absorber to blunt the slam of each hard landing. The bitch—in this case, *him*—was forced to press her tits hard against the outlaw's back while the rigid shuddered between her spread legs like the world's most powerful vibrator. Zinc felt as if he were being gang-raped in a prison yard.

Things were about to get even hairier.

Keith Road loomed ahead.

West to east across the slope of the mountainside, there were five major roads, and one of them was Keith. Here, just east of Victoria Park, where it intersected St. Andrews, Keith was a divided thoroughfare with a grassy swath down the center. The Olds shot through the stop sign on the curb, causing brakes to screech a moment before one eastbound car rear-ended another. Momentum carried the fugitives across that lane and the median, where, with a peel of rubber and a belch of smoke, the ragtop veered east in the westbound lane.

Now traffic was swerving and jumping both curbs to avoid head-on collisions.

The dominant brake on a chopper is the front-end one. Hit the rear brake too hard in a turn and you might skid out. Unlike a bicycle, which has little weight, a hog is heavy enough to keep hugging the ground. So Red Beard rode the front brake as they hit the intersection, leaning hard to the right to take the sharp corner, then he gunned the hog full-throttle in the eastbound lane so they could parallel the Olds on this side of the median.

Gaining . . .

Gaining . . .

Then out came the gun.

A block ahead, at St. Davids Avenue, the grassy median vanished and the lanes converged. Closing on the point where the parallel lanes joined, the Olds and its pursuers were on a collision course, when down slid the window on the passenger's side of the car so the hooker riding shotgun could blast at them. The gun in her grip was the piece the pimp had used to shoot up the bar.

Bwam! She fired as the Olds cut in front of the hog.

The biker leaned into a corner that didn't exist, angling across the rear of the Olds into the oncoming lane so they could put the car between them and the muzzle flash. That zig made the bullet miss its mark, then a quick zag realigned them with the backside of their quarry.

Ridgeway . . .

Then Moody Avenue whizzed by.

Ahead, Grand Boulevard met Keith on the left. Keith marked the southern toe of that wide green avenue up the mountainside. Queensbury—a much narrower road—took over on the right to descend the downhill slope. Responding perhaps to a shots-fired call from the bar, the flashing red-and-blue wigwags of a patrol car raced toward them on Keith. With squealing tires, the Olds took evasive action in another fishtail turn and detoured south on Queensbury.

The suicide run.

"Pull back!" Chandler shouted.

But Red Beard didn't hear.

The roar of the hog and the muffling of the Viking helmet squelched the cop's words.

Down this shallow canyon of single-story shops and single-family dwellings plunged the pursuing chopper like a bat *into* hell. Revved up to this speed at high rpms, his foot shifting up four gears to kick out all the stops, Red Beard was amazed that his baby didn't let him down, for she had a false neutral between her third and fourth gears. The wind whipped his long locks across the

Mountie's face. Through Sixth, through Fifth, through Fourth, they plummeted at warp speed.

"Pull back!

"Pull back!

"Pull back!" Zinc hollered, but to no avail. His shouting retreated in their jet stream.

Unfortunately for the fugitives, Queensbury ended at Third. Beyond that T-intersection was Moodyville Park, commemorating the settlement of Moodyville, from whence sailed the barque *Ellen Lewis* on November 24, 1864, carrying the first cargo of lumber from Burrard Inlet.

In a blur, the car was across Third and heading into the park. Passing a fire hydrant that signaled the start of an access lane, it barreled along the bumpy tract that L'd to the right, where—unable to take a curve at such a high speed—the Olds shot into space as the ground dropped away beneath it.

It wasn't the Grand Canyon, but it was drop-off enough. In a soar reminiscent of the climax in *Thelma and Louise,* the convertible was airborne in a graceful descending arc, until it slammed the hard reality of this less-than-sheer cliff. The nosedive had carried it fifty yards down the tree-studded slope, where it bounced and took off again, picking up momentum like a snowball rolling downhill. The gas tank blew in midair, and the Olds plunged toward the Low Level Road as a blazing fireball.

Unlike the Californians, Red Beard did know the lay of the land. On many a warm summer night, he'd gone for a putt with a bitch on the rigid, and he knew all the haunts—like Moodyville Park—where he could pull in, tear off her pants, lay her down and fuck her under the stars. So there was no need for Zinc to shout "Pull back!" as they roared across Third. The biker knew the chase was over, and he geared down.

The hog braked to a halt where the Olds had left terra firma.

Tanker trucks cannot use Third Street because of the runaway grade on the west-to-east hill. To skirt the harbor, they must use the Low Level Road between the cliff that plunges from Moodyville Park and the grain elevator by the railroad tracks near Neptune

Terminal. The trucker of one of those oil rigs had parked his tanker on the inside shoulder of the road at the foot of the cliff to check a shredded tire, and he stood there examining it as the Olds came flying in over him to hit the concrete and bounce like a fiery basketball toward the railroad tracks and a grain hopper being loaded with wheat from the silo.

The man was no fool. He ran like hell.

It seems laughable that something as wholesome as bread contains a deadly explosive. A grain-dust explosion unites four factors. The first is fuel, which is the grain dust itself. A solid fuel burns only at its surface, where there is air. A cloud of dust particles, however, has an immense surface area. As the size of the particles decreases, the chance of explosion increases, and where there's a concentration of between forty and four thousand grams of dust per cubic meter, as there was in the hopper tonight, watch out!

The second factor is oxygen, which was present too. Combustion results when oxygen and fuel are ignited.

An ignition source is the third factor. If a cigarette or welding spark is enough, imagine the combustion potential of a flaming car like the Olds crashing into a grain hopper.

The fourth and final factor is confined space, for explosions result from the instantaneous buildup and release of pressure caused by rapid burning. Here, amid the clanking and ratcheting from the heavy machinery, each bin, silo, conveyor housing, bucket elevator and hopper car offered itself as a pipe bomb.

The hopper blew apart when the Olds rammed into it. That blast set off a cascade effect as the pressure wave from the primary explosion billowed layered dust into clouds in other areas a microsecond ahead of the flame front.

BOOOOM!

The series of secondary explosions rocked the street as each blast set up and then set off the next. The ground shook like an earthquake at five points on the Richter scale. A ball of fire rolled out to wrap the fugitives in the Olds in a blanket of flames. As powerful as dynamite or natural gas, the combined force of the multiple grain-dust explosions hurled the car back across the Low Level Road, where what was left of the Olds pierced the parked oil tanker as blazing shrapnel, blowing it sky-high like a hellish geyser.

Heat from that eruption singed Red Beard's beard.

The shock wave almost knocked the biker and the Mountie off the hog.

All that remained of the fugitives rained down as ash.

"When you Mounties get your man, you *really* get him," the biker said.

DEAD END

The newspapers were spread across one of the three antique library tables that had been joined in a U to make up C/Supt. Robert DeClercq's desk at Special X. The papers were calling it a "miracle" that no innocent bystanders were killed in the high-speed chase. Denny the Barkeep had earned his fifteen minutes of fame through a series of inside-scoop interviews in which he recounted how he had "fingered both killers for the Mounted Police" because it was his "bartender's duty to protect the producers, directors and casting agents of the industry that I hope will soon employ me." As for those who'd been at work in the grain elevator that night, never had they been so thankful for labor strife. The threat of a wildcat strike fomented by two malcontents had pulled the staff away from their posts shortly before the Olds came in for a landing. Lucky too was the trucker who'd run from the rig. He had—to quote one reporter—"experienced an epiphany, the effect of which was to veer him toward a new career. He will either try out for the Olympic team as a sprinter or switch to transporting Brussels sprouts instead of flammables."

"Is it serious?"

"What, Chief?"

"Your new relationship?"

DeClercq tapped the photograph of Chandler on the front page of *The Province*. Snapped as Zinc and Red Beard arrived on the customized chopper at the scene of the explosion on the Low Level Road the night before last, it caught the inspector hugging the outlaw's back like a gang girl. The cutline for the candid shot read, "Strange bedfellows."

"I'm his bitch on a rigid."

"I don't want to hear," said DeClercq, wincing. "Your sex life is none of my business, Inspector. As long as whatever you do on his rigid is done *out* of uniform."

"You're a card," punned Zinc as he pinned a tarot card to the Strategy Wall in DeClercq's office, located on the second floor of the Tudor building at Thirty-third and Heather. Here, at the West Coast headquarters of the RCMP—a string of structures that stretched four blocks south to Thirty-seventh—the floor-to-ceiling corkboard that sheathed both windowless walls of this airy, high-vaulted corner loft was the operational heart of Special X. Fiftyish, lean and wiry, his dark hair now graying at the temples and flanking even darker, brooding eyes, DeClercq was, above all other skills, a military strategist, so when he worked a case, he worked it visually. The Strategy Wall was his equivalent of the campaign maps on which generals have moved toy soldiers around for centuries.

"He's a card too," Chandler said, pinning a photo of the vic found suspended upside down at the Lions Gate beside the tarot card depicting the Hanged Man.

"Déjà vu."

"I'll say."

"It reminds me of the Ripper."

The chief finished perusing the report from Internal that lay on his desk—searching for signs that witch hunters were out to crucify Zinc, DeClercq's second-in-command—then he pushed back his chair to join Chandler at the Wall. The chair was an antique from the early days of the Force, high-backed with a barley-sugar frame and the bison-head crest of the Mounties carved as a crown. A portrait titled *Last Great Council of the West* hung behind the desk. Guarded by the Mounted Police, their hands on their swords, the pith-helmeted governor general, the Marquess of Lorne, sat in regal splendor beneath an awning at Blackfoot Crossing in 1881, a tribe of feathered Indians squatting at his feet. In recent years, the Force had changed to embrace both founding myths. Now there were whole detachments of Native officers, and DeClercq's third-in-command was a full-blooded Plains Cree.

The modern Mounties stood side by side in front of the juxtaposed pinups. There was a time, way back in 1921, when this heritage building—once known as the Heather Stables—had been a barracks for 200 redcoats and 140 horses. Befitting its royal pedigree, DeClercq's office gazed out across a vast expanse of green lawn at Queen Elizabeth Park on the crest of Little Mountain. The morning sun beaming through the front windows highlighted the bloodshed in the photo of the dangling victim so that it glared as red as a Horseman's scarlet tunic.

"Quod superius," Chandler said as he tapped the tarot card.

"As above," DeClercq translated.

"Sicut inferius," said the inspector, sliding his finger across to the crime-scene photo.

"So below," the chief translated. "You even remember the Latin?"

"For the past two days, Alex and I have rehashed the Ripper case. And I reread *Deadman's Island,* her account of our ordeal."

Mentioning Alex, the Ripper and Deadman's Island flashed Zinc's memory back. Etched in his mind as vividly as if it were this instant in time was the first glimpse he had caught of Alexis Hunt. The floatplane was rocking at the dock in Vancouver's harbor. All but one of the crime writers invited to a mystery weekend at an as-yet-undisclosed location were aboard. The event had been auctioned off to aid Children's Hospital. The secret benefactor who had outbid all rivals had challenged the sleuths to match wits with a "real cop" for a $50,000 prize. If the cop won, the prize would also go to charity, so C/Supt. Robert DeClercq of Special X had been asked to provide a good detective for a good cause. Zinc Chandler had mostly recovered from a bullet to his head, but he was still suspended from active duty until the aftermath of the Cutthroat fiasco was sorted out, so that's how he found himself seated among the slew of writers in the float plane.

A Mickey Mouse assignment.

Or so he had thought.

Barely discernible through the rain was the city's downtown core. Huddled like an urchin at its feet was the shack of Thunderbird Charters. From the hut to the floatplane out on the water stretched a gangway and the heaving pier. The woman sea-legging down the gangplanks struggled against the Pacific squall, suitcase in one hand, umbrella in the opposite fighting the wind to block the slanted rain. Her black coat flapped about her like Batman's cape, revealing a black pinch-waisted jacket and black jeans tucked into black cowboy boots. Her blonde hair was pulled back in a ponytail and clipped with silver heart-shaped barrettes, but wayward strands dancing about her face masked her features. Only as she climbed up into the plane did Zinc grasp her beauty: eyes as azure as South Seas lagoons, delicate bone structure around a most kissable mouth, with the grace of a ballerina in every move. It was the cliché of love at first sight, and Zinc's heart was gone.

It still was.

Their destination had turned out to be the hellhole of Deadman's Island. Their secret benefactor was none other than Jack the Ripper. Not the *real* Ripper—for that monster was long dead—but a rabid psychotic who thought he could use the Magick of the Tarot to conjure Jack from the there and then of East End London in 1888 to the here and now of modern-day Vancouver.

The ensuing carnival of carnage had cut short the careers of most of the writers lured to the island. One by one, the psycho had picked them off in fiendish ways, and had Zinc not thwarted him before he could sign the final occult symbol in blood, there would have been no survivors to tell their tale of horror. That task had fallen to Alex, during the many months she spent at home in Cannon Beach, Oregon, nursing Zinc back to health from a stabbing at the hands of the psychotic Ripper. *Deadman's Island* became the title of her resulting book.

"I assume the Ripper's still locked away on Colony Farm?" said DeClercq, pulling the inspector's mind back to the Strategy Wall.

"Yes," replied Chandler. "I phoned FPH. He's confined in Ash 2, the high-security ward."

"What about visitors?"

"No one suspicious. His only visitors are his lawyer and support staff from that law firm."

"Wes Grimmer still his counsel?"

"Uh-huh," replied Zinc. "But the Ripper is so far gone that he may never be fit to stand trial."

"Is this the work of a copycat?" The chief forked two fingers of one hand at the Hanged Man card and the photo of the suspended corpse pinned to the Strategy Wall.

"It could be," said the inspector. "The Ripper's occult motive was all over the media at the time of his arrest. And Alex set it out in detail in her book."

"You don't sound convinced."

"The M.O. is different, Chief. Our Ripper hanged four women in Vancouver at locations selected to form an inverted cross on a street map of this city. That mimicked what Jack the Ripper might have done in the East End of London with his first four victims. Then our Ripper lured a final female victim to Deadman's Island to kill her at a 'Magick place' so that astral projection would propel his consciousness into the occult realm. Jack the Ripper might have done the same with his fifth and final victim in Room 13 of Miller's Court. But here we have a single victim who is *male,* and the cross seems to be formed in how the man was strung up."

"So it isn't the Ripper. And it might not be a copycat."

Chandler nodded. "The Tarot has enough influence on its own to spawn an occult killer."

"Refresh me, Zinc."

The Tarot, Chandler explained, is one of the great systems of divination. The others are the I Ching and Scandinavian runes. Tarot magic is "in the cards," as each symbol relates a seeker to the physical and spiritual worlds. Symbols evoke both conscious and subconscious reactions, so it is believed that each card opens a door to the occult mind. The word "occult" means "unknown" or "hidden." Occult manifestation occurs when subconscious insight enlightens the conscious reality of the seeker. Divination empowers the mind to bring the occult into being, so the cards reflect what is, has been and will be. The Magick is in the seeker's transmutation.

The origin of the Tarot is an unsolved mystery. The deck has worn many guises through the centuries, but the basic meaning of each symbol has remained the same. A tarot deck consists of seventy-eight cards. The fifty-six in the four suits are called the Minor Arcana, and they evolved into modern playing cards. The twenty-two symbolic pictures are the Major Arcana, and those images reflect the occult's Greater Secrets.

Occult power is omnipotent. That's the basic law. All things— including us—reflect a greater power—the greater power of the occult realm.

So what's "up there" . . .

Quod superius . . .

Projects "down here" . . .

Sicut inferius . . .

And manifests itself as what we call reality.

"As above, so below."

The Tarot hides the key to the occult realm. Find that key and a seeker will gain occult power. The Greater Secrets of the Major Arcana have been attributed to many sources. To Egyptian hiero-glyphics in history's oldest book. To the kabbalistic lore of ancient Hebrews and nomadic gypsies from India. To the city of Fez in Morocco, where symbols were used as the common language of diverse cultures. Even to refugees from Atlantis, who encoded dark wisdom in the deck as their doomed land sank into the sea.

"For Jungians," Zinc said, "tarot symbols represent the arche-types of our collective unconscious. Whatever their origin, the Greater Secrets were mysteries even back in the Dark Ages. The oldest deck found in Europe dates from 1392."

"That's the problem," said DeClercq. "The Tarot has stood the test of time. Anything that old takes on sacred meaning. The world is full of true believers seeking Greater Secrets. What motivates a suicide bomber to kill himself in the name of Islam? How many witches or heretics were burned at the stake in the name of Christ, and how many 'heathens' were enslaved by zealous missionaries? If that's the curse of divine religions espousing peace and harmony, what's the power of the Tarot, which is tied to the black arts?"

"Power enough to motivate murder."

"And captivate a psycho."

"Especially—" Zinc began.

"The Hanged Man," finished DeClercq.

The most obscure card in a tarot deck is the Hanged Man. To hang upside down is a time-honored symbol for spiritual awakening. Odin, the Norse god, so hanged himself on Yggdrasil, the wonder tree, so he could gain mystical power to read the fortune-telling runes. Yoga practitioners stand on their heads to move energy from the base of their spines to their inverted brains. Caught in a moment of suspension before all is revealed, the Hanged Man symbolizes sacrifice to gain prophetic power. Reversal in life is possible through reversal of mind. This card hides the key to the occult realm. That's why it encodes the most sought-after Greater Secret in the Tarot.

The Mounties studied the pinned-up card.

"Remember how it works?" Chandler asked.

"Sort of," said DeClercq. "It's been a while since I last read the Ripper file and *Deadman's Island.*"

"The seeker blindly picks a card from the Major Arcana—"

"His significator."

"—to reveal his inner being."

"In the case of our Ripper, that card was the Hanged Man."

"For Jack the Ripper too."

"Or so our Ripper thought."

"Because of the theory of the Golden Dawn."

The Order of the Golden Dawn was founded in nineteenth-century Britain by S. MacGregor Mathers. Members of the Dawn included Bram Stoker, the author of *Dracula,* Aleister Crowley, the notorious Satanist, and A. E. Waite, who designed the card of the Hanged Man pinned to the Strategy Wall. In 1888, the year of Jack the Ripper, Mathers penned *The Tarot: Its Occult Signification.* His theory—adopted by the Dawn—was that the Tarot was a door through which seekers could work their will on the universe.

How?

By astral projection.

Between the occult realm and its reflection as the here and now of reality lies what Mathers called the astral plane. Psychic vibrations pulse through that cosmic medium to create our physical world. The Dawn thought it possible, with the right key, to intercept those wavelengths before they reflected down here. If the Tarot hid the key to the occult realm, properly ritualizing its symbols would not only open the closed path to the astral plane, but also enable the seeker to project his own consciousness toward the occult realm so that his "astral double" could intercept and alter the psychic vibrations before they arrived to reflect as the here and now, thereby changing the illusion of our reality.

Heady stuff.

Do *you* want to be a god?

All it required was the right tarot card properly ritualized and the seeker could manifest occult power under *his* control.

"Did Jack the Ripper ritualize symbols in the Tarot?" wondered DeClercq.

"Our Ripper thought so," Chandler replied.

"That's the problem with symbols—they get ritualized. A symbol that captivates the imagination elicits a more profound response than the actuality it represents. A dying Catholic fears death and the afterlife until a priest gives him last rites and signs him with a Christian cross to open the door to heaven and everlasting peace. Did Jack the Ripper visualize a cross in the Hanged Man, and ritualize signing it in female blood to open the door to the astral plane and occult power?"

"I see a cross."

"So do I."

"And so did our Ripper."

"The intriguing question is, did Jack?" said DeClercq.

What's baffling about the first four killings by Jack the Ripper is that those four murder scenes—when plotted on a map of London's East End—symbolize the four points of an inverted cross. The chance of that being coincidence defies all odds, so did Jack the Ripper consciously kill four females at those *predetermined* spots?

By Scotland Yard's estimate, twelve hundred prostitutes haunted those streets, so finding a suitable sacrifice for his knife was no problem. Equally puzzling is why Jack was not caught. Despite the tight police dragnet and roaming vigilantes, the Whitechapel demon repeatedly vanished into thin air.

Where did he go?

Into the astral plane?

"That's what our Ripper thought," said DeClercq.

"And that's why he's at Colony Farm."

The Mounties switched focus from the pinned-up tarot card to the crime-scene photo beside it. Minus the Hanged Man's belted jacket, the naked corpse suspended upside down by one leg from the hotel room's ceiling beam mimicked the obscure card in the flesh. The body's left ankle was tied behind the right thigh to position it in place. The wrists were cuffed together at the small of the back. And a halo of nails—like a crown of thorns—was hammered into the skull.

"So," said DeClercq, "does the same psychology apply here? Like our Ripper—and perhaps Jack—did whoever killed this man find motive for murder in the Tarot?"

"A tarot card was left in the room," Chandler said. "The Hanged Man was used to chop six lines of cocaine. Traces were found on a table by the front windows."

"Three people?"

"Looks that way. Two lines apiece. One for each nostril of the vic and his two killers."

"Coke and the Tarot. A spooky combination. If the killers were in the grasp of cocaine psychosis, God only knows what motive they saw in the card."

"The pimp and the hooker were jitterbugged by blow. That's why they shot up the bar downstairs."

"What evidence do we have that ties them to the vic?"

"According to the barkeep, he saw the vic, Romeo Cardoza, who had just flown in from L.A., talking to the pimp and the hooker—whose names were Gord and Joey—in the bar on the night the vic was killed. Gord and Joey—the barkeep thought they were brother and sister—were also up from L.A. They had been hanging out in the bar for about a week."

"What did the three talk about?"

"He didn't overhear. But Gord was a pusher who was snorting his own supply, and Joey was an S&M hooker who was into rough trade and discipline. The pair could be hired for a two-on-one, and that's what Gill Macbeth thinks went on in the room. The base of Romeo's penis and his anus were raw."

"DNA? Forensics?"

"Nothing so far, Chief. Evidently, the killers cleaned up after they were through. The condoms used were removed. The body was scrubbed with chemicals where there could be telltale fluids. All fingerprints were wiped away. Even the bed was vacuumed of hairs and fibers. If we do find something forensic, there's nothing to match it with. The combined destruction by the grain-dust and tanker-truck explosions obliterated both suspects."

"Have you traced them?"

"Uh-uh. No prints or photos. The Olds was stolen in L.A. from a man who's out of the country. The owner didn't know it was gone until we told him."

"Does anything tie Gord and Joey to the murder in the hotel room?"

"Just the coke traces on the table and the tarot card. We obtained a sample—no questions asked—of coke the pair had sold to another buyer in the bar. Lab tests have proved that both drug samples came from the same supply."

"Can we link Gord and Joey to the Tarot?"

"They came from California."

DeClercq smiled. "That state does produce more than its fair share of New Age gurus, but I doubt that connection would stand up in a court of law."

"Manson found motive for murder in 'Helter Skelter,' the Beatles song. It's less of a stretch to imagine two L.A. coke fiends getting orders to kill from the Hanged Man."

"The halo of nails is significant."

"In more ways than one, Chief."

"How so?" DeClercq asked.

"They did double duty. Not only did pounding in the nails signify the nimbus on the tarot card, but they were hammered in while the three were having sex."

"Kinky."

"I'll say. And the nails were short. Long enough to pierce the skull and enter his brain, but short enough to kill him slowly, with a lot of clenches and spasms. His mouth was gagged to keep Romeo from crying out, and toxicology tests on blood drawn at the post-mortem revealed a heavy dose of Viagra in his veins."

"A *double* motive?" said DeClercq.

"Sex and the Tarot."

"What about the movie mentioned in the papers?"

"Bed of Nails?" Chandler said.

"An ironic title. How does that fit in?"

"The film's in trouble. Way over budget. Cardoza was a producer. He flew in from Hollywood on the day he was hanged, checked into the Hyatt downtown, then crossed the harbor to the Lions Gate to score the coke and buy sex."

"Where he died in a bed with nails in his head, just like the title of his troubled film?"

"Could be coincidence."

"I don't buy that. Do you?" asked DeClercq.

"The Tarot plays no part in the film. I checked."

"What was Cardoza here to do?"

"Crack some heads."

"But instead he got his head cracked," said DeClercq.

"Motive?"

"Why not?"

"Someone with his head on the chopping block, who's got an ax to grind?" said Chandler.

"You're mixing metaphors. But perhaps the motive for Cardoza's murder mixes metaphors too. Say someone involved with the production was going to lose his job. Or say there had been a fraud, so he might go to jail. What if Cardoza was the only one who knew, and he flew in from L.A. to confront the thief? Perhaps the thief was still back in Hollywood, and Cardoza flew in to gather evidence to nail the crook. The guy on the hot seat didn't want that, so he hired the kinky coke freaks in Vancouver, or had them come up from L.A. before Cardoza. Their contract was to snuff the producer in a way that masked the motive, so they mixed the metaphor of the Tarot up with *Bed of Nails* and finished him off in a coked-up orgy of blood and sex. Luckily for the contractor, the actual killers died while fleeing from you, and we're left scratching our heads, trying to figure out a bogus Tarot motive."

"Or maybe it's truly a dead end."

"Let's hope," said DeClercq. "We've got a man dead in his room, and we've got two innocent people shot dead in the bar. And we've got a lot of property damage on Low Level Road. The papers are convinced that a pair of psychos ran amok and—thanks to you— were taken down before more people died. Internal won't touch you as long as you're the hero, so quietly check out the various angles as if you were tying up loose ends. And if you hit that dead end, leave it at that."

"Let's hope," said Chandler.

"I know what you're thinking. What if the pimp and hooker only supplied Cardoza with the drugs, and the reason they bolted from the bar was because they were coked up and afraid you were going to bust them for trafficking?"

"That's possible."

"I agree. In which case, there may still be two psychos loose. But at the moment—based on what we know—that possibility is a dead end too. If the Tarot is driving them to kill, we won't know that for sure until they kill again."

ROOM 13

"Murder!" she cries as I muffle the word by clamping my left hand over her mouth. Already naked except for a dingy linen chemise, Mary Kelly sits on the edge of her corner bed in cramped Room 13 of Miller's Court, waiting for me to undress and join her on the bare sheet. The bedclothes, pushed down to the foot of the mattress, lie rumpled close to the chair on which her garments are neatly folded. By the guttering glow of the single candle on the bedside table, its flame flickering from the draft blowing in from the yard outside through a broken window, I see stark terror staring at me from her wide-open eyes. Up jerk her flailing arms to ward off the bite of my knife as I push her back flat onto the grubby sheet and wrench her head sideways to bare the carotid artery, which is pulsing wildly in her corded throat. Slash after slash is intercepted by her forearms, and the blade rips jaggedly through her shredding defenses until she cowers away from the pain. I go for the jugular, still exposed despite her struggling, and slit that half of her neck to the bone.

Blood sprays the wall on the far side of the bed.

I stood drinking earlier in one of the public houses on Commercial Street when Black Mary Kelly approached to ask if I would buy her a gin. "Make it worth my while and I'll buy us the bottle," I said, so that's why we left the pub and angled into Dorset Street to wend our way here. There's no better place in the East End for what I have to do, and I knew that the moment she told me we could drink and fuck in Room 13 of Miller's Court.

Room *13*!

Surely a Magick place.

Number 26 Dorset Street had once been a house. This three-story brick-front on the north side of the cobblestone road is now divided up into rooms let out to whores. Dorset Street has more than its fair share of common lodging houses, and the building across from the archway that leads to Miller's Court rents three hundred beds every night. Here in the shadow of Spitalfields Church and Market, Mary and I escaped from the midnight rain by ducking under the dripping arch into a narrow passage between Number 26 and the chandler's shop next door. We groped through the darkness toward the squalid cul-de-sac of open yard beyond. Miller's Court was deserted as we emerged, squared by six sooty houses with dirty whitewashed faces and begrimed green shutters. In the yard were dustbins and a pump. On our right as we quit the passage were two doors. The first accessed the upstairs of Number 26. The second, at right angles to it and facing us in the corner nook, was the door to Mary's crib.

Unsteady on her feet from drink, Mary opened the door.

Before Number 26 was converted into separate rooms, this down-and-out hovel was the back parlor of the original house. A false partition was all that cut it off from Number 26 now, but because it had a private entrance off the common yard, it was renumbered Room 13 of Miller's Court.

The harlot's crib we entered was about twelve feet square. As the door swung in to our right, it knocked against the table beside the corner bed. Mary struck a match to light the candle on the table, and by its glow my eyes surveyed Room 13. The only furnishings apart from the bed and the table were two chairs by the fireplace opposite the door. The wall on the yonder side of the bed was the added partition, and where it met the hearth in the far corner, an open cupboard yawned, revealing bits of crockery, some empty ginger beer bottles and a crust of bread. The sole decoration was a cheap print of *The Fisherman's Widow* above the fireplace, which, I noted, had a kettle but no fuel. So destitute was Mary that she couldn't afford coal. The pair of windows to our left gazed out on Miller's Court, the smaller one closer to the door having the broken pane. The makeshift curtain that covered the hole was an old coat, and through the opening I heard the gurgle of rainwater rushing down the pipe affixed to the bricks.

How pathetic.

Mary Kelly was a social parasite.

"Give us a drink," Mary slurred, extending her hand for the bottle of gin.

"And?" I said.

"Don't worry, luv. I'll do right by you."

I passed her the bottle and watched her take a swig. Much younger than the other whores I'd ripped, she was—I would say—about twenty-five. If not for the ravages of drink, she might have been a comely lass, with her fine head of hair, fair complexion and inviting blue eyes. Vanity kept her from covering that mane with a bonnet or a hat, and beneath her shabby dark skirt and the red knit crossover draped around her shoulders hid the most alluring figure Jacky's knife would ever gut.

"Let's see what you've got," I said.

And so I watched her strip.

The force of my attack has shoved Mary across the bed. The spurts from severed vessels create a blood-spatter pattern that forms an *M* on the far wall. The crown of her skull is in the corner where the headboard of the bed abuts that false partition, and the sheet beneath is saturated with so much blood that it is seeping through the mattress to pool on the floor. Patiently, I wait for the spurting to cease. Then, satisfied she's dead, I haul Mary's body back to this half of my feather-down dissecting table.

The curtains over the windows will keep outsiders from peering in at my work. The candlelight, however, might attract a nocturnal friend to Mary's door, for it would not be glowing if she weren't still awake. The safer illumination would be a fire on the hearth, since that might be lit to keep the harlot warm as she sleeps. There is no fuel, but there is laundry heaped on the distant chair: a boy's shirt, two men's shirts, a black crepe bonnet and a white petticoat. Stuffing it all into the fireplace, I ignite it with the candle, and once I have stoked a blaze suitable for work, I snuff the wick between my fingers.

It is almost four a.m. by my pocket watch.

Time constraints curbed Jacky's fun with the first four whores. To signify the cross hidden in the Hanged Man, it was necessary for me to kill them outdoors. Each was merely a quarter of the tetrad four, so each had to *add* to the occult symbol signed in blood on the cobblestones of London's maze of streets.

For the triad three, I can take my time.

Bloodlust overcomes me as I begin to rip. With all the time in the world, I revel in taking Mary Kelly apart piece by piece. So intoxicating is the absolute freedom to allow my mind to go berserk that hours of time have slipped away before I rein my *lustmord* in, and when—panting as hard as if I had just run a few miles—I once more flip open my bloody watch to check the current time, I find the hands aligned north and south as six a.m.

"Her face," I mutter. "I must sign the three on her face."

Before carving the triad into Mary Kelly's flesh, I sweep my eyes around the room to survey my handiwork.

Bong . . .

Bong . . .

The steeple bells toll the new day.

Bong . . .

Bong . . .

It's Lord Mayor's Day in London town.

Bong . . .

Sorry, Your Worship, but you'll be upstaged.

Bong . . .

'Cause Jack the Ripper will steal your show.

The room is a butcher's shambles. What a sight to behold! Mary's folded clothes are the only sign of order. The garments on the grate have burned down to ashes and embers, and amid their glow I can still see the rim of the black bonnet and a fragment of the under-skirt. Relighting the half-melted candle on the bedside table, I hover over what remains of God's creation.

Even God has finally met His match.

Wearing what are now the tatters of her linen slip, Mary lies faceup on this half of the bed with her head turned on its left cheek to stare blankly at the door. Her hair fans out through a welter of blood like kelp in a red sea. So deep are the cuts to her throat that the bones of her neck are notched. Circular incisions removed both breasts, and along with the mammary tissue went the muscles down to the ribs. Intercostals between those ribs were cut through too, and the contents of her thorax are visible in the crevices.

Both arms are mutilated by the jagged defense wounds. The right limb is slightly angled from the raw mass of her torso, and it rests on the mattress with its forearm supine and its fingers clenched. The left arm is close to the body, with its elbow flexed at a right angle so the hand lies across the open abdomen. Both legs are splayed wide apart with obscene invitation, the left thigh at right angles to the trunk and the right forming an obtuse angle away from the groin. My experiment in anatomy has laid her bare. From her cunt to her costal arch, I've ripped her open, and what was once inside her belly is strewn about the bed. Mary's uterus, kidneys and one breast are tucked under her head. Her liver and the other breast are down by her feet. The intestines coiling from the empty cavity slither like a nest of snakes at one flank, while across the pit, by her left side, is her spleen. Heaped on the bedside table is a mound of red flesh stripped in three large flaps from her pelvis and legs. The jumble contains skin, fascia and muscles removed from both thighs, part of her right buttock, and Mary's sexual wares. Her right leg, almost denuded of flesh, shows the white of its bone. Empty of viscera, her abdominal cavity now contains only the remnants of partly digested fish and potatoes from her last meal.

All in all, I'd say the slashing, skinning and gutting of this whore is a work of art.

Rembrandt in blood.

Having harvested Mary's heart from her pericardium by reaching in through the ripped diaphragm below her lungs, I have the meat for my victory feast. Signifying the tetrad cross in the blood of the previous four has opened the path to the astral plane, so all I must do to complete the full cycle of occult manifestation is to carve the triad three into Mary's face. As I repeatedly slash the Hanged Man's hidden triangle into her flesh, I hack off Mary's nose, cheeks, eyebrows and ears until she is beyond recognition. So frenzied is this gashing that the blood-soaked sheet on the far corner of the mattress where I initially slit her throat is shredded too.

Suddenly, the coat that serves as a curtain billows and a cold wind blows in through the open pane. The embers on the hearth explode into a spray of sparks that transmogrify into cosmic stars as the features of Room 13 turn hazy and fade to black. The gin bottle in one hand, the knife and the heart in the other, I feel my consciousness project into the astral plane, streaking along the wormhole that burrows through space and time, hurtling thousands of miles west from London's East End and more than a century forward from 1888, until I rematerialize in Room 13 at the Forensic Psychiatric Hospital on Colony Farm.

Drenched in blood, I sprawl on my bed and bite into Mary's heart, washing her sweet meat down with cheap gin.

———•——•———

Port Coquitlam

Along the hall from the Ripper's room, Rudi Lucke sat daydreaming at the desk in the nursing station. He saw himself pinned to the mat in a wrestling ring by Jock Ogilvie, the sun-bleached hunk who'd patrolled the wards with him on the night after Halloween. In Rudi's wakeful wet dream, the croc wrestler from the Australian outback had him face down on the canvas so that all he could do was squirm. To a roar of approval from the crowd swarming forward to ringside for a closer look, Jock tore the skimpy shorts off the vanquished nurse's magnificent ass. Lord knows how many cable subscribers would watch Rudi being conquered on the sports network—

But—*poof!*—those imaginary screens went blank when the call came in from Central Control.

Sighing, Rudi raised that magnificent ass off the chair and left the station to stroll to Room 13 of Ash 2.

The Ripper's psychosis was still in a florid state, but the killer was no longer locked away in the seclusion ward. This being a hospital, not a jail, the madman was back in his regular room. Rudi glanced in through the oblong judas window in the door, and there the Ripper lay on his back beside the left-hand wall.

In one palm, the Ripper held something he was eating. Whatever it was, the imaginary delicacy bestowed upon him more gourmand pleasure than any real food offered at FPH could ever give.

In his other hand, he seemed to grip a bottle. From the way he winced each time he guzzled a phantom swig to wash down his repast, Rudi surmised the liquid in the non-bottle was strong booze.

He's time-traveling, Rudi thought as he swung open the door, and his eyes followed the wormhole tunnel through the series of collages that ran from the math calculations beside the Ripper's head, spiraling around to the occult symbols on the far wall and ending up at the tarot cards and photos of Jack the Ripper's hapless victims snapped during London's autumn of terror in 1888.

"You have a visitor," Rudi said.

THE KEY

They met late this afternoon in the same interview room at the Forensic Psychiatric Hospital out on Colony Farm where they had conspired four days ago to commit bloody murder. The Goth was already seated on one of the two chairs flanking the bare table in the austere, anti-septic cubicle when Rudi ushered in the florid psychotic from Ash 2's Room 13. Like before, the Ripper was dressed in a dark navy-blue sweatsuit and Velcro runners. Again, his eyes were black holes that seemed not only to suck the flesh of his face into his skull, but also to tug the Goth out of the here and now and into the occult realm. Once more, an odor of rancid cheese permeated the claustrophobic nook.

The door closed.

The Ripper sat.

The psychos faced each other.

The one the Mounties knew about.

And the one they didn't.

The Ripper set the tiny hourglass down on the table between them so the sand of time could flow from the past to the future. Stacking the twenty-two cards of his Major Arcana facedown beside the egg timer, he pushed the deck toward the Goth and said, "Pick a card."

"I picked a card last time."

"Yes, the Hanged Man."

"That's my significator. I don't want another one."

"You have no say in the matter. The Magick is in the cards. If you are truly chosen, the Tarot will say so."

The Goth picked a card randomly from the deck.

"Turn it over."

The Goth obeyed.

What stared up at them from the table was the Hanged Man.

"Study your card," the Ripper said. "What number do you see at the top?"

"The number twelve. In Roman numerals."

"How many signs are there in the zodiac?"

"Twelve," the Goth said.

"That's why the Hanged Man is the most important card in a tarot deck. The twelve symbolizes a complete cycle of occult manifestation in the here and now of our reality."

"The number of *my* significator."

"Yes, chosen one."

"Yours too?"

"I thought so. But then I made a mistake."

"What mistake?"

"I saw one too many occult symbols in the card."

Using the index finger of his left hand—the Devil's hand—the Ripper outlined three hidden symbols on the face-up card. In the mind's eye of the Goth, the Hanged Man looked like this:

"One leg is bent across the other to form a human cross. The cross—or tetrad—signifies the number four. There are four points to the cross. You see that symbol in the Hanged Man?"

The Goth nodded.

"That's why I ripped the first four whores where I did in London. Back in 1888, when I was Jack the Ripper. Plot the sites on a map of the East End and you will see that Polly Nichols, Annie Chapman, Long Liz Stride and Catharine Eddowes were sacrificed where they were to signify the inverted cross in the Hanged Man."

"Did that work?"

"Sort of. Signing that occult symbol in blood opened the closed path to the astral plane."

"To a time warp?"

"If you like."

"To a wormhole?" the Goth added.

"I didn't know it as a wormhole back then. With Einstein yet to be born, there was no expounded theory of relativity. I thought in terms of the theory of the Order of the Golden Dawn—Mathers, Crowley, Stoker, and Waite, the member who drew this card. Wormhole, time warp, astral plane. It matters not what term we use—all lead to the other dimension of the occult realm."

"Why did you remove the organs?"

"To eat," the Ripper said. "But that doesn't matter. As long as the sacrifice sheds human blood."

"To sign the cross?"

"*And* the triangle."

The Ripper licked his lips as if savoring his last taste of blood. The tips of both canines peeked down from behind his upper lip like Dracula's bloodsuckers.

"Back to the card. You see the triangle hidden in it? Both arms are folded behind the Hanged Man's back to straight-line its base. The top of his inverted head—as indicated by the nimbus—is the tip of the obscure occult symbol. The triangle—or triad—signifies the number three. There are three sides to the triangle."

Another nod. "Did you sign that in blood?"

"Yes, in the way I ripped Mary Jane Kelly to shreds in Room 13 of Miller's Court."

"To do what?"

"Project my astral double into the astral plane."

"Your consciousness?"

"Or doppelgänger. Choose the term you like. The effect of signing the triad in her blood was my astral projection."

"How?"

"Four times three equals what?"

"Twelve," the Goth replied.

"The number of the Hanged Man. Multiplying the tetrad four of the cross by the triad three of the triangle equates to the Magick number twelve on this card to complete a cycle of occult manifestation. $E = MC^2$. Energy, mass and the speed of light are interrelated. By astral projection, I hurled the energy of my mind into the astral plane of the occult realm. *Quod superius, sicut inferius.* 'As above, so below.' Since what's 'up there' projects 'down here,' as soon as my astral double vanished into the other dimension of the time warp—of the wormhole—the past reality of Jack the Ripper's autumn of terror in London, 1888, disappeared as well."

"You vanished?"

"I time-traveled. That's why they didn't nick me. Jack escaped to the future reality of what is now present-day Vancouver."

"Why here?" the Goth asked.

"Because of my mistake."

"The *third* symbol?"

"Right. I read the nimbus wrong. See how the belt and the braid down the front of the Hanged Man's jacket form a second cross? And how his collar joins with the nimbus around his head to form a circle? Combined, they seem to signify an inverted Mirror of Venus, the ancient occult sign for the female sex."

"A circle atop a cross. The symbol's still in use."

"I know. Which compounded my error. The Hanged Man signifies sacrifice to obtain occult power. But sacrifice of whom? Of women, the symbol suggested. That's why I ripped those whores in the East End: to sign the third symbol in blood. When astral projection landed me here in Vancouver, I knew I had made a mistake."

"Why?"

"Because I didn't end up where I wanted to go. Yes, I'd found the time warp into the occult realm, but I couldn't control the power surging around me. Somehow, I had read the Hanged Man wrong. Tarot power is controlled by those who interpret the symbols in a proper deck correctly. Instead, the power of the Tarot controlled me, projecting me unwillingly here to serve *its* purpose."

"What purpose?"

"We're together, aren't we? The mistake I thought Jack the Ripper had made was in not *hanging* those first four women. The Hanged Man depicts the three symbols hanging from a T, so after I ended up here, I set about correcting my 1888 mistake by hanging four women in Vancouver to signify what I thought must be the proper tetrad four in the card."

"It wasn't?"

"No. That just compounded my original error. All that did was open this end of the *same* wormhole that projected me here from 1888. And I didn't get to finish signing the triad in blood on Deadman's Island thanks to the meddlesome cop who's responsible for locking me up in here."

"Which brought us together."

"What brought us together was the will of the Tarot. I was sent here to meet up with you and pass on the Magick key."

"Why don't you escape from FPH like you did from the East End? By astral projection?"

"I can't, because the cop stopped me *before* I could kill the female I slashed with the triad symbol on Deadman's Island. Botching the cross denied me control over my occult power, and failing to sacrifice the triangle here means I can corporally manifest myself back in 1888 London, but I can't vanish from the reality of here and now."

The Ripper flipped the hourglass over on the table.

"Back and forth . . ."

The hourglass flipped again.

"From here to there to here . . . That's all I can do. The Tarot has made me a prisoner of my past mistakes."

"So that's why you gave me a *different* key to the occult realm?"

"Yes," said the Ripper. "The proper key has to be the tarot card itself."

The madman tapped the Goth's significator displayed on the table between them. "You don't have to sacrifice four victims to sign the cross. Nor do you have to sacrifice a fifth to sign the triangle. That Mirror of Venus I thought I saw was just an illusion. The jacket worn by the Hanged Man is irrelevant to the key. Therefore, so is the female occult symbol. What matters is that you signify the tetrad and the triad in blood by sacrificing a man and hanging him upside down to *literally* manifest the symbol of the Hanged Man on this card."

"Like you told me to do?"

"Yes," said the Ripper. "The important detail is the nimbus around the head. Without it, the inverted triangle won't have its tip, and the sacrifice will fail to signify the proper Magick."

"Have you seen the news?"

"No, I just returned from 1888."

The Goth dropped a file on top of the tarot card and flipped it open. The file was full of clippings from several local papers about the murder at the Lions Gate and the subsequent high-speed chase.

"I did it," said the Goth. "I signed the key in blood."

The Ripper read the clippings. "And?" he asked when he had finished.

"I *am* the chosen one."

"You found the wormhole?"

"And time-warped where I wished. Astral projection took me back to the island of Tangaroa in the nineteenth century."

"Why there?"

"Like you, I have a hunger to sate."

"Have you warped elsewhere?"

"I go where I please. All the inspiration in the occult realm is mine to use."

The Ripper fingered one of the clippings in the file. "What about the two killed in the car chase?"

"Scapegoats," said the Goth. "They sold cocaine to the sacrifice I hanged *before* he met up with me."

"Why choose him?"

"That was my earlier ruse. He was producing a film called *Bed of Nails*. My plan was to sign the nimbus with a halo of nails pounded into the skull, so I figured that by picking someone at work on that movie, I'd fool the Mounties into suspecting the killer might be linked to that production. The film's being shot in North Vancouver. That's why I picked the hotel bar as my hunting ground. It's where all the movers and shakers in the industry hang out."

"A double ruse."

"Yeah, I lucked out. *Bed of Nails* and a pair of kinky dealers from L.A. The cops investigating the case will hit as dead an end as the pimp and the hooker did."

"How'd you lure the right cop?"

"The one you want killed?"

"Him!" snarled the Ripper, stabbing a finger at one of the tabloid photos in the file.

"The sacrifice I stalked in the bar had just flown up from L.A. Kill an American and that brings in Special X. As luck would have it, the Special X cop was him."

"Luck be damned," the Ripper cursed. "It's the will of the Tarot."

"A deal is a deal. I owe you," said the Goth. "That's why I'm here today—to pay up. Give me the go-ahead and the cop will be dead by tomorrow."

"Not so fast. Why rush? You have all the time in the world." The Ripper flipped the hourglass over between them. "Revenge like mine is a dish best served cold. Of all the ways there are to get even with someone who fucked you over, what's the most degrading death you can imagine?"

"Eat him alive."

"Why's that?"

"It's the ultimate horror. What better way to exact revenge than by consuming your enemy piece by piece in front of his eyes, and then flushing him down the toilet as a pile of your shit?"

"Could you do that?"

"Yes."

"Then set it up. And I want him to know that your meal is billed to *my* account."

"To do it right might take a year and a half."

"You have a plan?"

"Yes."

"And a place?"

"Tangaroa."

"Good," said the Ripper. "Take all the time you need."

The psycho clawed his fingernail across the face of the Mountie in the photo of him and Red Beard astride the hog on the front page of *The Province*. The same Mountie who'd stopped him from signing the triad on Deadman's Island, and the cop who had locked him up in here to rot.

"Eat him for me," said the Ripper.

PART ii
MorLocks

The bodies were hung from the rafters above,
While Eddie was searching for another new love.

He went to Wautoma for a Plainfield deal,
Looking for love and also a meal.

When what to his hungry eyes should appear,
But old Mary Hogan in her new red brassiere.

Her cheeks were like roses when kissed by the sun,
And she let out a scream at the sight of Ed's gun.

Old Ed pulled the trigger and Mary fell dead,
He took his old ax and cut off her head.

He then took his hacksaw and cut her in two,
One half for hamburger, the other for stew.

—"A Visit from Old Ed," anonymous "Geiner"
about the Plainfield Ghoul

AMAZING GRACE

Coquitlam
April 11 (Seventeen months later)

A few miles northeast from Colony Farm—where the Ripper was safely confined in Room 13—loomed the social and architectural anachronism of Minnekhada Lodge. *Minnekhada* was the Sioux word for "beside running waters," and the name was brought to the West Coast in 1904 when Harry L. Jenkins left the United States to make his fortune as a lumber baron in what were then the untamed wilds of British Columbia. His 1,650-acre Coquitlam farm—nestled between the heights of Burke Mountain and the marsh flats of the Pitt River—faced a panorama of natural splendor that stretched across the Fraser River valley to the snowy cone of Mount Baker, seventy miles to the south in Washington State. In 1932, the farm passed to another lumber magnate, a man who would four years later become the king's lieutenant governor here in Lotusland. To reflect his royal position, Eric Hamber built Minnekhada Lodge. Conceived as a stately British home rusticated by the realities of a besieging wilderness, the house was fashioned as a Tudor-style Scottish hunting lodge that lorded over the countryside from a commanding knoll.

A pair of Celtic towers thirteen feet in height flanked the gateway to the lodge on Oliver Road. The drive up the knoll passed to the right of a turquoise swimming pool, then looped behind the manor to a courtyard plaza. A statue of Pan playing his flute graced the fountain in front of the main door. That door opened into an entrance hall with a floor checkered by black and white tiles. The banquet room beyond was a double-storied vault. The redbrick fireplace just left of the entry faced Dutch doors and windows that opened on the veranda. Spindled oak staircases ascended both sides of the room to balconies beneath the arched trusses and cedar beams of the dormered Jacobean roof. The master bedroom was tucked beyond one balcony, and off the other, the lodge boasted a genuine royal suite.

A steady stream of royalty—including the Queen—had partied and slept beneath the roof of Minnekhada Lodge. Lord Tweedsmuir and his sons had played polo on the manicured lawns out by the stables. Hunting parties had ventured out onto Addington Marsh to blast shotgun pellets at the waterfowl while drinks were served from a nearby cabin, extending bar service into the wilds. Returning victorious to this banquet room, the royals would swap their deer-stalker caps and tweeds for black ties and fancy gowns aglitter with jewels. Served by cooks and maids in starched uniforms, they would dine on the game they had bagged while a pet monkey fetched them bananas from a fruit bowl in the center of the table.

Seeing how Her Majesty the Queen was still commander-in-chief of the Royal Canadian Mounted Police, what better site could the Mounties of Special X have chosen for tonight's regimental dinner than Minnekhada Lodge?

God save the Queen.

———•·•———

Time, they say, heals all wounds. That's the optimist's point of view. A pessimist will tell you that time inflicts wounds, too . . . and the past year and a half had not been kind to Zinc Chandler.

Emotionally and physically, Zinc was a wounded soul. Losing the love of his life to death had hollowed out his heart to leave him empty and alone. At one point, he had teetered on the edge of suicide, and he might have eaten his gun if not for a fortuitous call to duty from Insp. Bob "Ghost Keeper" George and Sgt. Ed "Mad Dog" Rabidowski. That call had ultimately flown the three of them to Ebbtide Island on a rescue mission. In the pyrotechnics that followed, the RCMP helicopter had crashed into the sea, knocking Zinc out when his head hit the fuselage. That downing had concussed his already injured brain and seen him hospitalized, spending weeks convalescing from the blow. Tonight's festivities marked his return to red serge, but though this dinner had been organized to honor the heroic three, as far as Zinc's zest for life was concerned, he too had passed away.

Going through the motions.

The wheeze of the bagpipes filling with air should have quickened his heartbeat with joyful anticipation. The drone pipes filled the entrance hall of Minnekhada Lodge with bass a moment before the tartan-draped Mountie began to finger the melody pipe in a stirring Scottish march to lead the thin red line of Horsemen to the head table. In the aftermath of a hard-fought battle, Scottish Highlanders would hold a regimental dinner at which their commanders were piped in to prove they had survived the conflict. As the last vestige of the British colonial army, the redcoats of the Royal Mounted retain that tradition, so as the banquet hall resounded with the bagpipes' tunes of glory, C/Supt. Robert DeClercq—the host of the dinner—followed by Dep. Comm. Eric Chan, head of the Mounties in B.C. and the Yukon, then Insp. Zinc Chandler, Insp. Bob George and Sgt. Ed Rabidowski—the heroic three—were led single file through the entry door into the vaulted room.

Except for the violin (and perhaps the saxophone), no instrument makes the human heart soar quite like the heavenly shrill of the bagpipes. It used to be that Zinc was moved to almost religious euphoria by the glory of this magic—for was there any greater affirmation of what it means to have a righteous soul than the sound of "Amazing Grace" brought to life by the piper?—but since the day that tune was played at Alex Hunt's memorial, the soaring of bagpipes had left him flat.

Going through the motions.

This hollow shell of a man.

Tonight, the redbrick fireplace was ornamented by a big stuffed bison head that had been removed from the stairwell that climbed to DeClercq's office on the top floor of Special X. Bordered by RCMP flags and red-and-blue banners, the hearth emitted a cheerful glow that burnished the rustic wood decor with coppery tints. The wail of the pipes echoed down from the shadowy peak as the procession to the head table doubled back and forth among the ranks of red serge. The banquet room was arranged to reflect a barracks mess, with the head table along the side wall to the right of the hearth and the rank and file of the Mounted facing them. Every diner in this hall but one had endured six months of rigorous training at Depot Division in Regina, Saskatchewan. Regimental dinners reinforced the camaraderie that glued them into the Force. Sure, there were other police forces around the world, but all cops knew *this* tradition was as good as it gets.

The thin red line.

They always get their man.

So why did Zinc feel so emotionally detached?

Who were all these people?

Nick Craven, Rachel Kidd, Rick Scarlett, Rusty Lewis—the gang was all here, but they seemed no more to Zinc than faces in a crowd. The procession reached the head table and two drams of Scotch were poured, then DeClercq locked arms with the Highlander to snap back both single malts in the time-revered tradition of "paying the piper." Parallel lines of red serge took their seats at the long tables, at which point it was time for another amazing grace. Zinc impressed himself that he got through the delivery of "grace before meat" without shaking his fist at God in anger for what He . . . She . . . It—whatever—had done to Alex.

You celestial psycho, he thought.

Satan damn You.

Burn in hell, God.

The first plate of roast beef and Yorkshire pudding was handed to the deputy commissioner. Mounted protocol demands that the commanding officer at a regimental dinner personally serve the most junior member present at the feast. To applause from comrades seated around the honored constable, Deputy Commissioner Chan carried the serving from the head table to place it before a Native rookie sitting at the rear.

Zinc's sense of detachment grew with each wave of alcohol. What had begun with hard spirits served before dinner continued with multiple bottles of wine uncorked throughout the meal. The overhead lights were dimmed as a lively dessert—mincemeat with blue brandy flames dancing a jig on top—was carried in ceremoniously and portioned out with vanilla ice cream or custard to cool it down. The head wound he had suffered in Hong Kong had put an end to Zinc's drinking—instead, he took Dilantin to ward off epileptic fits—so by the time port was being decanted for the "loyal toast," the inspector found himself surrounded by faces flushed as red as the sea of scarlet tunics.

It's no fun to be sober in a crowd of drunks.

As host, DeClercq was called on to test the "potability" of the ruby red, a ritual he performed with the panache of a natural showman. A barely perceptible nod of his head acknowledged the quality of the elixir, then a bottle was passed from hand to hand along each table. By tradition, port bottles are never set down.

Glasses filled, the redcoats rose to their feet. As six bars of "God Save the Queen" were played, Insp. Bob "Ghost Keeper" George raised his glass.

"The Queen!" the Cree declared.

"The Queen!" the ranks responded.

Coffee and cigars were passed around to end the formalities. High spirits reigned as the group broke down into small conversational circles. A regimental dinner is for members only. No spouses, significant others or hangers-on attend. There are, however, exceptions to every rule, and since Mad Dog Rabidowski was the hero of heroes tonight, someone on the planning committee had taken it upon himself to invite Ed's wife, Brittany Starr.

Brittany, the ex-stripper.

And ex-hooker.

Hemingway hero that he was, Mad Dog fell into that category once known as the man's man. With the brow of a Neanderthal and testosterone seething in his muscles, Ed seeped the musky smell of maleness from every pore. In a world of equal opportunity, Brittany Starr would qualify as the woman's woman. With breasts out to there and a waist in to here, with bleached blonde hair and a skintight gown scooped toward her navel, the ex-ecdysiast belonged on every pinup calendar in every grease monkey's shop from Coquitlam to Timbuktu. This, however, was a room in which all the other women had battled sexists in the Force for the right to dress like men. Having won that war, they were tonight all cinched into high-collared, straight-cut jackets and, from the look in their collective glare, were not impressed to have this creature in their midst. Especially not when Mad Dog gallantly offered his wife a phallic cigar, and Brit nibbled off the tip with her sexy mouth, then proceeded to lubricate the rolled tobacco leaf with her lips and tongue in a manner that had every male within reach offering her a light.

It's a funny ol' world.

"'Hello? Is this the RCMP?'" Nick Craven held his good hand up to his ear like a phantom phone, his pinky finger the mouthpiece and his thumb the receiver.

"'Yes,'" the corporal answered himself, mimicking the dispatcher. "'How can we help you, sir?'

"'I'm calling about my neighbor Joe Fitzpatrick. He's hiding bags of pot in his woodshed.'"

"I've heard this one," Mad Dog said.

"Shush, Ed," chided Brit.

Nick pressed on with his joke.

"The next day, the drug squad raids Joe's house. Members search the shed where he stores his firewood. They find nothing. Using axes"—Nick swung his arms as if chopping wood—"they bust open and split up every log round in the place. Again, the narcs find nothing. So, frustrated, they leave.

"Ring," said Nick, trilling his tongue. "Joe answers the phone in his house.

"'Hey, Joe, did the Mounties come?' the snitch asks.

"'Yeah, they just left.'

"'Did they chop your firewood?'

"'Every stick.'

"'Happy birthday, buddy.'"

Barks of boozy laughter punctuated the joke. Though an anchor of depression weighed him down, Zinc managed to muster up a weak smile for Nick.

Brit blew a smoke ring up to form a halo above her blonde head. "Whaddaya say, boys? Do you want to hear the one about the Mountie who stops the dumb blonde for speeding?"

Judging from the size of the circle of men coalescing around Brit, a lot of those present did want to hear—and watch—the ex-stripper tell a funny. In fact, they'd probably stick around if all she did was read stock quotes.

"'I pulled you over for speeding, ma'am,' the Mountie says. 'May I see your driver's license?'

"'License?' replies the blonde, revealing how dumb she is.

"'It's usually in your wallet,' the Mountie says.

"A lot of searching later, the blonde finds her license.

"'Next, I need your registration,' the Mountie says.

"'Registration?' says the blonde, proving she's really dumb.

"'It's usually in the glove compartment,' says the Mountie.

"After a lot of fumbling, she finally finds the registration.

"The Mountie takes the documents back to his car, where he calls dispatch to check her out. A moment or two later, a voice comes over the line. 'Um, by any chance is she driving a red sports car?'

"'Yes,' replies the Mountie.

"'Is she a drop-dead gorgeous blonde?' asks dispatch.

"When the Mountie confirms she is, the voice over the radio says, 'Trust me, here's what you do. . . . '

"The Mountie strolls back to the sports car and hands the blonde her papers. Then he drops his pants like the dispatcher advised and waits to see what happens. The blonde looks down, shakes her head and rolls her eyes."

Brit acted out the expression by way of illustration.

"'Oh, no!' the blonde says. 'Not *another* breathalyzer test!'"

Rain hammered down on the striped awning above Zinc's head, beating the canvas as if it were the skin of a kettledrum. The raucous laughter at his back beyond the Dutch doors indicated that Brit's joke was a hit with the men. Zinc had slipped away before the punch line was delivered, and now he stood alone out on the veranda that overlooked the hazy Pitt River marshes at his feet. Minnekhada Regional Park, the land surrounding the lodge, provided sanctuary for beaver, bear, fox, deer, bullfrog, eagle and Steller's jay. If any of those backwoods denizens was eyeing the inspector through the scrim of silver slants, what it saw was the black silhouette of a man backlit by glowing windows.

A door opened.

The door closed.

Now there were two silhouettes.

Seen closer, both Mounties were decked out in the colorful mess kit of commissioned officers: a waist jacket of red serge over a blue vest, with a white pleated shirt and a black bow tie above blue trousers with a yellow side stripe and black congress boots with silver box spurs. A gold crown on Zinc's epaulets signified his rank of inspector. The rank of the second Mountie had been raised to chief superintendent by the addition of two pips to the crown. Gold regimental crests sparkled on their lapels. Medals shone on their chests.

"Dreaming of the South Pacific?"

"No," said Zinc.

"Do you prefer rain?" asked DeClercq.

"I prefer work."

"Plenty of that will be waiting when you get back. Decided where you're going?"

"No," said Zinc.

"Genny and I honeymooned in Western Samoa."

"There's a big difference. Alex won't be with me, Chief."

"I know. But you'd get away from it all, and you might meet someone new."

"All I'd do is think of her. That's why I want to work."

"You need a rest."

"I'm okay."

"Then what are you doing out here? The party going on in there is for Ghost Keeper, Mad Dog and *you*."

"I need a breath of fresh air."

"You need more than that. I've had my eye on you. I don't think you're with us, Zinc. I've been where you are. I know what's going on in your head. I lost two wives and a child to the job. I thought I'd go mad from grief. But look at me now. Gill Macbeth and I are seeing each other regularly, and I found a wonderful surrogate daughter in Katt. A break to get perspective is what you need."

"I've been shanghaied."

"Really? How?"

"I woke up in the hospital after suffering a concussion, and what did I find all over the media? 'Insp. Zinc Chandler is off to the tropics for a well-earned rest.'"

"We discussed that before the chopper crashed."

"As I recall, the discussion was along these lines: 'You can accept my advice as a friend and go willingly, or you can force me as your boss to order you onto a plane.' The only choice I had was between the Caribbean or the South Seas."

"It's for your own good."

"I don't like being ordered around."

"Then you're in the wrong job. Policing is about taking orders."

"Orders to work."

"And orders not to. A tragedy like losing Alex exacts a heavy toll. Some can bury themselves in work, but not you. Sleep and four caps of Dilantin a day protect you from epileptic fits. Who kept you in the Force after you got shot in the head? And after the Ripper stabbed you? Now I say it's time for a rest, and you fight me?"

"I can't afford it, Chief."

"What? The money?"

"My brother's having trouble with the farm. I've been helping him out."

"Then it's your lucky day. Gill Macbeth, as you know, has money to burn. Despite the helicopter crash, the three of you saved her life on Ebbtide Island. As thanks, she's treating each of you to a vacation. Mad Dog and Ghost Keeper have graciously accepted. So, I'm sure, will you."

The chief left Zinc alone for five minutes for that breath of fresh air, on the understanding that he would join the others for the announcement of the beneficence of the pathologist Gill Macbeth. So there he stood, listening to the mournful tattoo of rain drumming down on the awning, gazing out into the inclement night that swallowed up Washington State, while—prompted by renewed laughter from the men surrounding Brit inside the lodge—he relived a memory of Alex from a year and a half ago. The recollection caused sorrow to gnaw at his hollow heart. Unknown to the inspector, at that very moment 150 miles away to the south, a scheme was unfolding so the Goth could eat the Mountie's heart, too.

TED BUNDY'S HOUSE

Seattle, Washington

Were it not for the constant rain, the population of the Pacific Northwest might rival California's. For sure, the natural splendor of God's country was in abundance here, but there is nothing like shitty weather to scare hordes of prospective settlers away. Too much rain was kosher as far as Detective Ralph Stein of Homicide was concerned, since fewer people milling around the city that Ralph called home, doing all sorts of atrocious things to each other, meant a shorter stack of murder cases piling up on his desk. There are, however, exceptions to every rule, including the one that says that constant rain helps squelch violent street crimes, and when it came to exceptions, the one that Ralph was responding to was shaping up as a doozie. It's not every night you get called out to investigate a severed head found stuck on a stake up in the U District.

Lake Union lies at the heart of Seattle. Montlake Cut, a ship canal, runs east to Lake Washington. The north bank of the cut is dotted mostly with marine businesses and academic facilities, for it marks the southern edge of the University District. This area used to be called Brooklyn way back when, but there was little future in that pilfered name, so once the University of Washington was founded here in 1895, Brooklyn became the name of the street one block west of University Way, and the campus and its surroundings became the U District, in student-speak. Today, the university—known as the U Dub in that same tongue—meshes with the surrounding neighborhood. Called the Ave by those attending the U Dub, the north–south artery of University Way is the hangout hub of the U District.

In cop-speak—Stein's lingo—this was the North Precinct.

Beyond the rain-streaked windshield of the unmarked police car, Stein watched a string of coffeehouses, cinemas, book and record stores, pizzerias, pubs, fast-food joints and cheap ethnic restaurants, clothing stores, newsstands, panhandlers and homeless people line the gutters of the Ave—exactly what you'd expect to see in a university district. To the west, between this main thoroughfare and the I-5 freeway north to Vancouver, most of the side streets were full of apartment buildings and old homes that had been converted into student flats. Such a street was Twelfth Avenue N.E., and as Ralph's car approached the 4100 block, the red-and-blue wigwags that flashed on the roofs of the first-response vehicles cordoning off the crime scene dyed the rain snakes slithering down the glass in front of the detective's eyes.

Ralph parked outside the cordon and stepped out into the deluge.

Popping his umbrella, he walked the rest of the way.

Det. Ralph Stein was a big man. Big as in blubber, not in brawn. Ralph was married to a make-your-mouth-drool cook, so keeping his weight under control had always been a problem. A regimen of exercise had helped him battle the bulge, but then Ralph had suffered a crippling accident. Before going to work for the Halloween-night shift, he had scaled a ladder to clean his second-story eaves. Some of the slimy sludge he had plucked from the gutter had fouled the rung of the ladder a step down under his shoes, with the result that Ralph's descent from on high had been swifter than planned. Two broken ankles had kept him in traction for weeks, and Ralph was damn lucky that he was able to walk again. But as for all that exercise that had kept down his weight . . . well, it had gone the way of all flesh. And where that flesh had gone was to Ralph's ballooning waist.

The blue guarding the barricade waved the homicide detective in. As Ralph splashed along the sidewalk toward a crowd of neighborhood gawkers watching a knot of cops huddled at one corner of a cream-colored two-story house close to the cross street, his ankles ached. The rain was pelting so hard on the umbrella over his head that mist came through the thin fabric to spray him anyway. On drenching nights like this, Ralph wished he were a gumshoe back in the forties. Gumshoes would, from the sound of the word, keep your feet dry. Combined with a waterproof trench coat and a wide-brimmed fedora . . . well, rain would be like water off a duck. Instead, Ralph felt like a sponge in his sopping pea jacket, soaked flannel slacks and squishy loafers.

Better yet, he decided, I wish I was that dog.

The hound and his master had matching yellow slickers. The man could be a lobster catcher in from the East Coast. The pooch was a long-bodied basset hound with stubby legs and a drooping belly slung close to the waterlogged lawn. In a cute parody of the lobster-man, the dog was strapped into a miniature plastic hood and cape.

Ralph was green with envy.

The dog was dry.

"I thought I owned a basset hound," the lobsterman was telling a blue who was trying to record his statement in a soggy notebook protected by his doffed hat. The cop's hair was plastered to his head. That was one of the drawbacks of being a uniform. Umbrellas weren't issued as part of the standard equipment. Not that it made much difference from Ralph's point of view. His bumbershoot was doing squat to keep him dry. "What I own instead in Murphy here," the lobsterman said, "is a sleuth out to prove he's a bloodhound."

Murphy barked, concurring.

"Hound of the bloody Baskervilles, that's what he is."

The blue kept scribbling.

Was he actually taking that down?

The cop had led man and dog away from the crowd of gawkers in front of the house to take his statement. Ralph reached them before he got to the crime scene. When he heard the blue ask, "How'd you find the head stuck on the stake, Mr. Gebhardt?" the detective stopped in his tracks to join the conversation.

"I'm busy, Mac," the blue said, waving the interloper away. "Wait your turn."

"The name's Stein," Ralph said.

"Everyone's Mac to me."

"*Detective* Stein," Ralph emphasized. "You new to the job, *Mac*? I don't recognize your surliness."

The young blue reacted as if the detective had put an electric cattle prod to the family jewels. "S-sorry, sir," he stammered. "I thought you were . . ."

Mr. Michelin? Ralph wondered with a wrathful scowl. His wife had called him that on that dark day when she made him swear solemnly on a plate of cheese blintzes to use her accursed calorie wheel to calculate the damage inherent in every blessed meal.

The detective angled his umbrella to keep the rookie out in the rain, bequeathing his largesse—in Ralph's case, a physical term—of shelter from the storm on the basset hound instead. "I'm taking over. Take notes, Mac."

The blue began scribbling as the image of a Big Mac popped into Ralph's head.

Food for thought.

"Hello, Mr. Gebhardt. I'm Detective Stein. Fine dog you have in Murphy. Sherlock Hound. Let's take it from the top. Where do you live, sir?"

"Up the block," Gebhardt said. "In the yellow house."

"Address?"

He gave a number in the 4100s.

"Telephone?"

He gave that number too.

"First name?"

"Rufus."

"Thanks," said Stein. "Now, what brought you and Murphy out on a night like this?"

"Do you have a dog?"

"No."

"Didn't think so. I take Murphy for a walk every night."

The word "walk" registered with the basset hound, and it glanced up at Gebhardt expectantly.

"That's the *W* word in our house. Mention the *W* word in his presence and Murphy heads for the door."

"I see," said Ralph. "Rain or shine?"

"Or sleet. Or snow. Or hordes of locusts. Or volcanic eruptions of Mount St. Helens."

"Murph," said Stein, addressing the hound, "it sounds like you're a pest."

Murphy barked.

"So tell me, sir, exactly how did your 'bloodhound' find the head?"

"See that bush growing at the corner of that house?" Gebhardt turned and pointed through the downpour toward the knot of cops standing in the teeming rain. "You might say that bush is Murphy's fire hydrant."

"It looks healthy."

"Fertilizer," Gebhardt said.

"So Murph wandered off to do his business, and you followed him to the john?"

"No, I waited out here on the sidewalk for him to return, and when he began to howl like the bloodhound he thinks he is, I went over to see what was wrong. And there it was, behind that bush, stuck upside down on a stake driven into the ground."

"Quite a shock, huh? Finding a severed head?"

"For sure," said Gebhardt. "It almost made me do my own business by the bush. In hindsight, it was predictable. Sooner or later, something was bound to happen at that house."

"How so?" Stein asked, the bloodhound in him sniffing around the question.

"That's the Bundy house."

"Does Bundy have enemies?"

Gebhardt frowned. "Lots, I would think."

"Ones who'd do him harm?"

The frown deepened. "Not unless they know how to get to him in hell. Bundy fried in Old Sparky, Florida's electric chair. That house is where Ted Bundy lived from 1969 to 1974, back when he was stalking coeds in Seattle."

Det. Ralph Stein felt like a buffoon. Who did he think Bundy was? W. H. Bundy, the Australian manufacturer of time clocks? McGeorge Bundy, the special assistant to JFK and LBJ on national security? True, it should be noted in Ralph's defense that Ted Bundy had just rented a room in the house and never owned the place. But still, Ted Bundy had ranked as Seattle's worst serial predator until the Green River Killer topped his body count. And it didn't help Ralph's attempt to forget his memory flub that Mac, the rookie taking notes in the rain, muttered in disgruntlement, "I knew that."

Luckily for Ralph, the cavalry arrived.

"So, Detective Stein, what new forensic challenge do you have for me on this enchanted evening?"

The detective turned to find the medical examiner approaching the trio blocking the sidewalk. Her car was parked behind Ralph's on the far side of the cordon. Known as Ruthless Ruth to homicide bulls, the M.E. was a mannish woman in dress and appearance. Bundled up in a trench coat like Ralph *should* have been wearing, and a brimmed hat that owed its inspiration to film noir, she looked about as feminine as Bogart would after a beating in *The Big Sleep*. Her pants were thick stovepipes capped by steel-toed boots. Her hands and wrists were those of a sumo wrestler. And her round face, devoid of makeup for maximum butch, resembled a ham.

"We've got a real doozie here, Doc," Stein said. "A severed head stuck on a stake outside of what was Ted Bundy's house. Mr. Gebhardt and Murphy—Murphy's the hound, not the water-logged youth taking notes—found the remains. You're just in time to catch the story of Ted Bundy's lair."

"Bundy!" Ruth exclaimed. "Is this where he lived?"

"Evidently. You were saying, Mr. Gebhardt?" Ralph continued, in a smooth handoff of the fumbled ball.

The lobsterman sighed. His was a tired tale.

"Bundy rented the large room in the southwest corner of the upper story from an elderly German couple named Ernst and Freda Rogers. He was studying deviant personality in the psychology curriculum offered at the U Dub. His roommate was a Boston fern that sat in the corner where the windows meet. He called it Fern, and he fussed over it. Bundy kept his stereo tuned to Seattle's classical music station to help Fern grow. Freda kept the rooming house in immaculate condition. Everything was orderly and spotless. The hardwood floor in Bundy's room was covered with an old pink-patterned carpet. A starched doily was stretched across the top of his dresser. The ceiling was high and airy, like those charming houses in Europe. For decoration, Bundy hung a raft over his bed and suspended a bicycle wheel from a chained meat hook. He was active in Republican politics. In 1968, he supported Rockefeller's campaign at the convention in Miami, and he kept a souvenir from it in his room: an imitation straw hat made of Styrofoam."

"You have a remarkable memory, sir."

"Not really, Detective Stein. When you have resided as long as I have on the block where Ted Bundy lived, have you any idea how many people pump you for details?"

"Tell us more."

"You're the detective."

"Bundy was before my time. Sure, I can look it up. But why should I, if I have a prime source in you? You don't want Murphy to come out of this as the hero of the moment."

Gebhardt laughed. "You hear that, dog? Should I tell him to take a walk?"

The hound barked again, wagging its tail in excitement.

"While Bundy lived here, the university doubled in size to thirty-five thousand students. That was the time of Vietnam, and there were protests down in Red Square."

"Named for its bricks," Ruth said to keep the record straight. "Not its politics."

And damn if Mac didn't write that down.

The lobsterman sighed again. Back to his tired tale.

"Early in 1974, Sharon Clarke was beaten with a metal rod as she slept in her home here in the U District. While she was unconscious, Ted Bundy raped her. Later that month, Lynda Ann Healy vanished from her basement room. That was also around here. Her bloody nightgown was found in the closet. Five more coeds disappeared in the next five months, the last being Georgann Hawkins, a U Dub student, who vanished from the back doorstep of her sorority house. That July, two more evaporated from Lake Sammamish Park. In the fall of 1974, Ted Bundy left Seattle. The abductions followed him to Utah and Colorado. Then Bundy met his Waterloo in Florida, after an orgy of sex and violence at the Chi Omega sorority. Old Sparky fried him in 1989."

"Spoken like a historian."

"I teach history, Detective Stein," Gebhardt said.

"So this house was the anchor point from which Bundy spread out to hunt his victims?"

"Yes, but there were never heads lined up on the mantel."

"Heads?" said Ralph, puzzled.

"That's my point. The severed heads are a bogus attempt to create an urban myth."

"What severed heads?"

"The story goes that Bundy, at one point in his rampage, had four severed heads lined up on the mantel in this house."

"What are you saying? That that story might have inspired some nut to stake a head out front tonight?"

"That's possible."

"Because the house is a shrine?"

"It might be to a copycat. To a Bundy clone."

"Is that why you stated, 'Sooner or later, something was bound to happen at that house'?"

"Lies become urban myths by capturing imaginations."

"You walk Murphy"—the dog barked expectantly—"every night," said Stein. "Have you spotted anyone suspicious near Ted Bundy's house?"

"No," said Gebhardt. "But the bus went by yesterday afternoon."

"What bus?"

"Spooky Seattle Tours. They're the ones trying to spread the bogus myth. What they tell passengers to spice up their tours is that at one point during Ted Bundy's stay in the Twelfth Avenue house, he had the heads of four women lined up on the mantel. How did he do that when the room he rented didn't even have a fireplace?"

The detective and the M.E. left Mac to tie up loose ends with Murphy and Gebhardt while they went to look at the head. The knot of blues around the crime scene moved aside to let Stein and Ruthless Ruth through. As the two approached the stake that had been stuck in the muddy ground behind the bush at the southwest corner of Ted Bundy's house, Ralph connected what he saw to a conversation he'd had with another cop during his convalescence from his two broken ankles.

The head mounted upside down on the stake belonged to a man. The stake was buried deep in the crown of the skull, but not so deep that it protruded through the raw flesh of the severed neck, which the driving rain had washed so clean of blood that the vertebra above the cut and the mess of tubes truncated by the blade were clearly visible in the pool of light cast by several flashlights.

Ruth crouched on her haunches, gathering in her coat flaps to keep them out of the mire.

"It could be a Christian crazy," she said.

Ralph squatted beside her. "So it seems. That ring of nails driven into his skull resembles a crown of thorns."

YOU ARE WHAT YOU EAT

Coquitlam

What caused Zinc to recollect this particular memory of Alexis Hunt
was the laughter echoing out of Minnekhada Lodge from the enrap-
tured male Mounties gathered around Mad Dog's wife, the ex-hooker
Brittany Starr. Standing alone where the overhead awning protected
him from the downpour that splattered the open veranda, the inspector recalled that noon a year and a half ago when he and Stan the
Accountant had joked with another humorous hooker, Moaning
Mona, at the Lions Gate. Between that midday laugh-fest in the hotel
bar and Zinc's return that night to question Gord and Joey, the pimp
and the hooker who'd rumbled off to die in the high-speed chase, the
Mountie had gone home for dinner with the now lost love of his life.
Erasing the past seventeen months, Zinc's mind traveled back. . . .

———·•·———

"What's for dinner?" Zinc asked, sniffing the aroma of exotic
cuisine as he entered the kitchen of the Kits Point house that he
and Alex shared in central Vancouver.

"Eloi," Alex said, referring to the human prey of the cannibalistic Morlocks in H. G. Wells's *Time Machine*. She was stirring a pot
of something that bubbled and let off delicious steam.

"Mmm, my favorite," Zinc replied, kissing her cheek and hugging
her from one side. "Is it female?" he asked as a morsel of succulent
meat bobbed to the surface. "If so, serve me a breast or a thigh."

"You pig!" Alex scolded, threatening him with the spoon.

"Hey, *you* chose the menu. If the way to a man's heart is through his stomach, expect cooking Eloi for dinner to bring out the cannibal in me."

"The cannibal's okay. It's the sexist I abhor."

"Blame Mona."

"Mona who?"

"Moaning Mona," said Zinc.

Alex rolled her eyes. "It goes from bad to worse. Who's Moaning Mona? Do I want to know?"

"Mona's a hooker."

"I *never* would have guessed. When'd you meet her?"

"Today. In a bar."

"Great," said Alex, and she rolled her big blues again. "I spend the day slaving over a hot stove to cook my beau something special, and he spends the day hanging out in a bar with hookers."

"Are you jealous?"

"In your wildest dreams."

The kitchen table was cluttered with books, scribbled notes and a pair of DVDs. Both were films of *The Time Machine*—the 1960 George Pal version and the remake by Steven Spielberg. Picking up one of the movies, Zinc read the back: "Rod Taylor stars as a young scientist whose ingenious machine propels him to a civilization thoroughly devitalized by war. Humanity has been reduced to a colorless passive race, the Eloi, who are held in the thrall of loathsome mutants known as Morlocks."

"Remember that?" Alex asked, stirring the pot of "Eloi."

"You bet," Zinc said. "One of my favorite stories."

"What do you remember most?"

"The Morlocks, of course. Such ugly, white-haired creatures, with glowing eyes and mouths pegged with crooked teeth."

"It's a fine dichotomy," Alex said. "The Eloi, a gentle, ineffective people, seem to have descended from us. They do no work and appear to spend their days in the Eden of the surface world in amorous dalliances and other pleasures of the flesh."

"You mean like me and Mona?"

"Careful, Zinc. I'm the one preparing the curry. Wells describes the insipid Eloi as having blond hair and finely chiseled features. Theirs is a Dresden china prettiness."

"That's Mona."

Alex twisted her face in a snarl. "The Morlocks, on the other hand, are a sinister, savage race of mutants who dwell underground. From time to time, they seize Eloi from the surface world and haul them off to work in their subterranean caves."

"I know the story, Alex."

"But do you know where I'm going with it?"

Zinc shook his head. "I'm afraid to ask."

"The Morlocks, as Wells describes them, have bleached hair, pale and chinless faces, and large, lidless, pinkish-gray eyes. He says they are nauseatingly inhuman, and they dwell in the darkness of their world of eternal night because they are blind and helpless in daylight."

"Don't be so hard on yourself," Zinc teased.

"When the Morlocks steal the Time Machine and drag it into their lair, the Time Traveler must descend down one of their wells. He barely escapes from their clutching hands up a narrow ventilation shaft. That's when Wells's hero is shaken by the memory of meat that he saw in the underworld."

"Eloi meat," said Zinc. "The Morlocks are cannibals."

"Well?" asked Alex, crossing from the stove to sweep her arm in a wide arc over the table.

"You're writing another book?"

"My, you're a good detective."

"Got a title?"

"Uh-huh. *You Are What You Eat.*"

"A cookbook," Zinc said. "A nice change from true crime. That's why you're in the kitchen. To get in the mood."

"Ah, but *what* am I cooking?"

"Uh-oh," said Zinc.

"*You Are What You Eat: Cannibal Killers.* That's the full title."

"And *The Time Machine?*"

"That's the motif. The Eloi are content to dance away their

golden days with fatalistic pleasure, while the Morlocks see them as fatted cattle—as merely a source of food."

"That's how you'll frame the book?"

"We're Eloi, with Morlocks among us. The difference is that my time machine goes into the past."

"How far?" Zinc asked.

"At least half a million years, to the days of *Homo erectus*. *Erectus*—the hominid that evolved into us—enjoyed supping on the brains of his fellow cavemen."

"I'm hungry," Zinc said.

"Eloi?" Alex asked. Returning to the stove, she spooned a morsel of meat from the curry and held it out for him to taste. "See if this whets your appetite."

"Mmm. Good."

"Eloi and Morlocks. A good theme, don't you think? Wells's *Time Machine* provides a grotesque reminder that the taboo urge to feast upon human meat lurks just beneath the surface of the comforting illusion that we have evolved into modern creatures who live a supposedly civilized life."

"Hannibal the Cannibal?"

"Precisely," said Alex. "Of all the horrors we associate with serial killers, cannibalism strikes us as the worst. Unless you've been living in a cave, you know that Dr. Hannibal Lecter's favorite meal is human liver served with fava beans and a nice Chianti. That's why he's become the icon of the genre."

"So what's on your menu?"

"The *real* thing," Alex replied.

Crossing to the table, the cook rummaged among the notes spread across its surface until she found a list of nations and names scrawled in her almost-illegible hand. "Here," she said, holding it out so the Mountie could read:

Britain:
  Jack the Ripper
  David Harker

Germany:
  Fritz Haarmann, "the Butcher of Hanover"
  Georg Grossmann
  Karl Denke
  Joachim Kroll, "the Ruhr Hunter"

France:
  Nicolas Claux
  Issei Sagawa

America:
  Albert Fish, "the Moon Maniac"
  Ed Gein, "the Plainfield Ghoul" (?)
  Edmund Kemper, "the Co-Ed Killer"
  Lucas and Toole (?)
  Stanley Dean Baker
  Daniel Rakowitz
  Albert Fentress
  Arthur Shawcross
  Gary Heidnik
  Jeffrey Dahmer, "the Milwaukee Monster"

Russia:
  Andrei Chikatilo, "the Mad Beast"
  Nikolai Dzhurmongaliev, "Metal Fang"

Canada:
  Dale Merle Nelson (?)

"Good lord," said Zinc. "That many?"

"I'm still working on it. The list is under construction."

"Jack the Ripper. There's no escape from him."

"We may not know who Jack was, but we know his predilections. We have the famous 'From Hell' letter accompanied by a human kidney, with the taunt 'Tother piece I fried and ate.' And we have organs missing from three of the Ripper's victims: Annie Chapman's uterus, Catharine Eddowes's left kidney and womb, Mary Jane Kelly's heart. He removed them for some reason. To eat is the likeliest answer.

"Jack the Cannibal. Who's David Harker?"

"A modern Brit. He strangled a woman with her tights when he got bored during sex. He chopped off her head and limbs, sliced skinned flesh from her thigh and cooked it with pasta and cheese. Tattooed on his scalp were the words 'subhuman' and 'disorder.'"

"When was that?"

"1999."

"Four Germans, huh?"

"Shows how hard their nation was shaken by the First World War. Many turned to Nazism. Three to cannibalism. Haarmann may have butchered as many as fifty young refugees who flooded into Hanover after the war. He lured each starving boy home from the train station with the promise of a meal, then attacked him like a werewolf, chewing at his throat. Death resulted from his almost biting off each head, an act that gave Haarmann a sexual climax. Later, he butchered the body and disposed of the leftover flesh as black-market beef. His near downfall was a dissatisfied customer who complained to police about the quality of his 'steaks.' The analyst, however, pronounced it was pork! So Haarmann was able to continue his nefarious trade."

"Selling 'the other white meat'?"

"Georg Grossmann, just after the war, ground fifty or more plump young women he met at the Berlin train station into sausage meat, which he sold the following day, on the same platform, as frankfurters. When he was arrested by police, Grossmann was butchering a trussed-up woman in his apartment."

"Sausages scare me," the Mountie said. "You never know what's in them."

"Karl Denke was an innkeeper in Silesia. He killed and consumed at least thirty of his lodgers. He chopped them up, ate certain parts right away and pickled the rest in tubs of brine for later feasts. He confessed that for three years he'd eaten nothing but human flesh."

"And Joachim Kroll?"

"Germany's modern cannibal. Between 1955 and 1976, he choked and raped fourteen females in the Ruhr. If the flesh was tender, he would cut steaks from their buttocks and thighs. Kroll was a lavatory attendant by trade, so it's ironic that he got caught because he plugged the toilet in his apartment building with guts: the internal organs of a four-year-old girl. In Kroll's flat, where he lived with a harem of rubber sex dolls, the police found plastic bags full of flesh in the deep freeze and, bubbling in a saucepan on the stove, a stew made out of the girl's hand, with potatoes and carrots."

"Two Frenchman?"

"One, in fact," said Alex. "Claux was a mortician who ate strips of flesh cut from the muscles of cadavers in a hospital morgue. He used to prowl graveyards and dig up fresh corpses to drink the blood mixed with human ashes and protein powder. Sagawa was a Japanese living in Paris who ate a Dutch woman. He said her flesh tasted like raw tuna. That's a sushi I don't want to try."

"Albert Fish was the old man who ate that young girl?"

"Grace Budd. In New York, in 1928. He turned her 'meat'—as he called it—into a cannibal stew, complete with carrots, onions and bacon strips. He spent the next nine days locked away in his room, savoring his dreadful meal and masturbating compulsively. Fish made the mistake of writing a letter to Grace Budd's parents, describing in sickening detail what he had done to their daughter. On arresting him in 1934, police found a collection of newspaper clippings about Fritz Haarmann, 'the Butcher of Hanover.' No one knows how many children Fish killed and ate during his travels through twenty-three states."

"As I recall," Zinc said, "when Sing Sing Prison tried to fry him in the electric chair, he short-circuited his execution because he'd inserted a phalanx of needles into his groin."

"Twenty-nine, I believe. He's the oldest man put to death in New York State."

"Ed Gein we all know. The man behind *Psycho*."

"And *The Texas Chainsaw Massacre*. And *The Silence of the Lambs*."

"Busy Ed. Why the question mark?"

"One respected author thinks he wasn't a cannibal."

"And you, Alex?"

"Before his first grave-robbing, Gein confessed, he'd been reading adventure stories of headhunters and cannibals. Psychotically fixated on his dead mother, he kept her room like a shrine. The headless and gutted corpses of the women he butchered were hung upside down from a rafter like dressed-out game. Inside his shambles of a house, police found soup bowls made from skulls, chairs uphol-stered with human skin, a shoebox full of female genitalia, faces stuffed with newspapers and mounted on a wall like hunting trophies and a 'mammary vest' flayed from the torso of a woman, which Gein would wear to pretend he was his mother. In a frying pan on the stove was a human heart. Since he draped himself in female flesh, I find it hard to swallow—no pun intended—that he didn't try to ingest Mother too."

"What was the name of those jokes?"

"Geiners," said Alex.

"Find any?"

"Sure. In a psychiatric journal. What did Ed say to the sheriff who arrested him? 'Have a heart.' Why won't anyone play poker with Ed? He might come up with a good hand."

"Macabre."

"We laugh to keep from crying."

"Kemper," said Zinc. "He was the giant?"

"Six-foot-nine. Three hundred pounds. He decapitated his sisters' dolls when he was a boy, then decapitated coeds after he became a man so he could have sex with the headless bodies. First, he'd strip them and pose them in a bath, so he could take Polaroids of them whole. Later, he'd chop up the bodies and store most of the meat in the freezer, except for what he would cook in a macaroni casserole. Having elaborately set the table, he would display the Polaroids behind his plate, then eat the meat, staring at them, until he reached orgasm. The frozen flesh would last him a month. On his arrest, he was asked, 'What do you think when you see a pretty girl walking down the street?' Kemper replied, 'One side of me says, I'd like to talk to her, date her. The other side of me says, I wonder how her head would look on a stick?' When convicted of eight murders, he told the court he thought a fitting punishment for him would be death by torture."

"When was that?"

"In the early 1970s."

"Lucas and Toole. Another biggie. Why the question mark?"

"We have only their say-so about eating flesh."

"The next four draw a blank."

"They're recent Americans. Stanley Dean Baker was stopped for a hit-and-run in California. 'I have a problem,' he told the officer. 'I'm a cannibal.' He was snacking on the fingers of a social worker whose heart he had devoured raw. Daniel Rakowitz lived on New York's Lower East Side. He killed his girlfriend in 1989, then boiled her head to make soup out of her brain. Scrawled on the door of his apartment was this gibberish: 'Is it soup yet? Welcome to Charlie Gein's Ranch East. Home of the Fine Young Cannibals.' Albert Fentress was in Poughkeepsie. He cooked and ate the testicles of a young man he'd chained in his basement. Arthur Shawcross fell from grace in Vietnam. The GI roasted and ate 'Nam kids. When he went back to New York, he switched to women. There, he ate vaginas, and not in the usual sense."

"Heidnik. The harem guy?"

"Right. Philadelphia, in 1986. He kidnapped and imprisoned six women in his cellar. One died in a pit filled with water and charged with a live wire. Another died after she was hung by her wrists for a week. He cut up that body, ground some flesh in a food processor, mixed it with dog food and made the others eat it. Police searching Heidnik's house found a charred human rib in the oven and a forearm in the freezer. His lawyer described him at trial as being 'out to lunch.'"

"Jeffrey Dahmer. The modern Ed Gein."

"There must be something in Wisconsin's water. Another charnel house. A human head on a refrigerator shelf. Skulls stashed in a closet. Body parts crammed in a plastic barrel. Hands decomposing in a lobster pot. An array of dry bones in cardboard boxes. A freezer full of viscera: lungs, livers, intestines, kidneys. Individually wrapped portions of hearts, thighs and biceps, some of which were tenderized, with the fat trimmed off. His favorite meal was biceps—he claimed they tasted like filet mignon. Dahmer killed seventeen men he picked up in gay bars."

"What I remember," Zinc said, "is the zombies. He drilled holes in the skulls of still-living men and poured in acid to dissolve their brains to mush."

"And more jokes."

"Geiners?" said the Mountie.

"Jeff 'the Chef' Dahmer's mom came over for dinner. 'Jeffrey,' she said, 'I really don't like your friends.' 'Then just eat the vegetables, Ma,' he replied."

"I remember one," added Zinc. "What did Jeffrey Dahmer say to Lorena Bobbitt? 'You going to eat that?'"

"Which brings us to Andrei Chikatilo—Russia's 'Mad Beast'—who lured at least fifty-odd victims into lonely woods and attacked them like a monster. In the twelve years prior to 1990, he cut out tongues, bit off nipples, sliced off noses, gouged out eyes and devoured genitals, which—according to his captors—left him with a gagging case of halitosis. He holds the record as the worst serial killer of modern times. Close behind is Nikolai Dzhurmongaliev of Kyrgyzstan. At least forty-seven victims were in the ethnic cuisine he served to his neighbors. Dzhurmongaliev told police that two women provided enough meat for a week."

"Why the nickname Metal Fang?"

"His false teeth were made of white metal."

"Nelson. The local guy. Does he count?"

"Is it cannibalism if you cut someone open and eat the *contents* of her stomach? Another question mark."

"That's a lot of Morlocks," Zinc summed up.

Alex nodded. "It's shocking to see so many people-eaters gathered in one place."

"Your book may end up too heavy for the masses."

"At least it will serve one purpose: if fiction readers come across a psycho-thriller involving cannibals, they'll have no difficulty suspending disbelief."

"Amen," said Zinc.

"So," said Alex, returning to the stove, "what say we have a hearty meal of Eloi curry, then settle back and watch a double bill of *The Time Machine*?"

"Sorry. I can't."

"Party-pooper. Why not?" she asked.

"I've got a tentative date tonight with two possible suspects at the Lions Gate."

"Mona's bar?"

"Afraid so."

"Will she be there?"

"An irresistible hunk like me, how could she not?"

"In that case, buster, you'd better come with me." Alex took Zinc by the hand and pulled him toward the bedroom. "By the time I'm done with you, you'll be of no use to Moaning Mona."

————•••————

Like the Time Traveler in Wells's novel, Zinc's mind was transported forward by a vibrating machine. In his situation, the device summoning him back to this rainy veranda at Minnekhada Lodge from the memory of Alex seventeen months ago was the silent cellphone vibrating in his pocket. It was one of those ironic coincidences in life—considering the secret plot that was currently unfolding in Seattle to turn the Mountie into the Goth's food—that of all the pleasant recollections Zinc retained of her, the one that had captured his mind tonight involved *You Are What You Eat*.

The inspector checked the number recorded on his cellphone. The area code was Seattle. The number didn't click.

"Hello?" he answered.

"Zinc, it's Ralph Stein."

"Ralph? It's been a while. I can barely hear you."

"Rain on my umbrella."

"It's pouring here too. Where you calling from?"

"Outside Ted Bundy's house."

THIRTEEN STEPS TO HELL

Twenty Miles East of Seattle

On bone-chilling nights like this, the undead do crawl from their graves. Charlie Yu could hear them moan in the wind that drove the rain through the skeletal trees, their gnarled limbs creaking overhead like rusty elbow joints, and he could see their foul breath from beyond the grave emerge in miasmic puffs that swirled in from the darkness around the flashlight's beam. Freddie, the torchbearer, led the way into the hidden cemetery from the deserted bypass that ran up to Maltby from Redmond, north of Lake Sammamish. Tommy, the map reader, was their middleman as the three skulked single file into the dark unknown, for he was the one who could understand the X–Y coordinates on the survey grid. Charlie, the pot supplier, brought up the rear. His task was to roll the joints that skyrocketed the anxiety level of the Zombie Hunters so their hearts were tripping like jackhammers in their throats as they penetrated deeper into the foreboding fright night of this verboten netherworld.

"Look," Freddie whispered, pointing dead ahead.

"Eureka!" Tommy crowed when he saw what was caught in the pool of light.

"What is it?" Charlie asked, trying to see around the pair, who were blocking his view.

"A gravestone."

"Eldritch!"

"There's another one."

"There should be fifteen gravesites, give or take," Tommy said.

"I can barely see them for the weeds," Charlie said, stepping aside to peer around his buddies.

"Speaking of weed," Freddie hinted. "It's time to roll them joints, Brother Charles."

"Whoa!" gasped Tommy. "What's that in the center?"

"Jesus H. Christ! It's got to be the pit."

"Do you see what I see set into the rim?"

"A step."

"A concrete step."

"The Thirteen Steps to Hell."

Once a year, the Zombie Hunters met somewhere in the States for a fright-fest. Charlie came in from Texas with the loco weed. They had tried acid once, but that was overload, and Freddie— though he denied it—had pissed his pantaloons. He came in from Rhode Island, the home state of the dark prince, H. P. Lovecraft, so Freddie considered himself a maestro of the macabre and, consequently, the natural-born leader of the Zombie Hunters. Usually, it was his job to pick a haunted destination worthy of conquest by the intrepid trio. But Tommy hailed from Seattle, and this year he was one of the organizers of the World Horror Convention, currently under way in his hometown, so it had fallen to him to choose the spookiest spot around.

Maltby Cemetery had won hands down.

Freddie, Tommy and Charlie had first met in Nashville, Tennessee, lured to that city's World Horror Convention by the opportunity to have Richard Matheson, the guest of honor, sign their well-thumbed copies of *I Am Legend.* Standing one behind the other in a line of fans slowly snaking up to the signing table, they had engaged in a lively debate about the merits of that novel. Was it the ultimate vampire story, better than *Dracula?* Was it the inspiration for *Night of the Living Dead,* which Freddie had called "The best goddamn fucking fright flick ever filmed, in my humble opinion"?

"Hear, hear," Tommy said. "Imagine what it must have been like to be in your car at a drive-in in 1968 when that black-and-white shocker flashed on-screen."

"Bet it's the only drive-in movie more memorable than what went on in the backseat."

"And to think it was shot for a measly hundred and fifteen thousand bucks," said Charlie, tossing in his two cents.

"Relentless," Freddie said.

"Just like *I Am Legend.*"

"What a book. What a theme."

"Robert Neville is the last man alive on earth," Charlie said. "And every other being—man, woman or child—is a vampire hungry for his blood."

"By day, he's the hunter. By night, he's the hunted," Tommy said.

"Barricaded in his home, praying for dawn—how long can he hold out?" said Freddie with obvious glee.

"Damn good question. How long must *I* hold out till I get to meet the man?"

Charlie stood up on his tiptoes. "I can see Matheson's head."

"You know what's wrong with vampires today?" said Tommy.

"Yeah, Anne Rice," Freddie replied.

"The books are all about chicks in gowns who yearn to get sucked while they're fucked."

"Romance and horror," Charlie scoffed.

"Yuck," said Freddie. "Give me relentless monsters who crave nothing more than to tear us limb from limb so they can gobble the raw flesh off our bones."

After the signing, the three had moved on to the bar. There, as pint after pint of beer foamed down their gullets, they had dissected the nitty-gritty of *Night of the Living Dead.*

"Know why zombies make the best monsters?" Charlie had said.

"'Cause the dead rising from the grave is one of our oldest fears," Freddie replied.

"Why's there no great zombie novel?" complained Tommy.

"'Cause zombies came out of voodoo and went straight to film, where all they did was lurch around like mindless robots."

"Until Romero. And *Night of the Living Dead,*" Charlie said.

"Not only are the dead rising from the grave, but for the first time on film, they are rising to *eat* us!" Freddie added.

"His zombies are as loathsome as movie monsters come. Not only do his living dead mimic us—returning with an insatiable hunger for our flesh, shambling and stumbling and lurching around to get their hands on you, grasping and clawing at anything that stands in their way until they can rip out your entrails and devour them with glassy-eyed intensity—but those who fall prey to them become zombies too," Charlie said.

"You a writer, dude?"

"I'm trying," Charlie confessed.

"It's *I Am Legend,* isn't it?" Tommy said.

"It's more than that," Freddie said. "It's the ultimate nightmare. In the *Dead,* you've got these desperate people trapped in an old farmhouse near a cemetery with zombie cannibals closing in all around. But all they do is panic, squabble and make stupid decisions that turn them into meat. Romero destroys every comforting notion we have. Family ties don't matter—"

"Yeah," rejoiced Tommy. "The dead brother tries to eat his living sister. The little girl kills Mommy with a garden trowel, then mindlessly munches on Daddy's remains."

"Courage isn't rewarded."

"Heroes don't triumph."

"What's the use? No one survives. Characters we've come to like are ripped apart and devoured bone by bone and organ by organ in front of our eyes. Even the black guy—our main man—gets through the night only to be mistaken for a zombie at the end," Charlie said.

"Shoot 'em in the brain," Tommy advised, imitating the voice of the *Dead*'s hick sheriff.

Freddie signaled the barman to tap them another round.

"It's nihilism run amok," he said.

"There is no logic in death," said Tommy.

"Death is nothing more than nonfunctioning flesh. The zombies' only reason for 'living' is to propagate death. Because its horrors break every taboo, the film reduces death to the loss of all we value," Charlie said.

The three contemplated their mugs.

Charlie belched. "We're deep, dudes. *Deep.*"

"Yeah," said Tommy, nodding. "I'm glad I met you guys. At last, a pair of geniuses who think like me."

"Genii," said Freddie.

"Huh?"

"That's the Latin plural. You gotta learn to speak a dead language, pal."

"To zombies!" said Charlie, raising his refilled mug.

"To cannibals!" said Tommy, upping the toast.

"To us!" said Freddie. "The fearless Zombie Hunters!"

Wobbly mugs clinked.

"Shoot 'em in the brain!"

So that was the first night these three had set out on a quest to test their mettle, abandoning the convention hotel to find somewhere spooky in Nashville where they could seek the paranormal. From sea to sea, America is rife with haunted enclaves and bad places. Each subsequent year, the three had converged at the World Horror Convention, first to score the John Hancock of the guest of honor on books and albums in their horror collections—in Stanford, Connecticut, Peter Straub; in Atlanta, Georgia, Alice Cooper; in Eugene, Oregon, Clive Barker; and now, in Seattle, Bret Lister—then to venture forth to the eeriest local place to face the evil dead.

Jeepers creepers.

Yesterday, Thursday, Tommy had greeted Freddie and Charlie at SeaTac Airport, where their flights from back east and down south had landed within ten minutes of each other. No sooner were the Zombie Hunters together in one place than he pulled the program guide for this year's horror convention out of his pocket and said, "Maltby Cemetery. Friday night."

Flipping through the six pages of panels and events scheduled for the next three days, and several more pages of short biographies about those at the convention, Tommy arrived at the closing article, "Spooky Seattle: A Ghost Tour of Haunted Sites," and jabbed his finger at this:

MALTBY CEMETERY—According to Ripley's Believe It or Not, *this is one of the most evil places on earth. Maltby Cemetery was founded in the 1800s by a family of Satanists so they wouldn't have to be buried in sacred ground. Fifteen gravesites surround a hole in the center and descending into that pit are thirteen cement steps that lead to nowhere. These are the infamous Thirteen Steps to Hell. It's said that if you count off the steps as you go down, when you reach the last step—Step Thirteen—you will suffer a glimpse of your spirit in hell. Local lore maintains that over the years, some have vanished into the pit, never to return, while others have crawled out stark raving mad. The cemetery is haunted by a woman dressed in ragged nineteenth-century garb. Because the graveyard is a magnet for Satan worshippers, it is omitted from local maps. Hidden away on the right side of the road up to Maltby from Redmond, it can be located twenty miles east of Seattle on a survey grid with these coordinates: T27N R5E.*

"Damn," Freddie said. "The program gives away the location. Half the convention will beat us there."

"No," Tommy assured him. "It's not on the bus tour. It's out in the boonies. And who knows how to read a survey grid?"

"Do you?" Charlie asked.

"I got it all worked out. I had a surveyor convert the coordinates to a tourist map. We'll be the only ones there," Tommy replied.

So, earlier tonight, the Zombie Hunters had ventured across Lake Washington on the Evergreen Point Floating Bridge and continued east on Highway 520 all the way to Redmond, at which point they turned north on the country bypass that led to Maltby, with Tommy reading the map until he said, "Stop here."

"I told you," Freddie groused. "Company."

An old VW van was parked off the road on the right.

"Naw," said Tommy. "It must be a breakdown. Who in their right mind would be out here tonight?"

"Us?" said Charlie.

"That's debatable, dude."

And so the fearless Zombie Hunters had ventured off the deserted road into the black woods, their only guide the flashlight sweeping back and forth in Freddie's hand. The beam caught ominous shadows lurching and shambling through the trees like zombies stalking them for the meat on their bones. This was their night of the living dead, and it was as if they were the last three survivors on earth. A shift in the wind had waved the limbs looming over them like clutching giants who could pluck them from the ground at any moment. Then, abruptly, Tommy had stopped them dead in their tracks.

"Hear that?"

"Hear what?"

"People talking."

"I don't hear a thing."

"Neither do I."

"Must be that raggedy woman who haunts the place, bro."

And that's when Freddie had spotted the gravestone.

So here they stood, shivering in the teeming rain, puffing on the fat joint that Charlie had rolled, their collars turned up against the cold and their bare heads bowed together in a huddle to keep the sparks at the lit end from snuffing out.

"Wow!" said Freddie, his voice warbling as he struggled to hold in the smoke. "That"—he exhaled the sweet billow—"is awesome shit, man."

"Everything's better in Texas."

"This weed's almost as strong as the hit of acid that made Freddie wet his pants."

"I did *not* wet my pants."

"You pissed yourself. Didn't he, Charlie? Remember, Freddie said he saw a psycho with an ax?"

"Man, am I stoned."

"Me too," Freddie agreed.

"So who's got the balls to follow me down those steps?"

"Lead on, Brother Tom."

"Let's fuckin' do it."

The Zombie Hunters wore a mismatched uniform. Underneath, the three were bundled up against the cold, but over top, each had pulled on a favorite T-shirt garnered at a past convention. "Bad Moon Books, Garden Grove" read Tommy's torso. "Shocklines" said Charlie's chest. "Cemetery Dance" prophesied Freddie's pecs.

Closing on the beckoning pit sunk into the muddy ground, the zonked Zombie Hunters paused at the edge of the abyss for a passing of the torch. Careful not to shine the flashlight down into the hole, for that would spoil the thrill, Tommy allowed the beam to creep forward to the step at the rim and no farther.

"Step One," he said, then down went his foot.

"Step Two. Step Three. You with me, fellas?"

"Roger," whispered Freddie.

"Aye," said Charlie. "Bringing up the rear."

"Step Four. Step Five."

The beam of the torch descended no deeper than the outer edge of the next step down.

"Step Six. Step Seven. Step Eight. Don't piss yourself, Freddie. Remember, I'm here in front of your stream."

"I did *not* piss myself."

"Step Nine. Step Ten. As I recall, it wasn't raining that night, dude."

"It's sure as hell raining now," Charlie said.

"Step Eleven. Step Twelve. This is it, guys. One more step down and we get a glimpse of hell on earth."

"Quit yakking, Tommy."

"Yeah. Let's roll."

"Step Thirteen," Tommy announced, planting his shoe in the mud at the foot of the sinkhole, then sweeping the beam forward to illuminate whatever lurked in the darkness beneath the Thirteen Steps to Hell. And that's when he saw the ax.

As the torch flipped end over end out of Tommy's grasp, it flickered a "now you see it, now you don't" nightmare in front of Freddie's eyes. When the psycho with an ax appeared in the blinking pit of light and shadow, Freddie thought it was an acid flashback to his prior bad trip. Then he remembered that Tommy had organized this trek into the hinterland, and he figured his conniving buddy had set up this shock to yank his chain. But then—

Whack!

The ax cracked down on Tommy's crown, cleaving his skull open in a spray of blood and brains.

Freddie pissed himself.

The maul, a fitting name for this ax-shaped weapon, was as wide at the back of its wedge as a sledgehammer. The descending blade sank as deep as Tommy's shuddering shoulders with a sickening crunch. When the axman jerked the handle up and down to free the steel V, the wedge squeaked against shattered bones and wrenched out of Tommy's bisected brain with a sucking sound.

The beam winked out.

As Freddie turned to scramble back up the Thirteen Steps to Hell, the last thing he saw before the tumbling flashlight hit the concrete were the gouts of gore splattered all over Charlie Yu's twitching face. Then it was pitch black down in this hellhole, and Freddie sensed he was an ax stroke away from taking a bone-crushing blow. So, with hands that clutched and clawed like those of the cannibal zombies in *Night of the Living Dead,* he grabbed hold of Charlie and tried to pull him down the steps so that he could crawl over his buddy and turn him into a buffer between the blade and himself.

Clang!

Too late.

Sparks and chips flew as the steel struck a step.

Freddie's shriek in the darkness echoed in the pit. Blood spewed as Charlie struggled to break free, flailing his limbs like an over-turned crab in a frantic attempt to climb the slippery steps back-wards. Freddie's hands still clutched him, so the terrified Texan swung his body from side to side to throw off the inhibiting drag. The result was that Charlie got whapped in the face by the mushy stump of a severed limb. Now he, too, was screaming.

Whack!

Clang!

The maul kept hacking at Freddie. His other arm suddenly let go, releasing Charlie to roll over onto his belly and clamber his way up the Thirteen Steps to Hell on hands and knees.

Step Eight.
Step Seven.
Step Six.
Step Five—
Then someone grabbed his ankle.

"Nooooooooo!" Charlie wailed as he bumped back down into the pit, his chin bouncing off each concrete step in turn. The dazzling glare of a heavy-duty flashlight lit up the blackness from behind his head, and as Charlie tried to push himself up from the bloody steps, a silhouette of his own head shadowed the cement under his eyes, and over that outline loomed a dark blur, descending fast.

Whack!

Clang!

Charlie never saw the sparks.

GHOST TOUR

Zinc Chandler was mildly surprised to find waiting at the arrivals gate for his flight from Vancouver a Seattle cop who whisked him from SeaTac Airport to a nearby helipad, where a police helicopter sat ready to fly him into the hinterland. It was still drizzling, but far less than the deluge overnight, and as the rotor whirling above their heads blew the rainwater on the Tarmac away, the chopper lifted up into the sodden gray sky.

The pilot gave Zinc a verbal tour through his cockpit headphones as they flew northeast over Seattle toward the Cascade Mountains. Puget Sound and the Pacific retreated on their left.

"Mount Rainier," the pilot announced, pointing to the snowy volcanic cone dominating the horizon thirty miles away to the southeast. "If that baby ever blows like Mount St. Helens did, it will be one of the deadliest eruptions ever.

"In 1947, an Idaho businessman flew a private plane past the peak en route to Oregon. Supposedly, that's when he saw nine circular objects hovering in single-file formation. He described them to a reporter as each being about the size of a DC-4, and he said they flew like a saucer would if you skipped it across water. That's where we got the term 'flying saucer.'"

Their flight path took them over the lower tip of Lake Washington to the upper tip of Lake Sammamish, farther inland. The Cascade Mountains formed a white backdrop. This morning, the overcast sky made for a brooding vista.

"Lake Sammamish State Park," the pilot said, indicating an area to the south of the dark body of water. "That's where Ted Bundy drove his VW Bug in the summer of '74 to rape and kill several women he picked up near the picnic benches.

"And that," he added, pointing farther east toward the Cascades, at a distance that Zinc estimated to be around thirty miles from Seattle, "is where you'll find Snoqualmie Falls. The water plunges a hundred feet more than Niagara. Remember 'Twin Peaks'?"

"Who killed Laura Palmer?"

"That's where it was shot."

The pilot set the chopper down on a country road to the north of Lake Sammamish. To prepare for the landing, a pair of county sheriff's cars angled across the pavement to block off a section. As Zinc removed the cockpit headphones from his ears, the pilot gave him a thumbs up. The Mountie stepped out into the drizzle, where Det. Ralph Stein of Seattle Homicide waited for him on the shoulder of the road.

The helicopter took off and banked its rotor southwest to return to Seattle. The sheriff's cars moved aside to reopen the road so that no fewer than four coroner's vehicles could drive in to park. Now, that was an ominous sign.

"Ralph."

"Zinc."

The cops shook hands.

"How are the ankles?"

"Wet weather makes 'em throb, and the added weight doesn't help. How you faring? Alex and all?"

"Up and down. You know. Losing her broke my heart. To cope, I threw myself into work, but the chief's not happy. He's ordered me off to the South Pacific for some R&R. I'll probably get my knuckles rapped for coming here."

"The South Pacific? I wish! Let me take your place?"

"Go pack."

"No need. On a day as wet as this, I'm wearing trunks instead of Jockey shorts."

"What's with the four meat wagons?"

"One for each vic."

"That bad?"

"Uh-huh. We don't want to mix up the pieces."

Det. Ralph Stein was bigger—*much* bigger—than when they had last met. Their cop-to-cop relationship went back several years, to an investigation into a blackmailing scheme run by a pimp who'd recruited underage girls for sex across the border. Later, Stein's accident had taken him out of the joint manhunt that came to be known as the Hangman case, whose repercussions had ultimately cost the Mountie the love of his life. In the aftermath of those personal tragedies, Zinc had paid a visit to Ralph while he was recuperating at home, talking shop for hours in Stein's kitchen.

"You bring 'em?" Ralph asked now.

"Yes," said Zinc.

"Where'd you get 'em?"

"From my locker."

"You said they were hold-back evidence?"

"Right. Key facts. That we found nails hammered into Cardoza's skull was released to the media. The halo was seen by the chambermaid, so it got out of the bag. But we managed to keep the style and dimensions of the nails under wraps for use as key-fact evidence to trip up any suspects we might interrogate."

"You still keeping that secret?"

"Yep. To thwart copycats."

"Let's hope that's what we have here. I'd rather go after a copycat than a serial killer."

"I'll show you mine, if you show me yours."

Ralph fished in his coat pocket and withdrew his hand as a closed fist. The Mountie foraged in his travel bag, then held out a fist too. They were like children playing the game of Rock, Paper, Scissors.

"Ready?"

"On three."

"One, two, *three*," said Ralph.

They opened their fists.

"Son of a bitch," said Zinc.

The nails on both palms were identical: non-galvanized flatheads of the same make and length.

"It reaffirms my faith in this," said Ralph, tapping his nose. "Hard to believe there was a time before computers and high-tech gizmos when cases were linked by instinct—cops discussing their cold ones, then putting two and two together if a similarity cropped up later. The moment I saw that head staked upside down with a crown of nails hammered into the skull, I recalled what you told me about your dead-end Hanged Man case from a year and a half ago."

"It just reopened."

"Here, take a look." The detective popped his umbrella to protect them from the drizzle, then withdrew a photograph of the head stuck on the stake from his shirt pocket.

"Déjà vu," said the Mountie.

Again, Ralph tapped his nose. "We'd have gotten there anyway, even if you and I had never discussed your case. I had HITS"—the Homicide Investigation Tracking System, developed in Washington State—"check for similarities in previous local cases. Nothing. HITS widened its search to VICAP"—the FBI's Violent Criminal Apprehension Program—"but a sweep of the United States struck out too. Then HITS went to ViCLAS"—the Violent Crime Linkage Analysis System, created by the Mounties—"and it came back with one link: your Hanged Man case."

"A cross-border serial killer."

"A killing up there. A killing down here. Is he yours or is he ours? Where does he call home?"

"I hope it's Seattle," said Zinc.

"It's probably Vancouver."

"So what have you found way out here?"

The detective led the inspector off the road into the dripping trees. Perhaps it was the weather—dismal, depressing and gray, with wisps that could be ghosts' breath condensing here and there—but Zinc felt a chill of Gothic morbidity about this bad place. The trees weren't healthy. They were diseased and gnarled. Claustrophobia closed in around the cops, and crooked limbs reached for their faces. The ground that squished beneath their shoes was wildly overgrown, and only when he almost tripped on a hidden grave-stone did the Mountie realize that he was in a cemetery that time had forgotten.

The smell of death grew stronger as they approached what seemed to be a yawning sinkhole in the center of the graveyard. Out of it rose a disembodied voice noting anatomical aspects. As Zinc neared the rim of the pit to gaze down the Thirteen Steps to Hell, Ralph cautioned, "Brace yourself. It's ugly."

The Thirteen Steps to Hell deserved their damned name. Littering the sticky staircase were the hacked-up bodies of three young men, the maul left behind on the bottom step. The skull of the lowest victim was cleaved in two. The arms of the middle man were severed from his body. The cranium of the uppermost corpse was reduced to mush.

Zinc's eyes, however, were riveted on the fourth body. In a hellish parody of the crucifixion of Christ, the Satanic crucifix faced the foot of the Thirteen Steps to Hell. Its crosspiece indented by blunt blows from the backside of the maul, the wooden T was stuck upright in the mud of the pit. Instead of the Roman soldiers who had stared up at the face of Christ on Golgotha Hill, forensic personnel squatted on their haunches to examine the remains of a naked man who'd been hung upside down, his right leg lashed to the beam, with his left leg tied in place behind it to sign a cross. Both wrists were cuffed at the small of the victim's back to fashion the base of a triangle. In every way except one, the victim at the bottom of the steps was similar to the hanged man displayed seventeen months ago at the Lions Gate. All that was missing here was the nimbus of nails, because this hanged man didn't have a head.

While driving back to Seattle in Stein's car, they stopped for breakfast at a roadside diner near Redmond. The café was a ma-and-pa affair, with her out front working the dining room and him back in the kitchen slinging hash. This was Zinc's kind of eatery, a comfy, cozy harbor off the beaten track where a man could sit back, relax and feel at home. To the Mountie's way of looking at modern times, one of the worst developments was the endemic cancer of franchising. It was beyond him how anyone could find succor in knowing that no matter where you went in North America, there was a Denny's or IHOP close at hand. If Zinc owned a time machine, he would return to the era before cloning took hold, when every restaurant was built to be unique.

"What in God's name are you doing?"

Ralph looked up from the menu. "Counting calories," he said.

"With that?"

"Uh-huh. It's a calorie wheel. What you do is turn this circle until the food you're considering appears in this slot, then you check here to see how many calories it contains."

"You're not telling me it's got the lumberjack breakfast in there?"

"No."

"So what do you do?"

"You find what ingredients go into the meal, then you check each one on the calorie wheel and add the numbers."

"The bulls in Homicide must love you, Ralph. Out goes the squad as a group for lunch, and you call the chef out of the kitchen at the height of the lunchtime rush to have him list the ingredients in the lasagna special."

"You're right," said Ralph. "Fuck it." He tossed aside the wheel. "I'll have the lumberjack breakfast," he said when Ma came to the table for their order.

"Make that two," said Zinc.

The diner had a jukebox biased in favor of country and western that patrons could feed with coins. No wonder Zinc felt at home in here. As a farm boy raised on the Prairies, he'd grown up on this stuff.

"So," said Ralph, "what's your take on the scene?"

"I see why you're out here. It has to be the other half of what you found at Ted Bundy's house."

"It is. The M.E.—"

"Ruthless Ruth? I saw her down in the pit."

"You know her?"

"She worked the Hangman case. She was on the cruise ship when Alex died."

"Ruth won't commit until she compares 'em in the morgue, but it seems the cut patterns on both stumps match. It's safe to say—given the nails in the spiked head—that it *was* hacked off the body we found strung up like the Hanged Man."

"Why two dump sites?"

"Why indeed? You got a theory?"

"Perhaps," said Zinc. "But first I need more info. What gives with the graveyard? It's unmarked, and it's ancient."

"That's Maltby Cemetery."

"Never heard of it."

"The graves go back to the 1800s. Local lore says it was founded by a family of Satanists. That staircase down into the sinkhole is known as the Thirteen Steps to Hell. Over time, the graveyard became a mecca for devil worshipers and vandalizing kids. Though it was erased from all local maps, the legend of Maltby Cemetery wouldn't die. According to *Ripley's Believe It or Not,* that graveyard is one of the world's most evil haunts."

"I could feel it."

"So could I. People still come looking for the site. But there's also an Old Maltby Cemetery around here, which recently converted its name to Paradise Lake Cemetery. The Internet—God bless it—is infested with false information. Someone assumed that name was changed to mask its scandalous pedigree, so now *that* cemetery has taken on *this* cemetery's Satanic lore."

"It fits," said Zinc.

"What? Your theory?"

"One of the motives attributed to Jack the Ripper was that his first four victims were killed in locations that formed an inverted cross hidden in the Hanged Man. The fifth victim—Mary Kelly—was ripped to shreds in Room 13 of Miller's Court; an inverted occult triangle was among the cuts that tore her flesh."

"So?" said Ralph.

"This killer may be trying to gain access to the occult realm too."

Ralph rolled his eyes. "I wish I'd become a plumber."

"Room 13, supposedly, was essential to that motive because thirteen, of course, is the Magick number. A witches' coven, with its twelve witches and a grand master, signifies thirteen. Jesus was doomed to crucifixion at the Last Supper, which was attended by his twelve disciples and him—to make thirteen."

"A Magick place?"

"Right."

"Like Ted Bundy's house and the Thirteen Steps to Hell?"

"Could be."

"Sounds crazy."

"We're dealing with a psycho."

"Crazy fits."

"Remember the Ripper? That psycho I told you about? The fellow who thought he was Jack the Ripper transported to modern times? Tarot Magick was his motive too. First, he hanged four women at specific sites in Vancouver to sign the occult cross. Then he lured a group of victims—including Alex and me—to Deadman's Island to whittle us down to a single survivor, whom he would rip apart in a Magick place to sign the occult triangle. The Magick place he thought would launch him through the gates of time and into the astral plane was an ancient Indian burial ground hidden in a cave on the island."

"Where's the Ripper now?"

"Locked away."

"So we have a copycat?"

"Possibly. Alex published a true crime book about the motive for Deadman's Island. Could be that someone read it and—like our Ripper—set out to copy the key."

"A copycat of a copycat?"

"It's the Tarot. Dark minds have been mesmerized by the Devil's picture book since the Dark Ages."

"Your case in North Vancouver—the vic in that hotel? What made it a Magick place?"

"Don't know."

"Was the hotel built on an Indian burial ground?"

"Not that I've heard. But I'll check it out. Until you came up with Ted Bundy's house and the Thirteen Steps to Hell, I thought this killer had rejected the theory of the Magick place. Since he signified both the four points of the cross and the three points of the triangle in *how* he hanged his victim to mimic the Hanged Man, I wondered if that, *by itself,* had made the hotel a Magick place. Four times three equals twelve, and twelve's the number of the Magick card."

Two lumberjack breakfasts—sausages, bacon, eggs, pancakes, the works—were set down on the table. Ralph smacked his lips. "Remind me not to eat for a week," he said, then wolfed into calorie overload as if this were his last meal.

"Opportunity," Zinc said. "That should be our focus. Motive and means we may have. But opportunity?"

Ralph mumbled something with his mouth full that the Canadian didn't catch.

"My take on what happened in Maltby Cemetery is that the Tarot killers—there must be two, from the exertion required—were hammering their cross together down in the pit with the sledge-hammer side of the maul so they could haul up the headless body to mimic the Hanged Man. They were interrupted by the three young men, whom they then hacked to death on the steps."

Savoring a sausage, Ralph wiped egg yolk up with a pancake as he nodded in agreement.

"You said Maltby Cemetery was erased from maps. From what I saw, the graveyard is unmarked, forgotten and overgrown. Without you as a guide, I'd never have guessed it was there. So how did you find the bodies?"

"You notice the car at the side of the road?"

"The blue Toyota?"

"A sheriff's deputy spied it and stopped to look inside. A severed arm lay on the front seat. He knew about the Thirteen Steps from trouble they've had there over the years, so he walked in to check the cemetery and found the four vics."

"Whose car?"

"Thomas Cribb's. One of the guys on the steps."

"Was he local?"

"Seattle."

"And the other two?"

"From ID found in their wallets, they were Charles Yu from Texas and Frederick Sanders from Rhode Island."

"Opportunity," Zinc repeated. "That's what we need. How did the killers down in the pit and the three vics on the Thirteen Steps know the location of Maltby Cemetery?"

"I'm out of sausages."

"So?"

"It's barter time," said Ralph.

"You know the answer?"

"It'll cost you one of your three."

The Mountie picked up the calorie wheel that Ralph had tossed down on the table, then spun it repeatedly as he muttered, "Sausages, sausages . . . Yep, there they are." His eyes shot wide dramatically, and he dropped the weight-watching device. "Take 'em all, Ralph. The fat in those bangers will clog you."

"Don't mind if I do." Ralph spiked the sausages on his fork. "Next time I'll order the ham."

From the inside pocket of his houndstooth jacket, the buttons of which strained to hold in his expansive paunch, the homicide cop withdrew a pamphlet and passed it across.

"World Horror Convention," said Zinc, reading from the cover of the program.

"We found a box of those in the blue Toyota. One lay folded open on the passenger's seat. There's a list of those attending the convention inside. You'll find the names of all three vics hacked up on the cemetery steps. Thomas Cribb was also on the organizing committee. Take a look at the back pages."

The Mountie flipped through the booklet until he came to the title "Spooky Seattle: A Ghost Tour of Haunted Sites." His eyes ran down the short takes on the city's famous ghosts. Princess Angelene, daughter of Chief Seattle, who haunts the Pike Place Market. The ghost of the little boy in the puppet shop who makes the marionettes move on their own. The man with the wax mustache who haunts the bank vault in Underground Seattle. The floating ladies in the Neptune Theater, adorned with heads depicting the god of the sea, complete with glowing aquamarine eyes. The hot spot of Northgate Hospital, which became Northgate Mall, the first shopping mall in North America. The tunnels under the parking lot are haunted by entities from the old morgue, and the homeless who later went in for shelter got lost and never came out. The printed tour moved on to ghosts outside Seattle and ended with a description of the Thirteen Steps to Hell in Maltby Cemetery, complete with X–Y coordinates from a survey grid.

"Opportunity," echoed Zinc.

"For anyone who can read them. A grid map marked with Maltby Cemetery and a road map with that information transferred to it were left in the blue Toyota under that program, which had been folded back to the page on Maltby Cemetery."

"So," said the Mountie, "the big question is, did the killers use the same grid coordinates in the World Horror Convention program to locate the Thirteen Steps?"

"Most likely. The severed head seems to corroborate it."

"At Bundy's house?"

"Uh-huh. That's a telltale clue. There's an urban myth being spread that Ted Bundy once lined up four severed heads on the mantel in that house. He didn't."

"You think that's why the head was spiked there?"

"It fits. A bus tour that periodically goes by the house uses the severed heads as a story to spice up the tour."

"The killers took that tour?"

"And I think I know when. The bus went past the Bundy house on Thursday afternoon."

"Why suspect that tour?"

"It was a private charter. I was about to check the charter party out when the sheriff called about the headless body hanging upside down in Maltby Cemetery."

Zinc snapped his fingers. "The horror convention."

"They chartered the ghost tour bus for the opening day. And guess what? The convention is still in town."

"I wonder what goes on at a horror convention?"

"Let's find out," said Ralph.

Horror Convention

"Just what the world needs," Chandler said as they traversed the parking lot of the Captain Vancouver Hotel. "All its ghastly horrors convened in one place."

Stein flipped open his cellphone and held it up to his ear. "I'll call the military and ask for a nuclear strike. Level this convention and we'll solve all the world's problems."

"The nerve of this hotel," Zinc huffed with mock umbrage. "What right does an American inn have to usurp the name of *my* hometown's patron saint?"

"Every right," Ralph replied. "*I* was born in Vancouver."

"You don't look Canadian."

"That's Vancouver, *Washington.*"

"Oh," said Zinc, scrunching his nose as if he smelled a pulp mill. "That pretender."

"We were first," Ralph said, putting up his fists.

"A ninety-pound weakling. A poseur. Which once had the balls to suggest that *we* change our name."

"Plagiarists."

In truth, Zinc Chandler stood on shaky historical ground, as Det. Ralph Stein proceeded to point out. In 1778, the legendary Captain Cook sailed to this coast, seeking the passage that was reputed to link the Pacific and Atlantic oceans. Fourteen years later, one of Cook's crewmen, Capt. George Vancouver, returned on the *Discovery.* His assignment was to map the area, so he dispatched Lieutenant Puget down the sound that leads to Seattle and now bears his name. Mount Baker got charted in honor of another lieutenant, and Mount Rainier was named for an admiral of the British navy.

"Lieutenant Broughton," Ralph added, "explored a hundred miles up the Columbia River and named a point of land for Captain Vancouver. That same point was renamed Fort Vancouver in 1825, when the Hudson's Bay Company established it as the oldest permanent non-Native settlement in the Pacific Northwest. The fort became the center of the fur trade, and in 1857 it was incorporated as the city of Vancouver in Washington State."

"Humph," snorted Zinc. "A likely story."

"Do you know where *your* city of Vancouver got its name?"

"From God?" wondered the Mountie.

"When your burg was incorporated in 1886, some railroad tycoon pulled the name out of thin air. So," said the American, opening the door with one hand and sweeping the other around his girth in a poor attempt at a Sir Walter Raleigh bow, "welcome to the Captain Vancouver Hotel, named for *our* patron saint long before you fuckin' low-down, snake-in-the-grass imperialists stole it."

Their worst fears about what goes on at a World Horror Convention were realized as Chandler and Stein stepped through the door, for what they encountered in the lobby was a creature— that was the best word—from another world, an alien being who made Zinc imagine Cher on bad acid.

Black was the color of this demon's garb. Her getup was tailored to sheathe her flesh with black leather skin, while tattered sleeves dangled, evoking a recent crawl from the grave. Her long nails were lacquered as black as vampire's claws, and her facial makeup hollowed her cheeks and sank her onyx eyes. Her lip gloss glistened like licorice goo, and her hair, cropped close on both sides, was woven into a two-foot-high black Mohawk that reminded Zinc of the helmet of a Greek warrior condemned to guard the River Styx.

"Mom!"

A child's voice.

The dark demon turned.

Slouched on a couch in the lobby was a five- or six-year-old girl wearing blue denim overalls and hugging a teddy bear. "What about me?"

"Sit there," the demon instructed, "until I return."

Zinc glanced at Ralph.

Ralph glanced at Zinc.

"That says a lot."

"That says it *all.*"

The reception desk was to the right of the common area. The cops ventured over to speak to a black man in a blue blazer with dreadlocks down to his shoulders.

"Bet the management loves this convention," Ralph said.

"Yes," the clerk agreed.

Stein scowled. "A *horror* convention?"

"They're well behaved. The WHC has a good rep in the industry. The Shriners—now there's a horror show. They get drunk and piss in all the corners."

"So what's that?" Ralph asked, cocking a thumb at the creature in the leathers.

"Pariah."

"No doubt."

"That's her name. She's a performance poet. Poets are usually the most outré of any creative group."

The clerk directed them across the common area and along a hall to the left. Opposite the doors through which the cops had entered, a boisterous bar ran the width of the lobby and served a scattering of tables that overlooked a swimming pool through the glass beyond. The turquoise pool was surrounded by several hot tubs for intimate bubbly soaks, and on the other three sides of that recreational square were four tiers lined with individual hotel rooms. The central court had a skylight canopy. By looking up, the cops could spy aircraft landing at and departing from the nearby SeaTac Airport, but the soundproofing built into the hotel was sufficient to kill the engine noise.

"Into the valley of death," said Ralph.

Judging from the hubbub spilling out into the hall, a contentious event had just wrapped up at the convention. A flood of dark-side aficionados engulfed the cops, most of them "normal-looking" people heading for the bar to argue and debate the undertones of whatever they had witnessed. Two fellows stepped aside to let the surge ebb. They paused long enough for the cops to eavesdrop. The shorter man had snow-white hair that cascaded over his shoulders. He sported a black T-shirt emblazoned with a white skeleton and the red words "Dark Delicacies, Burbank, CA." The tall man, lean and fit, wore all black with sartorial elegance. In his hand was an invitation to the all-night Borderlands Speakeasy, sponsored by the San Francisco bookstore.

"Those two hate each other," Dark Delicacies said.

"Word is, they used to be partners," Borderlands replied.

"Writing partners?"

"Law partners."

"Something sure went wrong."

"Professional rivalry."

"If looks could kill, huh?"

"How are they doing at your table?"

"*Halo of Flies* is outselling *Crown of Thorns* four to one."

"Same with us."

"The GOH is pissed."

"I'd be too if everyone was saying I should be Wes."

"Round two coming up."

"Yeah. What time's the panel?"

The tide had depleted, so the men walked on.

Three-quarters of the way along the wide hall, a registration table was set up against the wall. The young woman staffing it sat on a chair facing an open doorway across the corridor. On the board tented outside to lure in traffic were the words, written in big black letters, MORBID MAZE.

Zinc froze in his tracks.

"Y' okay, buddy?"

Ralph didn't get an answer.

"You look like you've seen a ghost."

Zinc shook his head, gaping at the young woman.

Alex? he thought.

If the supernatural was going to slip into his life, what better place for it to happen than at a horror convention? Was that the term for this? Doppelgänger? The ghostly counterpart or double of a living person? But what if that "living person" was dead, and it was the ghostly double who was sitting here in the flesh? Would that make Alex the doppelgänger of this woman? It wasn't just the hair, wayward and blonde. Nor was it the eyes, as blue as lagoons. It was also the way she moved, with a ballerina's grace. From what Zinc could see from this far away, everything about her was the spitting image of his lost love.

"Are you with me, Zinc?"

"Huh?"

"Snap out of it, buddy. Yeah, she's good looking. But I don't see the snakes it takes to turn a man to stone."

"Sorry, Ralph. Momentary lapse."

"You had me worried. I thought it was a heart attack. If a healthy guy like you drops dead, what hope is there for a fatty like me?"

You're right, thought Zinc.

It is a heart attack.

Punctured by Cupid's arrow, Zinc's scarred heart pounded wildly in his throat as he and the detective narrowed the gap between them and the siren seated at the registration table. The natural pout of her lips. The slightly turned-up nose . . .

"Know who she reminds me of?" Ralph said.

"Who?"

"A young Kim Basinger in that film with Mickey Rourke. What's it called? The one where Kim does a striptease to 'You Can Leave Your Hat On'?"

According to the tag encased in the square of plastic strung around her neck, Yvette Theron was the woman's name. With Gothic black the color of choice for most conventioneers' clothes, she stood out like a lightning bolt cleaving the night. Her top was electric blue and picked up the hue of her eyes.

"You're cops?" she said when they walked up.

"Yes," replied the Mountie. Zinc flashed his badge, and Ralph did too.

"We've been expecting you."

"Oh?" said Stein.

"First, the head spiked upside down outside Ted Bundy's house—a house our ghost tour passed on Thursday afternoon. And now, according to the radio, the rest of the body found hanging upside down in Maltby Cemetery, the graveyard in our program. We placed bets on how long it would take you to come looking for suspects here."

"This isn't what I expected."

"No?" said Yvette.

"I thought there'd be rabid fans running about made up like their favorite monsters."

"So did one of the networks. They were going to tape the con but chickened out when they heard we aren't Alice Cooper, Ozzy Osbourne and Marilyn Manson clones."

"Biting the heads off chickens?"

"Bats," Yvette corrected him. "Ozzy bit the head off a bat onstage in his prime."

"Why so staid?" said Zinc.

"Us, you mean? Except for the locals, for whom it's cheap, a trip to the con by fans from around the world costs the price of an airline ticket, four nights in this palace, meals, transport and the program itself, all in Yankee dollars. It's a fun-loving group. Practical jokes. Gallows humor. Drinking folks under the table. But for that sort of money, the fans who come want juicy discussions with meat on the bone."

"Discussions like . . . ?"

"Take your pick," Yvette said, reaching for a WHC program and folding it open to the list of today's panels. She held it out for Zinc to peruse while Ralph read over his shoulder:

How to Write a Horror Best-seller: Is There a Demon You Can Sell Your Soul To?

Eros and Thanatos: The Siamese Twins of Erotic Death.
Eldritch and Blasphemous: The Cthulhu Mythos Spawned by
H. P. Lovecraft.
Feminism and Horror: We've Come a Long Way, Baby.
Urban Horror: New Monsters for a New Millennium.
Psychological Horror: The Voices in My Head Told Me To.
Genre Blending: Mixing Horror and Mystery.
How Far Is Too Far?: The Moral Responsibility of Writers,
Filmmakers and Artists.

Though Zinc tried to focus on the print, his eyes kept flicking back to Yvette. True, he was face-to-face with a woman in her own right, but the features that his imagination superimposed on hers were those of his lost love, Alexis Hunt. His psychology—and he recognized it himself—was similar to that of the Hollywood director who was devastated by the murder of his Playboy Playmate love by the boyfriend who had "discovered" her and was unhinged by jealousy. In the end, the director married his love's sister, and the rumor was that he tried to remold her with plastic surgery. The rumor may have been false, but if not, Zinc understood, for that's what he was doing in his fantasy world.

Love hurts.

And lost love cuts like a knife.

"Your nerves good, Ms. Theron?" the Seattle detective asked.

"We're at a horror convention."

"It's a photo of a dead man."

"I've seen worse. One of the presentations here is 'What Happens to Dead Bodies?' An autopsy film."

A digital camera was ideal in murder cases like this. By capturing the severed head found spiked outside Ted Bundy's house on a memory card that was then fed into a computer, the police photographer was able to manipulate that image. The picture had been cropped to eliminate the stake and the sliced-through neck, then digital finagling had removed the ring of nails. In the same way an undertaker cleans up a deceased for viewing, so the tech had softened what began as a hardcore X-rated beheading into a PG one.

"Recognize him?"

"No," said Yvette.

"He didn't register at the con on Thursday or Friday?"

"Not to my knowledge."

"Would you know?" Ralph asked.

"Only if he registered while I was at the table. We work in shifts. Tickets are sold all day."

"Were you on the ghost tour?"

"No. I was here."

"Is there a list of those who were?"

"You'd have to ask Mort."

"Mort?"

"Mort Montgomery. Head of the convention."

"Where do we find him?"

"Try Tomb A. That's the big convention room around the corner. Mort caught the panel that just let out."

"The one that caused the hubbub?" interjected Zinc.

Yvette nodded.

"Why the buzz?"

"Our guest of honor is being eclipsed by his rival. That, combined with the Tarot murder that brings you here."

"Who's your guest of honor?"

"Bret Lister. Know him?"

"Yes," said Zinc. "The lawyer-turned-writer."

"Bret wrote a couple of psycho-thrillers based on his law practice. His third book has a publication date that coincides with this convention. He registered for the con as an attendee, but when our scheduled guest of honor died suddenly, Bret was asked to step in. He has the draw of having been committed to an asylum, and his latest book is a *roman à clef* about the Hanged Man murder."

"The death in Vancouver?"

"Uh-huh. A year and a half ago."

"What do the Romans have to do with it?" Ralph asked.

Yvette raised an eyebrow.

"That's a joke," said Stein.

"Do you know what a *roman à clef* is?"

"No, Ms. Theron. But if I had to guess, I'd say it's a novel about real events and characters under the guise of fiction. From the French for 'novel with a key.'"

"He's an etymologist," Zinc explained. "He studies bugs."

"Who are you two? Laurel and Hardy?"

"I'm Laurel," Ralph said.

"So I see."

"What's the title of Bret's new book?" asked the Mountie.

"Crown of Thorns."

"Publisher?"

"Grave Subjects. It's a specialty house. Dark fiction."

"Crown of Thorns. Sounds religious. Like *The Exorcist,*" said Ralph.

"The cop in the novel," Zinc asked, "what's he like?" If a *roman à clef* is about real events and characters, he knew he was probably in this one. Not only was he the investigator involved in the real Hanged Man murder in North Vancouver, but he and Bret Lister had crossed swords in several murder trials before the lawyer flipped out in court and was sent to Colony Farm.

"To be honest, I haven't read it. It just came out."

"Good timing," Stein said dryly. "Thanks to the new Hanged Man murder here."

"Thus the buzz," echoed Yvette.

"You mentioned a rival?" Zinc said. "A writer challenging Bret as guest of honor?"

"In a strange coincidence—almost a twist of fate—Bret's isn't the only novel being published this week about the Hanged Man murder in Vancouver."

"Another *roman à clef*?"

"Halo of Flies."

"Like the Alice Cooper song?"

Yvette nodded.

"Publisher?"

"Penguin."

"A major house."

"Two books. Same source. Guess who's playing second fiddle?"

"Bret Lister."
"There's more. They used to be law partners."
"Who's the rival?" Ralph asked.
"Wes Grimmer. Know him?" Yvette asked the Mountie.
"Yes," Zinc replied.
Grimmer was the Ripper's lawyer.

GOTH QUEEN

Morbid curiosity hooked its barb through Zinc's cheek, then tugged the Mountie across the hall toward the art gallery. As the cops had turned away from Yvette and the registration table to head around the corner to catch Mort—"That's French for 'dead,'" said Ralph—Montgomery in Tomb A, Zinc happened to glance through the open doors of the gallery and spot the lure.

"You go, Ralph. I want to check this out."

Stein followed Zinc's gaze. "I'll bet you do," he said.

"I wondered how long it would take you to notice Petra," teased Yvette.

"Petra," warned Ralph. "As in 'turn to stone.'"

"Careful," cautioned Yvette. "I'll sell you a garland of garlic."

"The cross will protect me," Zinc replied.

The cross in question was in the painting that lured him in through the doors. The grisly image was displayed on the outer wall of a maze of panels in the center of the ballroom. Fifteen feet of empty floorspace stretched from the doors to the painting, beside which was a vacant chair so ornate that it could only be a throne. In front of the throne stood a filigreed stool fanned with tarot cards.

The cross was a Christian crucifix that had been staked upside down on the crest of a Golgotha mound that could be Calvary. The naked man crucified to the wood was the Hanged Man. Both hands were joined behind his body at the small of his back. His left leg was pinned in place behind his right thigh. Instead of being crucified by nails pounded through his hands and feet, he was impaled on countless spikes that jutted toward the viewer as if the cross was a vertical bed of nails. The points that skewered through his flesh were red with dripping blood, and the sky beyond roiled with a deeper red that could be Satan's wrath. The figure's brow was pierced by a line of longer nails that protruded from his forehead like a blasphemous crown of thorns.

The image bore a title card.

The Antichrist, it read.

The Mountie noted the artist.

Petra Zydecker.

Zinc's curiosity was piqued by a puzzling detail. The painting was secured to the display panel by corner latches, and through the eyebolt of each was a padlock. Intrigued, Zinc craned his head around to one edge of the canvas, where to his further puzzlement he found that *The Antichrist* hid another painting.

Of what?

Something more profane?

Or obscene?

The Mountie's suspicion switched to an array of smaller paintings that had been arranged like an aura behind the throne. Each depicted a tarot card drawn at random from a deck composed of both the Major and Minor Arcanas. The Queen of Swords sat on a throne similar to this one, with her sword held high in one hand and the head of a man gripped by his hair and dripping blood from his severed neck in the other. The High Priestess was a black voodoo witch, zigzag patterns painted on her face, with a headdress of grass and animal horns. The Fool, as usual, had his back turned to the viewer so a cat could pull down his pants with bared teeth. The Wheel of Fortune was a rounded rack that spun off broken bodies while it snapped healthy ones. The Devil was a goat with a huge erect phallus, and chained about its hoofs was a harem of nude women. The Ace of Wands was a female hand whipping a cat-o'-nine-tails. The Ten of Swords was a naked man sprawled dead in a flood of gore, his chest run through by ten blades. . . .

And so it went. Card after card. Sex and violence.

Eros and Thanatos.

There was an ebb and flow to the Morbid Maze. The gallery must have cleared out for the toxic debate between the guest of honor, Bret Lister, and the spotlight grabber, Wes Grimmer. But having drained their bladders or chugged a beer in the bar, the fans were returning to the gallery for an interlude with the dark seers who exposed their malignant psyches in the maze of panels beyond. To keep ahead of the jabbering crowd, Zinc U'd around one side of the moveable wall backing the throne and entered the labyrinth of horror. Ghastly monsters lurked around each hinged corner, and he felt like Theseus stalking the Minotaur, that mutant with the head of a bull on the body of a man, through the bone-littered tunnels beneath the kingdom of Crete.

Creepy stuff, thought Zinc.

Fear. Despair. Superstition. Persecution. Paranoia. Captivity. Pain. Torture. Sex. Sadism. Madness. Death. War. . . .

Such were the themes.

One artist was fixated on damsels in jeopardy. His body beautifuls all wore clinging gossamer gowns with slits or tears that revealed garters and nylons above high heels. Each had her mouth open as if caught in a scream, for the perils that threatened her closed in like the jaws of a vise from both in front and behind. In fleeing from one menace, she would be snatched by another—damned if you do and damned if you don't. A hooded skeleton rowed a boat after a victim who was waist-deep in a lake of blood from which a dozen male hands emerged to claw at her clothes and grope her buxom torso. A horde of green-faced dwarfs with teeth filed to points as sharp as their dual-fisted knives came after a terrified woman about to plunge into a well of filthy, wallowing madmen. White-haired, toothless, dirty old men clutched at another as she climbed a ladder to an attic where hook-handed bald ogres were dissolving bodies in barrels of acid. Those already captured were in worse predicaments. A woman sat with her hands and thighs protruding forward through locked stocks as a buzz saw began to pass across the face of the wooden clamp. And finally, a reluctant bride stood at the altar in the grasp of a hunched giggler with burning eyes and twisted features, while a blindfolded priest with a noose around his neck joined them together for all time in unholy matrimony.

Zinc assumed the artist was male, but the signature read "Godiva."

"You've come a long way, baby."

The next artist was obsessed with the mask and the face. The mask was the false face presented to the world, the pie crust of civilization that hides the truth of human nature. The face was spawned by evolution out of primal ooze. Here, Dr. Jekyll faced a mirror reflecting Mr. Hyde, Dorian Gray faced the picture that exposed his debauchery, the Phantom of the Opera faced the false front of the mask torn from his deformed features, and the Masque of Red Death was discarded to show the putrescent flesh beneath.

Around the next corner, Zinc faced a blackout curtain. On parting the slit down its center, he entered a tent-like area with a canopy shutting out overhead light. The dark room contained just a single painting, but it was so big that the canvas covered the height and length of its wall. The stretch of art was entirely black except for two tiny figures in a spotlight beam. Only by approaching the center of the painting could the Mountie fathom who they were. He smiled as he recognized the naked Adam and Eve, complete with an apple in Adam's hand and a serpent coiled around the trunk of Eden's tree.

Without warning, a burst of black light lit up the canvas. Zinc had tripped a sensor by closing in on the panel, and what the rays brought to life in the black morass that spread beyond the boundaries of his limited vision was a panorama of such brutal bloodletting that he—seasoned cop though he was—recoiled in horror.

The atrocities faded.

Did he see what he thought he saw?

Only by tripping the sensor again could he dispel his doubt.

Which he did.

So vast was this slaughterhouse for pagan gods, so all-consuming was this abattoir of hell's demons, so terrifying was this butcher shop of macabre dread, that it would take a hundred bursts of black light to grasp its full potential. The painting was a visual dare—

How much of this can your mind stomach?—with "stomach" being the operative word. It was as if the entire cosmos fed on one food: bloody joints of human meat. And not just humans in the *Homo sapiens* sense, though there were plenty of those being cut up on butcher blocks—or spiked to hang from celestial hooks, or skewered to roast over cooking pits—but also the hominids who evolved into us: *Australopithecus, Homo habilis* and *Homo erectus.* Flesh-eaters from another dimension joined cannibals from this one, each rendered so that the outstanding features were fangs and demented eyes. One creature was a jumble of scales, warts, wounds and pustulate mush. Another was quasi-human but had gnashing teeth in those sockets that should have housed sight. Ghouls played with bones stripped of stewing flesh, like the one Zinc glimpsed who decorated each skull with a scalped wig. The roots of Eden's apple tree squirmed out like a can of worms, and through the dark woods that tangled from them pranced Pan-like fairies fingering flutes made from hollowed ribs. The adjectives that came to Zinc as he digested grisly bits of the overwhelming whole were bug-eyed, cackling, fetid, grotesque, howling, leprous, maggoty, noxious, oily, putrid, reptilian, scabby, teeming, vile, withered, yammering and zymotic . . . until he had seen much too much. Whoever had conceived this mind fuck, painting it must have consumed at least a year, and all that while, this labor of love was feeding off the theme of cannibalism.

You Are What You Eat. Alex's unwritten book.

Did this nightmare have a title?

Zinc searched for the card.

There it was.

Morlocks, he read.

And the artist?

The painting was signed "The Goth."

Zinc encountered a nightmare from his past as he exited from the maze. The pantheon of horror has three seminal myths: the vampire, as captured in Stoker's *Dracula;* the split personality, the origin of the serial killer, in Stevenson's *Jekyll and Hyde;* and the monsters from the occult realm, in Lovecraft's Cthulhu Mythos.

Howard Phillips (H. P.) Lovecraft was born in 1890. Three years later, his father was committed to an asylum. The boy and his mother went to reside with her parents in a crumbling old house in Providence, Rhode Island. Little Howard was eight when his dad died from the syphilis spirochetes worming through his brain. Sarah Lovecraft took her resentment out on her son, belittling Howard as an "ugly-looking" boy. He suffered from poikilothermism, an abnormal sensitivity to low temperatures, so the frail child was kept out of school. To cure him of his phobic fear of the dark, his unstable mom dragged him around the unlighted house at night. Imagining himself as a "nightgaunt," with ears elongated to points and horns sprouting from his temples, Howard began lurking in rooms with the curtains drawn during the day, then skulking about the streets of Providence after the sun went down, often sitting in the moonlight in St. John's Graveyard on the same flat tomb where Poe had once sat.

The seat of inspiration.

Lovecraft's mom was committed in 1919, and two years later, she died insane in the same asylum as had his dad. Struggling at the poverty line, H. P. began to sell horror stories to *Weird Tales,* the legendary pulp magazine. His ill-fated attempt at marriage soon ended in divorce. So repressed was he sexually that when his stories saw the only publication they did while he was alive, he tore off the covers with their scantily clad women and kept just the pulp. Aided by a diet largely of chocolate cake, he died of intestinal cancer and Bright's disease in relative obscurity in 1937. Eventually, the Cthulhu Mythos he created would evolve into the most influential force in modern horror fiction and transform Lovecraft into the horror writer's horror writer.

Déjà vu, thought Zinc.

The monsters of the Cthulhu Mythos were waiting for the Mountie when he emerged from the claustrophobic labyrinth of dark art on the far side of the maze. Wonders can be done these days with cold-cast porcelain and acrylic resin, as evidenced by the detailed models displayed on the tables in the sculptors' area. The exhibit was laid out beneath a banner blaring "LOVECRAFT'S REALM."

Wandering over, Zinc read the quote on its poster:

All of my stories, unconnected as they may be, are based on the fundamental lore or legend that this world was inhabited at one time by another race who, in practicing black magic, lost their foothold and were expelled, yet live on outside ever ready to take possession of this earth again.

The models on the table brought Lovecraft's realm to life, for each was rendered in exquisite detail. Zinc recognized the Nightgaunts—shocking black things with oily skin, horns and wings, and a suggestive blankness where their faces ought to be— posed so they clutched and flew and lashed their barbed tails. And Azathoth, the blind idiot god, that amorphous blight of confusion that bubbles and blasphemes at the core of infinity. And Yog-Sothoth, the all-in-one and one-in-all that isn't yoked to laws of time and space, but instead dwells in the interstices between the planes of the universe, a wormhole that waits as a conglomeration of iridescent globes, shifting and hovering like flying saucers. In the center of the table—befitting his place in the Mythos— crouched Great Cthulhu in all his glory—the dominating claws on his hind and fore feet; the long devilish wings on back of his scaly, gelatinous green, bloated and corpulent torso; the squid-like head. The sculptor left no doubt about the subconscious inspiration for this grasping creature. With its mass of tangled tentacles writhing around a labial-lipped maw, the face of Great Cthulhu was a carnivorous cosmic cunt trying to suck every man born of woman back into its ravenous black hole.

"Don't even think about it."

The threat emanated from behind the Mountie's shoulder.

"I'm buying that."

Zinc turned to face the voice.

"Hello, Bret."

"You slumming, Chandler? It seems they'll allow *anyone* into this convention."

The last time the inspector had seen the lawyer was during his final outburst in court. His wild, unruly hair prematurely white, his face ruddy from too much drinking after work, the fingers of the fist he shook at the judge nicotine orange from chain-smoking, Bret was screaming, "You fucking Nazi!" in the public gallery as sheriff's deputies waded through his circle of die-hard disciples to snap handcuffs onto the firebrand and wrestle him off to jail. Now in his late forties, and having switched careers from law to thriller-writing, Bret Lister, despite the passage of time, had not lost his intense demeanor. Pugnaciously, his face challenged Zinc with its thrusting chin. His phrases were delivered at a staccato clip, and his long and lanky body was strung tight with ropy muscles. His torso-hugging T-shirt, tucked into blue jeans, bore a stenciling of Petra Zydecker's *The Antichrist*. The same image was on the jacket of the book in Bret's hand, and emblazoned across both Hanged Men were the words "Crown of Thorns."

"I have an alibi," Lister said.

"For what?"

"Friday night."

"Do you need one?"

"That's why you're here."

"Is it?" Zinc asked.

"I'm way ahead of you."

"Are you?"

"Always. Here, as well as in court. I can read your mind."

"Can you?"

"You're Ted Bundy's favorite cartoon."

"How so?"

"Dudley Do-Right."

"Never seen it."

"It's about a bumbling Mountie and his true love, Sweet Nell, who is forever being tied to the railroad tracks by the cartoon's mustachioed villain, Snidely Whiplash. Ted Bundy could mimic the voices of all three characters."

"Is that a fact?"

"Look it up."

"Were you on the ghost tour?"

"I was. Along with a busload of other conventioneers."

"Did you stop outside Ted Bundy's house?"

"We did."

"And heard about the severed heads on the mantel?"

"That's bullshit, by the way."

"How do you know?"

"I've read several books about the Bundy case."

"An interest of yours?"

"Come on. I write psycho-thrillers. My plot ideas come by my delving into real-life murders."

"So I hear."

"Okay, I'll read your mind. We both know I spent time in a psych ward. A year and a half ago, an exec from L.A. was found dead in North Vancouver. Hanging upside down like the Hanged Man. A ring of nails around his head like a crown of thorns. I just published a psycho-thriller—*Crown of Thorns*—about that case, and while I'm in Seattle as guest of honor at a horror con, a similar crime occurs. A severed head ringed with nails is staked outside Ted Bundy's house after I am on a bus tour that drives by. The headless body—strung up like the Hanged Man—is found miles away in a long-forgotten graveyard, and directions on how to locate the Thirteen Steps are in the con's program."

"Well?"

"Coincidence."

"That's improbable."

"Why? Because I wrote a book? So did your murdered girlfriend. *Deadman's Island*. Which I read."

"Did you meet the Ripper on Colony Farm?"

"I did."

"And referred him to Wes Grimmer?"

"That fucking asshole."

"Is that a yes?"

Lister nodded. "And look what that self-centered, grandstanding prick is out to do to me. It boils my blood to think I made that egotistical backstabber."

"You were partners?"

"Not anymore. If you're looking for a killer, take a look at him."

"Why?"

"One, he's the Ripper's lawyer. Two, he also wrote a novel about the Hanged Man case. Three, he's in Seattle at this convention too. And four, I have an alibi for Friday night."

"Doing what?"

"Fucking."

"From dusk till dawn?"

"Isn't that how you do it?"

"What's her name?"

"A gentleman doesn't tell."

"Then where's the problem, Bret?"

The lawyer-turned-novelist held up his book and tapped it against his chest.

"Petra Zydecker?"

"Wow, what a detective! You'd think that answer was staring you in the face."

"Backup proof?"

"Sorry, no voyeurs. But we did call room service twice."

"To your room?"

"Hers."

"Remember what times?"

"Two. Four. Around there. Check with the hotel. I'm a big tipper. The waiters will remember."

"Where's Petra now?"

"Out front. At the tarot table. She was just sitting down as I came in."

With a Reuben sandwich in one hand and a Pepsi in the other, the Cthulhu Mythos sculptor returned to his monsters. A thin, sleek, reptilian man with the fragile fingers necessary to create such exquisite details, he wore black slacks and a bloodred shirt with a hand-painted illustration of the tentacle face.

"How much?" Bret asked, touching Cthulhu.

"A thousand bucks."

"U.S.?"

"Is there any other currency?"

"I'm Canadian," Bret said.

"Life sucks, my friend."

"I'll take it."

"Catch you later," said Zinc.

"You wish, Dudley."

And as the Mountie walked away, Bret called after him, "Want to bet Wes doesn't have an alibi?"

———————

"Want to know the future?"

"I'm afraid of what you'll see."

"The Magick is in the cards. The Tarot doesn't lie."

"If your cards are an indication, the future's a bloody mess."

"So's the past. And the present. What's your point?"

"The refuge of an optimist is to remain willfully blind."

"Are you an optimist?"

"No."

"Then pick a card."

"Will this do?" Zinc asked, flashing his badge.

The goth queen was seated on her throne at the gateway to the Morbid Maze. Earlier, while Zinc's attention was focused on *The Antichrist*, her image for the Hanged Man card in her personal tarot deck, she had slipped away into the labyrinth of paintings behind this display, and the Mountie had followed her through the maze without catching up. Only now did he grasp why Yvette had said, "I wondered how long it would take you to notice Petra." Having gathered up the tarot cards from the stool in front of her throne, the goth queen shuffled them from hand to hand as Zinc got an eyeful of what it would be like to live life beyond the pale.

"Vamp" was the catchword for this creature. Vamp as in vampire, and seductress. Her eyes smoldered in a pale-skinned face that could use the blush of a blood transfusion. Her black hair was parted down the middle and curved around her cheekbones like pincer claws. A black bustier laced down the middle flaunted her cleavage in its scoop-necked top and the one-inch-wide bare strip that plunged to her navel. The black miniskirt clinging to her curvy hips was about as short as a skirt can get. Her ankle-high boots were those of a punk, and tattoos littered her arms. Her lips were black, her nails were black, and the only detail that seemed out of whack was the choker of dainty pearls around her neck—until the Mountie realized the "pearls" were a string of baby's teeth.

Bret Lister, he thought, you're one brave man.

"Am I under suspicion?"

"Should you be?"

Petra flicked a wayward hand toward *The Antichrist.*

"That's a powerful image."

"It's my Hanged Man. It captures all the conventions necessary for that card."

"Why so gruesome?"

"That's fitting, don't you think? The Hanged Man is card twelve in the Tarot. Death follows. As card thirteen."

"When did you paint it?"

"A year or so ago."

"Under what inspiration?"

"You ought to know, Inspector. You were the main investigator in the case."

Petra crossed her legs and sat back on her throne. She was playing with him like a cat plays with a mouse.

"You're being watched."

"I am?" said Zinc.

The vamp peered over his shoulder.

Zinc turned, and there was Yvette, sitting at her table out in the hall, elbow on its surface and chin in the palm of her hand, gazing in through the doors of the gallery.

"She seems your type."

"What's that?"

"Missionary position."

"That's catty."

"No, that's a fact. Yvette and I met at Bible camp when we were little girls. I doubt she remembers, but I do. It seems Miss Yvette has a crush on you."

"What about Bret Lister?"

"What about him?"

The vamp uncrossed her legs. Zinc concentrated on her words, not her body language.

"You know Bret?"

"Sure. He was my lawyer."

"For what?"

"An obscenity beef."

"A rare charge these days."

"It was a private prosecution. Some religious kooks didn't like my art."

"Where was that?"

"Chilliwack."

"Do you live in B.C.?"

"Up the Fraser Valley. In the Bible Belt."

"What riled them?"

"I wasn't the instigator. A local priest was."

"Why?"

"He thought I was the Devil's spawn."

"Why?"

"The priest was my dad."

A portrait of Petra's psychology came into focus in the Mountie's mind. Christian fundamentalists embrace an uncompromising doctrine of the perfect nuclear family in a caring, nonviolent society with a puritan's repugnance of sex. Created in God's image, the human body is a temple to Him that must not be defiled. The Gothic rebellion is the antithesis of that. Just as the Goths—barbarian invaders from Scandinavia and eastern Europe—sacked Christian Rome in AD 410 to usher in the Dark Ages, so current goths seek to undermine the stranglehold of enlightenment on the here and now.

In art, accessories, atmosphere, books, music, movies and clothes, theirs is a realm of darkness where anything goes. Humankind needs fear and passion to feel alive, so goths turn anguish into delight. Their love of plunder, thirst for revenge and lust for domination puts the scare of hell into the meek, who shan't inherit the earth. Paranoia, goths believe, is the sane response to a chaotic world, where there is constant risk and nothing is protected. Decay is an obsession, graffiti an art. Immorality defies and subverts authority. To be trapped inside unchanging flesh is to live life in chains. Through piercings, tattoos and scarification, goths set themselves free. Self-reinvention, that's the key to the Gothic realm, and the way to post your declaration of independence is to flip your finger at God's design for humankind. Provoke reactions. Express who you are. Stand on the giddy edge of eternal damnation and stare defiantly down into the fire and brimstone that dances and bubbles in the volcanic crater of hell.

Petra Zydecker.

The priest's rebellious daughter.

Dressed in black, with pagan tattoos and a stud of a skull through her nose. Sitting wantonly on a throne carved with biblical horrors from the Old Testament. Backed by profane art that made her dad cry foul. A deck of hellish tarot cards in her hand.

"Did Bret win your case?"

"Easily."

"When was that?"

"Just before his breakdown and stint in the asylum."

"When'd you next see him?"

"Not until last year. By then he was writing novels and had retired from the law. For *Crown of Thorns,* he desired a striking cover. He'd seen my previous card for the Hanged Man, and he told me about the murder in North Vancouver. I designed this one"—another flick of the hand—"and it became the jacket on his new book."

"Did you come to the convention with Bret?"

"No, we met on the tour."

"The ghost tour?"

"Yes."

"The one that passed Ted Bundy's house?"

"Do you suspect *me*?"

"Not yet," said Zinc.

"Ahhhhh . . ." Petra drew out the sound like a succubus stealing the breath of a sleeping man. "You want to know if I spent last night fucking Bret?"

"Did you?"

"Yes."

"All night?"

"With breaks. Bret's a driven man."

"Can anyone corroborate?"

"Sure, room service. Ask the skinny kid to describe my tattoos. He stared long enough."

"What room?"

"Mine. Main floor. 104. Off the pool."

"You see the problem?"

"No."

"The facts defy the odds. The North Vancouver death. *Crown of Thorns*. Your Hanged Man card. Ted Bundy's house. Thirteen Steps to Hell. The horror convention. You and Bret."

"So?"

"That's beyond coincidence."

"What you call coincidence, I call fate. Life is preordained. That's the Tarot." Petra set the deck face down on the stool and fanned the cards for Zinc. "When doubters question fate—coincidence, if you like—I ask them to consider this: Lincoln was elected president in 1860, Kennedy in 1960. Each was concerned about civil rights, and each had a child die while he was in the White House. Each was assassinated on a Friday, in the presence of his wife. Each was shot in the head, and from behind. Lincoln's secretary, Kennedy by name, advised that the president not go to the theater. Kennedy's secretary, Lincoln by name, advised that the president not land in Dallas. John Wilkes Booth was born in 1839, Lee Harvey Oswald in 1939. Booth gunned down Lincoln in a theater and ran to a warehouse. Oswald gunned down Kennedy from a warehouse and ran to a theater. Both men were killed before standing trial. The successors of both Lincoln and Kennedy were named Johnson. Andrew Johnson was born in 1808, Lyndon Johnson in 1908. Both were Democrats from the South who served in the Senate. The names Lincoln and Kennedy both contain seven letters. The names Andrew Johnson and Lyndon Johnson thirteen letters. The names John Wilkes Booth and Lee Harvey Oswald fifteen letters.

"Well?" asked Petra. "Fate? Coincidence?"

"Touché," Zinc acknowledged.

The goth queen smirked.

"The locks on the corners of *The Antichrist*? What's hidden under that painting?"

"Another card."

"Which one?"

"For that, you'll need a warrant. I'm giving the secret away at the end of the con."

"To whom?"

"The Tarot will decide. Pick a card, Inspector."

Zinc hesitated.

"Come on," Petra coaxed. "Take a walk on the wild side."

Selecting a card, he flipped it over. The image exposed was that of an animate skeleton wielding a scythe. The Grim Reaper stood in a pool of blood, and floating in what could be a cauldron of tomato soup was an assortment of body parts that had been hacked off by the blade.

Number 13.

The Death card.

CROWN OF THORNS

Zinc Chandler and Ralph Stein were seated at a table in the café of the Captain Vancouver Hotel. Lunch was over, so they had the restaurant almost to themselves. Ralph, uncharacteristically, had ordered a salad. From the scowl on his face, it was clear the detective wasn't enamored with his rabbit food.

"That looks healthy."

"It's your fault, Chandler. I'm slimming down to draw the eyes of the lookers away from you."

"I'm single. You're married, Ralph."

"What future is there in a relationship with a woman who's always at you to slim down?"

"Incisive logic, that."

"If only women would see me for my beautiful mind, and not you for your hollow shell."

"Yoo-hoo," Zinc called out, waving to the waitress. "I've changed my mind. I'll have a plate of fries."

"You wouldn't!"

"Watch."

When the fries arrived, the Canadian sprinkled them with vinegar. The American winced at the travesty.

"I don't understand it."

"What? Vinegar?"

"Isn't that what they fed that poor schmuck on the cross? Not the Hanged Man. The other guy."

"It's better than gravy, Ralph." Zinc patted his flat belly. "Did you get a list of those on the ghost tour?"

"The names Mort could recall."

"Bret Lister?"

"Tick."

"Petra Zydecker?"

"Tick."

"Wes Grimmer?"

"Tick."

"Yvette Theron?"

"No. She was here, doing registration, while the bus was en route to Bundy's house."

"Good."

"You thought she was lying?"

"I keep an open mind."

"If there's a woman in the case, I'd bet on Petra."

"There's a problem with that bet."

"What?"

"Alibis. On Friday night, while the severed head was being staked outside Ted Bundy's house and the body was being hanged in the pit of the Thirteen Steps to Hell, Petra and Bret were here in her room making the beast with two backs."

"Conjuring?"

"Fucking. *Othello,* Ralph. 'Your daughter and the Moor are now making the beast with two backs.'"

"Hey, speak American."

"Sorry. That was English."

"Speaking of which . . ." Ralph reached out and snaffled one of the chips. "By the way, we have an ID on our Hanged Man. His name is Bev Vincent. A businessman from Texas."

"Here for the convention?" Zinc asked.

"No, he's a scientist. Crystal technology. He flew into SeaTac late yesterday but never reached his hotel."

"This one?"

"No. The Hilton downtown."

"How'd you make him?"

"Prints on file. They matched those of the body at the foot of the Thirteen Steps to Hell."

"Someone picked him off between the airport and the Hilton?"

"Looks like."

Ralph attacked Zinc's fries with lip-smacking relish. The vinegar had no effect in keeping him at bay. Catching their server's attention, he ordered a side of gravy.

"If not for their alibis," Zinc said, "Bret and Petra would be in the glue. He was her lawyer before all this started. Bret defended her against an obscenity charge brought by her father. Petra's a Tarot obsessive into *outré* art. Sex and violence. Her dad's a priest. A Bible-thumper and his wayward daughter. Get the picture, Ralph?"

"Did Bret win the case?"

"He routed Petra's dad. The white knight syndrome. But then Bret broke down."

"How bad?"

"He went crazy. And was committed."

"Know the cause?"

"I was there."

It was several years ago, the Mountie told the detective. Having been shot in Hong Kong, Zinc was on sick leave. The Supreme Court of Canada had ordered a new trial in one of the inspector's cases, so, to give evidence, he had to return to Vancouver from the farm in Saskatchewan where he was recuperating. That's where he was when a deputy sheriff burst into the courtroom to announce that a riot was shaping up in the case going on next door, and that the presiding judge had hit the panic button.

Bret Lister was a crusader. A lawyer on a mission. A Don Quixote tilting at windmills that other lawyers avoided. A self-appointed scourge of the justice system, Bret was a feisty scrapper who reveled in fighting unpopular cases for the little guy. He accused the government of stealing Native lands, and cops of systematically undermining civil rights, and doctors of using their patients for quack experiments, and churches of actively recruiting pedophiles. A renegade who refused to play by the rules, Bret argued with judges, displayed contempt for opposing counsel, and embraced the eccentrics that others dismissed as hopeless causes. In the end, law became his entire life. Sixteen hours a day and seven days a week.

Amphetamines kept him going, and booze put him to sleep. Overworked, over-fatigued and chronically sleep-deprived, Bret plunged into a paranoid state, and ultimately conjured up a vast conspiracy that cast the entire judiciary and the Law Society as traitors out to thwart him and his beleaguered clients.

"He hit the wall and crashed?"

"But not without a fight. Bret filed a lawsuit alleging that the courts and every lawyer but him was corrupt. When the Law Society brought an application to dismiss the suit as frivolous and vexatious, he packed the gallery with a mob of supporters: the eccentrics, leeches and malcontents gathered by his practice. What brought them out was a promise from Bret that he would expose the corruption responsible for their tragedies."

"Did he?"

"He tried, Ralph. In a filibuster speech."

"What happened?"

"The Battleax took the case herself."

"The Battleax?"

"Chief Justice Morgan Hatchett."

As Zinc described that legal donnybrook to Ralph, the one-on-one between the no-nonsense judge and the paranoid lawyer had degenerated like this:

"Sit down, Mr. Lister!" the chief justice ordered.

"Stand up, Judge."

"You're a disgrace to the bar."

"And you're a carbuncle on the ass of the law. I demand that you disqualify yourself for bias."

"Shame! Shame!" shouted the chorus in the gallery.

Chief Justice Hatchett was ready to spew lava. With iron-gray hair chopped in a severe cut, eyes tough enough to drill through diamonds and a mouth permanently pursed from years of reprobation, she looked to Zinc like Maggie Thatcher's wicked stepsister. He and the deputy sheriff had just entered the court.

"You're in contempt, Mr. Lister."

"I'm way beyond that. Contempt falls short of the disrespect I have for you."

"Arrest him," Hatchett ordered.

A court security officer moved toward Bret, who stood defiantly at the counsel table, but the deputy sheriff failed to reach the lawyer. As he was sidling along the rail that separated the counsel area from the public gallery, a fist flew out of the mob.

Whap!

Down went the deputy.

Another sheriff grabbed hold of the offending arm and hauled the man who threw the punch over the barrier.

"Rescue him!" Bret incited, vaulting over the rail into the gallery. "Follow me!" he shouted, like a First World War sergeant trying to coax his troops out of the trenches. His troops were having second thoughts about the waiting machine guns.

"You have no power over me!" Bret shouted, spittle flying, at the judge. "I'm standing among comrades!"

A wedge of deputy sheriffs stormed the gallery.

"Scum! Scum!" Bret yelled.

The court security officers grabbed hold of him.

"You fucking Nazi!" Bret screamed at Hatchett.

There was pushing and shoving on both sides before the deputies could snap on the cuffs. As they trundled Bret out of his mob of die-hard disciples and away to jail, the last words the firebrand lawyer heard from the hard-assed judge were these: "You're remanded to the Forensic Psychiatric Hospital on Colony Farm for a thirty-day assessment to determine if you are fit to be charged with contempt of court."

"Lawyers!" Ralph scoffed, shaking his head as the Mountie finished recounting what he had witnessed several years ago in the Battleax's court.

"That's the last I saw of Bret until today," said Zinc. "Later, I heard that he had slashed his wrist with his fingernail in jail and used the blood to scrawl a petition for his release on the wall of his cell. So convinced was he that authorities would try to poison him that Bret refused to eat until a nurse or guard had tested the food in front of him."

"Now *that's* how to diet," said Ralph.

"It was shortly after Bret's breakdown that the Ripper and I fought it out on Deadman's Island. He was motivated by symbols hidden in the Hanged Man to attempt to control the occult realm by signifying them in blood. He made a mistake in the signing and went completely mad. I was stabbed in the back and nearly killed. DeClercq landed on the island and made the arrest. Unfit to stand trial, the Ripper was sent to the Forensic Psychiatric Hospital on Colony Farm—"

"Where he met Bret," Ralph completed.

The waitress brought his gravy. Stein dug in. A drip dribbled onto his belly and stained his tie.

"While Bret was being psyched, the Law Society had to appoint a lawyer to oversee his practice. Wes Grimmer was a brash up-and-comer who could handle Bret's mishmash of oddball clients and the tough legal issues they clung to. Out of that assignment, Wes got a high-profile case of serial and multiple murder when Bret referred the Ripper to him from inside the hospital."

"Cozy," said Ralph.

"Therapy, supposedly, patched up Bret. After he was declared fit, the contempt proceedings advanced. Bret apologized to the judge for his behavior. Grimmer, who acted for him, offered psychiatric evidence to the effect that Bret had suffered a psychotic episode. Acute paranoia brought on by mental exhaustion from stress and burnout caused by a crushing workload. The court imposed a fine and barred Bret from practicing law for a year. The Law Society agreed. With four hundred B.C. lawyers seeking help every year for alcohol, stress and marital problems, it sees mental illness as a disease."

"So Bret began writing?"

"Horror," said Zinc. "He joined the long line of lawyers who jump ship from trials to novels."

"Fiction to fiction," said Ralph.

The cops shared a laugh.

"The last I heard, he and Wes had formed Lister & Grimmer. Bret didn't return to practice. He was the silent partner. With Wes working a client base fanatically loyal to Bret, it was worth his while to have Bret's name on the letterhead. And as for Lister, he could tap the files for story ideas and promote himself as a courtroom insider who still had a finger on the pulse of crime."

"Including the Ripper."

"So it seems."

The waitress brought them cups of coffee and a bowl of creamers. Sugar and artificial sweetener were already on the table. Zinc took his java black. Ralph took the works.

"A year and a half ago, when we found Cardoza strung up like the Hanged Man, I wondered if the Ripper had escaped from Colony Farm. I called the psych hospital and was assured not only that he was still there, but also that no one except his legal representatives had been out to visit him for years."

"You left it at that?"

"The M.O. was different from that in the Ripper's crimes. The Ripper's Tarot motive was out there for everyone to read in *Deadman's Island,* Alex's book on the case. And I had the pimp and the hooker."

"Who were dead."

"Running from the law. Besides, they fit the M.O. to a tee. Cardoza was the victim of a sex crime. The nimbus of nails was pounded in while he was the sandwich meat in a two-on-one. A woman in front and a man from behind was one scenario, and that was a service that the hooker and the pimp were known to offer."

"Case closed."

"Until your call. And when I arrive in Seattle, what do I find? Not only that your Hanged Man mirrors mine, but also that Bret and Wes are here."

"Theory?"

"Sort of. Consider this: Bret knew Petra from defending her on the obscenity charge. Petra is a hard-core goth, into the Tarot. Sex and blood. Bret broke down in court and was sent to Colony Farm. There, Bret met the Ripper and was told the secret in the Hanged Man. Bret got together with Petra after his release, and fell under her sexual spell. Bret told her what the Ripper had told him, so Petra seduced Bret into killing Cardoza to sign the Hanged Man symbols properly in blood. Their joint sex crime inspired Bret to write *Crown of Thorns* and inspired Petra to illustrate it with *The Antichrist.* The death wish is part of being a goth, so perhaps they came to Seattle to flirt with your death penalty. Bret and Petra were on the bus that drove past Ted Bundy's house, and they had a copy of the WHC program that located the Thirteen Steps to Hell in Maltby Cemetery. They killed your Texas businessman in a manner that would draw attention to *Crown of Thorns* at the convention, then gave each other an alibi for the overall time of the crime."

"Sounds good," Ralph said. "It fits the evidence. The three young vics died because they, too, followed the X–Y coordinates in the program out to the cemetery, and they interrupted the killers in the act of stringing up their Hanged Man."

"In the wrong place at the wrong time," said Zinc.

"The three could identify Bret and Petra for the police. They were all at the *same* convention."

"Our problem is that there wasn't enough time for Bret and Petra to be the killers. As guest of honor, Bret was on a panel at the convention last night. Countless horror fans heard him talk. There wasn't time for him to spike the head upside down outside Ted Bundy's house. Assuming Petra did it alone, there's another problem: Bret and Petra swear they were in her hotel room having sex all through the night. Room service confirms they were in the hotel at both one-forty-five and four in the morning. I don't see how they could have driven the distance to Maltby Cemetery to string up the headless corpse and ax the three young men."

"I'll have someone time it."

"So that leaves Wes. Lister and Grimmer had a falling-out, and the partnership broke up. Did the up-and-comer get too big for his britches in Bret's eyes? Not only did Wes get the Ripper and the rest of Bret's client base, but he had the nerve to write a thriller that rivals *Crown of Thorns,* and one that attracted a mainstream publisher. Is Wes feeding off Bret's Hanged Man murder of Cardoza, or was *Halo of Flies* inspired by Wes's own crime?"

"He knows the Ripper," Ralph said. "He was on the ghost tour. He has a copy of the program. And—thanks partly to the

Hanged Man crime down here—he and his novel are a hit at the convention."

"It says here in the program"—Zinc held it out—"that Bret Lister and Wes Grimmer are about to do round two in their bare-knuckle bout. 'How to Write a Horror Best-seller: Is There a Demon You Can Sell Your Soul To?'"

"I wonder," said Ralph.

"Wonder what?"

"If there is. And if one of them did."

Long Pig

Thanks to the Ripper's having provided the key to the occult realm, the Goth had thrown the gates of time wide open. For the past seventeen months—the length of time it takes a manic novelist to write and publish fiction—the Goth had wormholed at will through the astral plane, experiencing the cannibal horrors currently on display in the painting *Morlocks,* which hung in the Morbid Maze gallery at this hotel. As the Tarot killers had discussed the last time they met at the mental hospital on Colony Farm, it had taken a year and a half for the Goth to set up the Ripper's revenge. But now the trap had been baited with the new Hanged Man victim in Seattle, and the Mountie had been lured to the horror convention.

First, the bait.

Next, the hook through Zinc Chandler's cheek.

The Goth sat at a writing desk that faced a mirror that could have been the looking-glass to Wonderland. On the surface of the desk lay a blank sketching pad. The rancid odor of insanity began to fill the hotel room as the Goth's psychosis slipped out of hiding and into a florid state. Curtained windows along the wall that looked out at the swimming pool hid the antics of children in the water from the psycho's eyes. Slowly, the spark of consciousness in those eyes dulled, until their stare was as blank as the sheet of drawing paper.

The Goth was time-traveling.

Back . . .

Back . . .

Back . . .

Cries from the horizon announce the return of war canoes. Some of the double-hulled *drua* in the Bauan war fleet are so big that they carry 250 warriors along with cargo. The cargo this morning is *bakola* from a raid on the Rewa, a rival coastal clan. The anticipation of glutting themselves on "long pig" at the victory feast brings the islanders running joyously to the beach. What brings the reverend to the door of his small Christian mission on this side of the narrow stream that separates it from the god-house of the cannibal king are the screams of captured children hanging from their heels atop the masts.

The year is 1838; the place, the Fiji Islands.

I've traveled back to get ideas for the Odyssey.

Time travel is nothing like how it was described to me. No doubt that's because the Ripper signed the symbols in the Hanged Man wrong, and consequently he has to cope with the cosmic glitches that result from an incomplete cycle of occult manifestation. But for me, it's like casting a mental yo-yo into my personal wormhole through space-time. Unlike the Ripper, I can go wherever and whenever I want. Nothing but my free will determines whether I stay there physically forever or pull my consciousness back to the here and now.

I'm a free spirit.

And I have all the time in the world.

That's how I currently find myself in the yard out front of the Fiji mission. This mission church is similar to the one where I grew up in Mission, British Columbia, and to the one my ancestors built in the Cook Islands, back in times parallel to these. It's a white clapboard chapel with a steeple over the door. The god-house beyond the stream is a thatched temple with a heap of sun-bleached bones piled out back. The skull of each *bakola* eaten by the cannibal king—smashed open to add its brain to past feasts—sits atop a separate stone set in a line along the beach. History will later record the number of stones as 872.

Now the frantic rhythm of beating drums drowns out the mast-head screams. This is a special sound, never to be forgotten, for the *derua* pounding out of the slit drums on board and answered by drums on the beach is played solely before a village feast. *Thudda-thudda . . . thudda-thudda . . .* My heart thuds in time with the driving beat as the "long pigs" come into view.

The enemy dead are sitting up in the prow of each canoe. Arrayed in two rows along the bow deck, the corpses squat on their hindquarters with their knees cocked up and their hands lashed together around their jackknifed legs so there is space enough in the hind part of the bend for a long pole. Side by side, each body supports the others as the *bakolas* sit strung along the poles like shish kebabs. Vermilion and soot were used to paint the naked dead bound for the god-house ovens, so they still look like they did alive in battle.

The god of war has triumphed.

Times are good.

The beaching of the canoes sparks activity on deck. Unstrung, the *bakolas* are thrown into the surf for cleansing and purification. To keep the corpses from floating away, the Bauan warriors link each one to its boat by a vine stem tied around one wrist. As for the fifty living children hoisted up to the mastheads as victory flags, the rocking motion of the canoes has knocked some out, silencing their piercing cries. Conscious or unconscious, down they drop as the hoists are cut, then each is thrown into the water to sink or swim. Those who stumble ashore face a deadlier threat, as Bauan boys learn the art of Fijian warfare by firing arrows at them or bashing their brains out with clubs.

"'Suffer the little children to come unto me,'" the reverend prays as he holds a Christian cross high at the mission door.

"Fat chance," I say.

He turns to frown blankly at me. No doubt he's wondering how in hell I materialized in his yard.

"Magick," I offer.

What little clothing the warriors wear is shed as they jump off the boats and onto the sand. There, they begin to dance the *cibi* in unison in front of the god-house. Hundreds of naked cannibals strut their stuff for a horde of stripping women, the ceremony accompanied by the erotic rhythm from several villagers hammering on the end of a hollow log. Each trying to outdo the others in ferocious overkill, the men have painted their faces and bodies with hideous patterns. Amid terrific yells that punctuate their war chants, the victory dance is made up of a series of threatening and boastful poses with bloody clubs and spears. Their arms extended, some fall backwards onto the beach, only to spring forward to regain their feet. Others flaunt erections raised by all the excitement.

Now it's the women's turn to dance the lewd *dele*. The only Fijian dance for which they strip bare, it praises the prowess of their heroes and insults the *bakolas*. The men haul the bodies out of the surf and lay them faceup on the sand. While their breasts bob to the beat of the drums and their hips undulate, the women dance suggestively to mock the corpses. Killing and eating the Rewa isn't enough, so they prod the genitals of the dead with sticks as they sing.

I take note.

For the Odyssey.

Despite the overpowering heat, the reverend sweats it out in his suit of Bible black, as if the stifling garment is the armor of God. Watching him stare in horror at the ritual on the beach, I suspect he's more affronted by the sex than the violence.

"Father forgive them . . ." he mumbles.

His words trail off.

"Are we having fun yet?" I jest.

Brandishing their clubs and tossing them into the air like jugglers, some of the warriors lead a parade up the beach to the god-house while others drag the *bakolas* facedown through the sand like logs to be fed to a fire. The cannibal king and his high priest stand waiting at the temple. Both men are larded with layers of flab from lifetimes of consuming the fatty flesh of other humans. The *bakolas* are flung at the feet of the cannibal king as the high priest dedicates each in turn to the Bauan god of war.

The braining stone—the *vatu ni mena*—is a heavy column that has been erected on the grounds of the temple. As each *bakola* falls prey to the appetite of the god, his brain is sacrificed to the stone. A pair of burly islanders each grab hold of an arm and a leg to lift the corpse from the ground, then, using the body as a human battering ram, run with it at top speed to smash the skull open against the phallic column, the way they crack coconuts for their meat.

Crackkk!

Crackkk!

Crackkk!

The burly batterers carry the corpse back to the high priest. So fat he finds it difficult to bend over the remains, the priest combs hair away from the crown of the shattered skull so that his fingers, plump as sausages, can pluck shards of bone out of the tissue that has been bared by the braining against the stone. With a blade, he cuts the organ free from its calcium confines and drops it into the yawning mouth of the brain pot close at hand. There, the brains will boil in blood for the next few hours, until the flesh is reduced to a simmering savory stew swimming in a rich red gravy that's fit for a god of war.

A god who is fed through the mouths of the priest and the king.

To squeals of joy from the naked women crowding in front of the god-house, the priest slices the genitals off each enemy warrior. Females are barred from partaking in the cannibal feast, so they get their kicks in vicarious ways.

On the bank of the narrow stream flowing between the god-house and the mission, at the back corner of the temple grounds, grows a sacred grove. The *akau tabu*—the "forbidden tree"—stands in the center of the grove, surrounded by a ring of shaddock trees. The forks of the shaddock trees are wedged with trophy bones from previous cannibal feasts. I can make out the bones that garnish the nearest trophy tree: two thighbones, a jawbone, a shoulder blade and several ribs. Evidently, they date from a while back, for the bark of the tree has grown to incorporate them into its trunk.

The *akau tabu* is a large ironwood tree selected for its conspicuous location. From its limbs dangle countless scraps of skin that, if this were the Wild West, could be scalps. Belying that, however, is the kinky, curly nature of the hair, which matches that in the pile of sex organs sliced off the *bakolas* by the high priest.

When the pile is big enough to warrant a walk to the grove, one of the lesser priests conveys the genitals to the genital tree and proceeds to hang them along the hairy branches like Monday-morning washing along a clothesline. As a new supply of forbidden fruit is added to the already abundant tree, I watch the reactions of some of the women who cry out with ecstasy, and wonder what fantasies pass through the minds of these Eves in Eden.

Cannibalism and castration.

What a heady mix.

Those rituals concluded, it's time to cook the feast. The butchers of the temple have dug *lovo*—sanctified pit ovens—in the ground around the god-house. One by one, the brainless bodies stripped of their genitals are lugged by the burly pair to the *i sava,* a large flat dissecting stone. On it, the bamboo knives of the butchers go to work, segmenting the bodies into prime cuts. First, the heads are severed, low down on the neck so the shoulders of the torso are flat. The heads are sent back to the high priest, who keeps track of which *bakolas* the king eats to make sure that their skulls are added to the line of stones. Next, the limbs are cut off joint by joint: the hands at the wrists, the arms at the elbows and the armpits, the feet at the ankles, the legs at the knees and the groin. Assistants grab each piece as it falls away from the skill of the chief carver's knife and pass it off to an assembly line that ends at the ovens. Along the way, the raw flesh is wrapped in plantain leaves, and the most succulent segments—the thighs and the arms—land in special pits. Particularly with "long pig," those at the top eat high on the hog.

The culinary art of the chief carver holds me in awe. The knife he wields is a blade of split bamboo. Naturally effective for gross surgery, it is kept razor-sharp by tearing strips off the edge. This the carver does on the upswing with his teeth, and soon the rhythm of slice and tear has him drenched from head to toe in blood. He licks his lips as he works.

Butchering the torso is a sloppier task. Except for the heart— since the *mana* is there—the vital organs and the entrails are thrown aside. The discards are quickly gobbled up by pigs, which forage around the temple to scavenge scraps.

It occurs to me that there is irony here. "Long pig"—*puaka balava*—is strictly for men, while "real pig"—*puaka dina*—is fit for women to eat. But if the pigs around the temple can eat human meat, why isn't it taboo for women to eat the pigs?

That thought is broken by a shout from the king.

"*I sigana!*"

The big guy is hungry. He doesn't want to wait while bonfires heat the stones that go into the ovens.

To tide the king over, hors d'oeuvres are served. What elevates his majesty above his common subjects is the luxury of never having to feed himself. That's what the subservient women who make up his harem are for. In calling for *i sigana*—the choicest of pieces—the king sends his female retinue scurrying to the high priest, who harvests dainty morsels from his pile of severed heads.

"*Vinaka! Vinaka!*" extols the cannibal king after he is fed eyeballs freshly plucked from their sockets by a nude girl who drops them down his throat like peeled grapes.

As canapés, he is served the tips of several noses nipped off by the high priest and roasted like marshmallows on a stick over a fire lit to heat the oven stones. To feed the meat into the king's mouth in such a way that it won't touch his lips and be defiled, the server uses a peculiar wooden fork, a *culanibakola*. That's because the flesh isn't just for him but is also being fed directly to the *kalougata*, the spirit of the god of war responsible for the victory, who is physically present within the king at a cannibal feast.

The eating is in his honor, and the god wants his share.

The reverend, it would seem, can take no more of this blasphemy. He and the cannibal king are locked in a tug-of-war for the souls of these Fijians. The man of God still stands at the chapel door with his Christian cross held high in the air, as if that should be enough to bring the pagans to their knees. Inside the threshold of the church, I can just make out the sickly form of the old missionary on his deathbed. When he first set foot on this island years ago, he introduced a plague of biblical proportions in the guise of

European diseases. But now the old man is stricken with one of the local infections, and the reverend sent to replace him lacks the clout of a new germ-infested God.

"In the name of the Father . . ." the reverend shouts.

Some of the cannibals turn.

"In the name of the Son . . ."

Attracting more attention.

"In the name of the Holy Ghost . . ."

Including the cannibal king.

"Uh-oh," I say. "You've really done it now."

The advantage of being a time traveler to the past is that you enjoy the benefit of twenty-twenty hindsight. What the reverend has yet to understand is what he's up against. Historians will later unravel the inherent logic of Fijian cannibalism. I know, because I digested their books before I time-warped here.

Veikanikani—cannibalism—is founded on the worship of ancestor spirits. Spirits reside in the spirit world of Bulu and manifest themselves on this island through the cannibal king. As such, this cannibal king is a living god who, in exchange for raw women supplied to his harem in the form of island virgins, imports a plentiful supply of *bakolas* to bake into cooked men, which the islanders can offer as sacrifices to the spirits of Bulu.

Any man, if his spirit survives, can enter the spirit world. In battle, ancestor spirits guide their descendants. The spirit of a body clings to the corpse for four days after death. Sacrificing and eating an enemy's body destroys his spirit before it can enter the spirit world to become a power source for those trying to eat you. Killing means nothing. Eating brings glory. The more damage done to the *bakolas,* the better. Powerful is the cannibal king whose *mana*—effectiveness—is fed to his subjects. And nothing brings home the bacon in that regard better than long pig from victory in war.

That might not make sense to the reverend, but it makes sense to me.

Different countries. Different customs. Different gods.

"Vakatotoga!" the cannibal king yells, pointing one of his chubby fingers this way.

The big guy is really pissed off. The reverend has riled him to a pique of fiendish ferocity with that holy-roller rhetoric beneath the Christian cross. True, the missionary may be a disciple of the Lord, but the cannibal king is a *living* god among these man-eaters, and also the *waqa*—the vehicle—for the god of war.

"*Vakatotoga!*"

My blood runs cold.

I know the meaning of that word, and it scares the living bejesus out of me.

Somehow I doubt the reverend's cross will offer much of a shield against this horde of naked, war-painted cannibals thundering toward the mission, their feet splashing through the stream that separates there from here, each brandishing a weapon of some kind: spear; sling; bow; or club in one of two sizes, the heavy, wooden, two-handed type that pounds you into a pulp or the smaller missile club for throwing. It doesn't bode well that some warriors are still erect from having mixed sex with death, and now here's an opportunity to show off for the womenfolk.

Sorry, Rev.

I'm outta here.

Vakatotoga, I leave for you.

With a jerk, I feel myself yanked back into the astral plane as that cosmic yo-yo retreats through the humming wormhole in space-time and returns me to the here and now of Seattle today. . . .

Suddenly, the spark of consciousness returned to the Goth's eyes. The psycho was back at the writing desk that faced the mirror that could have been a window into the occult realm. The stench of insanity faded as the killer's psychosis slipped back into a latent state. The clock on the desk said 2:43. In fifteen minutes, the panel was set to convene in Tomb A. "How to Write a Horror Best-seller: Is There a Demon You Can Sell Your Soul To?"

The sketching pad still lay on the desk, but the top sheet was no longer blank. Judging from what was drawn on the paper, it had gone time-traveling too. The Christian mission in Fiji was rendered in minute detail, as were all the atrocities of the cannibal feast. In going back to do research for next week's Odyssey, the Goth had chosen Fiji from among the many cannibal islands of the South Pacific because Fiji was the source of eyewitness accounts dating back to the mid-1800s, a time when and the place where Western explorers recorded the utter horror of *vakatotoga*. Since *vakatotoga* was the fate planned for the Mountie, the Goth's research into how to perpetrate it would require another trip.

But now it was time to jab the hook through the cop's cheek and begin to reel him in.

The Goth cleaned up and left the room.

hALo of flIES

"Hello, everybody. My name's Wes Grimmer, and I'm the author of this book, *Halo of Flies*."

The lawyer-turned-writer held up his just-published novel so that the conventioneers packed into Tomb A could see it. The buzz from the earlier confrontation had lured them here in droves, probably hoping to witness one attorney-cum-scribe throwing a punch at the other. If nothing else, it was sure to be a hot debate.

"We're missing a moderator," Wes said, "so I'll get things going. The topic we're here to discuss is 'How to Write a Horror Bestseller: Is There a Demon You Can Sell Your Soul To?' My answer is yes. That demon is *you*."

Scattered laughs.

"How many of you here are really serious about being writers?"

A sea of waving hands shot up from the audience.

"Sinclair Lewis asked the same question of a room full of aspiring writers when Columbia University invited him to deliver a lecture on the writer's craft. On seeing the hands go up, Lewis said, 'Well, why the hell aren't you all home writing?' The lecture over, he walked back to his seat and sat down."

Laughter.

"Imagine that I have hurled the same scolding at you, so you've gone home to sit at your desk and write that best-seller. What are you going to write about so it rings true?"

Again, Wes held up *Halo of Flies*.

"I don't know *what* you'll write about," he said, "but I do know *where* you'll find it."

"Hold the book higher," Bret Lister piped in, "and repeat the title. Your blatant self-promotion is too humble, Wes."

"Here we go," Ralph muttered to Zinc. The cops were standing at the back of the room.

"Have some couth, Bret. You'll get your chance."

"When hell freezes over, if you keep hogging the mike."

The two men could not have sat farther apart and still been at the same table. The table was up on a dais at the front of the convention hall, with four chairs arranged behind it. Wes sat at the left-hand flank, Bret sat at the right-hand flank, and the chairs between them sat vacant. Heavyset and brawny, Wes—in his early thirties—was at least ten years junior to Bret. Though this was a horror convention, Wes wore a blue blazer with a tie, as if to let everyone know that he was a high-powered courtroom titan in his other life. But so as not to seem completely out of place, he chose a silk tie hand-painted with the jacket of *Halo of Flies*. His toughness was topped off with a skinhead's coif to give him the Yul Brynner/Telly Savalas/Vin Diesel look.

"So you're sitting at your desk about to write," said Wes, "trying to think of something to write about. That's when you recall what I said about selling your soul to the demon that is you, and you wonder what the hell I meant by that. Well, look at me."

"Surprise, surprise," said Bret.

Wes ignored him. "Who here knows what Creative Anachronism is?"

A few hands.

"Creative Anachronism is a worldwide organization of followers attracted to medieval times. As a hobby, they dress up in the costumes of pre-seventeenth-century Europe to reenact everyday life as they believe it was in that nonindustrial era. Born out of the late sixties, it appealed to the mind-set of back-to-the-land hippies, like my father and mother, who were flower children in the Haight."

"Peace, love and have a nice day," mumbled Bret.

"Thanks to LSD, my dad soon tired of playing that game. What he desired wasn't fairs and get-togethers but a time machine to take him back. Unable to obtain that, he moved my mom, my sister and me to the backwoods of British Columbia to cut us off from modern times. We dressed like they did in the 1600s, and lived in a house without electric power and running water. We had no machines of any kind. The Amish were futurists compared with us.

"Then one day, a black goat was born in our barn. My dad saw the meddling of witchcraft in that, and because my mom and sister were the only females around, he became convinced that they were possessed. In the end, he went berserk and hanged the two of them from the sturdiest limb of the oak behind our house. Overwrought by what he had done, my dad then hanged himself from the same tree. I was four.

"Three days later, a pair of lost hikers found me sitting on the ground, staring up at the three of them suspended in the air. My memory has shut out their faces. All I can recall is the ring of flies around my father's head."

Wes held up his book a third time.

"*Halo of Flies,*" he said, and this time elicited no snarky comment from Bret.

"The point I'm making," Wes said, "is that if you want to tap into horrors that will cause readers to shiver and shake, you must delve down into the landscape of your own damned soul. To be a bestseller, a book has to resonate. A year and a half ago, up in Vancouver, there was a murder in which the body was strung up like the Hanged Man card in the tarot deck. The tarot image has a nimbus around its head, and that got me thinking about the halo of flies around my dad's head. I transposed that personal horror to the characters in my book, and that's why I'm sitting up here in front of you."

"Wrong," said Bret. "It's because you cribbed my idea."

"Don't be an ass. The Tarot murder was all over the media in Vancouver for weeks."

"But I turned it into a novel."

"So did I."

"*Crown of Thorns* came first."

"Bullshit, Bret. The story of my dad hanging my family was in all the papers thirty years ago. What motivated me to write *Halo of*

Flies is there in black-and-white for you to look up. What motivated you to write *Crown of Thorns?* The belief you're Jesus Christ?"

Laughter.

"Now if Bret can find the courtesy to let me finish what I'm trying to pass on to you, the moral of my personal experience is this: You each have the genesis of a horror novel in your background. Perhaps you were sexually abused as a child, or you wandered off from a campground and got lost in the woods for a night, or like Clarice Starling in the novel *The Silence of the Lambs,* you had to listen to lambs having their throats cut out in the barn. It could be anything, so that's why I say I don't know the *what* of your personal inspiration, but I do know *where* you'll find it, and that's in your deepest fears. Do you want to know mine? Read *Halo of Flies.*"

Wes reached down beside him and did something out of the sight of the audience. The explosion of music that filled the room from a ghetto-blaster was so loud and unexpected that everyone jumped. What Wes was playing was Alice Cooper's "Halo of Flies."

Just as suddenly, the barrage stopped.

"Think about that," he said.

Ralph was breathing heavily next to Zinc.

"Y' okay, Ralph?"

"A shock like that, I could be dead of a heart attack."

"Cannibals!" Wes abruptly shouted. "Do I have your attention? If you want something to write about, write about that. 'Okay,' you're asking, 'what do cannibals have to do with me?' Well, you'll find a connection if you dig deep enough. I can tell you how to find it, but I'm sure Bret wants me to give up the mike."

"No!" yelled a voice in the crowd. "Feed us, Wes."

"Lunchtime," someone bellowed.

The room took up the chant.

"Lunchtime . . . lunchtime . . . lunchtime . . ."

"This guy's a natural showman," Zinc commented, trying to make himself heard through the din.

"Lawyers!" scoffed Ralph for the second time. "Selling snake oil is their trade."

Wes held up his hands. "Back by popular demand," he announced. "What I want each of you to do is to dig *waaaaay* back. Back to the days when hominids evolved from apes. Come on, people. Feel your DNA. In your skulls are three integrated brains, and the inner two are the ones we got from lesser beasts.

"Cannibalism is rare among nonhuman primates in the wild. But there is an exception: chimpanzees. Among chimps, cannibalism is a common act. Chimps are the most carnivorous of apes, and we share 99 percent of their genes.

"Are there any carnivores in the room?"

More palms shot skyward than at a Nazi rally.

"'Taphonomy.' There's a useful word. That's the analysis of human bones after death. The science that records the death history, as opposed to life history, of deceased individuals. By examining the tooth marks on ancient skeletons, taphonomists can identify the species that gnawed off their flesh. From *Homo erectus* in northern Spain eight hundred thousand years ago, to Gough's Cave at Cheddar Gorge in Somerset, England, twelve thousand years ago, to Fontbregoua Cave in southeastern France seven thousand years ago, to the Celts of Eton in Iron Age Britain three thousand years ago, to the Fremont Culture and the Anasazi Indians in the Four Corners region of the American Southwest one thousand years ago—time after time, scientific evidence establishes that man was eating man.

"Cannibalism, folks. Man-eaters evolved into us."

"I'm a vegetarian," a woman called out.

"Eat her!" a man retorted, to laughter all around.

Wes glanced down at the table. He was consulting notes. His facts and figures had been researched. Bret, on the other hand, faced an empty surface. Ill-prepared, he would wing it.

Oops, thought Zinc.

"Are there any Scots in the audience?"

"Aye, laddie." A new voice.

"Consider the case of your countryman Sawney Bean. Sometime in the 1600s, he and his incestuous brood hid in a cave on the Galloway coast, less than ten miles east of Edinburgh.

When the king's men hunted that clan down, their hideout was exposed as a charnel house with dried, salted and pickled people hanging on hooks.

"That's your background, Scotty. Build on it. Consider what goes into that haggis served at a Robbie Burns dinner and you've got a horror story.

"Who has Chinese ancestors?"

Several waving hands.

"Those hands I see. Ko Ku, anyone? Cannibalism was thought—and is *still* thought—to have a medical and nutritional purpose. Dating back to the Tang Dynasty of the seventh to tenth centuries AD, the remedy of Ko Ku dictated that a faithful child cut off a portion of his thigh or arm and serve it to an ailing relative as the last medicinal resort. Princess Miao Chuang offered her severed hands to her father, so she was deified.

"Now what about you, ungrateful child that you are? A traditional parent has slaved his entire life, day and night, in the family restaurant so that you can hang out at the mall. Now he's got brain cancer and thinks he needs a dose of that remedy to survive, so at night he tiptoes into your room with a meat cleaver from the kitchen to harvest the filial medicine you haven't offered to Dad.

"Chop. Chop. Munch. Munch.

"Don't like Ko Ku? Try Ko Kan. That's when you offer your liver instead, preferably by cutting it out yourself. Traditional Chinese medicine recommends thirty-five human body parts that will cure various ailments if consumed. China currently has a 'one-child policy' to curb population. The result is that on the mainland and in Hong Kong, there's a thriving black market in human fetuses to eat for rejuvenation. Today, an aborted baby costs three hundred dollars."

"Anyone for takeout?" someone shouted.

"Now, now," Wes said. "Westerners can't be smug. Surely you've heard of placenta-eating? Look it up. You'll find all kinds of recipes on the Internet. Supposedly, it reduces the effect of postnatal depression in new moms. Any women here ever suffered from that? Well, there's your story. The mother of a newborn has postpartum depression. So first she eats the placenta, and when that appetizer works—or doesn't work—she goes for her baby.

"In the 1800s, eating ground-up Egyptian mummy was a common cure-all in Europe. Ever had food poisoning? Use that experience. Curse of the mummy is a time-honored theme. A bad dose of mummy and the cure could be worse than what ails you.

"Do we have any teachers? Good," said Wes on seeing several hands. "Imagine you're teaching in Guangxi during the Chinese Cultural Revolution of 1966 to 1968. Mao set his fervent young Red Guards loose to express their class hatred, and in one school they turned on their teachers and ate them as food. Is the duty of a teacher not to feed young minds?

"Have we any sailors? All hands on deck."

More waving.

"Avast, ye hearties. 'The custom of the sea'—that's the euphemism for eating the crew to survive *in extremis*. In 1710: the *Nottingham Galley*, a clipper ship out of Boston. They ate the carpenter. In 1765: the *Peggy*, bound for New York. They ate the black slave. In 1816: the *Medusa*. It hit a reef off Africa, forcing a hundred and fifty people onto a raft. Only six men weren't eaten. In 1821: the Nantucket whaler *Essex* was rammed by a sperm whale halfway between Hawaii and the Galapagos Islands. The incident is immortalized in *Moby Dick*. The human body yields, on average, sixty-six pounds of edible meat. That was the food in the lifeboats. In 1845: the Franklin Expedition. While trying to find the Northwest Passage across Canada's Arctic, Franklin and his crew got stuck in the ice. A nine-hundred-mile death march to civilization degenerated into man eating man.

"So, sailors, ask yourselves what you might do if your only chance of survival was the meat on your buddy's bones. And hey, if you can't get your imaginations around that, ask yourselves what he might do to you.

"Are there any hikers or skiers in the room? The Donner Party. That's one you probably know. While heading west to California in 1846, they ran afoul of winter in the Sierra Nevada mountains. Of those eighty-seven pioneers, half were eaten in an orgy of cannibalism. Same with Alfred Packer in 1873. He ate four gold prospectors. Snow's a good setup for lots of horror stories. The famine in the Volga after the Russian Revolution, the siege of Leningrad by the Nazis in the Second World War—both forced Russians to eat Russians. The winter of 1999 saw meat shortages in the Ural Mountains, so Alexander Zapiantsev invited the residents of his apartment block in for a New Year's Eve dinner. Unknown to his guests, the roast he served was Valdemar Suzik."

Wes cupped an ear.

"Do you hear that? Sounds like a faulty aircraft engine to me. Is a plane coming down? Yep, it crashed in the Andes. Back in 1972, the Old Christians rugby team was marooned for seventy-two days in alpine snow. The sixteen who were finally rescued had fed off the flesh of their dead comrades. Though not a balanced diet, human meat had provided all they required to face one of the worst climates on earth. They consumed the heart, liver, kidneys, intestines, bone marrow and brain. The more squeamish ate just the muscles. Only the heads, skin, lungs and genitals were discarded. One of those cannibals went on to run for president of Uruguay."

While Wes was holding the floor, Zinc had his eye on Bret Lister. The elder author had painted himself into a corner by his lack of preparation for his challenger's onslaught. The room had called for Wes, and he was delivering the goods. So the only way Bret could jump back in the game was to intercept the ball, and he didn't seem to have the vignettes to rival Wes's command of the subject. All he could do was sit on the sidelines and watch Wes perform while the veins in his temples stood out and his jaw muscles jumped.

"Do we have any travelers? Any Conquistadors? There's no need to go far—just to Mexico. Imagine you're with Cortez, back in the 1500s, and you chance upon a pyramid when the Aztecs are sacrificing. Here is a culture where cannibalism sits at the heart of highly elaborate religious rituals. A priest is sacrificing a victim on top of the temple. He hacks out the still-beating heart and offers it up to the gods. The heartless remains tumble down the steep steps of the pyramid, then roll toward the priest's assistants, who are waiting at the bottom. Looming near them is a towering trophy rack with thousands of human skulls strung side by side on horizontal rods, rods tiered layer upon layer toward the sky. The body is spirited away to vaults underneath the temple, where others have the task of draining the blood and portioning off the flesh for high nobles to eat. Except for the skull, which will adorn the trophy rack, the bones will be used as kitchen utensils or musical instruments, for the Aztecs let nothing from a sacrifice go to waste.

"Do you know what Jeffrey Dahmer said when he was arrested? 'Maybe I was born too late. Maybe I should have been an Aztec.'"

A pause.

Wes let that sink in.

"Cannibals!" he said. "We began with that single word. I've tried to conjure up the multiple stories that might spawn from the personal demons within each of you. Will you write a best-seller? I can't say. But I do know you *won't* write a best-seller if you're afraid to sell your soul to whatever demon eats at your mind.

"Consider the reader. What do you share in common? Three fairy tales from childhood? Hansel and Gretel to be cooked in the oven of the old witch. Fe-fi-fo-fum. That giant smells the blood of an Englishman. Will Jack's bones be ground to make his bread? Little Red Riding Hood. That wolf in Granny's bed. 'My, what big teeth you have, Granny.' 'All the better to eat you with, my dear.'

"Why do those horrors captivate kids? Why do we recall them now? I'll tell you why. Because man is and always has been a cannibal. But we manage to suppress the urge—though not the fear—by means of the artificial construct of civilization.

"How many people here have ever seen a corpse?"

Not many hands.

"How many people here kill and butcher the meat they eat?"

No hands.

"Do you not find that strange? Eating and dying are our two most basic functions. So why have we obfuscated both into taboos? Hospitals and undertakers insulate us from death. We no longer buy meat chopped off by the butcher, but instead prefer chicken breasts wrapped in plastic and burgers frozen in boxes. What is it about visceral content that makes it taboo? Our inclination?"

Wes tapped his index fingers against both sides of his head, above his ears. "The temporal lobe. Home of the id. Psychiatrists consider it to be the primitive instinctual part of our brains. Anger, fighting, fleeing, sex and violence. Irrational behavior lurks here. And so do those prehistoric cannibals who became us."

Wes tapped his forehead. "The frontal lobe. The censuring device that keeps the id under control. If there's damage to the frontal lobe, our capacity to inhibit primitive urges fails, and that can release the horrific monsters we encounter in the news.

"Nature or nurture? That debate is bullshit. A troubled childhood can make matters worse, but modern science gives us a glimpse into our brains. And what we see in PET scans—positron emission tomography—of serial killers' brains is a lack of activity in the prefrontal cortex. That's like having a broken emergency brake on your car. If primitive behavior manifests itself, there's no way to stop aggressive, outrageous acts. What cannibal killers are doing is traveling back in time to the era before there was a man-eating taboo.

"'Taboo,'" continued Wes, "was a term used by Freud. To him, it meant forbidden acts for which there nonetheless exists a strong unconscious inclination. Incest was Freud's focus. We all have that impulse buried in our minds. Cannibalism too. That's *why* it's taboo. Because we all know unconsciously that it's a human tradition, an urge from deep within our primitive past. Where there's taboo, there will be taboo-breakers.

"I know that.

"You know that.

"And so does the reader.

"Consequently"—Wes held *Halo of Flies* aloft—"what you aim to do is what I hope I've done in this novel. Tap into your own fear of what is taboo so that what you write will activate your reader's dread, since we all share a collective unconscious. The baggage of evolution.

"Now back to the beginning, to my initial question. How many of you are really serious about being horror writers? Because if you are and you want to venture to the heart of cannibalism, you can still sign on for the Odyssey. The word 'taboo' wasn't coined by Freud. It was picked up by Captain Cook in the South Pacific. The Polynesian word *tapu* refers to things you cannot do, so if you want to accompany me to the realm of the most ravenous cannibals in history—"

Wham!

Bret slammed his palm down on the table with such force that the notes in front of Wes jumped off its surface.

"Now just a goddamn minute!" Bret exploded. "That was *my* idea! The Odyssey is *my* group! *I* booked the flight! *I* made the arrangements! And I don't need some johnny-come-lately hijacking the trip that *I* put together!"

Wes stared at his watch. "My time's up, folks," he said. "I see that many of you have *Halo of Flies* in your hands, so what I'm going to do is leave this hothead to rant, and if you want your books signed or have a question arising out of my advice, come on out and join me in the hall. If you don't have the novel and you want to invest in my stock, *Halo of Flies* is on sale in the dealers' room."

A mass exodus followed Wes out of the room.

Bret looked apoplectic.

"A blood feud," Ralph said.

"A blood feud," Zinc agreed.

ELDER GODS

After round two of the punch-up between Lister and Grimmer, Zinc and Ralph separated. The Seattle detective left the hotel to attend the autopsy on both parts of the Texas businessman, which he hoped would provide Homicide with helpful forensic clues. In addition to the Canadian suspects Zinc had identified, there were—to guard against tunnel vision, the curse of several well-known botched cases—other avenues to pursue. Numerous ghost tours had driven past Ted Bundy's house, and the WHC pamphlet with the X–Y coordinates for Maltby Cemetery had been openly distributed in print and on the Internet to draw attendees to the horror convention. As for the Tarot motive, not only was *Deadman's Island,* Alex's book on the Ripper case, still in print, but detailed coverage of the North Vancouver Hanged Man killing a year and a half ago was also out there in cyberspace. Consequently, there was no need for the Seattle Tarot killer or killers to be conventioneers at this hotel. In fact, if the matching nails recovered from both victims' skulls was one of those quirky Lincoln/Kennedy coincidences that defy all odds, it could be that the two Hanged Man killings weren't connected at all.

And then there were the murders of the three young men who were hacked apart on the Thirteen Steps to Hell. True, they probably interrupted the Hanged Man killers at work and had to be snuffed because they could identify them from the horror convention. But what if *four* young men had set out to commit the Hanged Man crime—spiking the head outside Ted Bundy's house because of the ghost tour and hanging the body in the cemetery because of the WHC pamphlet found in their car—and then one of the four had freaked out on drugs and butchered the other three? A bag of powerful pot was found on the remains of Charles Yu, up from Texas (the same home state as that of the Hanged Man victim), and Yu had a past conviction for possession of LSD.

So while Ralph departed for the autopsy and to put a task force together, soon to return with a squad to interview those at the hotel, the Mountie remained at the horror convention to investigate the Canadian connection. To that end, but also for personal reasons, Zinc returned to the registration table to speak to Yvette. The new man on duty informed the inspector that her shift was over and she had gone for a swim in the pool, so Zinc booked a room for the night, went up to change into trunks he purchased in a hotel shop and rode the elevator down to the central aquatic court.

The pool and its satellite hot tubs were encircled by a green belt of potted vegetation. A path of Astroturf wound through the artificial jungle from the elevator to the steamy oasis in the middle of the quadrangle. Zinc was close to emerging from the faux foliage when an Amazon stepped onto the path. Decked out in a wet bikini that barely kept her in, her body glistening with moisture from a dip in the pool, her upper arms tattooed with enigmatic designs, it was the Tarot's goth queen who blocked his way.

"Stripped for action, Inspector?"

"Hello, Ms. Zydecker."

"Petra, please. May I call you Zinc?"

"Inspector is better."

"As you wish. What brings you to the garden of Eden?"

"Surely your cards know the answer?"

When Zinc's eyes flicked past her shoulder, Petra craned to follow his momentary glance.

"Adam and Yvette in Eden? The missionary position? Take my advice: don't eat the apples," she teased.

The goth queen's breast brushed Zinc's arm as they crossed paths.

"*Hisssss!*" Petra sibilated, flicking her tongue like a sexy serpent before she walked away.

With so much going on at the convention, few swimmers splashed in the pool. Sunlight slanting in through the skylight gave the man-made lagoon a tacky tropical glaze. Only one of the hot tubs was in use. Yvette sat soaking in a roiling boil of bubbles.

"What's cooking?" Zinc asked.

"Me," Yvette replied.

"May I join you?"

"Petra went thataway."

"I know. She brushed by me."

"How exciting."

"Not really."

Yvette beckoned. "Join the stew."

Zinc stepped into the hot tub and slowly submerged up to his chin. The fizzing water spat in his eyes. Yvette was sweating and her hair was plastered to her brow. He imagined that's what she would look like after making love.

"Welcome to the cannibal pot."

"Please," said Zinc. "I've heard enough about cannibals to last me the rest of my life."

"Bret and Wes?"

"Uh-huh. I sat in on the rematch."

"I missed it. Had to work. Who won?" asked Yvette.

"Wes, hands down. What gives with those two?"

"Have you spent much time around writers?"

"A past girlfriend wrote true crime."

"That's not the same as fiction. With fiction, it's *you* being judged for what goes on in your mind. You don't have the defense of saying the subject let you down. Fiction writers are a factious mix. There have been some great spats. Best-seller lists establish a hierarchy. The ones lower down resent those higher up. The ones higher up believe they're smarter than those beneath them. Things get written. Things get said. That's why the questionnaire we sent around to organize the panels at this con asks if there's anyone you don't want paired with you."

"Fragile egos."

"They're *writers,* Inspector."

"Do you speak from experience?"

"I'm a wannabe."

"A writer in training?"

"On a long apprenticeship."

"How long?"

"Do you really want to know?"

"Yes."

"Ever since I can remember. I wrote a lot of juvenilia in my teens. Derivative stuff, copying favorite writers. Then I got serious and went to UBC. I have an undergrad degree in creative writing and fine arts. Like Clive Barker, I want to both write and illustrate my books. College taught me the basics of how to do it, then I set out to experience things for me to write about."

"Such as?"

"I worked as a morgue assistant."

Zinc raised an eyebrow.

"What? You think I'm a wimp? It worked for Patricia Cornwell. I learned about death and forensics."

"That's commitment."

"Readers these days aren't stupid. A book is a waste of time if you don't come out the far end knowing more about the subject at hand than you did going in. Too many writers are lazy."

"And after that?"

"I went to Cap College and qualified as a paralegal. With so many lawyers writing successful thrillers, I figured that was a must. As a fly on the wall of the legal profession, I took it all in. The cops. The killers. The victims. The witnesses. The scientists. The lawyers. The judges. They're all in my notes, just waiting for the right plot to let them step onto the page."

"Do you have it?"

"I think so."

"Give me a hint?"

"Can you keep a secret?"

"Try me."

"It's about a brutal murder and a pair of lawyers-cum-writers who have a falling-out."

Running her fingers through her hair to slick it back from her face, Yvette rose out of the swirl. So suddenly did her near-naked figure appear in front of Zinc's eyes that the Mountie caught his breath and sucked in a couple of bubbles. As she legged up out of the hot tub for a dip in the pool, Yvette's bikini clung to her buttocks like a fresh coat of paint.

Her jackknife dive radiated a wake of concentric ripples. Close on her heels, Zinc plunged into the cool depths. The shock to his nerves was bracing. Surfacing, he found Yvette hanging on to the side of the pool.

"Is that why you're at the convention? To study Bret and Wes for a *roman à clef*?"

"I didn't know they were at odds until today. I heard about the tiff they had at the earlier panel shortly before you arrived at the registration table. That got me thinking about the possibilities, and the plot came out of that."

"So what brought you here?"

"This is my group."

"The WHC?"

"You sound surprised. Writing's a lonely chore. You sit in a room and tell yourself a story, then you send it out into the ether and wonder if strangers will like it. The best way to tell is to go to a con. And this con is by far the most fun-loving lot."

"But you're not published."

"Hey, I'm preparing. And I know a good party when I see one. This is my third World Horror Convention."

"Why horror?"

"This group is the loosest. Anything goes: pranks, practical jokes, the Gross-out Contest."

"Gross-out Contest?"

"The heart of this convention. Stick around—it takes place tonight. There's an open mike, and you get four minutes to revolt everyone with your imagination."

"Sounds weird."

"It's a hoot. And then there's the tale of the wandering hat."

"What hat?"

"I'm glad you asked. One of the con regulars had this old base-ball cap. It was labeled for some defunct team from his distant past. He wore it as a lucky charm or something like that. Anyway, the hat went missing at a con a few years ago. Some months later, he received an anonymous photo in the mail. There was his hat on the head of a camel in front of the Egyptian pyramids. Time went by, and he got another photo. Now his hat was on the head of one of the hookers in the red-light district of Amsterdam. Photo after photo, he still gets them. His hat shows up in the most bizarre places."

"Who's the culprit?"

"No one knows. But it's probably someone he's rubbing shoulders with at this con."

Zinc grinned. "That's a good prank."

They were interrupted by the sounds of a commotion approaching the pool. Two boys, nine or ten, came barreling in. The chubbier one leaped off the deck and clasped his knees to his chest, then—*whoosh!*—cannonballed into the deep end.

"Time to get out," Zinc said.

"You first," Yvette replied.

His forty-year-old butt was less alluring than hers, but gentleman that he was, Zinc preceded Yvette out of the pool. Standing on the deck, he gallantly offered her a hand up, enjoying the sight as water cascaded off her emerging torso.

"Is this where you met Petra?" Zinc asked.

"Actually, we first met years ago at Bible camp. I doubt Petra remembers me, but I remember her. Even as a little girl, she was a hellion. I'm not surprised that Petra became a goth. She's a regular in the goth contingent at horror cons."

"What do you think of her art?"

"It captures attention. If my fine arts professors saw it, they'd need smelling salts."

"Have you read 'Pickman's Model'?"

"Yikes! A cop acquainted with Lovecraft? I thought you Mounties were straight arrows."

"It's a long story."

"I'll bet."

"Pickman is an artist whose work upsets viewers, right? The monsters in his paintings appear to incorporate the actual anatomy and physiology of our primal fears in such a way that they conjure up our survival instincts and hereditary memories of frights too fearful to face. Because it rings so true, one painting, *Ghoul Feeding*, gets him thrown out of art circles. In the end, we learn that Pickman has discovered a way to unlock the forbidden gate to the occult realm. The reason his paintings upset us profoundly is that his models are monsters drawn from real life."

"The elder gods," said Yvette.

"The ones that scare the hell *into* us."

"Petra's not *that* good."

"Someone is. In the Morbid Maze of the gallery, an artwork titled *Morlocks* had that effect on me. The painting is signed 'The Goth.' Whoever he or she is, the Goth sees Pickman's models."

"That's a spooky picture."

"Who's the Goth?" asked Zinc.

"No one knows. Except Bret. He brought the painting. And set up its exhibit."

Goose bumps pimpled their skin from standing out in the open air, so they eased into the hot tub farthest away from the deep end, where the two young boys kept up their cannonball barrage.

"How do you know Bret? Is he a regular at cons?"

"As far as I know, this is his debut. Bret was no longer in practice when I was a paralegal. I met him at a Vancouver signing for his first two thrillers. When the guest of honor originally slated for this con suddenly died, I put Bret forward as his replacement. The final step in my apprenticeship as a writer was supposed to be my picking his brain at this convention. But then I heard about the Odyssey."

"What's that?" Zinc asked, remembering that the Odyssey was the detonator that caused Bret to explode during his most recent bout with Wes.

"Bret has put together a trek to the South Pacific for an in-depth writers' workshop for lawyers on how to create a marketable thriller. A lot of lawyers, as you must know, burn out from stress."

"Bret included," Zinc said.

"Which got him writing. Bret disgraced himself in the eyes of the profession with his outburst in court, then went on to build a fresh career as a novelist. Stressed lawyers see thriller-writing as a ticket out of law. I suspect that Bret came up with the idea of the Odyssey as a means to redeem himself with his legal colleagues."

"Why the Odyssey?"

"It ventures into the realm of the cannibals."

"You've lost me."

"The Odyssey is an allusion to Homer. *The Iliad* and *The Odyssey*? You with me that far?"

"Yes, dumb cop that I am."

"Odysseus sails into danger from two tribes of cannibals: first, the Laistrygonians, these giant, ugly man-eaters who hurl rocks down at the Greek ships so they can devour castaways from the sinking wrecks; and next, the Sirens, seductive sea-nymphs who lure the Greeks ashore with their irresistible singing so they can feast off the men who fall prey to their charms."

"Okay," said the Mountie.

"Ulysses is the Latin name for Odysseus."

"Double okay."

"So imagine you're a burnt-out lawyer who wants out of the law. The Odyssey offers you a chance to get away from it all: a trip to the idyllic South Seas, an opportunity to learn to write a thriller that could be your ticket to freedom. And also immersion in inspiring stuff to write about, for you're at the heart of where Captain Cook encountered the cannibals with elder gods."

"Sounds expensive."

"It is. But I have a trust fund."

"You're going? I thought you said it was for lawyers?"

"The Odyssey isn't exclusive. The remaining spaces are open to anyone."

"Did you know Wes Grimmer is going?"

"I saw his name on the list."

"Wes just invited those at the con to join *him* on the South Seas trek. That's sure to make for explosive fireworks with Bret."

"And inspire my plot."

"How do you view what's going on between Bret and Wes?" Zinc asked.

"There's ten years between them. It's an ego clash. Bret isn't up to the challenge posed by Wes. He's like an older chess player who's afraid he'll lose the game to a younger player. Instead of playing it out to the end he dreads, he upsets the chessboard in mid-game."

"Good analogy."

"Poor Bret. Here's a crippled lawyer whose practice is usurped by an up-and-comer. To stay in the game, he assumes the role of mentor to the neophyte. Wes comes into his own as a lawyer by feeding off Bret's clients. That doesn't scare the mentor, because he has gone on to become a successful novelist. With two books under his belt, Bret writes a *roman à clef* about a horrific murder. The publication date coincides with his being the guest of honor at the World Horror Convention. But when he goes down to Seattle to have the spotlight focus on him, who muscles in from out of nowhere with a bigger book from a major publisher on the same horrific murder? His usurping student."

"Dog eat dog."

"Survival of the fittest."

"Too bad you missed the action. Both bouts."

"Unfortunately, we drew lots for who works when. And there was no warning that Bret and Wes would clash. I'll get to watch them duke it out in the Cook Islands—the Odyssey flies to the South Seas this coming Tuesday—and meanwhile, I have you to fill me in on everything you saw and heard at the second bout."

The killers of the hanged men—both the victim in North Vancouver and the victim in Seattle—stood at the window of the hotel room on the third floor and gazed down at those bubbling in the aquatic center of the quadrangle. One of them focused binoculars on the hot tub farthest away from the two boys splashing into the pool's deep end.

"What's Chandler doing?"

"Conversing with Yvette. Her lips aren't moving. The Horseman's doing the talking."

"You ready for tonight?"

"Sure. The nails are extra long."

"If the Mountie knew what's coming, he'd piss in the pool."

"First things first. We stick to the plan."

GROSS-OUT CONTEST

Be it the chest-bursting horror in *Alien,* or the girl throwing up green bile in *The Exorcist,* or the movie mogul waking up to find himself in bed with the severed head of his prize thoroughbred in *The Godfather,* or the shower scene in *Psycho* that changed movies forever—if the image makes us recoil from shock, it goes into our long-term memory banks. That's the gross-out factor.

The Gross-out Contest, Yvette had told Zinc by the pool, is the heart of the World Horror Convention. So tonight the Mountie found himself packed into Tomb A with hundreds of hard-core conventioneers, all of whom hoped to be disgusted, revolted, sickened and nauseated by each contestant who got his or her four minutes of infamy in front of the open mike. A motley crew of three mock-serious judges sat at a raised table spread with an assortment of cheesy prizes. The judge in the center picked up a set of chattering false teeth and slipped them under the table in the vicinity of his crotch, rolling his eyes and lolling out his tongue in lustful pleasure like the village idiot.

The crowd cheered.

"Does it count as head if there is no head?" a wag shouted.

The judge who served as MC consulted his roster. A stocky fellow with a black goatee, he wore black suspenders over a black T-shirt above black jeans. Rising from the table, he approached the stand-up mike. His introduction was short. "Next, Wes Grimmer."

"Aw right!" someone hollered.

An aisle down the middle of the room separated two ranks of chairs. From his seat on the aisle, Wes made his way to the podium with a sheaf of papers in hand. Positioning himself behind the mike, he waited for the hubbub to abate. Once the room was quiet, he announced the title of his offering to the crowd.

"'My . . . Horny . . . Prick.'"

"The story of my life!" the wag called out.

"Let him speak!" came the chorus from the audience.

"The moral of my story is," Grimmer began, "never take a piss in the Amazon. I know what you're thinking: it serves me right. A veteran traveler like Wes Grimmer ought to know that the world is full of unexpected dangers. Yes, I heard about the fellow who explored China to research a book. When in Rome, do as the Romans do, they say. So he ate a local delicacy called a thousand-year-old egg, which infected him with a bone fungus that ate his skeleton. His bones slowly turned to mush, until finally they could no longer support his organs. The would-be epicurean caved in on himself and smothered to death.

"And yes, I heard about the guy who stood barefoot on a riverbank in the Amazon jungle and wiggled his toes to squish mud between them like he used to when he was a kid. Unfortunately, loa loa worms lurked in the mud. They burrowed into the flesh of his feet and wriggled in his bloodstream until they found a suitable swimming pool in the ocular fluid of his eyes. There, the worms squirmed and grew until they were several feet long. First, their reluctant host went blind from overcrowding as the parasites usurped the space within his eyeballs, then, when the expanding pressure could no longer be contained, both orbs bugged out and blew a slew of slugs in someone's face."

"Mine eyes have seen the glory—" someone yelled out.

"Let him speak!"

"But hey, I'd been drinking beer all day on the deck of the boat as it snaked its way up that tributary of the Amazon River, and I had to take one hell of a piss. So I set down the research notes for my next novel and ventured to the stern of the boat to relieve myself over one side. There I stood, legs apart, draining the snake in my hand, sighing a little sigh as the beery stream arced forth, when—was that the sparkle of sunlight in my piss?—I caught a glint of silver.

"No, it wasn't sunlight.

"It was a little fish.

"My warm pee hitting the cooler water must have been the lure. It scooted up the yellow cascade like a salmon fighting its way upstream to spawn—a fitting simile, as things have turned out. A moment before that sleek minnow vanished into my piss hole, its gills and fins, barbed with needles, shot forward to form a phalanx of spikes. It felt as if a cactus had been rammed up my prick—one of those ones with the needles that break off as soon as they pierce your skin, then fester and itch like crazy until you dig them out. My scream was shrill enough to be heard in Seattle. My urethra and my bladder were pincushioned on the inside, so there was no way to dig those slivers out in the Amazon jungle, where it was a four-day junket to the nearest hospital. I spent the remainder of the cruise curled up in a fetal ball from the pain.

"By the time I got to a doctor, bad had slipped to worse. The doc pulled on latex gloves while I dropped my crusted pants, then he recoiled in shock from what assailed his horrified eyes. My prick—bloated twice the size it ought to be—was turning the sickly color of gangrene. The rot emitted a gagging stench. The spines that had broken off inside me had somehow sprouted, and now they stuck out through the skin of my prick like the bristles of a thorny thicket. The gunk that oozed out with them was a mix of blood and pus, a pukey yellow concoction of vile bile if ever there was one. And as for those squiggly white worms . . . yes, they were maggots.

"One look at the doc's face and I sensed that worse was heading for worst. After the blood tests, he gave me the prognosis. 'There's good news and there's bad news,' he said gravely. 'Gangrene has set in, so we must amputate.'

"'God, no!' I gasped. 'What's the good news?'

"'That *is* the good news,' he replied."

The audience—including Zinc—burst into laughter. Grimmer had to wait for it to die.

"'The bad news is that the needles can regenerate. Some have traveled through your bloodstream to your heart and your brain.

Less than a week will see those spikes begin to grow, and soon both organs will suffer the fate of your genitals.'

"'How can this be?' I wailed.

"'It's the Amazon.' He shrugged.

"Every doomed man deserves one last wish, and my wish was for a final all-night fuck. By then, my balls were swollen as big as my prick, but there was no way—thanks to the needles—to get a little relief. What I desperately needed was the company of like-minded friends, so that's why I hopped a flight to Seattle to catch the tail end—you might say—of the World Horror Convention."

Hoots of laughter.

"The pants I'm wearing hide the fact that my putrid, scabby, itchy, oozy, abscessed, wormy, horn-spiked prick is permanently erect. Special plastic diapers taped to my waist and thighs keep in not only the retching stench but also the rancid drippings. Hundreds of barbs protrude from the sloughing skin, each ready to pierce and snap off at any human contact. So much festering jizz juice has built up in me that I wouldn't be surprised if I could come a dozen times. All that's missing is the right receptacle.

"Look! There's Petra Zydecker!"

The mob howled as Wes pointed her out.

"What a foxy lady. Perhaps she'll play Beauty and the Beast with me."

Hamming it up, Petra ducked out of sight.

"Look! There's John Pfeiffer!"

Wes swung around and cocked a finger at the MC.

"What a sweet mouth in the hair of that Freudian goatee."

Like a "speak no evil" monkey, the master of ceremonies whipped his hands over his mouth.

"Look! There's Bret Lister!"

Zinc followed the cocked finger.

"Doesn't Bret have a regal ass? And, buddy, do I have a crown of thorns for you."

The laughter exploded.

"In fact," said Grimmer, shielding his eyes with one palm to gaze around the room, "everyone here has two—or three—raw pink holes that will do. So when it's time for beddy-bye and you go back to your room, slipping the card into the slot to release the lock on the door, that sound you hear behind you just before you catch a whiff of chloroform . . . well, that sound could be me.

"I'm Wes Grimmer.

"My prick is horny as hell.

"And I've got something to pass on!"

Most were laughing. All were clapping. Some were nudging each other. But whatever the reaction, Grimmer was a hit.

Except with Bret Lister, who slunk out of the room with a scowl.

MASQUERADE

"A trickle of blood?" Yvette suggested, holding up the tube of stage blood.

"No thanks," the Mountie replied.

"I thought the role of an undercover was to blend in."

"I'm not undercover. I'm plainclothes."

"Suit yourself. How do I look?"

"Dead," he said. "As a doornail," he added.

"You say the sweetest things."

Blonde and fair-skinned in her natural state, Yvette had blanched her flesh beyond pale with a cadaveric base coat. Her clinging, gossamer gown was whiter than a shroud, and the only color she sported other than her blue eyes was the insipid blue of the lipstick that dyed her mouth the pallor of death.

"Why so white?"

"Virginal, don't you think?"

"If you're saving yourself for a wedding in the afterlife."

"It's so I'll stand out."

"By bleeding yourself of color?"

"The Vampire Ball is a goth affair. With everyone in black except me, I'll be a neon sign."

The two had met up again outside the Gross-out Contest. Zinc had invited Yvette to have a drink with him, and she had agreed as long as she could first dress for the ball. So here they were in her hotel room on the second floor, where Yvette was transmogrifying from the living into the undead, while the Mountie pondered if he should step across the line from being an objective observer so he could escort this vampire to the midnight fest.

"Chicken," she taunted him with the tube of stage blood.

"I'll think about it."

"You can't be my date if you won't shed blood."

"Do puncture wounds count?"

"Where? On your neck?"

"I'll be your victim. You can nibble off me."

"Be careful what you wish for."

"I wish," said Zinc.

Yvette squirted the edible liquid into her mouth and slackened her lower lip until one side began to dribble. Tilting her head curved the line down her delicate chin. She went into the bathroom to spit the excess in the sink. The bloodsucker who emerged had a pair of jutting fangs. So shocking was the red dribble against her pale skin that it shrieked louder than a blood-curdling scream.

"About that drink?" she said.

If you love horror, you love the Cthulhu Mythos, so as a result, the convention was earning the Cthulhu sculptor multitudinous bucks. Al Savory was the birth name of the model maker who ran the Lovecraft's Realm exhibit in the Morbid Maze gallery, but the *nom de guerre* he used for his artwork was Dexter Ward, taken from H. P.'s eerie novel *The Case of Charles Dexter Ward*. Horror fans are a collecting breed—the plethora of specialty houses that offer deluxe editions of popular works proves that—and exquisite Cthulhu monsters of cold-cast porcelain or acrylic resin mounted on heavy metal brackets make ideal bookends. Collectors are obsessive. Rarity counts. So the ones with real money want those treasures that are one of a kind. Dexter Ward cast severely limited signed-and-numbered runs from his monster molds, and if you had the money to buy the only copy, he would let you smash the die and all the clones.

Big bucks in artificial rarity.

Plus it can be fun to destroy.

It tweaks the id.

One of the sculptor's best works was *Pickman's Model,* his Gothic rendition of himself as Lovecraft's tormented artist, painting the real-life monsters from the occult realm that he can use as models because he has opened that other dimension. Well, Savory had a buyer, and this guy had the wherewithal to buy the only copy. They were to seal the deal in the bar in half an hour, then carry the prototype out to the parking lot, where the collector would smash it with a hammer.

Al Savory's hotel room was on the ground floor, tucked away in a short hall blocked by the delivery area. Seen from the aquatic center, it was off in the far corner, just around the bend from the long side stretch. His was the only door off this angled nook, so as Al struggled to make his keycard spring the reluctant lock, he was hidden out of sight by the maskers who came and went from their rooms along the straightaway side.

In went the card.

Out it came.

Finally, the green light blinked.

This time the door popped open.

"Having trouble?"

Al turned toward the voice.

A figure draped in a black cape that swept down to the floor and a black hood that masked its face stood at the corner. A goth in costume for the Vampire Ball.

"Oh, it's you," Al said, recognizing the voice.

Zap. Zap.

The Taser darts hit.

With fifteen feet of take-down power, the handheld stun gun had more stopping force than a .357 Magnum. It released compressed nitrogen to hurl a pair of electric darts at a speed of 135 feet per second. Both 3/8-inch needle points jabbed into Al's chest like the fangs of a vampire. Akin to that jolt of juice that galvanized the Frankenstein monster into life, a fifty-thousand-volt zap shocked the artist. The effect of this pulsating current on Al was opposite to the effect of that jolt on the monster. It penetrated the neural net that sheathed Al's body and shut down communications between his brain and his muscles. Incapable of performing coordinated actions, Al's wildly contracting muscles turned him into a spastic marionette with jerky arms and legs. Dazed and confused, the stunned artist succumbed to spinning vertigo.

Al was vaguely aware of being propelled in through the open door to his room, and of crumpling in convulsions at the foot of his made bed, and of a cape being swirled away to expose a near-naked body, and of a figure bending down with something in both hands—a hammer and a long spike aimed at Al's forehead.

———◦—◦———

"The world is a masquerade," the artist Goya once wrote. "Face, dress, voice, everything is feigned. Everybody wants to appear what is not; everybody deceives, and nobody knows anybody."

The idea behind a masquerade is that you dress up in a costume to hide who you actually are. But Zinc had the feeling that this masquerade turned that notion inside out. Goth was the essence of who these conventioneers really were, so tonight's masquerade allowed them to shed the false face that masked their dark souls.

The elevator that brought Yvette and the Mountie down from her room opened into a corridor throbbing with heavy industrial music. Zinc was transported back to those gender-bending days in the early seventies when the clergyman's son Vincent Furnier spawned the phenomenon of shock rock by cross-dressing in black leather, transforming his face with clotty black mascara and renaming himself Alice Cooper. Onstage, Alice was the best theatrical performer in the rock business. In a camp, grotesque pantomime of anguish, excess, bloodletting, horror, ruin and warped sexuality, he hanged himself on a gallows in a mimic of the cover of his classic album *Killer*, cut off his own perverse head on a guillotine, simulated tearing off the head of a chicken and—his *coup de théâtre* in the annals of infamy—dismembered dozens of plastic dolls for the song "Dead Babies."

Shock rock begat new wave. And dark new wave begat goth.

Goth is a mind-set that goes back centuries. Constantly rein-venting themselves so they can luxuriate in death, doom and deso-lation, the "new goths" who stalked the halls and shadows of the convention hotel tonight sucked inspiration from all that had gone before. Theirs was the gathered esthetic of Byron, Poe, Dracula, Hyde, Jack the Ripper, James Whale, Poppy Brite, David Lynch and the Chapman brothers. Excessive was the norm. This was the fashion for those who would never be conventionally attractive. The black hair, black eyes, black lips, black nails, black satin, black velvet, black brocade, black leather, black fishnets, black tattoos, silver chains and fetishistic body piercings smacked of S&M. Over the top and almost operatic in intensity, this group conjured images of a fang club congregating in the dark to use razors, syringes and eye teeth to drink each other's blood.

No wonder frontal-lobe puritans dread this genre.

Because that's the fear, isn't it? Fear of the weak reed. It's all very well for dark fantasists to indulge their Gothic inclination, as long as they keep a firm eye on the line that divides the occult realm from the reality of everyday life. But what about those deluded psychos who believe they have actually broken through to the other side and are now possessed by whatever lurks beyond? Hyde took over Jekyll while Jekyll still believed that he was in control, and that's what Zinc had seen happen too often in his job. A breakthrough to the other side that was in reality nothing more than a psychotic delusion.

"Who's that?" Zinc asked Yvette, pointing out a woman on the edges of the throng.

"Your guess is as good as mine. She set up in the dealers' room to sell spankings at a buck a slap."

"You're joking!"

"I jest not," said Yvette. "A horror con is bound to attract a lunatic fringe."

The female in question had no face. From their table in the bar, at the window that overlooked the pool and its satellite hot tubs, Zinc and Yvette watched the Blank enter their watering hole, stop to sweep the pub with her invisible eyes, then retreat. A black stocking hugged her head as tightly as the black leotard that sheathed her figure. Fluttering behind her was a black cape with a bloodred lining.

"I feel like I'm at *The Rocky Horror Picture Show,*" Zinc said.

"Goths are theatrical."

Yvette was sipping a Bloody Mary while Zinc nursed a ginger ale. His drinking years were over, thanks to the scar in his brain. The goth at the table next to theirs had a sculpture of *Pickman's Model* in front of him. From the way he kept checking and frowning at his Rolex, it was safe to bet that he had been stood up. Finally, the man and his model left the boisterous bar.

Some of the conventioneers were cavorting around the pool. They shed their costumes to splash in and out of the hot tubs and the turquoise deep. Protecting his precious sculpture from the man-made water spouts, the jilted goth with *Pickman's Model* emerged from the artificial jungle to skirt one side of the party pool and vanish into the phony thicket off in the far left corner.

"I thought vampires were afraid of water."

"Times change," said Yvette.

"The network that balked at covering this con should have come. Lots of 'bites' here."

"Ouch!" his date winced. "That pun sucks."

"Where were we?"

"Death as theater."

"And speaking of theater," Zinc said, nodding to an impromptu drama of some sort that was being staged below. Poolside had turned into an amphitheater, with gesticulating actors and more exits and entrances than a bedroom farce. At the heart of it all, still clutching *Pickman's Model* as he pointed toward a room in the far corner, was the goth from the bar.

"Something's wrong," said the Mountie.

———————

The Seattle police had an interview room set up at the horror convention. So, responding from different directions, Det. Ralph

Stein and Insp. Zinc Chandler crossed paths by the swimming pool. Both held their badges up to establish authority. No need to ask the goth from the bar to guide them to the corpse. The stampede of gawkers dripping pool water had polluted the path through the jungle.

"Christ!" Ralph fumed. "Forensics are fucked."

"What a place for a killing."

"A cop's nightmare."

"With so many maskers spattered with fake blood, a faceless killer stained with real blood blends in. And the con gives everyone an excuse for having been in and out of the murder room if we do locate a clue that fingers a suspect."

"Police!" Ralph barked. "Let us through!"

The swimmers on the patio parted to let the cops reach the sliding door to the murder room. The room was the first one from the left along the back side of the pool's quadrangle. The suite around the corner abutted it at a right angle. On its other flank was a delivery area. Thanks to a thicket of faux foliage out front, no one could see into the murder room. Despite that, it seemed odd that the killer had left the lights on and the door to the pool ajar. Unless . . . unless he wanted the crime discovered soon because he—or she—had an alibi in place.

But what sort of alibi?

Swimming? wondered Zinc.

That would be a good blind, the Mountie thought. Kill your victim in a room that opened on the pool. Do it in a bathing suit so the blood is on your skin—a stain-resistant bathing suit to repel wayward drops. Then exit from the murder room and head for the pool. Splash around with the other swimmers to wash off the blood. And when the alarm is raised by someone who spots the crime— someone who you know in advance will go to the room—rush back with the others from the pool for a spectator's look. The result is that, one, you contaminate the murder scene; two, you invalidate forensic traces you might have overlooked; and three, if blood is found on you, it could have come from anyone you brushed up against in the crush.

One look at the murder scene, however, and Zinc's suspicion shot off in a different direction. The victim lay sprawled at the foot of the bed with blood pooled around his head. With so many spikes hammered into his face, the man had had his features mutilated beyond recognition. But his identity could be deduced. An artist by the name of Al Savory—*nom de guerre* Dexter Ward—had checked into the room. The room was full of Cthulhu Mythos molds and models identical to those that Zinc had seen on display at the Lovecraft's Realm exhibit in the gallery. The physique of this corpse was similar to that of the thin, sleek, reptilian dealer who had returned, lunch in hand, to sell the exhibit models. He was clothed in the same black slacks and bloodred shirt with a hand-painted illustration of Cthulhu's tentacle face. His mutilated face was a mimic of that monster, for the spikes, each about a foot long, had been hammered into the skull around his gaping mouth to fashion a yawning maw ringed by steel tentacles. And what this surreal squid face conjured up in Zinc's mind was an image of Bret Lister buying the Cthulhu model in the gallery where Petra Zydecker lurked.

Bret and Petra?

Where were they now?

Cooking up another sexual alibi in her room?

The killing of the Cthulhu sculptor banished any concern about tunnel vision from the Mountie's mind. The spikes hammered into his face were of the same make as—albeit longer than—the non-galvanized flatheads that had been pounded into the skulls of both Hanged Man victims. That information was still hold-back evidence known only to the police. Therefore, Ralph's concern that the killer or killers might have passed Ted Bundy's house on any ghost tour, and might have located Maltby Cemetery by using one of the WHC pamphlets distributed to the public, evaporated in Zinc's mind.

The killer or killers definitely haunted this convention.

The most likely suspect was Bret Lister. He had spent time with the Ripper in a mental hospital. He'd written a book about the Hanged Man victim in Vancouver, Bret's hometown. He was here in Seattle, when occurred both subsequent killings where nails were also hammered into skulls. He'd purchased a Cthulhu model from the sculptor whose face now resembled that occult monster. And he was at the Gross-out Contest earlier tonight, when Wes had spun his tale about a hotel room ambush like the one that happened here. What a good way to frame his rival—turn the tale back on Wes. There was only one problem. Bret had an alibi for last night's Hanged Man crime.

So was he currently alibiing up for this crime, too?

Zinc advised Ralph that he had something important to check out. Then, retracing his steps to the pool, the Mountie traversed the central court to the other side of the quadrangle. There, he entered the path through the green belt marked "Room 104." As he closed on the unlit patio hidden by the foliage, Zinc caught sight of two pint-sized silhouettes scrambling away. He recognized these peeping Toms as the cannonballers from the swimming pool, the young boys who had lobbed themselves into the water as he and Yvette cooked in the hot tub.

The little buggers were spying at a crack in the curtains.

The same crack to which the cop now applied his eye, and through which he spied sweating lovers making the two-backed beast on the bed. Petra was on the bottom, with her long legs wrapped around the buttocks of the lawyer-turned-writer on top, her claws digging into his back while he humped and pumped as if this was the last fuck he would have before going to the gallows.

Her stud wasn't Bret Lister.

It was Wes Grimmer.

THREE-BACKED BEAST

April 13 (The next day)

It would be hard for next year's World Horror Convention to surpass the excitement of this one. Last night's festivities had segued into "the dead dog party," a WHC tradition in which all the food and booze remaining at the dying con is gathered together in one suite for a final gabfest until participants break away to fly home. The five horrific slayings linked to this convention gave them loads to talk about. Meanwhile, Seattle police had locked the hotel down tighter than a submerged submarine exploring the ocean's depths. No one was going anywhere before running the gauntlet of a witness interview, so that's how Zinc and Ralph spent the wee hours of the night.

Sunday morning, at just after ten, the Mountie was strolling along the hall past Morbid Maze when a sideways glance through the open doors of the gallery made him screech to a halt. The locks at the four corners of *The Antichrist*—Petra Zydecker's design for the Hanged Man card in her bizarre tarot deck—had been unlocked in order to remove that image from the panel facing the hall. What stopped Zinc in his tracks and drew him into the gallery was the sight of the goth queen standing in front of the painting underneath.

"Did I win?" he asked.

Petra turned around. "Sorry, Inspector. The Tarot chose another."

"May I inquire who?"

"Wes Grimmer."

"That makes sense."

"The Magick is in the cards."

"And in bed?"

"Are you ready for that walk on the wild side, Zinc?"

"You're a lucky charm."

"Oh?"

"The man who takes you to bed always seems to have a convenient alibi."

"Did you read my statement about last night?"

"I'd rather hear it from you."

"Before the Gross-out Contest, Wes asked if I would allow him to use my name in his entry. I said sure. After he was such a hit, he thanked me for being a good sport. One thing led to another until we ended up in bed. You may not want to believe me, but I understand we were peeped by witnesses."

"Two little voyeurs."

"Three," said Petra. "*Three* voyeurs. Two little boys and a big one who deserves a spanking."

"At a buck a slap?"

"I'd rather do it myself."

"The problem is, we don't know when the sculptor died."

"That's weak, Inspector. Al was in here, selling models, until after the Gross-out Contest began. Not only were Wes and I at that event, but so were you. And as for the period after the contest, there wasn't enough time for Wes—or me—to fuck *and* kill."

"What about Bret?"

"What about him?"

"He left the contest in a snit. Did you see him after that?"

Petra laughed. "Three voyeurs aren't enough for you? You want to add a fourth?"

"Is that a no?"

"No, I didn't see him. What does Bret have to say?"

"You didn't ask him?"

"We're estranged at the moment."

"Because of Wes?"

"You may have noticed that those two are in a pissing contest."

"It seems Bret was all over the place. He went to the contest. Had a drink in the bar. Took a dip in the pool. Danced at the Vampire Ball. A lot of people saw him. But few recall at what time."

"Is that not what you'd expect at a lively convention?"

"What about Friday night?"

"I told you. I fucked Bret."

"Is that the truth?"

"What more do you want? Did you check with room service?"

"Yes. They back up your story."

"Did you time how long it takes to drive to the cemetery?"

"Yes."

"And?"

"Getting there'd be tight."

"How tight?"

"Real tight."

"Well, that does it. Unless you think we flew there on my witch's broomstick."

"No."

"Accept it. I fucked him. Like that." The goth queen pointed at the painting on the panel, the image that Petra had locked away behind *The Antichrist*. It was a graphic depiction of a male and a female having sex. The legs of the male arched like those of a spider toward the top of the canvas, and between them—seen from the rear—his grossly enlarged genital organs were poised to thrust into the vulva of the female, who was spread below him. Her legs curved up to meet his at both sides of the canvas, and together they could be the jaws of a ravenous shark. Her genitals were drawn with obsessive gynecologic detail, and her engorged clitoris bore the face of a grinning skull.

"The title?"

"Jaws of Death."

"And which card in the Tarot does that represent?"

"The Lovers."

"I should have guessed. Are you heading home?"

"Yes," said Petra.

"Stick around Vancouver. I may have more questions to ask."

"Better be quick."

"Why?"

"I'm off on Tuesday."

"Where to?"

"The Cook Islands. In the South Pacific."

"You're not a writer."

"No, I'm a writer's muse."

"To inspire Wes?"

"Uh-huh. He invited me last night. Right after I told him the Tarot had selected him for the Lovers."

"I feel jilted."

"Then come along. There's space left on the Odyssey."

PART III
ELOï

Fe-fi-fo-fum
I smell the blood of an Englishman!
Be he live or be he dead,
I'll grind his bones to make my bread!

—Jack the Giant Killer

GET AWAY FROM IT ALL

"You're in trouble," Ghost Keeper cautioned Zinc Chandler on Monday morning. The Special X inspectors crossed paths at the foot of the stairs that climbed to the chief's office on the upper floor of the old Heather Stables at RCMP H.Q.

"I have my shield," Zinc replied, hiding behind a book.

"You need a sword, not a shield," the Cree advised as he glanced at the book's title. "By the way, from *my* point of view, that biography is about one of the bad guys."

"Good," said Zinc. "That makes it an *offensive* weapon."

Climbing those stairs to DeClercq's inner sanctum was like taking a ride in a time machine, for hung sequentially on the walls up both sides of the staircase was a series of paintings that captured great moments in the history of the Force. One of the paintings, titled *The St. Roch in the Ice,* was a rendition of the RCMP vessel skippered by Sgt. Henry Asbjorn Larsen that had finally conquered the Northwest Passage to extend Canada's sovereignty to the North Pole.

The *St. Roch* gave Zinc another idea.

A backup weapon.

"I know where I'm going," the inspector announced as he knocked on the chief superintendent's door and entered, wielding the book as if he held Excalibur in his hand.

"Where's that?" his boss asked frostily, looking up from the piles of paperwork spread around his horseshoe-shaped desk.

"The Cook Islands," Zinc said, pointing to the title *Captain Cook* in his other hand.

"The last time I checked, the South Seas weren't off the coast of Seattle, Inspector."

"I had to detour, Chief."

"Why?" DeClercq asked skeptically.

"To see for myself. Remember our brainstorming session in this office after Gord and Joey—the pimp and the hooker—were killed in the high-speed chase that started at the North Van hotel where the Hanged Man murder occurred?"

"Vaguely."

"You said that Internal wouldn't touch me as long as I was a hero, so what I should do to protect my own ass was check out the various alternatives as if I was tying up loose ends, and if I hit a dead end myself, leave it at that."

"I'm listening," said DeClercq. He sat back and locked both hands behind his head, a signal that Zinc was being given enough rope to hang himself.

"So that's what I did," Zinc explained to duck the noose. "Nothing came to light that switched my focus away from Gord and Joey as our prime suspects for that murder. Internal was kept at bay because I remained the hero, and eventually the case became yesterday's news. However, you'll recall the worry that nagged at me. What if the pimp and his hooker had only supplied the vic with drugs, I asked you, and they bolted from the bar because they were coked up and afraid I was going to bust them for trafficking? Remember your reply?"

"No. But do turn my own words back on me."

"You said, 'In which case, there could still be two psychos loose. But at the moment that possibility is a dead end too. If the Tarot drove someone else to kill, we won't know until the phantom psychos kill again.'"

"Have they?" DeClercq asked.

"A troubling question. Do you understand why I had to see for myself?"

"Yes. A serial killing would open up that can of worms."

"Am I off the hook for going?"

The chief sat up straight and motioned Chandler to one of the two minion chairs in front of his desk. "How did you get involved this time around?"

"Ralph Stein called."

"Who's he?"

"A Seattle detective. We go back a few years to a cross-border sex case. One day, while Ralph was recuperating from a ladder accident, we chewed the fat about bizarre homicides. I happened to mention the M.O. in the Hanged Man murder, and Ralph recalled it when he responded to an eerily similar killing on Friday night."

"So he called you?"

"Uh-huh. On my cellphone. He caught me out on the deck of the lodge at the regimental dinner, a few minutes after you and I spoke in the rain."

"I see," said DeClercq.

"I had to go myself. If the Seattle killing matched the Hanged Man killing here, that meant that two innocent patrons died in the Lions Gate bar because of me, because I freaked out two armed cokeheads who weren't involved in the murder. If the phantom psychos had now materialized, it would be my ass in the wringer. I was at the murder scene in North Van a year and a half ago, and I had to see the murder scene in Seattle with my own eyes."

"I understand," DeClercq said. "You're off the hook with me."

"But I've dropped into the can of worms."

"It's the same M.O.?"

"Damn close. A male victim. Same sex as up here. Strung up like the Hanged Man, albeit in two different places. And the nails hammered into his skull match those used up here. The type and length of nails used was hold-back evidence."

"Sex assault?"

"Ralph's waiting on forensics."

A sudden *bang* caused both Mounties to wince. It sounded like a bullet had passed through the window, which was now vibrating. There was no bullet hole, however, so it had to be something else, and the clue that solved the mystery for them was a tiny feather stuck to the shimmering glass. Because DeClercq had the corner office at Special X, the world beyond the windows on one side could be seen from outside the panes of the other angle. A bird had tried to take a shortcut across the room.

Zinc saw a fortuitous opening. "We got it right, Chief. Back when we discussed the Hanged Man killing a year and a half ago. It's all about trying to break through to the other side."

"The Ripper?"

"Uh-huh. It all goes back to him."

"He's still at FPH?"

"Securely locked away. When we discussed the Hanged Man case after Cardoza was killed, the Tarot connection raised the same question. But when I checked with the hospital to see if anyone suspicious had spoken to the Ripper, the response I got was that no one had visited him except his legal representatives. Next, we discussed the possibility of a copycat. I said something like, 'Is that necessary? The Tarot has enough influence on its own to spawn a Tarot killer.' So that's when we left it at Gord and Joey . . . until I got the call from Ralph."

"Now you're back to suspecting the Ripper?"

"He's the source of the motive."

"A puppet master?"

"Right. With the key to the occult realm."

"Who's the puppet?"

"Don't know. One of two lawyers."

"Wes Grimmer?"

"Possibly. He's the Ripper's lawyer. That put him above suspicion on the FPH visitors' list."

"Why suspect him now?"

"He was in Seattle. At a World Horror Convention that is tied to the sites of the Hanged Man murder down there. Did you know that he just published a novel about the Hanged Man murder up here?"

"No. Title?"

"*Halo of Flies.* The title refers to the nimbus of nails pounded into Cardoza's head."

"And the other lawyer?"

"Bret Lister."

"I thought he left practice."

"He did, after he wigged out in court and was sent to Colony Farm on a psych remand."

"Where he met the Ripper?"

"And referred him to Wes for legal representation. Bret was in Seattle. At the same convention. Did you know that he, too, just published a novel about our Hanged Man? *Crown of Thorns,* a title that also refers to the nimbus of nails."

"Sounds like competition."

"It is. They loathe each other. And it doesn't help that they're both bedding the same woman."

"Who?"

"A goth named Petra Zydecker. She's the rebellious daughter of a priest with a church up the Fraser Valley. Petra's the artist who designed the cover of Bret's book. The image, titled *The Antichrist,* depicts a man spiked upside down on a bed of nails shaped like a Christian cross. That, too, was inspired by our Hanged Man murder, and it doubles as the Hanged Man card in her tarot deck."

"*Bed of Nails,*" DeClercq said. "Cardoza's movie."

"So many tie-ins."

"I see why you suspect them. That explains the cleanup."

"Lawyers and forensics. DNA is the nightmare of defense lawyers these days. That's why condoms were used and removed, the victim was scrubbed with chemicals to destroy fluids, fingerprints were wiped away and the bed was vacuumed."

"Describe Petra."

"Mid-twenties. Oversexed. Hard-core goth. Tattoos, piercings— the works. Schooled in the Bible. Hooked by the Tarot."

"The tarot card in Cardoza's room?"

"Used to chop coke."

"Sex, drugs and the occult?"

"That's how I see it," said Zinc. "Bret Lister or Wes Grimmer fell under the combined spell of the Ripper and the goth queen. Whichever it was, he and Petra stalked Cardoza in the bar of the hotel and lured him upstairs for a two-on-one with lots of coke.

Before the three got into bed, Cardoza was slipped Viagra. They cuffed him, gagged him, screwed him in front and behind, then hammered nails into his brain to get off on his death throes. Having signed the triad of the Hanged Man with his cuffed arms and the nimbus of nails, they suspended Cardoza from the ceiling beam with his legs crossed to signify the tetrad. Then the pair cleaned up the room and snuck away."

"Leaving us with *Bed of Nails*."

"What you'd expect from a lawyer. How better to bamboozle cops than with a false motive?"

"Clever cover-up."

"It was the perfect location. A hooker bar with drug dealers is full of suspects. The coke snorted during the crime did come from Gord. The lawyer knew we'd match the traces."

DeClercq fell silent.

He contemplated the window.

The feather from the bird fluttered in the breeze.

"It might be helpful to check the FPH visitors' list again," said DeClercq. "Let's see exactly who talked to the Ripper around the time of the Tarot killing of Cardoza."

"I phoned this morning. No luck, Chief. Their computer's down. Some sort of worm or virus got into their database and gobbled up past records. The hospital doesn't know how long it will take to retrieve the lost information."

DeClercq frowned. "We're not seeing the whole picture."

"How so?" Zinc asked.

"Why get reckless? Wes and Petra, Bret and Petra—take your pick of suspects. Having got away scot-free with the Hanged Man killing up here, why would either pair go out of their way down in Seattle to make themselves prime suspects, not only in that murder but also in our killing?"

Zinc shrugged. "They're crazy?"

"We're missing something. I want you to tell me everything that happened in Seattle."

So Chandler told DeClercq about everything.

Except the Odyssey to the Cook Islands.

"So tell me about the Cook Islands," DeClercq said after Chandler had finished his narrative.

Zinc blinked.

Could the chief read minds?

Was his subterfuge about to be exposed?

"What made you pick them as your destination to get away from it all?" DeClercq added.

Zinc recovered quickly. He had planned for this. "Revival of the Ripper case reminded me of Captain Cook's link to Deadman's Island. And the fact I've heard you say Cook is history's greatest explorer."

"Ah, the Northwest Passage."

"And the *St. Roch*."

It's surprising what you can do with a limited budget and limitless history. Formed in 1873, the Royal Canadian Mounted Police dates from the height of the British Empire. Early detachments were furnished with what were now antiques, so DeClercq had rummaged through storage rooms from coast to coast, commandeering treasures from Queen Victoria's realm to turn the lower floor of Special X into a museum.

Here, in the main squad room at the foot of the stairs leading up to the chief's office, cops worked with state-of-the-art computers and high-tech forensic data in an environment reflecting their frontier tradition. Mannequins displayed the changes that had been made to the classic red serge uniform over time: from the pillbox hat to the white pith helmet to the wide-brim Stetson. On the walls hung an armory of Wild West weapons: the Adams, Enfield, Colt, and Smith & Wesson sidearms; the various rifles carried in a sling that attached to the pommel of the California stock saddle; the cavalry swords of officers. Off in one corner by the coffee machines, which had enticed DeClercq and Chandler down for a caffeine fix, stood the Maxim machine gun, acquired in 1898 to police rambunctious miners in the Yukon during the Klondike Gold Rush.

History was the best training for a homicide cop.

The now of each person's life is the sum of his or her existence history. Every murder has a motive rooted in the personal histories of its participants. A homicide detective ferrets out the scattered pieces of each history and looks for clues from back then to solve the puzzle presented by the now. A flatfoot with one hand scratching his noggin as he tries to muddle his way through the conundrum "What in hell's going on here?" doesn't stand a chance against a trained historian. Every criminal trial is a history book.

There was no need for Zinc to sketch in the historical background to his ruse for the chief. DeClercq had written several history books, one of which—*Men Who Wore the Tunic,* his history of the Force—detailed the epic voyage of the *St. Roch.*

The Northwest Passage was the Holy Grail of the Age of Discovery. Ever since John Cabot had bumped into North America's mainland during his unsuccessful quest for a western route to Japan in 1497, merchants had dreamed of charting a northwest passage to traffic in a fabulous wealth of gold and furs. Jubilant over the success of Captain Cook's two voyages to the South Seas, Britain sent its finest mariner in search of that mythic Arctic route across the top of the globe. With William Bligh—of mutiny fame—and George Vancouver—whose name now graced both Ralph's and Zinc's hometowns—in his crew, Cook sailed to the far side of the New World.

In March 1778, Cook's ships—the *Resolution* and the *Discovery*—finally reached the coast of Oregon. Foul weather forced them out to sea as they sailed north, and about two-thirds of the way up the west coast of what is now Vancouver Island in British Columbia, Cook dropped anchor in the sheltered inlet of Nootka Sound. The *Resolution* required a new mizzenmast, so the British spent four weeks among the Nootka Natives doing repairs. When they left on April 26 to head north to Alaska, the ships sailed past Deadman's Island, which was used by the Nootka as a burial ground.

"It's layered, isn't it," Zinc said.

"What? History?"

"There I was, trapped on Deadman's Island with the Ripper, and I didn't know that Captain Cook had sailed past that hellhole over two hundred years before. Likewise, when Cook was sailing off to Alaska, he didn't know he was passing a Magick place."

"The Nootka Whalers Washing House, the West Coast shamans' shrine."

"Later, the Ripper's door to the occult realm."

"Or so he thought."

"The best-laid schemes . . ." said Zinc.

Not until 1942 would the Northwest Passage finally be conquered by the RCMP. The Mounties dispatched their floating detachment— the supply vessel *St. Roch*—on a two-year voyage across the frozen Arctic from Vancouver to Halifax to assert Canada's sovereignty in the North. In 1944, the ship sailed back, and by passing through the Panama Canal in 1950, the *St. Roch* became the first vessel in history to circumnavigate North America. Today, the ship is on display at the Vancouver Maritime Museum.

"Born too late," Zinc said. "I could have sailed with Larsen."

"Now there was one tough sergeant."

"Imagine finishing the voyage Cook didn't complete."

"And freeze your balls off doing it? You want to follow in Cook's wake, go to the South Pacific."

"Good idea."

"When does your flight leave?"

"On Wednesday," Zinc said. "But after what occurred in Seattle, I think I should stick around."

"No!" emphasized DeClercq. "That's what you *shouldn't* do. The shit is going to hit the fan in the media over this. They'll say we botched the North Van case a year and a half ago, resulting in the deaths of those two innocents in the bar. Not to mention the crash that killed Gord and Joey and destroyed so much property on the Low Level Road. That left the real killers free to kill again, which they did in Seattle over the weekend."

"But we had no evidence."

"Think they'll give a damn? Your bones are much bloodier for the media to feed on than having no one to blame. Eating you alive will sell papers and fill airtime."

"You want me out of the way?"

"You're damn right I do. If only to put off the feeding frenzy for a few weeks. From what you just told me, the Seattle police don't have a case. Both the ghost tour past Ted Bundy's house and the directions to the Thirteen Steps to Hell were advertised beyond those attending the convention. Just as they used hookers and drug dealers as a smokescreen up here, the killers chose horror fans as the haystack in which to hide their needles in Seattle. The deleterious influence of the macabre has always been a convenient scapegoat. Many would see that gathering as a massing of unstable freaks, any one of whom could flip out and kill. A convention inherently destroys forensics because those attending mill in and out of each other's rooms."

"The permutations are mind-boggling," Zinc concurred.

"Now add two wily lawyers to that mix. The Hanged Man killings are linked by the identical nails. The M.O. is slightly different—in that the nails were pounded into the victim's face as opposed to around his head—but the Cthulhu murder is also linked to the Hanged Man killings because of the make of nails and the connection to the World Horror Convention. Agreed?"

"Yes. All three murders are linked."

"Bret has an alibi for Friday night. He was in bed with Petra while the head was being spiked at Ted Bundy's house and the body was being strung up in Maltby Cemetery. Agreed?"

"That's what they say."

"Backed up by room service and the lack of sufficient time to commit the crime."

"Yes," said Zinc.

"Wes has an alibi for Saturday night. He was also in bed with Petra while the Cthulhu sculptor was being killed. Agreed?"

"That's what they say."

"Backed up by two peeping Toms."

"That's why I need to be here. To find out who's lying about who was with whom when."

"Until we have our ducks in line, we're not taking on two lawyers. If Bret hates Wes and Wes hates Bret, each will try to portray the other as the Seattle killer. And if *you* are the investigator trying to straighten that out, each will also accuse you of harassing him to try to shift the media's attention away from your own earlier foul-up. So that's why I want you away from it all."

"What about the case?"

"I'll take over."

"Do I have to go to the Cook Islands?"

"That's an order."

Zinc sighed with resignation. "You're the boss," he said.

MAN MEAT

Mission, British Columbia
April 15 (The next day)

The sketching pad on the Goth's lap was folded back to a blank page. The psycho sat in the center of a huge bed that had been set up in the sanctuary of what was once a church. From the outside, this structure still looked like a mission, but on the inside, it now served different gods. Elder gods worshiped long before the Christian God was born.

The killing of the second Hanged Man victim in Seattle was the bait designed to lure Insp. Zinc Chandler toward the hook that was waiting for him at the World Horror Convention. The killing of the Cthulhu sculptor at the convention was the tug on that hook, a tug intended to yank the Mountie toward the suspects who were about to embark on the Odyssey to the South Seas. Now it was time to reel Zinc in and gaff him into traveling to the cannibal island so that the Ripper's cold revenge—after a year and a half of scheming by the Goth—could reach its bloody climax.

To that end, the Goth was time-traveling again, wormholing back through the astral plane on a follow-up research junket to the Christian mission in Fiji in 1838, in order to witness firsthand the fate the Tarot had in store for Zinc.

Back . . .

Back . . .

Back . . .

"Vakatotoga!"

That's what I'm here to see.

The yard in front of the chapel was deserted when I materialized a moment ago, for the time warp has returned me to where I stood before, but not at that instant when the cannibals were at the gate. Instead, I have moved the clock forward long enough for the blood-crazed man-eaters to seize the reverend from the threshold of the church and drag him, along with the old missionary inside, across the shallow stream that separates the mission from the god-house.

Black smoke belches from the oven pits dug in the temple grounds as bonfires heat the stones that will bake the meat. At least one hundred *bakolas* have been butchered on the dissecting surface, and human flesh wrapped in plantain leaves lies waiting to feed those fiery mouths so that human mouths might eat. Except for those heads retained by the high priest to mount on top of the counting stones, the cut-off noggins are passed around like tins of chewing tobacco. Warriors tear off the ears and masticate them raw, then finger dollops of the goo onto the lips of their toddling sons to ensure that the boys acquire an early taste for long pig.

But now attention shifts to the sacred grove. There, amid the bone trees wedged with their skeletal trophies, both missionaries are being stripped of their clothes. The chief carver cuts their garments away piece by piece with his butcher knife, then tosses them into the narrow stream that runs red with discarded offal. How white the naked pair seem under this harsh sun. Their skin is unaccustomed to its rays.

Now the king himself waddles into the sacred grove, his multiple layers of consumed human fat jiggling like Jell-O with each jouncing step. Behind him skulks a bloated vulture: his high priest.

The old missionary is too weak to stand on his own. He is held up by the burly pair who dashed the *bakolas* against the braining stone. The king smirks in triumph as his archenemy is bound with vines, the upper and lower halves of his legs cinched together and lashed to his body, his arms secured in a similar fashion by tying both elbows to his knees and a hand to each side of his neck.

Locked in a sitting position by those restraints, the white *bakola* is carried across to the high priest. As the old missionary mumbles prayers to his God, the pagan priest mocks him with insults intoned loudly enough to be heard by the bloodthirsty mob crowded on the beach in front of the grove. My view across the stream is kept clear by the foul water. I watch as temple assistants decorate the new *bakola* to resemble the enemy dead who were brought home for the feast. His face and body are painted with obscene designs, and a fan is stuck in one hand for ornamentation. Then the burly brain-bashers hoist their human cargo shoulder-high and parade it around the trophy grove.

The king's cooks have dug a special *lovo* within the grove. The pit oven is deep enough to bake a man whole. Volcanic rocks are thrown atop a bonfire of ironwood stoked in the bowels of the pit and left there until they glow red hot. Now those cooks are leveling the bottom of the hole, removing unburned branches so the oven won't explode after it's closed. Fresh banana leaves are smashed to layer on the rocks, then the greens of palm fronds are crosshatched on top. That done, the oven is prepared to receive its meat.

The gibbering starts as the old man is lowered into the pit.

Though he tries to be as brave as Jesus on the cross, sickness takes its toll on the missionary's resolve. As I watch him slowly sink into that hellish furnace, I imagine my granddad in the old man's place, and that puts a smile on my lips every time he screams.

But soon the shrieks are muffled by more banana leaves. To close the oven, the cooks layer them on top of him, followed by four thatches of coconut greens. The greens act as a buffer between the *bakola* and the top level of his underground coffin, for what buries the missionary alive to stew in his own juices is a thick crust of sand.

Four and twenty blackbirds?

Naw, it takes just one.

And when—after four to six hours of subterranean baking—this pie is opened to set a dainty dish before the king, somehow I don't think the blackbird will sing.

But I'm not here for nursery rhymes.

Vakatotoga is my lure.

That shout from the cannibal king galvanizes ghastly action in the bone grove. The reverend I saw last time on the threshold of the mission chapel still grasps the Christian cross despite his nakedness. He will be a tougher nut for the king to crack, but if there is a fate worse than this, I'd like to see it.

The burly head-smashers take custody of the reverend from those who currently hold him, then, each grasping an arm, run him over to one of the trees as yet unadorned with trophies. The chief carver follows with his bamboo knife. In times of war, the carver doubles as a battle surgeon, for no one knows the human body like a cannibal butcher, which makes him an anatomical expert in the art of *drusu.*

"Lord, no!" the missionary beseeches as the blade cuts a slit in his belly. The carver reaches in and pulls out a glistening coil of the priest's small intestine. Fijian sail needles—*saulaca*—used for boat construction have been fashioned from the shinbones of prior human meals. The carver uses one of the long, slender needles to nail the intestine coil to the trunk of the shaddock tree. Then, with blows to his back from their muscular arms, the burly pair wind the reverend around the tree in a grisly version of Here We Go 'Round the Mulberry Bush, played with his unraveling bowels.

In effect, he ties himself to the trunk.

Like Fathers Brébeuf and Lalemant in the hands of the Iroquois, the priest tries to pray himself into martyrdom. He speaks to God as if he is standing in the crowd, and urges his Christian converts to suffer along with him that they might die well and join him in the everlasting peace of paradise. It's the same bullshit my granddad used to preach at home in Mission, until I fixed him.

The king has obviously had enough crap too. A wave of his flabby arm prompts the carver to jab a fishhook—also created out of human bone—through the tip of the priest's wagging tongue. No more will he take his Lord's name in vain, for a tug on the fishing line yanks out the offensive flesh like a toad going for a bug. The slash of the bamboo blade vanishes in a mist of blood.

A separate blaze is being stoked for this barbecue. The reverend's silenced tongue is spiked on a long stick in the same way a hot dog is at a weenie roast, then it's broiled over the flames. At the same time, a skull fashioned into a drinking cup is held under the priest's chin to catch his gushing blood. Once the tongue is cooked enough for a royal palate, the meat and drink are fed to the cannibal king. Not only does the Fijian eat the blackened tongue in front of its previous owner, but he instructs his priest with another wave of his jiggly flab to stuff a portion back into the mouth of the reverend.

It's the last supper for the holy man.

"Vakatotoga," taunts the king.

Is the reverend praying? Pleading? Screaming for his life? From the mewls and gargles he utters, it's hard for me to tell. What I do know is that his message isn't getting across, for nothing affects the relentless cutting of the carver's knife. As each successive joint of meat is severed from one of the reverend's living limbs, it is passed to the cook who has caught the blood shed in a basting dish. As with an assembly line, cooks come and go to and from the barbecue, where each joint is flamed in the ironwood blaze. Then each joint is taken to the king, who is fed a morsel in front of the shrinking man's eyes before what remains of that flesh is salted and packed away in the royal snacking chest, to be chewed on like beef jerky for weeks to come.

After each bite, the cannibal king points to his mouth.

It is the ultimate insult.

"Your flesh is caught between my teeth" is what that means.

Vakatotoga is the torture of being eaten alive. The reverend dies from loss of blood and brings it to an end. His head is handed to the high priest to add to the counting stones. The bones of his torso are harvested to wedge in the crooks of the tree.

There is nothing more vivid than seeing something with your own eyes. Thanks to my deal with the Ripper, I have the key to the wormhole that time-warped me here. Thanks to having witnessed *vakatotoga* in the flesh, I now have enough inspiration to come up with a suitable South Seas revenge to satisfy my half of the bargain with the Ripper.

So, turning from that scene of carnage in the trophy grove, again I propel my consciousness up into the astral plane and travel back through the occult realm. . . .

The sketching pad on the Goth's lap was covered with horrific details drawn during the trip. The psycho still sat in the center of the huge bed. On the sheet of paper that captured the fates of the two Christian missionaries, the facial features of the old man being lowered into the oven pit were those of the priest who had preached in *this* church before it was converted to the worship of the elder gods. The features of the reverend being eaten alive were familiar too: switch his stripped-off black suit for a red serge uniform and you would have the spitting image of Insp. Zinc Chandler.

"It's time," said a voice from the pillow on one side of the bed.

"Time flies when you're having fun," said the Goth.

"The flight leaves at three-thirty."

"Right. Let's pack."

They were off to the Cook Islands.

On the Odyssey.

CAPTAIN COOK

Over the Pacific Ocean
April 17 (Two days later)

"The almost certainty of being eaten as soon as you come ashore adds not a little to the terrors of a shipwreck," noted the botanist Joseph Banks in his journal during Captain Cook's first voyage around the world in 1768, when a storm threatened to sink the *Endeavour* off the coast of the cannibal islands that became New Zealand.

Now *that,* thought Zinc, is adventure.

As a farm boy marooned on the flats of Saskatchewan for all those years of misspent youth, Zinc had escaped by daydreaming himself into the skins of the great explorers he studied at school and the even greater superheroes he encountered in the movies, in the comic books and on the TV programs produced by the over-whelming behemoth of American pop culture.

As Radisson, Zinc was tortured by the Iroquois.

As Tarzan, he swung from vine to jungle vine.

As Davy Crockett, he went down swinging at the Alamo.

Adventurers, in this day and age, are a doomed species. It used to be that all a bored youth had to do was follow that sage advice to "Go west, young man." But whether Christopher Columbus or Buffalo Bill, point your compass in that direction and you could end up as dinner or lose your scalp. In the case of Columbus, west gave us a new word: "cannibalism."

That noun was first used by Columbus in his journal on November 23, 1492. On his initial voyage to the New World, the great explorer met the peaceful Arawak. *Caniba*—an Arawak term—was a corruption of *cariba,* meaning "bold," the label the Caribbean Indians of the Lesser Antilles used to describe themselves. When their neighbors, the Arawak, cribbed it for their own use, the term became an insult meaning "extreme barbarity." Columbus misinterpreted *caniba* as *Khan-iba* because he was searching for the Orient to meet the Great Khan of the Mongols. He also linked it to *canis*—the Latin word for "dog"—and since Pliny, the classical author, had populated the far edge of the world with man-eating Cyclopean and dog-headed tribes, Columbus put two and two together to equal three after the Arawak warned him of man-eaters too. "I therefore repeat," he journalized on December 11, 1492, "what I have said several times already: that the Caniba are none other than the people of the Great Khan, who must be neighbors to these. They have ships, they come and capture these people, and as those who are taken never return, the others believe that they have been eaten."

Columbus returned to the New World in 1493. On that voyage, he finally met the Caribs on the island of Guadeloupe. There, he discovered mutilated body parts and a severed head in an abandoned Carib village. That seemed to confirm the accusations of the Arawak, and when Columbus's adventures were widely disseminated in *De Orbe Novo* in 1511, Europeans learned how "the wylde and mysterious people called Canibales or Caribes . . . eat mannes flesshe." From then on, it was seared into the collective consciousness of Europe that cannibal tribes plagued such newly discovered lands.

Which was true, as Captain Cook found out.

How Zinc Chandler wished that he had a time machine. Oh, to be Marco Polo or David Livingstone. Oh, to be free to go where no one had gone before, to venture into the great unknown beyond the outer edge of all current maps. He knew he should be thankful to have been born Canadian. At least his country still had a frontier, and that—truth be known—was why Zinc had joined the Mounted Police. Yes, he'd had far-flung adventures on duty with Special X—his body was marked by the scars he'd brought back as souvenirs—but somehow that experience wasn't as satisfying as *pure* adventure.

Air New Zealand's Flight 53 from Los Angeles to Rarotonga in the Cook Islands had left the City of Angels for the South Seas at ten-fifteen p.m. this Thursday night. The inspector's travel plans were in disarray, thanks to a bomb threat at Los Angeles International Airport yesterday. Three days before that, in the final hours of the World Horror Convention in Seattle, Zinc had sought out Yvette at "the dead dog party"—that farewell blowout at which all the remaining booze and food is consumed by those conventioneers who stay until the last dog is hanged—to tell her that he wished to venture out on the Odyssey.

"You want to be a writer?" she had asked.

"I've had enough of copping."

"Why don't I believe you?"

"You tell me."

Yvette cocked her head, closed one eye and arched a quizzical eyebrow on the other side. "I think you think that either Bret or Wes is a killer."

"I do?" said Zinc.

The blonde nodded. "You think one of them killed that producer in North Vancouver a year or two ago, then used the experience to plot his novel. You think the same person killed the businessman whose head was found spiked upside down at Ted Bundy's house and whose body—the rest of him—was strung up like the Hanged Man at the bottom of the Thirteen Steps in Maltby Cemetery."

"Why kill him?"

"To promote the killer's book."

"That's insane."

"Exactly," said Yvette. "You think the same madman hammered a slew of nails into the face of the Cthulhu sculptor who was killed here in his room last night."

"Why kill him?"

Yvette shrugged. "The killer's running amok."

"The problem with your insight is their maze of alibis. Bret was in bed with Petra when the headless victim was killed. Wes was in bed with Petra when the Cthulhu monster came calling."

"Someone's lying."

"Who?"

"Probably Petra. And that's why you want to join the Odyssey. To find out for sure."

Drifting away from the party, they had moved out to the pool area to escape from eavesdroppers.

"There could be another reason."

"Oh?" said Yvette.

"I don't think you're safe on a trip with Bret, Wes and Petra. You need someone to watch over you."

"Someone like you?"

"Perhaps."

"I doubt if I'm in danger. You may have noticed that all the dead so far are male."

"So far," Zinc said. "But winds do change."

"There could, of course, be another reason why you want to come along."

"What's that?"

"To seduce Petra . . . or *me*."

"Petra maybe. But you, I doubt."

"You never know," Yvette replied, "unless you try."

And so she had conspired with Zinc to turn him into a stowaway on the Odyssey. The wannabe writers and their published gurus were set to fly out of Vancouver—by way of L.A.—for Rarotonga on Tuesday of that week. At 5:00 a.m. on Wednesday morning, they would land in the Cooks, and after spending a day recovering from jetlag and loss of sleep, the group would island-hop to Atiu at 11:00 a.m. on Thursday. Because Zinc had a budget conference at Special X on Tuesday, his departure would follow twenty-four hours later. Air Canada would land him in Los Angeles at 6:35 p.m. on Wednesday evening, then he would connect with Air New Zealand at 10:15 that night, and when he landed in Rarotonga at 5:00 a.m. Thursday morning, he'd hop a ride to the resort where the Odyssey members were snoozing, and be there to surprise Bret, Wes and Petra when they awoke. Off the group would fly to Atiu at 11:00 a.m., and he would set foot on Cannibal Island with the Eloi and the Morlocks.

That was the scheme.

But you know what the poet said about "best-laid schemes."

The bomb threat at LAX was one of those terrorist future shocks still rattling from 9/11. The result was that Air Canada didn't touch down in L.A. until Air New Zealand had hightailed it out of town. The Kiwis being the only carrier to the Cook Islands, Zinc had to wait another day to connect with Thursday's flight, which meant he would land in Rarotonga too late for the hop to Cannibal Island. The upside was that he got to fill a gap in his life experience by finally spending a day on Tom Sawyer's Island and in the haunted house at Disneyland.

So here Zinc sat, in seat 20J on Flight 53 while the flight attendants cleared the remains of the late-night after-takeoff meal for *The Count of Monte Cristo,* the first of multiple in-flight movies. Instead of watching swashbucklers skewer each other with épée and foil, the Mountie dug out that book about Captain Cook that he'd used as a shield against the chief's wrath over flouting his no-work order, and he settled in to set sail for the South Seas.

Avast, ye hearties!

In an obscure village and of obscure parents—a local girl and a Scottish farm laborer—James Cook was born in Yorkshire in 1728. At seventeen, the youth left home for a life at sea, which would be his all-consuming passion for the next thirty-four years as it carried him off to the uttermost ends of the earth.

In Whitby, Cook apprenticed with shippers in the coal trade. Time off was spent studying navigation, astronomy and mathematics, until he was self-educated to a level of expertise. Eventually, in 1755, he joined the Royal Navy.

The following year saw the outbreak of the Seven Years War, a bitter and bloody conflict between Britain and France over which Crown would reign supreme in North America. The opening move of that chess game was the Royal Navy's blockade of France, which occupied Cook until he was shipped off to Canada in 1758. The British were losing the war in the hinterland of what is now the eastern United States, and the best way to relieve the pressure on General Braddock's tattered army was to launch an attack on France's center of military might in the New World, the fortified clifftop citadel of Quebec.

Every student in Canada—Zinc included—studies the outcome of the most consequential struggle in the country's history: the battle on the Plains of Abraham at the gates of Quebec. He or she learns how General Wolfe, the British commander, seized the French fortress of Louisbourg, which protected the entrance to the St. Lawrence River, then sailed his armada of more than two hundred ships up that waterway to besiege the enemy in their commanding stronghold. Under cover of darkness, Wolfe snuck his army up the steep river cliffs to storm Quebec by surprise from the rear, drawing the Marquis de Montcalm and his troops out onto the battlefield to meet their bloody Waterloo.

Wolfe was killed, as was Montcalm. Those facts students study.

But what is always overlooked is the Traverse.

For between the British and the French and their date with destiny lay one of the deadliest inland navigational hazards in the world. Deep-water traffic up the St. Lawrence from its mouth to Quebec City must follow the northern shore, then, a few miles short of the fort, veer across the waterway to approach the basin of Quebec itself along the southern shore. That stretch of water where the crossing is made is known as the Traverse, and because it is a hazardous maze of submerged rocks, hidden shoals and ever-shifting sandbars, the channel is a navigator's nightmare unless it's accurately buoyed. To keep the British at bay, the French had removed all the buoys.

In Cook, however, Wolfe had a navigating genius. So honed were his skills at conquering the sea that in barely two years he had advanced from able seaman to master's mate to boatswain and finally to master in charge of running a ship. He was given the task of re-charting and re-buoying the Traverse within range of French guns, and so trustworthy were his weeks of toil (performed largely at night) that not a single ship was lost during the final leg of the British armada's sail up to Quebec.

If not for Cook, Zinc wondered, where would we be now?

Would France have triumphed in North America?

With no King George—and because the French aren't addicted to tea—would the Boston Tea Party have been canceled because of reign, and with it the American Revolution?

Would the wealth of the New World have helped feed the peasants of France, and having no need to "eat cake," might they have let the aristos escape the guillotine?

Would New England now be New France, and would all of North America be savoring frogs' legs on croissants?

Food for thought, thought Zinc.

The aftermath of the fall of Quebec saw Cook mapping the St. Lawrence and Newfoundland to create charts that were so good that they would be used for more than a century. So when, in 1768, the British decided to send an expedition to the newly discovered South Seas island of Tahiti so that scientists could observe the transit of Venus across the face of the sun, the Royal Navy selected Cook as the seaman to sail them there. His secret mission, however, was to thwart France, which, having been pushed out of North America and India, was seeking to annex new territories in the unknown vastness of the South Pacific. Up for grabs was a mythical land, the huge Southern Continent, which no one had seen.

Cook set sail from Plymouth on August 23 with Sir Joseph Banks (of the cannibal comment) and ninety-two men. The *Endeavour* was the kind of ship that Cook knew best, a Whitby collier designed for hauling coal. With its wide bows, raised poop and square stern, the bark was a stubby little vessel, but what it lacked in sleek beauty it made up for in sea-keeping qualities.

Cook's ship was all brawn.

Crossing the equator, the *Endeavour* headed for South America. As the ship approached Cape Horn, at the southern tip of that continent, the weather turned nasty. An icy gale pitched and rolled and yawed and corkscrewed the *Endeavour* about, draining the men of energy from bracing themselves against the motion. Finally, on January 24, 1769, Cook sailed around the Horn and into the South Pacific. From that date on, the history and future of the South Seas changed forever.

Cook arrived in Tahiti on April 13, after a voyage from Britain of eight months. What he found was a sun-drenched paradise of blue skies and bluer lagoons, where white torrents gushed down forest-green slopes and palms nodded lazily over sandy beaches. Tahitian females practiced free love, so while the scientists set about observing the transit of Venus, the *Endeavour*'s crew were off fucking their brains out. Two of Cook's men—Gibson and Webb—took leave of their senses, and when it was time for the ship to sail, they deserted to the hills with their girlfriends. The method Cook used to force their return was to seize half a dozen local chiefs and hold them hostage until the Tahitians betrayed both deserters. Once the men had been handed over for punishment, the *Endeavour* set sail with two agreeable islanders, Tupia and his boy servant, Tiata. Launched with a rousing send-off by hundreds of Polynesian canoes, Cook ventured out into the great unknown.

The ship sailed fifteen hundred miles south to forty degrees latitude without sighting the mythical Southern Continent. The weather was abominable in the Roaring Forties, so, having reached the limit imposed by the lords of the Admiralty, Cook turned north and west. On October 7, the British spotted land. The ship was off the east coast of New Zealand. Hoping for a welcome like the one they had received in Tahiti, the first Europeans stepped ashore—and met venomous hostility from the Maoris. With tongues stuck out as their way of expressing defiance, armed warriors with tattooed faces and feathers in their hair attacked Cook and his men. In a series of bloody skirmishes, the British shot ten Maoris, then were shocked to learn that their adversaries *ate* enemies killed in battle.

These were cannibal isles.

Cook spent six months circumnavigating and mapping the North and South islands. Banks named the waterway between them Cook Strait. In January 1770, Cook, Banks and Tupia went ashore, and passed the body of a woman floating in the water. The Maoris disposed of their dead kin by weighing them down at sea, so that was obviously a corpse that had slipped free from its ballast. On the beach, the landing party met a group of natives. In his journal, Banks recorded:

The family was employed when we came ashore in dressing their provisions. Near were provision baskets. Looking care-lessly upon one of these we by accident observed two bones, pretty clean picked, which as appeared upon examination were undoubtedly human bones. Tho' we had from the first of our arrival on the coast constantly heard the Indians acknowledge the custom of eating their enemies we had never before had proof of it, but this amounted almost to demonstration: the bones were clearly human, upon them were evident marks of their having been dressed on the fire, the meat was not entirely picked off from them and on the grisly ends which were gnawed were evident marks of teeth, and these were accidentally found in a provision basket. On asking the people what bones are these? they answered, The bones of a man.—And have you eat the flesh?—Yes.—Have you none of it left?—No.—Why did you not eat the woman who we saw today in the water?—She was our relation.—And who then is it that you do eat?—Those who are killed in war.—And who was the man whose bones these are?—Five days ago a boat of our enemies came into this bay and of them we killed seven, of whom the owner of these bones was one.

Cook picked up the tale in his own journal:

One of the cannibals thereupon bit and gnawed the human arm which Banks had picked up, drawing it through his mouth and showing by signs that the flesh to him was a dainty bit. Tupia carried on the conversation: "Where are the heads?" he asked. "Do you eat them, too?" "Of the heads," answered an old man, "we eat only the brains." Later he brought on board Endeavour *four of the heads of the seven victims. The hair and flesh were entire, but we perceived that the brains had been extracted. The flesh was soft, but had by some method been preserved from putrefaction, for it had no disagreeable smell.*

Cook's voyage home was grueling. The *Endeavour* left New Zealand on April 1, 1770. A few weeks later, he discovered the east coast of what is now Australia. On the night of June 11, the ship ran aground when its hull was pierced by coral on the Great Barrier Reef, and it foundered in shark-infested waters twenty miles from shore. While some men pumped around the clock, others carried the anchors a distance away by rowboat, then, having secured them, used capstan and windlass to kedge the ship off the reef into deeper water. By a miracle, the coral spike broke off and helped plug the hole.

Having been careened on shore and the gash in her bottom repaired, the *Endeavour* struggled west to Batavia—now Jakarta—in the Dutch East Indies. What works in Europe doesn't necessarily work in the tropics, and because the Dutch had built the city to mirror Amsterdam, the stagnant canals of that outpost on Java seethed with fatal diseases. Cook, who in over two years had not lost a single man to sickness, watched thirty-five members of his crew die because of that stop. Finally, on July 12, 1771, a month short of three years after sailing out, the *Endeavour* anchored in the Thames estuary and Cook was home.

New Zealand and Australia were added to the Crown.

———

Zinc was deep into Cook's second voyage—the most monumental ever undertaken by man—by the time his fellow passengers stirred and breakfast was served. Having passed north of Tahiti on its long flight west, the tiny plane on the screen in front that charted their own voyage was closing on Rarotonga in the Cooks, beyond which was Auckland, New Zealand, where Flight 53 would terminate.

Choosing the omelette over French toast, Zinc read on.

Never again would Cook sail with just one ship. That close shave with being marooned in Australia settled that. The *Resolution* and the *Adventure,* both Whitby colliers, left Plymouth on July 13, 1772, with Cook having carte blanche to explore wherever he desired. Reaching the tip of South Africa, the ships pressed on, crossing the Antarctic Circle to head farther south than anyone had sailed before. In that world of toppling icebergs, pack ice, penguins and whales, the vessels lost contact with each other in dense fog.

Four months later, they rendezvoused in New Zealand. Sailing on to Tahiti—where Cook and fifteen veterans from the *Endeavour* received a tumultuous welcome and took on Odiddy and Omai as interpreters—the ships swept around the South Pacific toward the Friendly Islands, which are now Tonga. Along the way, they passed through what would later be called the Cook Islands, which Cook named the Hervey Islands in honor of a British lord of the Admiralty, but didn't take the time to stop and explore.

By late October, they were nearing the east coast of New Zealand when a full-scale storm blew the *Adventure* back out to sea. Cook managed to battle his way to Cook Strait and sail the *Resolution* into Queen Charlotte Sound, the rendezvous point for both boats if they got separated. It was there that Cook witnessed cannibals eating.

On November 21, some of the local Maoris with whom Cook had made peace embarked on a plundering raid to the east for the purpose of looting new booty so they could barter with the *Resolution*'s crew. After their victorious return, Pickersgill, an officer, and some of his shipmates crossed to a part of the shoreline where wailing women were cutting their foreheads with rocks as *haehae*, a sign of grief. Nearby, a band of warriors was slicing apart the remains of a youthful enemy they had killed in the raid. One of the Maoris, to tease the Europeans, skewered the lungs of the dead man on the end of his spear and raised them to Pickersgill's lips. The officer refused the human meat but bartered for the severed head of the cut-up corpse to take back to the ship as a souvenir.

Cook was ashore, checking the progress of a vegetable patch. On his return, he witnessed a cannibal feast on the deck of the *Resolution*, then recorded the grisly event in his journal:

Calm light airs from the north all day on the 23rd November hindered us from putting out to sea as intended. In the afternoon, some of the officers went on shore to amuse themselves among the natives, where they saw the head and bowels of a youth, who had been lately killed, lying on the beach, and the heart stuck on a forked stick which was fixed on the head of one of the largest canoes. One of the gentlemen bought the head and brought it on board, where a piece of the flesh was broiled and eaten by one of the natives, before all the officers and most of the men. I was on shore at this time, but soon after returning on board was informed of the above circumstances, and found the quarterdeck crowded with the natives, and the mangled head, or rather part of it (for the under-jaw and lips were wanting), lying on the taffrail. The skull had been broken on the left side, just above the temples, and the remains of the face had all the appearance of a youth under twenty.

The sight of the head, and the relation of the above circumstances, struck me with horror and filled my mind with indignation against these cannibals. Curiosity, however, got the better of my indignation, especially when I considered that it would avail but little, and being desirous of becoming an eyewitness of a fact which many doubted, I ordered a piece of the flesh to be broiled, and brought to the quarterdeck, where one of the cannibals ate it with surprising avidity. This had such an effect on some of our people as to make them sick. Odiddy, the native who had embarked with us some time before, was so affected with the sight as to become perfectly motionless and seemed as if metamorphosed into a statue of horror.

Cook could wait no longer for the *Adventure*. A voyage into the polar wastes had to be done in high summer, so on November 25, the *Resolution* left Queen Charlotte Sound. A few days later, the *Adventure* arrived, and the crew set about repairing the ship in the safety of that cove. On December 16, Furneaux, its captain, sent two officers and eight men ashore to fetch vegetables and greens from the garden patch. When they did not return, a search party set out the following day. What it discovered was that the sailors who went for veggies had ended up as human meat. All ten had been killed and consumed by the same Maoris whom Cook had watched eat the severed head on board the *Resolution*.

Nothing remained but bones.

By now, Zinc's flight was descending toward Rarotonga. The seat-belt sign was on. The screen up front showed an overview map to orient passengers.

South of the equator and just east of the International Date Line, the Cook Islands sit midway between American Samoa and Tahiti. With Tonga, Fiji, New Zealand and Australia farther to the west, the Cooks are directly south of Hawaii, at about the same distance below the equator as Hawaii is above it. The total landmass of the fifteen islands is equal to that of Rhode Island, the smallest U.S. state, but they are scattered over some two million square kilometers of sea, an expanse equivalent to the size of Western Europe. The population is less than nineteen thousand. Some of the islands remain uninhabited.

The final words Zinc read as he marked his place in *Captain Cook,* just before the wheels touched down on the runway of Rarotonga and the engines of the jet roared to brake it to a crawl, were printed in a footnote on the page with Cook's comment on cannibals having eaten some of his men. It informed the reader that New Zealand was one of the last island groups in the South Pacific to be settled by Polynesian migrants, and that the ancestors of the Maoris Cook encountered in New Zealand had canoed from Rarotonga in the Cook Islands.

Closing the book, Zinc glanced out the window.

All he could see of the island was blackness masked by darkness.

Born too late for pure adventure, he thought.

Actually, Zinc was wrong.

For the cannibals were waiting.

BUSH BEER

Rarotonga, Cook Islands
April 18 (That morning)

The first sense engaged by this tropical isle as Zinc stepped out of the plane was his sense of smell. A fragrance of flowering humidity intoxicated him while he descended the staircase on wheels that had been rolled up to the plane. What a welcome relief it was to escape from the sinus-cracking dry air in the fuselage. The Tarmac under his feet glistened from overnight rain as the inspector crossed the apron from the 767 to the Polynesian airport.

The airport was a bare-bones shell of simplicity. The strumming of a ukulele and a singing voice that was a cross between Elvis Presley and Don Ho greeted Zinc at the door. The festive atmosphere belied the fact that it was just after five in the morning and dawn had yet to break, but you had to give the islanders credit for laying out the welcome mat. The immigration agent was a friendly woman in a colorful pareu—those wraparound dresses of the South Pacific—whose main focus was to ensure that Zinc had his ticket home. When you guard the gates of paradise, there is no such thing as a one-way trip.

Having cleared customs—he just strolled over, picked up his bag and walked away—the Canadian changed some money for New Zealand dollars at the Westpac bank, then he was directed outside to the minibus going to his resort.

Cook Islanders drive on the left-hand side of the road. Hoping to get a feel for the island along the route, Zinc sat in the front seat over the wheel well beside the driver. The Ara Metua—also called the Great Road of Toi, though today no one knows who Toi was— was built around the coast of Rarotonga in the eleventh century. The modern road runs parallel to it along the beach, so a bus that leaves from the airport has one of two routes to follow. The sign in the windshield will tell you if it is heading "Clockwise" or "Counterclockwise." From the bumpiness of the ride he took through the sticky predawn night, Zinc would have sworn the bus had wandered onto the Ara Metua by mistake.

The airport—a single runway along the north coast—was about a mile west of Avarua, the capital of the Cooks and the island's principal town. The clockwise journey bounced Zinc along the main street of what would turn into a lazy little South Seas port and trading center in the heat of the day but was now abandoned. Past the Punanga Nui open-air market with its fruit and vegetable stalls; past the rinky-dink national police headquarters that made the Mountie grin (for it seemed barely big enough to house enough officers to patrol the island on bikes); past the central traffic circle with its Seven-in-One Coconut Tree, a ring of palms that legend says grew out of one nut with seven sprouts; past the harborfront wreck of the SS *Maitai,* the old Union Steam Ship vessel that used to trade between here and Tahiti before it went down with a cargo of Model T Fords in 1916, but which is of far greater historical importance for bequeathing its name to the rum cocktail; past the inland Papeiha Stone, upon which the first missionary stood in 1823 to preach the initial gospel to the cannibals; and past the lordly CICC church, a lovely whitewashed mission made of coral that the London Missionary Society erected in 1853 on the site of the most sacred *marae*—or religious meeting ground—in Rarotonga, just to make certain the islanders understood who was taking over and replacing their gods.

So tired was the Mountie from his sleepless flight that the bus ride that circled southeast from the edge of town through rural countryside to Muri Beach slipped by his peripheral vision in a surrealistic blur. Zinc was vaguely aware that mountains rose inland to his right, and that waves broke on the reef to his left. At

Matavera, about halfway to his destination, the fine old Christian church was lit up white in the blackness, but the graves that should populate its graveyard were scattered far and wide. Converts they might be, but Cook Islanders still clung to their old cannibal ways in that they dug the graves of their ancestors next to their houses, instead of discarding them in some common dumping ground. And just this side of Muri Beach, the site of Zinc's resort, another weird dichotomy lurked in the dark.

He caught sight of the large white Ngatangiia church looming on the inland flank of the shoreline road. Off the coast and to the south, four smaller islands—or *motus*—lined the reef. North of the northernmost of those *motus,* between it and a headland on the Rarotongan coast, a deep passage through the reef led into Avana Harbor. A popular mooring spot for visiting yachts and small fishing boats, the harbor marked the starting point for one of the great epic voyages of the South Pacific. It was here, in about AD 1350, that a fleet of canoes from throughout what are now the Cook Islands embarked on the Great Migration, which resulted in the settling of New Zealand by those Maoris whose cannibalism so shocked Captain Cook.

Though Zinc couldn't make them out in the dark, a circle of seven stones dotted the grassy park opposite the Christian church. Each stone represented one of the seven Great Canoes that completed the voyage. Out on the point of land that abutted the harbor could still be found the well-preserved *marae* where the mariners sought help for a safe journey by sacrificing humans to their gods.

———•—•———

"Kia Orana"—"Hello"—said the wooden sign over the open entrance to the Muri Lagoon Resort. Lining the lot out front was a string of motorbikes, the transport of choice for the island's few good roads. A walkway ran between two ponds fed by fountains to guide the bleary-eyed guest to the reception desk inside the thatch-roofed villa. With several high stools to sit on, the desk belonged

more in a bar than it did in a classy hotel. As the solitary night clerk checked him in, Zinc looked around. A basket of umbrellas waited by the door for those who ventured out into the sudden squalls that could blow in at any time in the South Seas. Time itself was tracked by a line of clocks on one wall: Rarotonga, Auckland, Sydney, London, Frankfurt and Los Angeles. Such labels spoke volumes about who frequented the Cooks.

"Mosquitoes bad?" Zinc asked.

"No," replied the clerk.

"Then why the mosquito coils?"

"Precaution, sir. There's dengue fever on the island, and that you don't want to get."

"Oh," said Zinc. "So play it safe at night?"

"No, sir. Play it safe in the morning with a spray of DEET. That's when the bug bites."

"Symptoms?"

"Headache, fever, severe joint and muscle pain, and rash. Some of those bitten require a blood transfusion."

"Is that all?"

A pause.

"Death if you're unlucky."

Zinc made a mental note to buy some DEET.

The unit assigned to the Mountie was one of the lagoon villas, so he followed the night porter–cum–security guard past the book-exchange shelf (where beach reading was swapped) and the one communal TV, out into lush gardens ripe with night scents, to wend their way through the dark foliage toward the lulling sound of surf breaking on the reef.

"Just one TV?"

"Yes, sir."

"How do you prevent fights over what to watch?"

"We get only one channel in the Cooks, and it broadcasts just some of the time."

His villa was hot and stuffy from lack of air-conditioning. To conserve electricity, which on some of the outer islands works in fits and starts, the AC operates only when activated by the tag of your room key. Ergo, if you're not in the room, no cool air. The porter showed Zinc the ins and outs of his accommodation, then wished him a good night's sleep—or what was left of it. It seemed strange to the Canadian not to tip the man. Tipping was discouraged in the Cooks.

The siren call of the South Seas lured Zinc out through the sliding glass door while his villa cooled down. The patio that bordered the beach was arched by coconut palms, and strung between two of the trunks was an inviting hammock. Swinging his exhausted body into the meshed net, he gazed up through the swaying black fronds at the pinpricked dome full of stars. The warm wind off the reef had a velvet touch as it rocked him in this Snugli slung around Mother Nature's neck. Waves lapped the sandy shore of the lagoon, while out there where starlight glinted on the crests of breakers, the sea rolled over the coral barricade with a constant low rumble. A whiff of coconut oil from the palms and their scattered nuts took the raw edge off the salty scent of brine. Like those feathered fans used by Las Vegas showgirls to reveal and cover themselves in striptease revues, the fronds above opened and closed with a soft clatter with every gust of breeze.

Zinc remembered how as a lad he used to stretch out on the grass of the Saskatchewan farm and stare up in wonder at the summer stars that shone down on the golden flatlands. The longer he gazed, the more insignificant he felt, and that made him ask those age-old questions that perplex all of us: Where did I come from? What am I doing here? Where am I going? There was a night, he could recall, when he peered *too* hard into the vastness of the cosmos and almost lost his grip on the here and now. The earth had begun to spin as if he were dizzy drunk, and Zinc felt as if his mind were being sucked into another dimension.

He was out there for the blink of an eye. It was almost an occult experience.

Twice as many first-magnitude stars illuminate the heavens of the southern hemisphere. Lying in the hammock rocked by the trade winds, Zinc peered up at the awesome stellar display. He took in the Milky Way, which spilled across the celestial vault, and the Clouds of Magellan, which floated away, and the bright bulbs of the Centaur and the Southern Cross, out in front. With no pollution between him and them, the stars seemed to have multiplied a hundredfold. So bright were the diamonds dazzling his eyes that Zinc could believe the light of heaven burst through those pinpricks in its black screen.

Are you up there, Alex? he wondered.

And drifted off to sleep.

———•—•———

"Zinc?"

She was calling to him from the great beyond.

"Zinc?"

He struggled to open his eyes against the blinding glare.

When he did, he saw Alexis Hunt gazing down at him, the nimbus around her head as auroral as an angel's halo.

"Wake up," she said. "*Tempus fugit*, Mr. Van Winkle."

Zinc blinked.

"Yvette?"

"The one and only, Sleepy. Who did you think it was? The Hunchback of Notre Dame?"

He tried to sit up and almost flipped out of the hammock onto the sandy beach.

"It was tempting," Yvette said. "What with you sleeping as sound as a baby in that Dennis the Menace slingshot. How I would have loved to pull you back in your elastic pouch, then let go to catapult you into the sea. I'll bet that would have woken you up."

"What time is it?"

"Time for a quick dip. Then time for breakfast. Then time to catch a plane."

"What are you doing here?"

"Bad beer," she said. "It's a long, sad tale of woe. I'll regale you over breakfast."

He managed to swing out of the hammock and gain his feet, a Herculean effort that made every joint ache. With one hand in the small of his back, he moaned as he stretched out the kinks. How did Cook's crew sleep for years in those nautical hammocks?

"Oh-oh," Yvette teased. "Is your body seizing up? Perhaps there's someone younger here to play with me."

Backed by the blazing disk of the sun above the offshore horizon, Yvette was a dark silhouette encased in solar light. But as she retreated and sidestepped a pace or two to search up and down the arc of sand for Mr. Youthful, the shadowed apparition came into her own in the Mountie's eyes.

The sight took his breath away.

Even without her in it, the vista was a stunner. Glaring white sand stretched left and right as far as he could fathom. The inland edge of the pristine beach danced hypnotically with the shade cast by swaying palm fronds. The closer the wide swath of shore got to the lagoon, the brighter and bluer the shimmer that rose with its heat, until the sand slipped away beneath the lapping water where hermit crabs skittered through bits of coral. Bluer and bluer its hue became as the lagoon deepened, and Zinc had no idea which tint best described such allure: azure? turquoise? aquamarine? or a palette of all three? So transparent was the tranquil sea within the reef that he could see heads of brain coral submerged beneath its surface and the colorful tropical fish that swam around them like lazy ideas. Out where the Pacific foamed white over the underwater ramparts of the sunken reef, the protective barrier surfaced as a line of four green islets—the *motus*—ringed with sand and crowned by palms. Farther still, puffs of white cloud dotted a light blue sky that stretched forever across the endless deep blue sea.

But all of that was just the frame around *her*.

If Yvette Theron had stopped the Mountie dead in his tracks at the Seattle convention, that was a prelude compared with the whammy that flattened him now. As lithe and lean as only youth can bestow, her body was accented by electric blue. The flimsy triangles that held her breasts were tied at the back of her neck and cupped their bounty in such a way that she needn't have worn a top. The bottom of her bikini was hidden in the hip-hugging wrap of an ankle-length matching blue pareu, except that its cloth was patterned with white hibiscuses and flame-shaped red leaves. Was the bottom beneath as skimpy as the top? he wondered. Around her ankle was a bracelet of tiny white shells.

"Nope," she said. "No better playmate."

With a languid move as calculated as Gypsy Rose Lee's, she tugged the pareu free from her waist. Closing in on Zinc, who still stood by the hammock, she looped the garment around his neck like she might a lasso. Her sunglasses were pushed up on top of her head. Her blonde hair, ruffled by the offshore breeze, had a life of its own. A bloodred flower was tucked behind her ear. And those eyes, the shade of one of the hues in the lagoon beyond, seemed to tug him into her like a magnetic dream.

The pareu slipped through her fingers until it hung free around her captive. Turning, Yvette strolled away toward the beckoning lagoon. His eyes slipped down her hourglass figure to her long and shapely legs, then back up to the bikini bottom.

Suddenly she stopped and looked over her shoulder.

"Well, are you going to join me?"

"Sure," he said, and followed.

"If I were you," she said, "I'd change into my trunks. You might sleep in your clothes. But swimming in them is a little much."

———◦◦———

"Here's to bad beer," he said, raising his coffee cup.

"I can't toast that, Zinc. It made them *really* sick."

"Made who sick?"

"Most of the Odyssey writers."

"Bad beer?"

"*Bush* beer. Bad home brew."

"Where was that?"

"On Atiu. At the *tumunu*."

Refreshed by that morning frolic in Muri Lagoon, Zinc and Yvette were eating breakfast in the beachfront restaurant. The open-air octagon-shaped hut sat at the point where a stream that snaked through the lush resort fed the sea. In the light of day, the dark grounds through which the Mountie had followed the night porter a few hours ago were bursting with the riotous red, yellow, orange and pink blossoms of torch gingers, fruit salad, monkey tails, hibiscus, frangipani, golden trumpets and tropical snow planted in a manicured jungle of green, green, green. Beyond the railing beside their table on the perimeter deck of the hut, a school of mullet fish swam in lilied waters stalked by a predatory eel.

"Eat up," Yvette said. "We have to catch a plane."

"The Odyssey continues?"

"With diminished ranks."

"Who survived the bad beer?"

"Bret, Wes, Petra, me and two lawyers-slash-wannabe writers."

"Where are they now?"

"On Atiu. Waiting for us."

"*Us?* They know I'm coming?"

"I spilled the beans. That's how I got to accompany the poisoned ones back here. To pick you up."

"Poisoned?"

"Get your food. Time is tight."

The buffet breakfast was laid out in the center of the thatched hut. The roof was supported by several poles sheathed with green fronds, the ribs of each palm radiating out from a vertical spine. Suspended over the table spread with tropical fare, an old wooden outrigger canoe hung in a fishing net. As he stocked his plate with fresh papaw, starfruit, guava, pineapple, coconut meat, and grapefruit that tasted like lime, Zinc prayed that the meshes above weren't rotten from brine. The cop knew he was Down Under—in the case of the boat, *literally*—by the Kiwi and Aussie voices he heard using colloquialisms like "poor bloke" and "mate" and "bit of a shocker" in accents that complemented tossing another shrimp on the barbie. That this was a parallel world to his was obvious from brand names. Nothing was packaged as it should be. They had Ricies instead of Rice Krispies, Skippy instead of Corn Flakes and Weetabix instead of Shredded Wheat. And why all the Germans?

Yvette was shooing the mynah birds away as Zinc returned to their table. He maneuvered around a pair of chickens pecking crumbs up off the floor, and reclaimed his seat while the pesky mynahs took to the air in a flap of white stripes on brown feathered wings and tails, amid caws of protest from their yellow beaks. A second later, they were landing on the next table.

"Damn birds," Zinc swore. "It's like that Hitchcock film."

"There's a story in this."

"Yeah? Pray tell."

"Mynah birds are native to India. Tahiti imported them in the 1800s to control coconut stick insects. The mynahs were so successful at the job that the Cooks imported them in the 1900s. They saved the coconut trees and multiplied so quickly that now they have pushed out most of Rarotonga's native birds and drive diners like us mad."

"You're a font of knowledge."

"I want to be a writer. Dig deep enough and there's a story waiting to be mined from everything."

"Can you tell me another story?"

"Sure." Yvette rubbed her hands.

"Why are there so many Germans on the island? One of the clocks in reception tracks Frankfurt."

"Easy," she replied. "The curse of *Treasure Island*."

"This I gotta hear."

"Captain Cook sailed the South Seas and grabbed lots of sand for Britain. The French colonized Polynesia too. By the time Germany came looking for its place in the sun, there was squat left. Only Samoa, which was independent."

"That was Germany's Treasure Island?"

"No, I meant the book."

"By Stevenson?"

"Yes, Robert Louis. By then, he was famous for *Treasure Island, Kidnapped, Jekyll and Hyde.* But the climate of Scotland was doing him in, and he was dying of consumption. So Stevenson left Edinburgh on a round-the-world quest to find somewhere that would alleviate his T.B. In the end, he chose Samoa.

"The Samoans took instantly to their new guest. The Scot learned their language quickly so that he could enthrall them with stories. By the time the Germans landed to stake their claim, not only was he 'Tusitala,' the Samoans' teller of tales, but they had built him a magnificent estate—Vaima—in their midst. Not impressed, the Germans ordered Stevenson off their island, and that's when the islanders pulled their knives. 'That's our Tusitala,' they said."

Zinc grinned. He could picture it.

"When Tusitala died, the Samoans hacked their way up a pinnacle of rock to bury him near the heavens. The curse of *Treasure Island* cost the Germans their colony after the First World War. So ever since, they've been forced to wander the South Pacific in search of sun under a foreign flag, and that was the *real* cause of the Second World War."

Zinc laughed. "I think your plot needs work."

"That's my story," Yvette said, "and I'm sticking to it."

He felt as if he could sit and listen to her forever. It was one of those idyllic junctures in life when everything comes together: setting, company, conversation, weather, the works. For the first time since Alex died, he was reveling in love, lust, infatuation, the whole mirage. If fate had sent the Reaper to harvest him instead of Alex, this is the outcome that he would have wished for her. To find someone new to dispel crippling memories so that life could move on.

Tempus fugit.

But still he felt guilty. Yvette was *too* young and *too* sexy.

"I'll give you another chance. Tell me the story behind bad beer," he said.

"Do you know what a *tumunu* is?"

"No idea."

"The bush-beer drinking school that survives on Atiu. As planned, the Odyssey arrived in Raro on Wednesday. The next morning, we flew to Atiu, the cannibal island. Since that's where the initial writing seminar was to be held, Bret thought it a good idea to pass his literary wisdom on to us neophytes in the traditional way."

"At a *tumunu?*"

"Uh-huh. A makeshift pub in the bush. That word actually refers to the trunk of the coconut tree—the round, thick part that's closest to the ground and can be hollowed out to make a container that holds up to forty gallons of drink."

"Of bush beer?" said Zinc.

"Not originally. In the years before Captain Cook put Atiu on his map, kava was the drink prepared in the trunk. It was made from the root of the pepper plant. Though nonalcoholic, it packed a punch. Depending on your tolerance, you got a mild buzz or were knocked flat on your butt. The *tumunu* was strictly for men. They'd sit around, get zonked, eat and talk about life."

"Eat like cannibals?"

"I suppose. When the missionaries hit the beach in the 1800s, they suppressed kava *tumunus* with their blue laws. But they also introduced oranges as food, and soon the islanders learned from white Tahitian beachcombers how to brew orange beer. If the natives thought kava was potent, that stuff was Kickapoo joy juice."

"No doubt the Bible-thumpers reveled in that."

"They tried to stamp it out, of course, but the *tumunus* moved into the bush. Word would spread as to where and when, like it does now for raves back home. The boozing was done in the bush, so it became 'bush beer.' And because the drinking sessions were how the elders passed on their wisdom, the *tumunu* became known as the 'bush-beer school.' So that's why Bret suggested it for a seminar."

"And the poison?"

"Bret paid some of the locals for use of their *tumunu* site, and for a few gallons of brew. The thirteen of us gathered in the bush to drink and talk. A bush-beer setup consists of a ring of stools cut from coconut logs, with the hollowed-out trunk in the center. The barman, or *tangata kapu*—which was Bret, in our case—sits beside the beer. He scoops a cupful out of the *tumunu* with a small coconut shell and hands it to one of those on the stools to swallow in a gulp. The drinker returns the cup to the barman to refill, then it's passed to the next in line."

"Everyone drinks from the same cup?"

"Yes," said Yvette, "unless you wave the cup by. No one is forced to drink what they don't want."

"Is that what happened there? Bret controlled the drinking?"

"Right. He filled the cup from the trunk and passed it to each of us in turn. Until most began throwing up."

"Did you drink?"

"No."

"Did Petra?"

"Don't think so."

"What about Bret and Wes?"

"I know Bret had a few. Someone made a joke about our ending up with a drunken barman."

"How does that make sense? If it was bad beer in the *tumunu,* why didn't he get sick?"

"Good question."

"Could Bret have poisoned the others?"

"What, you mean could he have scooped a cupful inside the trunk, then added poison of some sort while it was out of sight, before drawing the cup from the trunk to pass it to someone on the stools?"

"That's what I mean."

Yvette shrugged. "I guess so. But why would Bret do that? Travel with us to the Cooks, then reduce the group?"

ODYSSEY

Zinc was still packed from his overnight flight, so all he had to do to get ready to fly on to Atiu was take a quick shower and dig out fresh clothes: a tropical patterned short-sleeved shirt worn with the tail out over khaki shorts and sandals. To top it off, he plunked a wide-brimmed safari hat on his head and contemplated fastening one side up, Australian-style, but then concluded that would be geek chic in a tourist. Besides, it seemed illogical to bare one side of your face to the sun, when the purpose of wearing a hat was to protect yourself from its rays. By the time he carried his bag out to the beachside patio, Yvette sat waiting for him in a lounge chair. She had switched her hip-hugging pareu for a full-body one worn like a dress. The curvy sheath was navy blue with royal-blue marbling and a pattern of bright red-and-yellow flowers. The actual flowers behind her ear matched the print.

"Why do men always keep you waiting?" she asked.

"I had to paint my toenails."

"Excuses, excuses. One thing I'll say about the tropics is no fuss, no muss. Fuss with your makeup, muss with your hair, and you look like a clown."

"Another story?"

"Try me."

"What gives with all the tattoos?"

With breakfast over, the sand was the place to hang out. The Kiwis and the Aussies were staking their claims to wide-open plots of beach. True, this was the age of new tribalism, when body piercing, scarification and tattooing were back in vogue, but even so, the

Down Under folks were addicted to taking ink. Both genders were human canvases.

Most of the males wore surfing shorts with muscle shirts. Splotches of color on their shoulders were in, as were barbed-wire rings around their upper arms. The funny thing about guys with tattoos is that they appear to swagger, as if their balls are a little too big to fit between their thighs.

"The Kiwis are a snap," Yvette said. "Their islands once belonged to the Maoris. The Maoris were the tattooingest culture on earth. Horrific designs on their faces and full-body cover. As for Aussies, Oz began as a prison colony for transported Brits. Cons love tattoos, so ink's in their descendants' genes."

"Shh! Keep your voice down! You'll get us creamed!"

"That's my story, and I'm sticking to it."

The tattoos on the females were much subtler. The scent of exotic lotions wafted up the beach as—having set up shop with sand towels, sandals, paperbacks and peeled-off pareus—they slathered creams onto their tanned bodies in preparation for another bake. A Chinese girl had a snake tattooed the length of her spine. From his case in China and Hong Kong, Zinc recognized the symbols at top and bottom as "good luck" and "dragon." The peekaboo brigade was out in force too—those women who tucked half-hidden etchings away in their wispy bikinis, like the Amazon who stretched out facedown on the sand nearby and undid the top of her swimsuit to flash a creamy patch on the side of her patterned breast.

"You have a tattoo?" Zinc asked.

"Maybe," Yvette replied.

"I doubt it. I've seen most of you."

"But not *all* of me."

"Then I guess I'll never know," he said, sighing.

"You never know," she said.

They accompanied his luggage through the garden of Eden in the center of the resort, depositing his bag beside hers in reception while Zinc checked out. A handsome Cook Islander in a blue Polynesian shirt with a name on his tag that the Mountie couldn't pronounce processed his Visa card, then Zinc and Yvette boarded the airport bus.

"*Kia Orana*"—"Hello"—read the overhead welcome sign at their backs.

The literal translation was "May you live."

Which was more to the point.

------•-•------

The bus continued clockwise around the island, in the same direction as that driven when Zinc had arrived. As it rounded the west coast to reach the airport along the northwest shore, it passed a big white missionary church in Arorangi village, the first to be built on the island, in 1849. Just up the road from it and before a nine-hole golf course, Yvette pointed down to the beach.

"Black Rock," she said.

"I saw that film."

"*Bad Day at Black Rock*? I saw it too."

"Spencer Tracy."

"The one-armed man. He lays Ernest Borgnine flat with a karate chop."

"You like old movies?"

"Better than the shit Hollywood turns out these days," she replied.

"Why so much crap?"

"They ceased buying novels. Instead, Hollywood churns out plots with no foundation. Like buildings, they topple."

Not only did Yvette *look* like Alex, but their interests ran parallel too.

Another writer.

Another retro addict.

"Petra's the expert on missionaries." Again, Yvette indicated the passing beach. "I think it's some sort of *danse macabre* between her and her dad."

"The preacher's daughter," said Zinc.

"It can really screw you up. Anything you need for a plot, just ask her. Black Rock is where the spirits of the dead departed from Rarotonga for their voyage back to Avaiki."

"Hawaii? A land of ghosts? I thought that was where zonked-out surfers went to wear puka shells?"

"It sounds like Hawaii, but it's not. In fact, Hawaii takes its name from the mythical Avaiki. Polynesians viewed the universe as the hollow of a vast coconut shell. Avaiki was at the center. They had no conception of a creator. Instead, they believed that their islands had been dragged up out of the depths of Avaiki—the Netherworld—otherwise known as Po, or the Night. These islands were merely the gross outward form, or body, so the spirits of the dead returned to Avaiki and added their ethereal essence to the other world."

"From Black Rock?"

"Uh-huh. From the beach below. So imagine what Cook Islanders must have thought in 1823 when Papeiha, the first Christian missionary, waded ashore to the same beach clasping the Bible over his head to bring the word of God from a distant realm."

"I'll bet there's a story in *that*," Zinc teased.

"Tinomana was the local cannibal chief. He challenged Papeiha to eat a banana roasted on a burning idol from his sacred *marae*. When the missionary didn't drop dead on the spot, the chief became the first Cook Islander to convert. Within a year, all the idols on Raro had been overthrown and burned. Tinomana gave the missionaries the land for the church we just passed. Papeiha is buried in the center of its graveyard, beneath the giant monument erected by his descendants. The missionary married the daughter of the chief, but Tinomana isn't buried at the church. Instead, his bones are up on the hill behind Arorangi, near the old *marae* from his cannibal days."

"Is there a moral?"

"There's certainly a question. Did the chief have second thoughts about the new religion?"

Daylight had downscaled the Rarotonga airport appreciably. Gone was the Air New Zealand Boeing 767 jet from the single runway's ramp, and in its stead sat a tiny eighteen-passenger Air Rarotonga Bandeirante turboprop. The plane was a dainty little thing. The white fuselage ran back to a two-toned blue tail patterned with three pink flowers. The pilots looked like a pair of kindergarten kids strolling toward a toy plane in their schoolboy duds: blue shorts and white kneesocks, gray shirts with blue epaulets, and aviator shades. Zinc felt like Gulliver in Lilliput, for everything about this island was on a miniature scale. The building beside the runway and closer to the shore was erected in 1973 as a hostel for the New Zealand workers who had been imported to construct the airport to bring tourists to the islands. It was now the Cook Islands Parliament, and the bedrooms were the offices of the prime minister and other officials.

The interisland check-in was an open-air shed. The boarding gate was a hole in a hedge. A swath of grass with benches served as a waiting lounge. The red Coke machine had an "Out of Order" sign. Beside it was a green doghouse with round holes cut in the roof. "Cans Only" said the sign above a red maple leaf; the words "Canadian International Development Agency" were written on the side.

"Typical," said Yvette.

"How so?" asked Zinc.

"The Americans make the litter, and we clean it up."

"Shh!" he shushed. "You'll get us creamed!"

Security did not involve a rectal search. Instead, the Mountie and Yvette simply walked through the hedge and across the scorching Tarmac to the stairs up into the plane, which pulled down out of the fuselage like a stepping stool. If it was hot outside, it was an oven within. A single file of seats flanked each side of the aisle back to a bench in the rear. Sweat was dripping off Zinc by the time he buckled himself into the front row. His seat was 1G, which made no sense. The turboprop was just outside his window. He knew of a case in North America where a prop had spun off a plane and slashed into the fuselage to decapitate a passenger sitting in the front row.

The Bandeirante buzzed like a hornet on takeoff. Sunlight glinted off the silver nose cone of the prop as they lifted up, up and away. Since the takeoff was out to sea to the west, and the island of Atiu was back to the east, the plane banked sharply and gave Zinc a bird's-eye look down on Rarotonga. Being the only high volcanic island in the Cooks, it was a mountainous maze of razorback ridges, steep valleys and tumbling white cascades. The mountains were what remained of the rim of the volcanic cone, and except for a jutting spike of rock known as the Needle, the highlands were covered with dense green jungle. As Zinc's eyes plunged down the inclines to Muri Lagoon, they picked out white goats and black pigs grazing in papaw patches and citrus groves, and men with shovels digging out swampy taro fields.

"See where we were?" Yvette asked, leaning across the aisle. She had to shout over the droning of the engines and the whooshing of air that did little to quell the oven heat.

"Yeah, I see the *motus*. And the passage through the reef."

"There's a story behind that."

"Do I want to know?" Zinc joshed.

"In less than forty-five minutes, we'll land on Atiu. Both Bret and Wes are going to wonder why you're there. Your cover story is that like the burnt-out lawyers on the Odyssey, you hope writing will be a ticket out of your current job. The theme of this junket is cannibal plots. Does it not behoove you as a cop to show as much interest in your new career as possible?"

"Feed me," Zinc said.

"The Cook Islands are the crossroads of the South Pacific. What's ironic is that Cook all but ignored them. His paradises were Tahiti to the east and Tonga to the west. The only Cook Island that Cook actually set foot on was the deserted atoll of Palmerston. He named them the Hervey Islands, after some insignificant British admiral. Half a century later, the Herveys were renamed the Cooks by a Russian cartographer to honor the captain who had sailed them."

Zinc knew that. But he loved to hear her talk. And it didn't hurt to see down her neckline while Yvette leaned over.

"What would you call the Cooks?" he asked.

"I'd call them the Blighs."

"After the *Bounty*?"

"Yes," she said. "Captain Bligh discovered Aitutaki to the north in 1789. Seventeen days later, en route to Tonga, the mutiny occurred. The *Bounty,* under Fletcher Christian, discovered Rarotonga while sailing the South Seas to find a place to hide from the British navy. Their hunters—Captain Edwards on HMS *Pandora*—came through too. And a few years later, Bligh returned. A lot of thrilling history played out here, so I think Captain Bligh should get the nod."

"Is that your story?"

"No, that's the buildup. The *Bounty* discovered Rarotonga, but the mutineers didn't land. The next ship that passed by found sandalwood in the sea, a valuable commodity in Asia for making incense joss sticks. So an Australian sandalwood company sent Capt. Philip Goodenough and the *Cumberland* to Rarotonga in 1814 to harvest that plant. Goodenough took his female companion, Ann Butcher, along, so she became the first European woman in the Cooks. The whites came ashore at Muri Lagoon and stayed for three months. Eventually, a series of squabbles arose. The sailors hauled local women off to the ship for sex. On discovering *nono,* a plant that produces yellow dye, they dug it up in front of the sacred *marae.* And when they tried to steal a hoard of coconuts from the wrong man, all hell broke loose. One by one, the whites were chased down, hacked apart and eaten. Ann Butcher was abducted by a cannibal named Moe. His plan was to take her as a lover, but another lust got the better of him. As Goodenough sailed away to save his sorry ass, she was being butchered and roasted on a spit."

"That was the layer of history under our feet?"

"What do you think? It's a true story."

"With a lot of play on words. Ann got cooked in the Cook Islands. Goodenough's girlfriend was good enough to eat. And the cannibal who abducted her butchered Ann Butcher."

"Mind if I use that?" Yvette asked.

"Be my guest."

"That's the story I plan to write out of this Odyssey. I'm going to tell it from Ann's point of view."

Sunlight streamed into that side of the plane. Through the opening into the cockpit, Zinc watched the pilot wedge a square of cardboard into his side window as a sunscreen. After read-justing a dial to trim the plane, he went back to reading a binder entitled "Operating Manual." Zinc hoped he was studying to upgrade to another model, and not to learn about the one they were in.

Glancing out his window, he gazed down at the dark blue sea. The shadow of the plane slipped across it like a sleek-nosed shark. The bright blue sky was wisped with white clouds, behind which peeked the face of a faint moon.

Zinc's ears popped as the plane began its sharp descent. Ahead, he spied a flat verdant island, with no visible settlements around its rocky coast. Foaming white, the narrow reef seemed more like a shelf in the sea, as if the entire island had been jacked up a notch or two. Here and there, a shallow bay indented the shore.

"Cannibal Island," Yvette announced, a mite too loud on account of her plugged ears.

Zinc craned around in his seat to assess if any islanders behind him had overheard, then realized to his chagrin that he and Yvette were the only tourists on board. The rest of the passengers were Polynesian, and probably flying home. Most of the females were heavyset, because starches make up all the staple foods. They were dressed in free-flowing shifts with bright flower patterns, and some were wrangling fidgety kids with topknots in their hair. With their golden skin, dark locks, broad faces and fingers as plump as sausages, the men looked unlikely to run from a fight. The hulks behind both Yvette and Zinc could wrestle as a tag team with the WWF. One wore a straw hat with a chevron band that matched the tattoo etched around his neck. The other could be a pirate from bygone days, with his shaved head, goatee, bandana, earrings and similar tattoos.

"*Kia orana,*" the Mountie said.

The Cook Islander smiled. "Don't worry," he soothed. "We won't eat you."

The killers of both Hanged Man victims and the Cthulhu sculptor stood beside the makeshift runway of crushed rock, shielding their eyes with the palms of their hands to watch the plane that carried Zinc and Yvette descend out of the shimmering sky.

"Think we gaffed him?"

"We'll know soon enough. What about the spearguns?"

"They're in that carryall."

"Did you see the sign above the departure gate? 'Please Check All AK-47s, Hand Grenades and Nukes at Security!'"

"Someone has a sense of humor. You'd never see that back home. Spearguns are common, so we're okay. Spearfishing is widely promoted to draw sportsmen to the Cooks."

"We're going after *bigger* fish."

"That we are. Get spiked with one of those barbs and you'll bleed like a stuck pig."

"Pun intended?"

"Our pig is gonna squeal. Are you sure you're able to go through with this?"

"What? Eat him alive?"

"It's a big step. The last taboo."

"A year and a half went into planning the Ripper's revenge. You know what he says about revenge being a dish best served cold? I'm here to party. Bring it on. You fuck her. I'll fuck him. Then we'll eat that fucking pig's pork down to the bone."

CANNIBAL ISLAND

Atiu, Cook Islands

Petra Zydecker was waiting at the foot of the dinky stairs that had been lowered out of the plane. As Zinc stepped down onto the hot concrete slab that acted as an airport apron, she draped a lei—called an *ei kaki* in the Cooks—around his neck. The white-and-yellow flowers of the garland necklace emitted a pungent scent.

"In your golden years," Petra said, "you can tell your grandkids that you got leied by the goth queen of Cannibal Island."

"Thanks," said Zinc.

"Meitaki ma'ata."

"You look . . . comfortable."

"I'm the scandal of the island. You won't believe how religiously repressed Atiu is. If you stroll through town in a bikini, the locals worry that you're walking past their church in your underwear. You'd never guess I'm a preacher's daughter, eh?"

"Actually, you would," Zinc said dryly.

Black was still her color, even when she was almost stripped to her skin. The black silk that slinked around her body at the World Horror Convention had been shed like a black mamba snake's scales for a black bikini and a black pareu the size of the miniest of miniskirts. Cleavage to rival Morticia's or Vampirella's was wantonly on display, while her pale flesh, pinking from the sun despite a slather of sunblock, oozed sweat in the most erotic way. Her glossy black hair, still parted down the middle and still curving around her face like pincers, couldn't rein in those wayward hanks that stuck to her damp cheeks. Despite the heat, her lips and nails were lacquered black, and that all-consuming color was picked up by her tattoos, delicate Gothic designs etched on her upper arms. Even the lei around her neck that hid the string of baby's teeth was of natural or dyed black flowers.

"I'm hurt," pouted Petra.

"Oh? Why's that?"

"Did I not invite you down here at the horror convention? Instead, you jilted me to fuck Yvette Goody Two-shoes."

"I'm not fucking her."

"Not yet. But somehow I doubt you came down here for the glare of the sun."

"I came to learn how to write. What about you?"

"Write? Me too. You may have heard it said that a picture is worth a thousand words. Cannibals and converts—that's what Atiu is about. Let me tell you, Officer, there's *dark* inspiration here. On the part of both the people-eaters and the missionaries."

"So who's your current patron of the arts? Bret or Wes?"

"Bret. Wes. Both. Neither. What does it matter? In my realm, I'm my own woman. I fuck who I want to fuck."

"Not me," said Zinc.

"Uh-huh. That depends on Yvette. If she doesn't feed your libido, I may just eat you up."

Lord knows what the Atiuan passengers thought as they filed past the *papa'as*. *Papa'a*—"four skins"—is what the islanders call Europeans and other foreigners. It refers to the four skins—jacket, shirt, singlet and their own skin—that the first explorers wore. Also, because Cook Island males are circumcised in a manhood ritual at age twelve, the term can be derogatory.

As the first person off the plane, Yvette was already shaded in the terminal, which was nothing more than an open walk-through shed beside the rural runway. It served as a gathering place for passengers and baggage. The baggage on this plane was stored in a compartment behind the left-side wing, and while Zinc and Petra were sparring by the steps in front, the ground crew—such as it was—had unloaded the cargo onto a pull cart powered by human sweat. The *papa'as* followed their bags into the terminal.

"Well, well," Lister said. "Who do we have here?"

"Hello, Bret," Zinc replied.

"Come to extradite me?"

"No, to learn how to write. You did offer an Odyssey opening to those at the convention, didn't you? Well, I got to thinking about it and decided what the hell."

"So here you are?"

"Here I am."

"Sneaking aboard like a stowaway."

"How so? I asked Yvette to make arrangements for me. Should I have gone to you? Besides, you're lucky I showed up. The rumor is you put half your students in the hospital."

"That was bad beer."

"I'm glad I don't drink."

Bret Lister looked like a high-strung man teetering on a tightrope. Though it was high noon in the tropics and everyone else was feeling the heat, the lawyer-turned-writer was pacing the shed like a doomed man at the hour of his execution. The black bags under his eyes cried out for sleep; it was as if he hadn't stopped going since the Odyssey began, which made the Mountie wonder if Bret was hyped on coke or speed. The wild and glassy glare of his eyes suited the weed patch of stubble sprouting from his bony jaws, while the sinews in his long and lanky frame—revealed around the edges of his open sweat-stained shirt—had bowstring tautness. Bret was ready for action and itching to have it start. He was also in need of a shower, not having bathed for days.

"Ignore him, Chandler. His time has passed. Bret's not the *ariki* he thinks he is."

Wes Grimmer had entered the terminal through the opposite door. He and two white men Zinc didn't recognize—wannabe writers who had survived the bad beer—were lugging baggage in from a truck parked outside. The name of a local guest house was painted in fading letters on the driver's door.

"Gone native, Wes?" the Mountie asked.

"You've heard of method acting? Try method writing."

The Stanislavski method of acting says a performer must identify with the character he is to portray. Zinc had once heard a funny anecdote about Dustin Hoffman and Laurence Olivier on the set of *Marathon Man* in 1976. To prepare himself to play the character of Babe and attain the necessary frazzled state for a scene, Hoffman hadn't slept for days. When Olivier—the greatest actor of his generation—showed up for his role, the Old School thespian was unimpressed. "Good lord, old boy," he said. "Why don't you try *acting*?"

It was hard to fathom what role Grimmer was trying to immerse himself in for his art, but whatever it was, his method was permanent. Not only had he shaved his head down to the scalp, but his bare biceps flaunted old tattoos in the repeated blue-black chevron pattern of Atiu cannibals from the time before Captain Cook. Seeing him now in a loose green muscle shirt and khaki safari shorts, Zinc grasped how powerfully built the younger lawyer-turned-writer was. If they shoved each other to the brink of throwing punches, the Mountie would bet his life's savings on Wes, not Bret.

"Hi," Zinc said to the two unknowns. "I'm Zinc Chandler."

"Miles Yeager."

"Bill Pigeon."

The three men shook hands. The two lawyers, both in their forties, had the bearing of button-down paper-pushers suffering midlife crises. Zinc could picture them toiling in cubicles in any one of the firms that occupy ten floors of the phallic towers that litter every city's downtown core. Tied to computers that assess every billable hour against what the minions actually bank, the ones seen as underachievers would have their ears boxed by the board. Likely, this pair dreamed of writing that humongous best-seller so they could shove their ground-down misery up the butts of their corporate tormentors and listen each morning to the traffic report that applied to commuting grunts before getting down to writing a paragraph or two.

"You look macho, Wes."

"*Mana,* Bret. *Mana.*"

"So you're the new *ariki?*"

"*Taunga,* fella."

"What's up with you two?" Zinc said. "Are you going to go *mano a mano* for the entire trip?"

"*Mana a mana,*" Petra corrected. A sketch pad in her lap, the goth queen had plunked herself down on a bench with her back in one corner of the hut. From how she kept eyeing him, Zinc suspected that he was being rendered for posterity.

"Would you guys speak English?" Yeager bristled.

"Yeah," Pigeon agreed. "I didn't pay all this money for a squabble that needs subtitles."

Yeager nodded. "What *are* you talking about?"

"Good question," Grimmer said. "And one that goes straight to the heart of why we're here. Let's get this gear on the baggage cart, then I'll tell you a story."

The check-in area was kitty-corner to where they were now. The *papa'as* were in the far corner, beside the exit out to the road. As the men relayed the pile of gear across to the ground crew's station for transport out to the plane, Yvette came out of the primitive toilet. Glancing in her direction put a smile on Zinc's face. Some wag had posted a sign on the departure exit that read "Gate 2." The matching sign for "Gate 1" was above the door into the toilet Yvette had used.

"April 3, 1777," Grimmer said, once the seven had gathered again in the back corner, "Captain Cook discovered Atiu." He held aloft a map of the circular island. "We're up here." He pointed to the runway along the north coast. "Cook's crew—but not Cook himself—went ashore at Orovaru beach, down here"—his finger arced around to the west coast—"to fetch feed for the animals on the *Resolution* and the *Discovery.* Three boats of white sailors landed, along with the Tahitian interpreter whom Cook had taken back to England on his previous voyage."

"Omai," said Zinc.

"Someone's done his homework."

"I told you I came to write."

"Anyway," the lawyer continued, "they were met on the beach by armed Atiuans, who escorted them into the jungle along a paved path to the Orongo *marae*. The *marae* was an open-air ritual grove where sacrifices—including human sacrifices—were made to pagan gods. Vestiges of that *marae* can still be seen."

"How come we missed them?" Pigeon asked.

"Medical emergency, thanks to Bret's bad beer. I'll take you there when we return."

"What happened to Cook's crew?"

"The Atiuans sat them down to watch a day of dancing. They met the *ariki*—the high chief—while his people worked themselves up into a frenzy. You saw how Cook Islanders dance our first night in Rarotonga. All that sexual energy, with knee-knocking and hip thrusts, displayed by the men. As for the women, they shimmy their booties so fast that you can barely see them because the historical root of all dancing was to honor Tangaroa, the god of fertility and the sea. In the pantheon of Cook Islanders' deities, he was one of the two cannibal gods that kept an oven for humans."

"Tangaroa?" Yeager said. "That's where we're going."

"The island named for him."

"Who was the other cannibal god?"

"Rongo, the god of war and ruler of the invisible world."

True to Gothic form, Petra carried a black beach bag. Setting aside her sketch pad, the goth queen rummaged in the bag until she withdrew a miniature souvenir idol of Tangaroa. The squat, ugly, but well-endowed figure was the symbol of the Cooks, and as such was on the islands' one-dollar coin. Petra's tiny idol was as tacky as they come. Hung like a bull, so to speak, its spring-loaded pop-up penis jerked erect with a flip of her finger.

"Show and tell," she said.

"A huge idol of Tangaroa stood in the center of the Orongo *marae* as Cook's crew watched the dancers. When the Atiuans began to dig a big underground oven for a feast, Omai freaked out. So worried was he that they were about to become part of the menu that he asked the *ariki* flat out if they were going to be eaten. The chief expressed shock at such an outlandish thought, but that was enough for the *papaas,* and they got the hell out of there. The crew safely aboard, Cook sailed away. It would be forty-odd years before the next whites came, and when they did, in 1823, what the Reverend John Williams of the London Missionary Society saw on Atiu and the nearby islands was an all-out bloodbath being waged by Rongomatane, a voracious cannibal chief."

Now back at her sketching, Petra stuck her thumb out toward Zinc and closed one eye.

"Rongo?" said Yeager. "Any relation?"

"Rongomatane, the cannibal chief, was Rongo, the cannibal god, incarnate on Atiu."

From the glowering scowl around Bret's eyes, it was obvious to Zinc that he was the odd man out. Here, as at the horror convention, Lister's star position had dulled in the glare of the center-stage limelight that Wes focused relentlessly on himself. Seeing how the Odyssey was Bret's idea to start with, that in itself would have been galling enough. But added to that volatile mix was the sexual put-down, for it was certain from the way the goth queen exchanged conspiratorial glances with Wes that, having tried out both lawyers-turned-writers in bed, Petra had rejected Bret in favor of his virile young rival.

"What Wes is trying to get across in his muddled way is this," said Bret. "'Write about what you know' is the rule of thumb in the scribbler biz. To write, you must have something interesting to write about. What the Odyssey has done, is doing and will do for you is lay out an overload of cannibalistic details that you can weave into a story. The technique used in writing courses to allow the natural writers to shine is to give the class a smattering of uncon-nected details—say, a wedding ring, a dead crow, a bolt of lightning and an old stove in an antique store—from which to pen a story in a set length of time. Well, on the Odyssey, you're getting the goods without the time limit. What you create is up to you, but look at the possibilities. Not only have you escaped from the stress of your everyday traps to this paradise in the South Seas, but you also have the spare time, the perfect location and the ideal inspiration to produce a thrilling story. Cannibalism is the last taboo. Not for nothing is Hannibal Lecter an icon for our age. Remember *Robinson Crusoe? Swiss Family Robinson?* Tom Hanks in *Cast Away?* Well, let those be your inspiration on Tangaroa. If you can't concoct fiction out of this trip, don't give up your day job."

"I'm going to write about Ann Butcher," Yvette stated.

"Who's she?" Pigeon asked.

"The first white woman eaten in the Cooks."

"Thank you, Brother Bret, for that clarification," said Wes. "As I recall, you had the floor yesterday at the *tumunu,* until your deadly brew sent half of us to hospital. Now it's time for someone else to have a say. But I do appreciate your giving us a good example of why Cook Islanders ate their neighbors."

"Get to the point," said Bret.

"*Mana,* folks. *Mana.* Focus on that word. *Mana* is the Polynesian concept of spiritual power or influence. Everyone has *mana* to a certain degree. But because the ancient islanders believed that the *ariki*—their high chief—was chosen by the gods, he wielded *mana ariki* through control of *tapu.* When Captain Cook first heard that word, he wrote it down as 'taboo.'"

"Same meaning?" Yeager asked.

"Yes and no," said Grimmer. "We use 'taboo' to mean that which is prohibited or banned. That which is bad. In the cannibal Cooks, it meant that which for supernatural reasons was sacred and forbidden for general use. Since the *ariki*—as the gods incarnate on earth—could determine on a day-to-day basis what was or wasn't *tapu,* that—in combination with his inherent *mana*—gave him control over his people even though he lacked the physical means to enforce his will."

"Get to the point," Bret goaded.

"The point is that cannibalism may be the last taboo for those who control us in modern times, but to Cook Islanders back then, cannibalism was never *tapu.* Why? Because in the islands, unlike other parts of the world, humans weren't eaten as a protein supplement. By consuming the flesh of an enemy killed in battle, not only did you add his *mana* to your own by supernatural acquisition, thereby increasing your power in this world, but you also exacted delicious revenge. What greater insult could there be than to devour him down to the bones and defecate him out as a pile of shit? Revenge was the fuel that fired vendetta raids for generations. Every insult had to be avenged by pillaging the *mana* of your enemy. If satisfaction couldn't be attained right away, a tattoo mark was recorded on your throat. If a father died unavenged, the tattoo mark was transferred to his son. Such marks could descend for generations, as nothing would obliterate the original injury but the killing of someone in the family of the original insulter. Some Cook Islanders had two or three marks, and some had so many that their throats were entirely covered. Is it hard to imagine the level of carnage that might result from that sort of revenge?"

The muse bit Yeager. He began scribbling notes.

"That's why Rongomatane was a voracious cannibal chief. Power and revenge required constant man-eating. Atiuan raids to supply the orgies of gluttony that Rongomatane offered his people on the island of Tangaroa all but wiped out the populace on the neighboring islands of Mauke and Mitiaro."

"What's there now?" asked Zinc.

"We'll all see soon enough. But if *mana* could be gained, it could also be lost. In the same way that Bret set himself up as the *mana ariki* of this Odyssey"—Grimmer formed a fist, palm up, and pumped his arm once in the machismo way—"but then came crashing down by feeding his people bad beer, so Rongomatane lost his power by making a stupid mistake."

Wes waited.

And waited.

And waited.

Until someone blinked.

Ever the lawyer, thought Zinc.

"What mistake?" Yeager finally asked.

"He *didn't* feed someone poisoned sugarcane."

"Who?"

"The Reverend John Williams," Petra said.

FALSE IDOLS

Mano a mano, mana a mana—it must have been quite a battle. Fought not with weapons in the classic sense, but with the power of God or the gods behind each man.

A clash of the titans.

With Atiu up for grabs.

As the rebellious daughter of a preacher with a church in the Bible Belt of British Columbia, Petra was the Odyssey expert on missionaries in the Cooks. That was evident from the way she described the arrival of the Reverend John Williams of the London Missionary Society off the coast of Atiu on July 19, 1823. Zinc had to give Wes and Petra credit for their preparation. Working in tandem, they painted a vivid picture in words of the fiction potential surrounding the wannabe writers. It was like having a time machine to travel back to the era of cannibals and converts. As he listened to Petra describing that collision of cultures out on the sea, Zinc could picture it clearly in his imagination, and that made even him contemplate taking a stab at writing a story.

Ladies and gentlemen, in this corner, weighing in at who knows how many pounds of ingested human fat, wearing the *maro kura*—the sacred scarlet loincloth of *ariki* chiefs—and the *pare kura*—the grand conical headdress of his rank, woven from sennit fibers and adorned with the red tail feathers of the tropic bird (that color being the color of the gods)—sat Rongomatane, the human shrine of the invisible and immortal gods on earth. His corner was actually the elevated seat on the royal canoe, which paddled out to meet the ship that waited off the coast. Accompanying him were eighty canoes of cannibal warriors. Eight or nine months earlier, an Atiuan prophet named Uia had foretold the arrival of a huge canoe with no outrigger, manned by people with their heads, bodies and feet covered. Theirs would be a mighty god, and the gods of Atiu would burn with fire. So out came Rongomatane to show them who was boss.

In the other corner, wearing black from head to foot, the Reverend John Williams stood waiting. Two years before, the zealous crusader had brought the word of God to Aitutaki, where, thanks to the Good Book he raised aloft in his hand, the missionary had triumphed over cannibalism, infanticide, idolatry, debauchery and polygamy. So when Rongomatane climbed aboard to size up his next feast, he was surprised to find none other than his neighboring counterpart, the cannibal *ariki* of Aitutaki, under Williams's control. That *ariki* took him down to see his *marae* idols stored in the ship's hold, and he told him how Williams had burned other idols to build a big white house of burnt rock in which the islanders now worshipped the new God.

A church, he called it.

The new *marae*.

"Williams preached a special sermon for the *ariki* of Atiu," Petra said. "He read from the Bible, the Book of Isaiah 44:9: 'They that make graven images are all of them vanity; and their delectable things shall not profit; and they are their own witnesses; they see not, nor know, that they may be ashamed.'"

"What in hell does that mean?" Pigeon asked.

Wes responded, "Those who fashion and worship idols will be put to shame."

"Williams told Rongomatane that his idols had no power because they were made out of wood, which has no life in it. Then he showed the cannibal the face of God," said Petra.

"You mean like Moses and the burning bush?" asked Yeager.

"Exactly. Want to see?"

"God?"

"Uh-huh."

"God hangs with you?"

"Got him in my bag."

"A dollar says you don't."

Petra put down her pad and got up from the bench. Rummaging in her black bag for the second time, she withdrew one of those old Bibles with the gilt-edged pages. The cover was new, Zinc assumed, since the cross embossed on it was upside down.

Turning her back on the group, she walked outside into the glaring sun that beat down on the dusty road. With the Bible held at arm's length from her body, she swiveled 180 degrees to face the others in the terminal, then ran her thumb across the pages so their gilt edges fluttered and flashed in the dazzling light.

"There's your burning bush," the Mountie said to Yeager.

"Blinded by the light," Grimmer added.

"It's worth a buck," the lawyer said. "I'm born again."

Returning to the shed, the goth queen collected her dollar. Both it and the Bible went into her black bag. "The cannibal chief was told that God himself was jumping around on the pages. The Cook Islands were still in the Stone Age. Both metal and books were unknown. Rongomatane was impressed, but he was also shrewd, so he challenged Reverend Williams to a test of his own. He dared the missionary to follow him to his *marae* and eat sugarcane from its *tapu* grove."

"Like the banana," said Zinc.

"You know about that?"

"Yvette told me on Rarotonga."

"Actually, the incidents are linked. The same missionary, Papeiha, was involved in both. Williams was hunting for Rarotonga when his boat stopped at Atiu. Off they went to the chief's *marae* to eat the sugarcane. 'If you do not die,' Rongomatane told Williams, 'I will believe in your God and burn my idols. But if you die, that will be the end of both you and your God.' Papeiha, Williams's right-hand man, knew sugar cane from Tahiti, so he gobbled it up with relish, and that was that."

"It wasn't poisoned?" said Pigeon.

"No need. It was *tapu*."

"It would have been poisoned if Bret had been the *ariki* of Atiu," joked Wes.

"What a blaze it must have been," Petra continued. "Rongomatane decreed that all the idols on this island be gathered together for burning. As Papeiha preached the gospel, questions were asked and answered. 'Is the fire of the god of darkness below like this?' 'Tomorrow, this fire will die, but that one burns forever.' 'What kind of firewood burns forever?' 'Those who refuse to believe in Jesus are the firewood.' 'But what is the fire?' 'It's the anger of God.' 'Will the fire never die?' 'When all of you believe in Jesus, then the fire will die.'"

"Amen," punctuated Wes.

"Having converted Atiu, Williams set sail for Mauke and Mitiaro with Rongomatane in tow. The last time the cannibal chief had landed on their shores, here's how those inhabitants ended up. This passage is from William Wyatt Gill, one of the early missionaries in the Cooks. I call it the shitty end of the stick."

A third rummage in her black bag produced a clip of photocopies. Handed one, Zinc read:

It was customary to prepare the body in this wise: The long spear, inserted at the [anus], ran through the body, appearing again at the neck. As on a spit, the body was slowly singed over a fire, in order that the entire cuticle and all the hair might be removed. The intestines were next taken out, washed in seawater, wrapped up in singed banana leaves (a singed banana-leaf, like oil-silk, retains liquid), cooked and eaten, this being the invariable perquisite of those who prepared the feast. The body was cooked, as pigs are now, in an oven specially set apart, red-hot basaltic stones, wrapped in leaves, being placed inside to ensure its being equally done. The best joint was the thigh. In native phraseology, "nothing would be left but the nails and the bones."

"Given the choice between that and Christianity," said Petra, "how eager do you think the cannibalized residents of Mauke and Mitiaro were to convert?"

"That fast," Yeager said, snapping his fingers.

"With those three islands converted, Williams was ready for more. Rongomatane had attacked Rarotonga several times, so he had Williams sail his ship around to the same beach on which Cook's crew had landed almost fifty years before and line the stern up with the rock that is still in the lagoon. Off they sailed in a beeline—"

"To Black Rock," completed Zinc, "where Papeiha waded ashore with the Bible held over his head and cooked that banana on the burning idol of the *ariki* of Rarotonga."

"*Banzai!*" said Pigeon, the cry of the kamikaze. "There was no stopping the guy."

"Sure there was," Petra replied, rotating her hand as if barbecuing a roast on a spit. "Eventually, everyone's luck runs out. The pagan gods got their revenge in 1839, when Williams was killed and cannibalized on the Vanuatu island of Erromanga."

"Or what about Charles Darwin?" Grimmer said. "He sailed through the Cooks on that famous voyage of the *Beagle* in . . . in . . . When was it that he was here, Petra?"

"It was 1835, I believe."

"*The Origin of Species. The Descent of Man.* Earthshaking books came out of that trip. The law of the jungle. Survival of the fittest. What if Darwin went ashore to explore the flora and the fauna of these islands, and what if the island he selected was one of the stragglers yet to be converted? Is that what inspired his theories? Did he write another book about his adventures, a book he had yet to publish at the time he died, a book that was suppressed for some mysterious reason, and only now has come to light because *you* found it?"

"I like that," Zinc said.

"If you want it, it's yours," offered Wes.

"Put that in writing?"

"You bet."

"If I was a writer," Petra said, "the tale I would tell is about a cult that challenges the blue laws. No sooner did they convert the cannibals in the Cooks than those London missionaries imposed a Christian police state. The people on Rarotonga lived inland, so the zealots uprooted their villages and moved them to the coast, where each could be controlled by the ring of churches we saw. Here on Atiu, the local villagers lived near the coast, so they were hauled inland around a central church, and that's why they all dwell on five landlocked streets today. A street for each village. Like a five-armed octopus."

Wes held up the map again and jabbed the center of Atiu with his finger as Petra elaborated.

"Christianity always comes with a price. That's why they pass the collection plate around. Along with the gospel came smallpox, whooping cough, dysentery, measles and flu. The population shrank by two-thirds. Cook Islands' mourning was something to behold. Death was referred to as 'going into the night.' When someone ill died, relatives went berserk. They gashed their flesh with sharks' teeth until blood gushed down their bodies. They blackened their faces and cut off their hair. They knocked out some of their front teeth as a token of sorrow. They shrieked a death wail until they lost their voices. And they shuffled about in grave clothes dyed red with candlenut sap and dipped in the black mud of a taro patch to give them a reeking stench that was symbolic of the putrescent state of the dead.

"The missionaries, of course, knew a good thing when they saw it. So there they stood, in the midst of all that suffering, with Bibles held high as they beseeched the islanders to cast out sin and join the church to drive away the plagues."

"Praise the Lord!" Wes intoned, mocking an evangelist at a revival meeting.

"And what about the blue laws?" Petra said. "What was it like to live in a Christian heaven on earth? Sunday—the Sabbath—was strictly observed. A curfew was levied at seven in the evening to force people to pray at the church. Since Sunday was a time for worship and nothing else, children were banned from playing and making noise of any kind. Instead, they were corralled in Bible schools and had to learn the Old and New Testaments by heart.

Sunday observance was so strict that it was illegal to walk from one village to another, and food for the Sabbath was cooked on Saturday so smoke wouldn't desecrate the air."

"Praise the Lord!" Wes repeated, banging the map as if it were a Salvation Army drum.

"Dancing was prohibited. Tattooing was outlawed. And as for sex, that became *tapu*. It was illegal for an unmarried woman to be pregnant. An unmarried couple who slept together were paraded up the main street to the beat of a gong, in front of a priest who denounced their offense. A man who strolled with his arm around a woman after dark was forced to carry a torch in his other hand. The blue laws were enforced by a system of paid snitches. Fines imposed on sinners were split between police and judges. Policing became such lucrative work that one of every six people was a cop on the take."

"Praise the Lord!" extolled Wes.

"Christ!" said Petra, flashing with anger. "Have you any idea what it's like to live under a jackboot like that? My dad was a holy-roller, so I know only too well. It makes you want to lash out at whoever grinds you down. The missionaries had free rein in the Cooks, until the British took formal control in 1888."

The year of Jack the Ripper, Zinc thought.

"As soon as word got out that there were souls to save down here, they all came stampeding in to lasso their share. The London Missionary Society became the CICC, the Cook Islands Christian Church, still by far the largest denomination. Others include Roman Catholics, Seventh-Day Adventists, Mormons, Jehovah's Witnesses, Assembly of God, Baha'is and Apostolic Revival Fellowship."

"You missed one," Bret said, a voice from the wilderness.

"No," said Petra. "I saved them for last. True Gospel Mission was the harshest of all. They turned Tangaroa into a leper colony. If I was a writer, my story would go like this: In came the Bible-thumpers to battle the elder gods. By desecrating Tangaroa with disease, they not only defiled the gods' sacred *marae,* but also spawned a cannibal cult bent on revenge. For generations, the insult has passed from parent to child in the form of a tattoo that is etched on each successive throat, and now is the time to settle the score."

"I'll write it!" enthused Pigeon.

"First come, first served," she said.

"Okay, folks," Wes said. "Time to go back in time." Their unscheduled flight to Tangaroa had just been called.

"The new *ariki*," Bret grumbled venomously.

"*Taunga*, Bret. *Taunga*. That's more my style. Why go for half the power if you can have it all?"

"What's a *taunga*?" Pigeon asked, busily scribbling notes. Revved up by the plot that Petra had outlined for him, the paper-pusher pursued his ticket out of law.

"The *taunga* was a god-box. The priest who talked to the gods. He would go into convulsions to communicate with them. On returning to a rational state, the god-box would voice the gods' will. If he declared that the gods no longer lived in the *ariki*, that was the end of the current leader's reign. Since there was no appeal from the word of the priest—after all, it was the will of their gods—the *taunga's mana* was more powerful than the *ariki's*."

"The power behind the throne."

"Right. As I am to Bret. After he shamed himself by poisoning us with bad beer, the gods abandoned Bret to reside in one of you. Which one will be revealed by sacrifice on the *marae*."

"Hey, Wes."

"Yes, Bret?"

"See this, pal?"

The taunted lawyer-turned-writer held up his ballpoint pen. For an instant, Zinc thought Bret Lister was going to stab himself in the Adam's apple. But instead, the insulted man marked his throat with an ink streak black enough to be a tattoo.

As Zinc was about to leave the terminal hut for the plane, Petra crooked her finger to summon him. Tearing the top sheet off her sketching pad, she handed it to him and walked away.

The illustration was a cartoon along the lines of those produced by Gahan Wilson for *Playboy* magazine. Macabre, but with a wicked sense of humor. The skillful drawing depicted a stretched-out pig skewered on a barbecue rod turning over a fire. The pig—a play on the sixties epithet for a cop—had Zinc's features caricatured in porcine form, a Mountie's Stetson plunked over its ears. Down in the bottom corner was the cutest little cannibal you ever saw: Petra Zydecker bare-breasted and wearing a grass skirt. A knife in one hand, a fork in the other, she licked her tongue around her lips with gourmet gusto.

The cartoon's caption read "Long Pig."

The words in the dialog bubble that ballooned from the cannibal's mouth were "I may just eat you up."

TIME'S ARROW

Late yesterday, a package had arrived at Special X. In it was Det. Ralph Stein's report, complete with backup documents and photographs, on the current status of the Seattle investigation. DeClercq had spent last night and this morning in front of the Strategy Wall in his office, pinning witness statements and forensic reports to the corkboard as a rapidly expanding collage gobbled up adjacent space. Colored threads connected links like a spider's web, and by the time the chief was finished, he could have been Spider-Man; but if so, his plate would have had no juicy fly on it for dinner, because the Seattle dragnet as yet had caught no one inside its meshes.

There was lots of buzzing, but nothing stuck to the glue.

And so it was, this afternoon, just after lunch with the pathologist Gill Macbeth, that DeClercq had taken his aging Benz out for a spin. Driving east on the Lougheed Highway as it wormed inland up the Fraser Valley along the north bank of the river, he'd squinted through the gray drizzle that blanketed this dismal day until he spotted the line of diminishing elms that stretched south to the water. The Benz had turned off the highway at Colony Farm Road. Flanked by the mushy marsh of the Fraser and overhung by dripping trees, his car had humped the bumpy pavement of the spookiest mile on the West Coast until it parked at the riverside hospital for the criminally insane.

"It's the Ripper, Chief. It all goes back to him."

That's what Zinc had told DeClercq on Monday morning, after the inspector returned from Seattle. The chief had hoped that Stein's report would throw up a lead for Special X to pursue. It hadn't, so the Mountie was here to time-travel back for a motive.

The nurse who opened the unlocked door to the interview room to usher in the patient he had escorted from Room 13 in Ashworth 2 was an effeminate fellow in his forties named Rudi Lucke. Rudi gave the chief a glance of casual assessment, then stepped aside so his charge could enter the eight-by-ten-foot cubicle with its bare-bones furniture. Though he didn't know it, DeClercq sat on the same seat the Goth had occupied a year and a half ago, when the pair of like-minded psychotics conspired to set the trap that was about to snap in the South Pacific.

DeClercq could smell him before he could see him.

The odor of rancid goat cheese was a stench the Mountie had sniffed before. On more than one occasion, he'd been in the presence of a borderline psychotic when the suspect's latent madness turned florid in front of his senses. He had seen that shadow of vacancy pass behind the psycho's eyes, had smelled that metallic stench seep from his pores and had felt the hackles rise on his own skin, for he knew he was face to face with the darkest threat in the world: a human mind powered with an awesome potential to kill and destroy, but with no rational being to keep it under control.

It had been years since the chief last faced the Ripper. From one side of the doorjamb, he moved into the frame, and the first thought DeClercq had was, He's cannibalizing himself. Like a terminal anorexic, the Ripper was skin and bones, an animate human skeleton who moved into the room. Little wonder, for he seemed to eat imaginary food. In one hand he gripped a tarot deck that was real enough, but the bony fingers of his other hand gripped empty air. Whatever he thought he held in it, the meal was delicious, for as he lowered his scrawny body in baggy blue sweats onto the chair opposite DeClercq's, he sucked the juice out of his phantom food with lip-smacking relish.

The nurse shut the door.

The stench permeated the room.

"I'm Chief Superintendent DeClercq."

"I know who you are."

The Mountie set the two nonfiction books he had published down on the table between them.

"I'm not here about your case. I'm here about a book."

"A book about what?"

"Jack the Ripper."

"You're writing a book about me?"

"That depends."

"Depends on what?"

"Whether or not you're the Ripper."

"I am."

"Prove it."

The psycho held out the nonexistent food in his empty hand and flashed his werewolf fangs.

"What's that?"

"What does it look like?"

"You tell me."

"It's a human heart."

"Whose heart?"

"Mary Kelly's," the Ripper said, biting into the fantasy flesh and tearing off a piece. Both pupils had blown their irises to form black holes that sank forever into his diseased brain. So intensely did he concentrate on that internal wonder that the fleshless skin of his skeletal face seemed to be sucked in too. To look at the Ripper was to look into a living skull that was forsaking its hold on life in the here and now in favor of existence in another dimension.

Could he time-travel?

Let's find out, thought DeClercq.

"The greatest unsolved puzzle in the annals of crime is the identity of Jack the Ripper. Though Scotland Yard mounted an extensive manhunt in the East End, Jack came and went as he pleased, ripping apart five hookers and tearing out their organs. Then he vanished into thin air, and despite the attempts of literary Ripperologists over the years, his identity remains a mystery today."

Munch . . .

Munch . . .

Munch . . .

The Ripper chewed and listened.

"The courts say that you're too insane to be tried. That's why we have you locked away in here. You say that you're Jack the Ripper incarnate, and that you found a wormhole through the astral plane from 1888 to now. If that is Mary Kelly you're eating—Jack's fifth and final victim—how did you get her heart unless you can travel *back* as well? You didn't have the heart when I arrested you on Deadman's Island."

The Ripper smirked.

Munch . . .

Munch . . .

Munch . . .

"If you're insane, I'm wasting my time. If you're Jack the Ripper, I have a blockbuster of a book to write. So which is it? Are you a nut or the Ripper?"

DeClercq had thrown the gauntlet down on the table. He paused a moment so the question could sink in. The Mountie knew the history of this Ripper in real life, the psychology of the killer who had trapped and murdered all those writers on Deadman's Island, so he felt confident that the psycho's craving for personal worth would compel him to go for the bait.

"Time travel into the future, that I can accept. All it requires is the means to travel fast enough. Einstein proved that time is elastic. It can be stretched, bent and warped. He also proved that gravity slows time, that time isn't fixed. Time is relative. And to top it off, Einstein showed how portals could worm through space-time."

The Ripper leaned forward. The hook was in. DeClercq was itching for a chance to jerk the line.

"Experiments in space have proved Einstein right. Because forces of gravity and speed warp time, time runs faster in space. Atomic clocks on rockets and long plane rides have picked up microseconds. A Russian cosmonaut who spent two years in orbit speeding around the earth in the Mir space station leaped one-fiftieth of a second ahead in time. So if we could find a way to hurtle ahead at a rate anywhere near the speed of light, we could travel through time."

"The twin effect," probed the Ripper.

"Exactly," said DeClercq. "A space traveler with an identical twin living on earth blasts off aboard a rocket that flies at close to the speed of light on a ten-year trek to far-off stars. The twin will age a decade in the time his sibling is gone, but the astronaut will be just a year older on his return. In effect, the spaceman has leaped nine years into the future. The result is that he has traveled through time."

"Like me," said the Ripper.

"That I can accept. How did you do it? By astral projection back in 1888?"

"Is that a guess?"

"Not really. I've read your file. You laid out how you did it on the walls of Room 13. Nice touch: Room 13. Here and in Miller's Court. But there lies the practical problem for me. Going *back*. Time travel into the future is nothing more than a technological challenge. But time travel to the past undermines the laws of physics."

"The grandmother paradox."

"Exactly," said DeClercq. "What happens if I go back in time and shoot my granny dead when she's a little girl? One consequence is that I will never be born. But if I were never born, how could I go back and shoot my granny dead? If we could tinker with the past, that would undermine every notion we have about cause and effect. That would produce causal chaos. Instead of our actions today influencing tomorrow, our influence would be on yesterday. It's all very well for you to believe that you have opened a wormhole and can tunnel back and forth through space-time at will. But if *I* give in to the idea that you can loop back into the past, then every notion I have about the nature of reality and my relationship to the physical universe is overturned. If you can mix up the past, present and future, what happens to free will?"

"It doesn't exist," said the Ripper. "Except in the occult realm."

"Ah." DeClercq sighed skeptically. "The timeworn debate between astrology and self-determination. Is my destiny sealed, so I have no vote? Or is it in my own hands, so I can alter it if I want to? No, I don't buy it. Life isn't mapped out. I'm not following some screenplay written in the occult realm. Time's arrow points in one direction, and that's toward the future."

The Ripper set the tarot deck down on the table.

"Pick a card," he said.

"What for?"

"You'll see."

The Mountie chose a card from the twenty-two spread out facedown across the surface.

The Ripper gathered up the rest.

"I know your card."

"How?" asked DeClercq.

"A glimpse into the future. I saw you turn it over."

"That's impossible."

"It's the Hanged Man. The key to time travel. And the key to free will."

DeClercq flipped the card.

It *was* the Hanged Man.

"I'll be damned," he said. "But there's a practical problem. If time can be warped in both directions, why aren't we overrun by Terminators and Marty McFlys? Where is Wells's Time Traveler? Why is there only you? If time travel was possible, surely there'd be other time tourists. That's why you're not the Ripper. That's why you're just a nut."

That got to him, as DeClercq had known it would.

"I'm *not* the only one!"

"How do you know?" snapped the Mountie.

"Because I *showed* someone how to open the way."

"Who?"

"Wouldn't you like to know?"

"I already do. It's either Bret Lister or Wes Grimmer."

The Ripper blinked, suddenly realizing that he had been duped. But instead of exploding in rage over having been thwarted again, the psycho began to giggle. His pores opened wide to fill the room with a gagging stench. The black holes behind his eyes grew more vacuous, and the skin of his face drew in taut. His lips receded to expose his jutting fangs, and the hand that held the phantom food curled toward his mouth, his bony index finger extending to pick at his ivory grin.

"I have your flesh between my teeth," the Ripper taunted.

Then he grabbed the Hanged Man card off the table, stood up and left the interview room. DeClercq could hear him laughing all the way to Room 13.

On his way out to the parking lot, the chief stopped at Central Control.

"I hear you have computer problems," he said to the security guard. "A virus or worm ate your visitors' record?"

"Swallowed it but didn't digest it," the man replied. "A tech stuck his finger down the system's throat, and it coughed up the missing data earlier today."

"Check a patient for me?"

"Give me the name and I can tell you everyone who's seen him. Plus the date and time."

The Mountie gave the guard the Ripper's real name.

The guard pulled up the record.

"Thanks," said DeClercq, then he returned to his car.

From the parking lot in front of the psychiatric hospital, the chief placed a cellphone call to Special X. He asked the cop who answered to find an address for him, an address that matched a name he'd seen twice today: in the record of the Ripper's visitors and back at the office on his Strategy Wall in the pinned-up report from Ralph Stein on the World Horror Convention.

With the address in hand, DeClercq drove through the marshlands on Colony Farm Road until it intersected with the Lougheed Highway. A turn left would take him back to Vancouver, but instead the chief angled right. From here, the road followed the Fraser River inland up its valley, along a route known as the Bible Belt.

WRATH OF GOD

Tangaroa, Cook Islands

Again, the engines revved up to a screaming pitch, and the plane was off down the runway and climbing up into the blue. Seen from the air, Atiu resembled a low-crowned hat with a flat outer rim. It lacked the soaring skyline of volcanic Rarotonga, for the uplands were nothing but a domed plateau. Smack-dab in the center of everything was a big white building with a bell tower in front, the largest mission church in the Cooks. Five limestone roads radiated out like tentacles wrapped around the cluster of five converted villages. The cannibal Rongomatane had built a *marae* for the first missionaries, and a stone marked the spot—as one did on Rarotonga—where Papeiha had preached the first gospel sermon on Atiu. Back then, human bones had littered Atiuan *maraes,* but today a hundred *tivaevae* quilts in as many appliqué colors hung on clotheslines strung across the green common in front of the big CICC church for the current priest to judge.

The unscheduled flight from Atiu to the deserted satellite island of Tangaroa took less than ten minutes. The only passengers on board were those on the Odyssey. The lights of the cockpit's instrument panel barely had time to change from orange for takeoff to green for leveling out. No sooner did Zinc hear the undercarriage retract beneath the engines than it was time for the wheels to lower. He had to admit that he was falling in love with this Brazilian plane, with its quaint windshield wipers on the outside of the cockpit windows.

His first glimpse of Tangaroa took his breath away. The island itself was a jungle-green volcanic hump surrounded by the eroded remains of an uplifted dead coral reef. Like a string of pearls or blossoms on a lei looping out into the sea, a new reef had formed on one side. The surf-topped necklace, dotted with the sandy islets of a dozen *motus,* encircled the dazzling turquoise pool contained within the endless blue depths.

Then up, up, up the magnificent atoll seemed to rise to meet them, until—*bump . . . bump . . . bump*—the plane skipped along a crunched coral airstrip that hadn't jounced wheels for months, or more likely years. With a whistle, both turbo engines died. One of the pilots emerged from the cockpit to open the door and lower the self-contained staircase. But if Zinc thought that would release him from the fuselage oven, escape was not to be. So witheringly hot was it outside the portal oval that he might as well have been an ant tracked across the ground by a sadistic kid with a magnifying glass. Luckily, the safari hat that had seen Zinc through Africa was designed for this. He plunked it on his head for respite from the glare.

Ahhh! Shade!

No need for the kid with the magnifying glass in Bret Lister's case. The lawyer-turned-writer was already burned out. As he and Zinc lugged the last of the luggage from the hold behind the wing to the edge of what was supposedly a runway, the cop opened a conversation with "This has to be one of the most beautiful lagoons on earth. Hard to believe it hasn't attracted a resort."

"Tangaroa is cursed."

"How do you know that?"

"I was in the Cooks a few years back."

"Doing what?" Zinc asked.

"Recuperating. After I got out."

The words "of the nuthouse" went unsaid.

"Were you here?"

"No, on Atiu. Until I was flown to the hospital on Rarotonga."

"An accident?"

"Uh-huh. I got struck by lightning."

"You're kidding!"

"Nothing funny about it. All I heard was a noise like the snapping of a twig, then I lost a few seconds of my life. My next recollection is of hitting the ground."

"How did it happen?"

"You saw Atiu. Everyone lives up on that domed plateau. Including tourists. The freshwater supply comes from rain collected and stored in tower tanks. A thunderstorm raged over the island while I was there. It rained so hard that gardens got pummeled flat. The woman who kept the guest house asked me as a favor if I would check the rain gauge for her. I waited for the downpour to subside before I popped an umbrella and went outside. Big mistake. We were in the eye of the storm, with the thunderhead right above, so the next bolt of lightning went straight for the spike of my umbrella. The shortest distance to the ground was achieved by zapping down my spine. Knocked flat, I soon got up and moved around for half an hour as if I had escaped unscathed, then I collapsed and couldn't move a muscle for three weeks."

"Was that in the Raro hospital?"

"Yeah. They flew me there to recuperate from my recuperation on Atiu."

"How'd you get home?"

"I sent for Wes. The Law Society had him looking after my clients while I was suspended. That was before we had a falling-out. So that fucker flew in to take care of me, and instead of accompanying my crippled body back home, he put me on a plane by myself and took three weeks off to skin-dive in the Cooks."

"On Tangaroa?"

"Ask him. But I doubt that. This place is cursed. It's not on tourist maps."

"Cursed how?"

"Ghosts, to start. Do you have any idea how many people were killed, butchered and eaten here?"

"No," said Zinc.

"Perhaps thousands. Then after the Christian missionaries flooded in, the Bible-thumpers who took control of Tangaroa turned it into a leper colony."

"True Gospel Mission?"

"Uh-huh," grunted Bret. "The threat of leprosy is a biblical curse. It's like that island in Hawaii."

"Molokai," the Mountie supplied.

"Right. Father Damien, the Martyr of Molokai. Well, that proves the curse, eh? Even with Jesus as his savior, the priest still succumbed to leprosy. Same here. They might as well have staked a skull and crossbones on the beach. And Lord knows they had enough of those to use."

"Did True Gospel own the island?"

"No one owns land in the Cooks. It belongs to the Cook Islanders. It can't be bought and sold. The best you can do is lease it from them for a maximum number of years."

"Does True Gospel still hold the lease?"

"I have no idea. But from what I heard on Atiu from the guy who sold me the bad beer, Tangaroa is still cursed. Archeologists from Japan came here to study the *marae,* and they all came down with dengue fever on the dig. Of course, they may have got that on Rarotonga, but it makes a better story if it was here."

Damn, thought Zinc. I forgot to buy DEET.

"Did the lightning strike have any after-effects?"

"Yes," said Bret. "I *see* things."

"What sort of things?"

"Read my novels," he said.

———•••———

Crossing the *makatea* was like treading on shattered glass. Bret Lister was in a talkative mood born of nervous tension—every so often, the muscles of his jaw would clench spasmodically—so Zinc let him ramble in the hope that Bret might give something away. The jilted man who "saw things" explained that Tangaroa is a geological anomaly. Eleven million years ago, it began as a volcano cone that rose out of the sea. Over time, the pyramid eroded and slowly sank, while coral grew on the submerged rim to form a reef.

Then two million years ago, Rarotonga, the youngest island in the Cooks group, was born from volcanic paroxysms that caused a buckling of the adjacent seafloor. That upheaval raised Tangaroa above sea level, and it left the fringing coral reef high and dry to transform itself into the rugged and holey *makatea* beneath their feet. However, unique among the Cook Islands, Tangaroa tilted, and the seafloor on the downside created a new coral atoll with a string of sandy islets ringing the turquoise lagoon seen from the plane.

"Watch your step," Bret warned, "or you'll be cut to ribbons. Fall and you'll land on a bed of razors."

"It looks like rock."

"It isn't. It's millions of skeletons. Do you know how coral reefs form?"

"Yes," Zinc replied. "Small jelly-like polyps secrete limestone casings around themselves. Their exoskeletons combine to create coral formations."

"Even the minutest of creatures can build a gigantic structure. The Great Barrier Reef of Australia is the largest structure on earth. It can be seen from outer space. Working together, polyps have built a home for great white sharks. Weird creatures, polyps. Each has a central mouth surrounded by tentacles. Sound familiar?"

"Cthulhu," said the Mountie. "Lovecraft's monster."

"How well do you know the Mythos?"

"Just the basics," Zinc lied.

"See the parallel?"

"No. Sketch it for me."

"Cthulhu dwells in the corpse city of black *R'lyeh,* which is sunk deep in the dark depths of the Pacific. There, he sleeps entombed with the others of his monstrous race. Someday, we're told, that city will rise above the waves, and the call of Cthulhu will summon the widespread members of his cult to the uplifted corpse city so that we might throw open the black door behind which he slumbers. Freed, the elder gods will slay their way around the world until they have retaken the realm from which they were once expelled."

"*We?*" said Zinc.

"Learn to role-play, Chandler. There are millions of stories around us waiting to be told. But if your mind's eye can't see them, you'll never be a writer. To be a writer of fiction, you must see the unseen. So tell me what we're standing on."

Bret stamped his foot on the *makatea*.

"Dead coral?"

"No, *R'lyeh*. Underfoot is the corpse city where Cthulhu sleeps, lifted up from the bottom of the sea."

"So where's Cthulhu?" Zinc asked, playing along.

"In his cave."

"What cave?"

"Inside the *makatea*. Think about it. We're standing on limestone. After this reef uplifted, the polyps died and were flushed away, leaving holes like in Swiss cheese. What remained behind to fossilize were their exoskeletons, now as hard as rock and as sharp as knives. Stub your toe on the *makatea* and you'll lose it. The volcanic core of Tangaroa is higher than down here. What happens to runoff when it rains or there's a hurricane? Water runs into the dead end of this *makatea* ring, and it has to burrow and erode a tunnel to the sea. The result is that the dead coral becomes riddled with caves."

"I don't see any."

"You will when we land on the beach. The Eyes of Tangaroa stare at the lagoon."

He's been here before, Zinc thought. I feel it in my bones.

The Mountie recalled his first glimpse of Bret Lister at the World Horror Convention, when this human lightning rod staked his claim to the Cthulhu model. He also recalled the dead sculptor, who'd had all those nails hammered into his face to fashion the maw of Cthulhu in a pincushion of human flesh.

Role-playing was one thing.

Acting out was another.

So now Zinc knew whodunit.

The psycho who "saw things."

The Lovecraft obsessive.

The barman who served spiked beer.

The motive was easy: Bret was psychotic. By definition, he had suffered a break with reality. First, the lawyer had lost sight of the dividing line between what was real and what was paranoid delusion, and his outburst in court resulted in a custodial remand to Colony Farm. There, he had come under the evil influence of the Ripper and his psychotic theories of the occult realm. Upon being released, Bret had taken that secret with him back into the world. Then, while convalescing in the Cook Islands, he had been struck by a bolt of lightning akin to the wrath of God, and that bolt not only fried his brain but also made him believe that he was given a second sight to gain glimpses into the Lovecraftian landscape of another dimension.

Like Cthulhu's realm.

Or Rongo's realm.

Or the realm of the elder gods.

Seeing is one thing. Experiencing is another. Bret had inserted the Ripper's Hanged Man key into the lock of the door to the occult realm by hanging the Hollywood producer Romeo Cardoza upside down in the room at the Lions Gate. Did Petra Zydecker team up with Bret for the North Vancouver murder? Were they the couple having three-way sex with Cardoza when someone pounded the crown of thorns—the nimbus of nails—into the American's skull? Or did Bret waylay Cardoza *after* the producer had snorted coke and cavorted as the sandwich spread between Gord and Joey, the drug-pushing pimp and the lounge lizard hooker who died in the dead-end chase?

Either way, Zinc was now convinced that Bret was the North Van killer.

The experience of having committed that murder had obviously inspired Bret to write *Crown of Thorns*. The year and a half needed to finish the manuscript and get it published had created an interval that had also been sufficient for Bret's ex-partner—Wes Grimmer—to write a rival thriller—*Halo of Flies*—about Bret's Hanged Man murder, and to have it published in the same month by a more prestigious house.

A weak reed anyway, Bret Lister snapped.

So why the Hanged Man murder in Seattle last Friday night? And why the separate displays of the corpse—spiking the head upside down in front of Ted Bundy's house and hanging the headless body upside down at the foot of the Thirteen Steps to Hell in Maltby Cemetery? Was Bret hoping to rectify an error he thought he had made in signifying the Tarot symbols in North Vancouver? Or was that just a madman's crazy way to promote his novel? Or—because Bret had an alibi for that murder—did he hope to frame Wes Grimmer for the crime?

And what about Petra?

How did she fit into Bret's scheme?

If the goth queen was a party to the North Van death, then she was undoubtedly also a party to the Seattle murder. Bret's alibi, in that case, was no alibi. Instead of making the two-backed beast in bed at the hotel, they were both off committing murder and dumping the body at two sites.

But what if Petra wasn't involved in either murder? Then the alibi in Seattle could be true only if she had fallen asleep before Bret crept out to kill, or had been drugged so she wouldn't wake up while he was gone.

Once he had that alibi for whatever reason, Bret was free to strike again at the horror convention. Killing the sculptor was easy. Bret was already a customer of the artist—with Zinc himself a witness to that, owing to their previous conversation at the sculptor's display in the Morbid Maze gallery—so not only did he have a cover story that freed him to approach the victim at the door to his room, but if forensic traces of Bret were found at the murder scene, who could say they weren't left behind after a *prior* business meeting?

But why kill the sculptor? How did that make sense? Unless the motive was only rational within the irrational fantasy of Bret's psychotic mind. Something unhinged, like acting out "Pickman's Model." In that Lovecraft story, the artist finds a way to paint Cthulhu Mythos monsters from real life, and they end up taking his. If Bret thought he had opened the path to the occult realm, where he could commune with the Mythos at will, then, when his psychosis was in a florid state, he may have killed the artist for any number of delusional motives, such as to get even with him for the blasphemy of depicting his occult subjects wrong.

Blur the line between fantasy and reality, and anything goes.

The outer limits are limitless to psychotic minds.

And what could be safer than escaping from the murder room? Since blood-spattered masqueraders milled through the hotel, a blood-spattered killer was just part of the scene. So off Bret went for a simmer in the hot tub and a cleansing dip in the pool while Zinc was playing peeping Tom outside Petra's bedroom.

All the pieces fit.

Except for Petra's role.

Crack that, the Mountie thought, and I'll crack the case.

——•·•——

Twenty feet or so behind Zinc and Bret, the Goth was in the group that trailed the cop and his prime suspect. Close by was the carryall in which the pair of spearguns were being lugged across the dead coral. The Goth used the trek to examine the Mountie with a butcher's eye, trying to determine the order of cuts that would keep Zinc alive and screaming for mercy the longest.

MARAE O RONGO

Crossing the *makatea* was like walking through a lush jungle. Pockets of volcanic soil had clogged some of the holes left by decomposition of the polyps aeons ago, so now the alien landscape of the fossilized coral was a dense tangle of tropical greenery. This wild vegetation included the ever-present coconut palms, for all it takes to grow one of those hardy trees is a dropped coconut shell rooting in some sand. Pandanus leaves, used for weaving thatch and mats throughout the South Pacific, interwove with vines, ferns, mosses and other scrub plants to shield the Odyssey team from the hammer of the pounding sun. The shade over the quarter-mile trek was a welcome relief.

Eventually, the seven seaward hikers zigzagged single file down a foothold path cut into a crevasse that cleaved the fifty-foot-high face of the gray *makatea* cliff. As Zinc set foot onto the dazzling beach at the bottom, a wicked-looking red-and-yellow wasp alighted on the bare skin of his arm. Dropping the carryall in his other hand, he brushed the insect away before it stung.

"Whew!" exclaimed Yeager. "Is this place for real, or am I dreaming?"

"It's the dead of winter back home," Pigeon said, "and you're about to wake up to another day of Vancouver rain, before going to work for another boring day of corporate finance."

"Don't wake me!"

The vista that enveloped them had to be seen to be believed. There are panoramas in travel brochures that lure sun-seekers away from home in the blahs of winter, but this lagoon was so heart-stopping in its surreal splendor that it would be a siren call away from a perfect summer. What Muri Beach had in sun, sand, water, reef and fish, this ultimate Eden had a hundredfold. The shore that stretched from the towering *makatea* to the achingly azure lagoon was bleached whiter than white. So clear was the water where the sand slipped into the sea that even from here they could see the coral garden wonders that awaited them on the gleaming floor of Tangaroa's swimming pool. Out beyond the surf-topped reef with its sprinkling of languid *motus,* the visibility would be hundreds of feet into the depths of the sea.

"Is that the Hilton?" Yeager asked, pointing left.

Halfway along the shore to where the lasso of the coral reef joined that edge of the deserted island, a shelf stuck out from the *makatea* like a disrespectful tongue. The outcrop was surmounted by the ruins of the old True Gospel Mission, basically four lime-stone walls with a caved-in roof of rotting thatch. Faded from the erasing glare of the blistering sun, faint words and a colorful wall painting could still be made out over the door. *"Tapu! Tapu! Tapu!"*—"Holy! Holy! Holy!"—harked several heralding angels in the mural.

Stuck on wooden stilts above the lagoon in front were three over-water *kikau* huts. The classic Polynesian dwellings of getaway fantasies, their frameworks were lashed together with coconut hemp sennit ropes, their peaked roofs thatched with platted pandanus leaves. The Japanese archeologists had no doubt fixed them up prior to their dengue fever sabotaging their expedition. Each hut had a deck with stairs descending to the water, so all that was missing was a fleet of three outrigger canoes for the Odyssey members to paddle.

"Let's check in," Wes said, "then gather at the *marae.*"

As the group swiveled to follow his pointing finger in the oppo-site direction, a chattering kingfisher dive-bombed the lagoon and speared a fish with its bill. Flipping the catch in the air, the bird opened wide to let the fish slide down its gullet.

The expanse of shore to the right was longer and blindingly bright. It also ended where the loop of reef joined the island. Burrowed into the gray *makatea* cliff about a third of the way along were two round black caves that yawned like hungry mouths. Equidistant between them was a huge flat rock, and laid out on its rectangular surface and flanked by gallows palms were the remains of an ancient idol *marae* dating back to cannibal times.

"Kopupooki," Grimmer announced.

"Translation?" Zinc asked.

"Stomach Rock."

————•+•————

Wes spread his arms to take in the *marae*.

"Marae O Rongo," he announced.

"Here is where the Atiuans performed blood sacrifices. Back then, this *marae* was a rectangular meeting place where the Atiuans erected fifteen-foot-high phallic idols carved from ironwood trunks to honor their elder gods. The four sides were delineated with triangular stones that jutted up like sharks' teeth and had been harvested from stalagmites within the flanking Eyes of Tangaroa caves. The inland boundary of the *marae* still has the *ariki* throne on which Rongomatane once sat, but the passing of time—or the weight of the man himself—has cracked the seat in half. As you can see, the pieces don't match. The half we found on the *marae* is ghost white, and the half we retrieved from the shade behind has gone brown."

Having stored their gear in a nearby shaded thicket, the Odyssey members had stepped up onto Stomach Rock, where they now sat among the remains of the cannibals' ritual grove. Two rows of lesser stones ran along each side, from the *ariki*'s throne at the head to the tail end by the sea. On them, the leaders of lower rank than the king—the *mataiapo* and *rangatira* of the royal gentry—had sat face to face, while commoners watched what went on from the beach. Today, in the heat of the afternoon sun, those who sat sweating on the ancient stones were the six listeners.

Wes, playing the role of *taunga,* stood in the center.

"This *marae* was dedicated to Rongo and Tangaroa. Huge idols of both cannibal gods stood where I'm standing when the first missionaries landed. They were toppled and burned during the

Christian conversion that led to that"—Wes swung his arm around dramatically to point along the beach at the ruins of True Gospel Mission—"but I have a replacement."

Stepping out of the *marae*, Wes jumped the few feet from the rock down to the beach and fetched a Nike carryall that had been stored with the rest of the gear the group had carried across the *makatea* from the plane. Returning to the ritual ground, he unzipped the long sausage-like bag and pulled out a three-foot-high wooden idol of a Polynesian god.

"Tangaroa," Wes announced, erecting the carved image in the center of the *marae* so it faced the reef.

The big-browed head resembled that of an Easter Island monolith. With squinty eyes, a flat nose and a monstrous mouth, the idol also had a potbelly whose prominent navel seemed about to burst open from having gorged on human flesh. The tiny arms and powerful legs were as out of proportion as the limbs of *Tyrannosaurus rex*. And dangling proudly between its legs so the massive circumcised head reached its ankles was a truly humongous cock.

"Ooh-wee," Petra said. "Is he well hung."

"I posed for it," Wes said, winking at the goth queen.

"In your dreams," scoffed Bret.

"No, Bret. He's in *my* dreams," Petra teased.

Lister sat across the *marae* from Zinc. The sexual innuendo turned his face a deeper red. It was already flushed from a volatile mix of anger at Wes, insomnia, sunburn and the arduous effort he'd expended to schlep his luggage across the *makatea*. Instead of countering Petra's comment, the fried man turned in on himself like an ingrown toenail. With his ballpoint pen, Bret added not one but *two* ink tattoos to the revenge mark that already marred his throat.

"In their zeal to erase all vestiges of pagan idolatry, the Christians outlawed carving of the elder gods," said Wes. "When the islanders began to carve again, the idols were as sexless as Ken and Barbie dolls. But as you can see, they now have their *mana* back."

"I'm getting hungry," Yeager said.

"For food, let's go to war," responded Wes. "The first thing we must do is consult the appropriate gods. Rongo is the god of war, so he demands blood. For that, the Atiuans kept slaves on hand. A sacrifice was hauled to the center of the *marae,* where the *taunga* gouged both eyes out of the screaming man. The priest handed Rongomatane the eyeballs to swallow raw, to feed the cannibal god who lived inside his namesake. The eyeless sacrifice was then offered to the Rongo idol on the *marae,* now that his eyes were 'open' to the ruler of the invisible realm. A needle of human shinbone was rammed through both ears to thread a rope that was then used to hoist him up, like a man hanged from the gallows, into one of these coconut palms. Finally, the sacrifice's entrails were pulled out to divine the appetite of the god of war. This was followed by a chant to Tangaroa, god of the sea."

Wes cupped both hands around his mouth and called out to the reef.

"*Tangaroa e . . . me oro koe ki te moana nui . . . numinumia.*"

He's really into this, thought Zinc.

"Translation?" the Mountie asked.

"*Tangaroa ho . . .* When you go to the big ocean, keep it calm."

Petra clapped.

"Well done, Wes," said Yvette.

"Now what?" Pigeon asked.

"We launch our war canoes and row across the Moana Nui o Kiva—the Big Blue Ocean—to storm the shores of Mauke, Mitiaro or Rarotonga to get us some man meat."

"We need a sacrifice," Yeager said.

Without a word, Bret stood up and jumped down from the *marae.* The others watched him rummage in debris scattered around the trunk of a coconut palm. When he found what he was looking for, he returned to Stomach Rock.

At four and a half pounds, the blue-gray coconut crab is a monster of a crustacean. Each takes twenty years to mature. A nocturnal attacker, it eats at night, scaling palms to snip off their nuts with enormous pincers that can easily crack open shells that don't split from the fall.

Without stooping to place the crab on the *marae,* Bret dropped it in front of Wes's idol and crushed the crustacean with such a pulverizing stomp of his hiking boot that the guts of the creature splattered the Odyssey members.

"Jesus Christ, man!" Yeager swore as he was sprayed with shards of shell and strings of meat.

"There's your sacrifice."

"Sushi, anyone?" Petra asked.

If it was hot before, it was blisteringly hot now. As midday wore on, the sun baked down on the *marae* with growing ferocity. Zinc began to feel lightheaded from the relentless heat, while the buzzing of nearby insects took on a metallic drone. As the Mountie listened to Wes recount the Atiuans' cannibal raids on neighboring islands to hunt for man meat, his overheated imagination transported him back to experience the attacks that Wes captured in words. . . .

"Mei te piri-rangi, ki Ana-lo!

"Mei Ana-lo, ki te piri-rangi!"

That was the cry that rang out from the top of an ironwood tree as the Mauke watchman looked out to sea.

"From the horizon to the landing passage!

"From the landing passage to the horizon!"

Already the Atiu cannibals, armed with spears and clubs and slings, were moving from canoe to canoe before jumping onto the reef. There was no time lost in paddling or beaching the outriggers, as surprise was the essence of successful attacks for these deadly warriors of the pre-Christianity Cooks. What misled the watchman into assuming there were more boats than there actually were was the tactic of lashing the stern of one canoe to the bow of the next, in effect fashioning a floating bridge from the open sea to the landing. Paddlers held each in position as the warriors leapfrogged to the Mauke beach, and within minutes the neighboring islanders were running for their lives.

The Battle of Akaina was under way.

This was a revenge attack for a previous slaughter by Maukeans of an Atiu chief. In earlier times, the Atiuans had come to Mauke under the false pretense of a friendly visit and lured the cowering populace out of their *makatea* caves by inviting them to an *umukai,* a feast cooked in an underground oven. The feast took place as promised, with the Maukeans the food, and henceforth they were known as *Mauke kaa-kaa,* Mauke the easily fooled.

With Mauke under the domination of Atiu, an Atiuan chief named Akaina had settled on the island and taken the wife of the local *ariki* as a concubine. Livid at being cuckolded by his conqueror, the Maukean had killed Akaina and all but one of his cohorts. Escaping in a small boat, the sole survivor had braved the perilous crossing back to Atiu. Not one to stomach such a challenge to his power—not when he could stomach the affronter instead—Rongomatane had rowed to Mauke at the head of an armada of eighty canoes, an armada whose Atiuan warriors were now storming the beach.

"Imagine you're a Maukean under attack." Zinc absorbed Wes's voice into his mental fantasy like a voiceover in the movies. "A wave of cannibals out for revenge are on your island. What a fearsome sight the man-eaters are to behold. Their bodies are blubbery with human fat that is both their own and that of your ancestors. The invaders fight naked except for loincloths at their waists and helmets of hardened sennit protecting their heads. Around you, family and friends are being skewered on spears or clubbed to death. Those seeking refuge in the caves are being hauled out kicking, screaming and begging for mercy. Females are killed or spared according to their looks. Plain women suffer the same bloody fate as the men. Pretty women are hog-tied and carried off to the boats. Imagine you are one of them after that slaughter. There you sit among the corpses of your father, mother, husband, children, relatives and friends as the cannibals row you *here.*"

Again, Wes spread his arms to take in the *marae.*

Then Zinc was off on another fantasy raid.

Unlike the Maukeans, the Mitiaroans didn't hide in caves. Instead, they built the fortress of Te Pare on the southeast coast to thwart Atiuan invaders. With an underground shelter below and a lookout tower facing the sea above, the stronghold was protected by a ring of sharp pointed rocks from the *makatea*. To get across it should have required reef shoes, but hunger for the human flesh quaking inside the fort inspired the cannibals to devise another tactic. By laying their spears two by two across the rocks to fashion a makeshift footpath, each pair connecting to another pair until all their spears were in use, the Atiuans crossed the barricade with bare feet. Scaling the lookout tower, the attackers rained fire down on the defenders cowering in the shelter and burned them alive. So complete was the annihilation of the populace of Mitiaro that those who live on the island today are mostly descendants of Atiuan victors from the Battle of Te Pare.

Survival of the fittest.

A different tactic succeeded on Rarotonga. There, Atiuan warriors attacked in a triangular formation: *te tara*. The deeper you drive a wedge into wood, the more the wood splits, because the force is concentrated at one point. And so it was with the Rarotongans who engaged the invading Atiuans on the coast of what is now Avaavaroa, near the resort where the Odyssey had grouped at Muri Beach. That name derives from *aue-roa*—the "long wailing"—for that's what the women did there as they watched the wedge sunder the ranks of their men, allowing the Atiuans to cut the defenders down and then cut them up for meat, which was packed into their outriggers for the long voyage home. The leftover joints were hung from palms as a grisly calling card.

What brought Zinc back to the reality of the *marae*, here and now, was that the voiceover in his fantasy suddenly stopped.

Wes was staring up at one of the palms from which he would have hoisted the eyeless sacrifice to Rongo if these were cannibal times. The self-appointed *taunga* of the Odyssey had ceased talking after describing the Atiuans' raid on Rarotonga, and now he was in one of those trances that takes a snap of the fingers to bring us around. For a moment, Zinc was unable to fathom what held Grimmer's attention. But then he recalled the childhood trauma that Wes had related to his audience at the horror convention, and the pieces of this puzzle fell into place.

A hanging tree.

The buzzing of flies.

A memory from the past.

Flies like those that buzzed around the head of his dad on the day Wes Grimmer had found him hanging from a gallows tree.

Is the heat getting to him? wondered Zinc.

"Rongomatane's cannibals had their victory feasts here," Grimmer said, snapping out of it. "The bodies that came back whole were hung by the heels from all these trees until the sand around turned red from the blood that rained from their cut throats. The idols taken from the *maraes* of the vanquished were offered to the gods of Marae O Rongo as thanks for the victories, along with trophies seized during the raids. The severed heads of important warriors and the bones gnawed clean during the cannibal feasts littered this *marae* for months after the celebrations. How many humans were butchered and eaten on Stomach Rock? Thousands, I would guess. Their idols may be gone, but what about the elder gods and the ghosts of those consumed? Is this *marae* haunted? Are you defiling a sacred place? It was *tapu* to tread on a *marae* without permission of the gods. The penalty was death. So there's another plot for you to consider. Which of you will craft the tale that crowns you as our new *ariki*? Who will sport this headdress of bloodred feathers that signify both cannibal gods?"

Wes pulled a plumed helmet out of his Nike bag.

"And who will wear the *maro kura,* the sacred red loincloth of the *mana ariki*?"

Wes held up a red diaper.

"This sounds like 'Survivor,'" Yeager said.

"Red's my color," commented Yvette.

"Phew, it's hot!" Pigeon said, dripping sweat.

Zinc gazed up at the blazing sun. This heat could indeed drive you crazy. Usually, the Cooks were cooled by tropical breezes, but today that ocean fan was on the fritz.

"Who's for a swim?" Petra asked.

"Good idea," said Wes. "Let's get our snorkel equipment and go raid the reef."

When the Odyssey regrouped at the lagoon a few minutes later, Wes was armed with a compressed-air speargun.

"I'll spear dinner," he said, "while you guys float around."

Uh-oh, Zinc thought. I don't like the sound of that.

The Mountie knew enough about spearfishing to grasp the potential danger. A speargun is like a crossbow that hurls a barbed shaft. The power source can be a steel spring, rubber bands, a CO_2 cartridge or—as was the case here—pneumatic power. The speargun in Grimmer's hands had what appeared to be a pistol grip at its back end. Extending forward from the grip was a long metal tube with a piston barrel inside. The insertion of a spear shaft into the muzzle rammed the piston back until it was caught by the trigger hook and held in place. The portion of the tube behind the cocked piston in the upper part of the hand grip was an air chamber. A valve at the rear of the hand grip was used to pump compressed air into the gun. Pull the trigger and the piston was released to shoot down the barrel until it hit a shock absorber inside the muzzle, hurling the barbed spear forward through the water. Or through the air, if the gun was fired on land.

"That looks deadly," Zinc said.

"You can never be too safe. See that reef?" Wes said, pointing the barrel across the lagoon. "There's nothing between it and Tahiti but the deep blue sea. Past that protective barrier, the drop-off is twelve thousand feet. *Anything* can happen out there. Some very scary monsters lurk beyond the reef."

SPEARGUN

Click . . . click . . . click . . .

The sound of tiny hermit crabs lugging their adopted shells as they clambered over bits of broken coral that littered the shoreline greeted the skin divers who were wading with masks, snorkels and fins into the tepid aquamarine waters. Were it not for the blistering heat of the sun on the sole-scorching sand, entering the lagoon might have felt like stepping into a bathtub. But with more sweat trickling down their bodies than would be sucked out by a sauna, the cooling dip evoked a collective "Aaah!" from the Odyssey group.

"That looks nasty," Yvette said.

"What?" asked Zinc.

"The scar near your spine. How'd it happen?"

"I was stabbed in the back."

"Who stabbed you?"

"Some psycho on Deadman's Island."

"An inch more to the side and he'd have finished the job."

"I'm sure he'd still like to."

"Where is he now?"

"Locked away in a psych ward on Colony Farm."

"Good riddance."

"I'll say."

From the corner of his eye, Zinc kept a bead on Grimmer. As he watched the spear fisherman arm the gun by ramming a barbed shaft down the barrel, he also saw Bret Lister bend at the waist and scoop both hands into the lagoon. The older lawyer was a few feet in front of the younger, who had paused to prepare his weapon for action. In Bret's fist was a slug-like creature known locally as a *matu rori,* a sea cucumber. Slippery and slimy, it resembled the guts of a snail. Lister tore the skin open and squeezed out the innards as if they were toothpaste in a tube. Then he threw back his head to drop the spaghetti entrails into his mouth, and with a gulp of gourmet's relish, he tossed the black skin away.

"Hey, *mana* man," he said, scooping up another and holding it out to Grimmer. "I dare you."

"Bon appétit," Wes said. "They're your bowels, Bret. But I'm not a bottom feeder."

"We'll see," Lister sneered as he waded back to shore.

For easy visibility during a masked dive, Yvette had strapped a sheathed diver's knife—serrated along one edge and razor sharp on the other—to the inside of her left calf, opposite her dominant hand. Zinc wished in hindsight that he had armed himself on Rarotonga as planned, but catching up to the Odyssey had moved things along at too fast a pace. As Wes had warned the Mountie back on the beach, you never know what dangers lurk beyond the reef . . . and Zinc's concern as he and Yvette prepared to swim out to sea was that the greatest of those possible dangers might turn out to be Wes himself.

Using the water to buoy him up, Zinc pulled on full-foot flippers. Just before Yvette lowered her mask of tempered glass and stuck the J-shaped tube of the snorkel into her mouth, she cocked a finger at Zinc and said, "Should I insist that you swim *ahead* of me?"

"So you can look up my trunks?"

"So you can't look up mine."

"I'd say Bill Pigeon is more of a threat." Zinc nodded toward the lawyer in the hibiscus-patterned trunks who was sneaking a surreptitious peek at the goth queen's breasts each time her head was turned.

"He'll stick with Petra," Yvette said knowingly. "Water magnifies peeping vistas."

"Gee, maybe I should stick with Petra too."

"It's your choice, Zinc. But if you do, that will kill your chances of ever seeing my tattoo."

And with that, she stuck the snorkel into her pursed mouth and dove cleanly into the wavering mirage of Neptune's turquoise realm, the color of which changed constantly according to the angle of refraction of the sun's beams. Beneath the dazzling sparkles that glinted off the surface, and above the glistening white sand that carpeted the bottom of the shimmering lagoon, Yvette's lithe figure scissor-kicked toward the beckoning reef.

From the corner of his eye, Zinc saw Wes dive in.

Splash!

Zinc got wet too.

＊ ＊ ＊

To dive in the South Pacific is to enter a different dimension. The tunnel vision of your face mask opens up a view into an alien world teeming with exotic creatures. As Zinc followed Yvette's flapping fins out to the barrier reef, he watched reality slipping further and further away from him. At first there was just his shadow on the pristine sand, which was dotted here and there with the sea slugs that Bret found delectable. Then clumps of phosphorescent coral came into view, around which swirled halos of brightly colored tropical fish. As the living corals fused together to fashion intricate ridges, caves, canyons and shelves, the sandbars sandwiched between the underwater gardens shrank. Yvette appeared to have discovered a trough through the coral barrier, a gap that flowed over the submerged ramparts and out to the open sea. As the Mountie caught up to his siren at the far edge of the reef, she bent at the waist for a tuck dive and threw her legs straight up in the air so the weight of her lower limbs would drive her body underwater.

Down she dove into Davy Jones's locker.

Viz, divers call it, for "average underwater visibility." Today, that viz was exceptional: up to two hundred feet. For the first few seconds that Zinc gazed down into plunging infinity, he was seized with a giddy sensation of vertigo. It was as if Wells's time machine had transported him back to the birth of life on earth in some primordial volcanic soup. The drop-off from the rim was layered like an archeological dig, with new generations of the ever-evolving reef tiered upon the foundations of those laid down before. The solid, big-knuckled corals that buttressed the top of the wall swarmed with the shimmering colors and flamboyant patterns of a mind-boggling palette of abundant fish that slashed through pools of trembling light amid ominous shadows.

The deeper he looked, the more Zinc fathomed.

This coral wasn't just coral. It was a multitude of shapes. He spied brain coral, mushroom coral, grape coral, plate coral and shelving coral. The bright, sulfur-yellow ones with smooth surfaces were stinging coral. Interspersed with the limestone heads were the vacuum cleaners of the sea: water-filtering sponges. The fish flitting around the reef were of such myriad species that they had evolved colors and designs for sexual recognition. To mate takes joining up with a genetic partner, and if your pattern doubles as camouflage to hide you from predators, so much the better. So here, passing in front of his mask, Zinc saw butterfly fish, goatfish, angelfish, damselfish and unicorn fish flash by as electric spectrums. He saw lionfish with orange and white stripes, their fins tipped with poisonous spines. He saw triggerfish with "attitude" that tried to scare him off. He saw parrotfish with beak-like teeth that chewed up hard coral to get at the delicate polyps within, venting the waste through their anuses as a shower of sand. It made him wonder why everything was named for something else, then he realized that was because such reefs were truly an alien realm.

You compare to what you *know.*

Including unicorns.

The monsters of the deep began down where Yvette was exploring the drop-off. Red sea whips and fans called gorgonians after the Gorgon, a snake-haired monster of Greek mythology, swayed in the currents that buffeted the coral wall. Giant clams with their wavy lips agape to reveal blue insides seemed poised to gobble her up. The tentacles of an octopus undulated in a hidey-hole, beneath the jutting ledge of which a school of purple-and-yellow fairy basslets swam upside down. Protruding from the crevice below that, its head weaving back and forth like a cobra's, its jaws hinged wide to expose rows of sharp needlelike teeth, a moray eel sought an opportunity to sink its fangs into something. When it went for the eye of a nearby fish to clamp onto what should have been its head, the prey got away because its tail was patterned with a false eyespot and its real eye was masked by a dark band at the other end.

As Yvette was coming up for air, Zinc espied pelagics—open-ocean creatures—in the depths beneath her.

A large green sea turtle gnawed on a sponge.

Other deep-water denizens pulled up along the reef like cars at a service station for work by "cleaner fish," the tiny parasites that feed off others' scale detritus.

Way down under at a hundred feet or more, a graceful manta ray slipped like a stealth bomber through the blue abyss by slow, rubbery beats of its broad wings.

And deeper down, where the viz faded into shadows, there slipped what might be a shiver of reef sharks.

Well, well, wondered Zinc. What do we have here?

For as his eyes followed Yvette up the face of the underwater cliff, the Mountie caught sight of a graveyard of dead coral. All that remained of what had recently been a colony of colorful polyps were the bleached bones of their limestone skeletons. In a twist of irony, the polyps in this coral reef were falling prey to a nocturnal raider with the same name as Bret Lister's newest book: a crown of thorns. Hiding among the rock nooks until it ventured out tonight was the purple starfish, two feet across, with thirteen to sixteen arms—Zinc couldn't see them all to count—its top side prickled with short, sharp, toxic spines.

The depths in front of the Mountie's mask were suddenly suffused with the shade of blood, until both the crown of thorns feeding off this reef and Yvette, nearing the surface, were submerged in a red sea.

Blood?

Sharks . . .

The cop craned his neck around.

Several feet behind Zinc, the terrified gaze of Miles Yeager stared out from the window of his face mask, air bubbles leaking from the seals around his quivering lips, blood pumping out from the puncture wound in his chest, which had been caused by the steel spear-gun shaft that was rammed spine to sternum through his heaving torso.

Yeager went into spasms.

Blood . . .

Sharks . . .

Thrashing!

Get out of the water! thought Zinc.

Like a whale spewing out through its blowhole, Yvette blasted the brine from her snorkel as she broke to the surface. Tearing the tube from her mouth as Zinc did the same, she yelled, "What happened? He's been speared!"

"Did you see any sharks?"

"Sharks!"

"Beneath you on the dive?"

"No."

The blast of another snorkel-clearing blew skyward from the water beyond the speared man. Wes Grimmer surfaced just inside the turquoise edge of the lagoon and yelled across the pool of blood that reddened the gap in the reef.

"Did you see that? Bret's mad! The fucker tried to kill me! That spear he fired missed by inches."

"Missed you," Zinc shouted back, "but it hit Yeager. Help me get him out of the water before he's shark bait."

"Sharks! You see sharks?"

But the Mountie was already swimming.

Soon, a gory streak of blood stained the idyllic powder-white sand of the nearest *motu* as Zinc, Wes and Yvette hauled Yeager ashore.

The skewered man's mouth gaped like that of a fish out of water. Each gulp of air bubbled blood around the spear shaft that had been driven through his lung. The spearhead that tipped the missile rod spiking out of Yeager's chest was a wicked one known as a Tahitian, with a "flopper" barb: the hinged barb hugged the shaft as it rammed through, then flopped wide so there was no struggling free. Normally, a shaft was strung to its speargun with a line, but this one was free to go with anything it hit because the shooter didn't want to reel in his catch.

This was for blood sport, not for food.

As Yvette and Wes saw to the dying man, Zinc stood on the beach and skimmed the glassy lagoon to get a fix on where Lister was from his snorkel. Facing him on the opposite shore were the Eyes of Tangaroa, those side-by-side caves burrowed into the *makatea* cliff on both flanks of the nose between that was Marae O Rongo. Rising out of the lagoon as the tide ebbed toward the sea was a sandbar in the shallows. Her back to the reef and unaware of the drama, Petra surfaced and waded from the water onto the hump of sand. And sure enough, on the heels of the bathing beauty, Bill Pigeon splashed out of the lagoon like a faithful dog.

Then . . .

"Look out!" Zinc yelled.

Bret Lister surfaced waist-deep in the shallows behind them like the Creature from the Blue Lagoon to let loose another spear that skewered Pigeon in the back.

As Petra swiveled in response to Zinc's warning, the speared man clutched hold of her in a futile attempt to stand fast on his buckling legs. Clinging desperately to her, the lawyer let out the sort of squeal you'd hear from a stuck pig and dragged Petra down with him as he crumpled to the sand.

Now Bret was out of the water and approaching the sprawled pair. As Petra looked up from beneath the burden of the mauling lawyer, Bret seemed to smash the back end of the gun down on her head. Zinc didn't see the blow hit because Bret blocked his view, but Petra's feet ceased digging into the sand as soon as the weapon descended.

Then Bret pulled a diver's knife.

Moments after he had bent over and slashed at the sand, then sawed back and forth several times, Bret straightened up with Pigeon's severed head in his hand. Holding it out toward the idol erected on the *marae* like Cook Islands cannibals used to do with their sacrifices to the elder gods, the psycho gouged one of the eyes out of its socket with his bloody knife.

"Rongo!" Bret offered in a voice loud enough to conjure that god from the invisible realm.

Throwing back his head, Lister gulped the eye down his gullet like Rongomatane had done.

"Rongo!" he summoned.

And gouged out the other eye.

And then gobbled it.

Then—the severed head and the speargun in his other hand—Bret grabbed hold of Petra by one arm and began to drag her toward the Eyes of Tangaroa.

bLEEDiNG BAiT

Petra's role in all of this was still unclear.

If she was a killer, then Bret's turning on her might be rough justice. But if she wasn't . . .

The Mountie had to act.

Staunching the blood flow from Miles Yeager's wound necessitated the removal of the spear from his torso. Wes had laid down his speargun and was busy unscrewing the Tahitian barb at the front end of the steel rod so the shaft could be extracted. Commandeering the weapon from the sand, Zinc splashed back into the lagoon as quickly as the fins flapping on his feet would allow, then, getting wet again, he headed for the sandbar that humped from the sea.

Keeping the fins underwater so they didn't break the surface, Zinc kicked from the hip for sleek propulsion. His arms were of no use in this torpedo run, so they hugged his streamlined sides, with one hand trailing the pneumatic gun. Several times, the Mountie bobbed his maskless face to see where he was going, and as soon as his chest hit the sandbar like that of a beached whale, he rolled over on his back, sat up in the shallows, yanked the fins from his feet and scrambled ashore.

Bill Pigeon's headless corpse lay sprawled on a stretch of churned sand that crested the hump that was rising out of the ebbing waters of the sun-drenched lagoon. The saturated red sand had soaked up his blood as fast as his heart had gushed it out. A trail of blood from the severed head Zinc had seen in Lister's grasp ran up the isthmus linking the sandbar to the island's permanent shore. Parallel to the drips that drained from the lawyer's brainpan were a set of footprints impressed by the psycho's soles and ragged drag marks gouged out of the sand by Petra's heels.

The spoor led the cop to a patch of coconut palms near the *marae,* where Bret's gear was piled with that of the others on the Odyssey. Footprints turned to shoeprints at that point, so Bret had shod himself before venturing on. The gout of blood that stained the spot where he had set the severed head down on the sand was now overrun by an army of red ants. Zinc rummaged through his own gear to retrieve a pair of shoes.

From the shade, the tracks led Zinc to the cave that sank into the *makatea* as the right Eye of Tangaroa. There, the prints, the drips and the drag marks were swallowed up by the darkness in the deep throat of the yawning mouth. With runners now on his feet, a flashlight in one hand and Wes's armed speargun in the other, the Mountie pursued the psycho into the Morlocks's wormhole.

A cave is a cavity in solid rock, a naturally burrowed void in the ground. The caves in the Cook Islands were hollowed out of the *makatea* by millions of years of corrosive action by rainwater percolating through the acidic vegetable matter growing on top, before seeping down into the dead coral to dissolve an interconnecting maze of tunnels, chambers and caverns out of the sedimentary limestone raised from the bottom of the sea.

Crouching to make himself as condensed a target as possible, Zinc scurried into the entrance zone of the beach cave. Backlit by the brilliant glare of tropical sunlight striking and reflecting off the lagoon, the round mouth was a shooting gallery with him as the only duck. Fully expecting a spear to come flying out at him from the dark gullet of the huge cavern beyond the hole, Zinc darted in around the side edge of the coral lips to seek refuge in the shadows.

No spear.

Nothing.

So he let his eyes adjust.

Like photographic paper developing a hidden picture, the contours of this subterranean vault slowly materialized. *Stalactite* is a Greek word for "oozing out in drops." All stalactites begin as "soda straws," like the cluster of dripstones hanging above Zinc's head and raining drops down on him.

On gazing up, it seemed to Zinc as if the world hung upside down, as if the soda straws were an inverted bed of nails. On gazing down, the Mountie saw the trail of blood across dry patches on the rocky floor, and he followed them from the sunny entrance zone of the cave into the dusky twilight zone of perpetual shade.

What was that?

A cry in the dark ahead?

Was it a scream?

Or was it maniacal laughter?

The deeper reaches of the drippy cavern thickened into a labyrinth of vertical speleothems. Block the central holes of soda straws and they filled out into carrot or tapered stalactites like these, fattened by deposits of calcite dribbling down their sides. Each narrowed to a drip point at its bottom, and where drops of dissolved limestone splashed down to spread out on a flat surface, built up mounds with rounded tops and no internal canals. Where stalactites and stalagmites fused together, they formed columns like this petrified forest around Zinc. The drops that had dripped onto the slope slanting into the tunnel at the back of the cavern formed a slick tongue of flowstone across the uneven floor beneath the Mountie's feet.

A single stalactite hung like an uvula at the deep throat. It marked the point where the twilight zone of perpetual dusk gave way to the dark zone of pitch-black night.

As he crooked his arm and swung behind the stalactite as if it were a square dance partner, Zinc glanced back at the mouth of the cave. Seen from here, the upper and lower speleothems could be fangs in a set of gaping jaws. Where the sunbeams hit crystals in the glistening formations, they sparkled like pearly whites in a toothpaste commercial.

What was that?

Another cry?

The Mountie stepped into the dark.

The switched-on beam of his flashlight took over from the sun. He was courting suicide by caving in the Cooks with just this single source of light. The rule of thumb was to carry three. Some of the caves through the *makatea* were known to go on forever. One of them, Teruarere—meaning "jump," because you had to jump down to get in—snaked into the earth on Mangaia for at least a mile, and probably a lot farther, since no one had ever reached the end. Other caves were festooned with endless chambers. On Mauke, Motuanga Cave—or the Cave of 100 Rooms—extended out toward the sea and under the reef. You could hear the waves crashing above you in the outermost reaches.

The extent of this cave could be similar to those. Barring a sinkhole where the ceiling had caved in, every vault from here on was born in perpetual blackness and would never see a smidgen of the light of day. With each step Zinc took, the maze would grow more convoluted. The main "going" channel might bifurcate, or branch off. Such multiple passageways might twist, turn, double back, loop, intertwine and reconnect. Crawlways, fissures, pools, sumps, pits, potholes and slides might lurk ahead. There are many ways to die in a cave: you can drown, fall, be crushed to death by loose rocks or simply get lost and starve. So what if he were to drop and smash his only source of light? Or what if the batteries ran out of juice? Here, in the bowels of this island, Zinc would be smothered by a blackout, with no escape but to *feel* his way out.

Imagine that.

Or better yet, don't. For little fears beget bigger fears and can then spin out of control.

Especially if your biggest fear is fear of being buried alive.

What was that?

Click . . . click . . .

Movement overhead.

Jerking the beam of the torch up, Zinc thought he spied a bat. That was all he needed: rabies underground. The flashlight struck a stalactite, but it didn't break. The dripstone rang with a deep organ tone. Flitting past it was a tiny swift-like bird. Called a kopeka, it nested in the caves. When kopekas flew outside to hunt insects, they never landed. Only in here did they rest. By chattering a series of clicks and listening for the echoes, the birds used echolocation to navigate among the dripstones the same way a bat does.

Click, click, click, click . . .

The cave was suddenly alive with birds.

And there it was.

Yet again.

Definitely a laugh.

Two tunnels led out of the kopeka cavern. Like the bird, Zinc used echoes from the laughter to choose which route to take. There had to be a catchment basin of some sort above, for halfway along the passageway to the next belling-out, water began to drip copiously into the tunnel. By the time Zinc reached a cool grotto that domed above a mineral pool, the floor was a wallow of orange mud. The ooze clung to his runners, letting go reluctantly with slurps, burps and gurgles. Tree roots and vines hung down from the ceiling like fairy-tale ladders, as if this were a subterranean mimic of *Jack and the Beanstalk*.

With no trail of bread crumbs like the one Hansel laid down so Gretel and he could find their way back through the wicked woods from the gingerbread house, and with no ball of string like that Tom Sawyer used as a guide to return him home from his underground adventure, Zinc would have to rely on his own sense of direction. So at every junction along his descent into the belly of Tangaroa, the Mountie glanced back to store a memory of this route in reverse.

It pays to have been a Boy Scout.

From here on, the Grimm Brothers' realm took on a grimmer tone. Eerie apparitions seemed to hover just beyond the reality of the glow of the flashlight. The dripstones closing in on Zinc transmogrified into gargoyle demons. Creeping and crawling, slithering and scuttling in the blackness beyond the beam, cave-dwelling troglodytes skulked in the nooks, unseen by the spelunking Mountie. Protruding from the razor-sharp walls of honeycombed coral skeletons that were hemming Zinc in as he passed along this tube like waste down a cancerous intestine were the fossils of prehistoric denizens of the deep.

Look at the teeth on that one.

It made him shiver.

Deep in the dark zone of this cave system, where the temperature remained constantly cool no matter how hot it got outside by the lagoon, Zinc was on a journey to the center of the earth. The cop knew he was on the right trail from the blood drops and the heel scuffs on the man-made crushed coral path that had smoothed the way in since the end of the flowstone.

The jolt of suddenly seeing the hacked-off head facing him at eye level in the stygian dark made Zinc jerk back. The hand that held the flashlight brushed against the tunnel wall. Wherever his skin touched the blades of dead coral, a red slit opened into his flesh.

The flashlight tumbled.

Smash!

The beam end broke.

The lens shattered.

But not the bulb.

Gingerly retrieving the torch from the floor, Zinc shone the naked beam into the next cavern. Bill Pigeon's severed head was mounted upside down on a stake in the same manner as the head displayed outside Ted Bundy's house. The plucked-out eyes had cried bloody tears down both cheeks, and now the inverted cranium was weeping them down its forehead. The spike of the sharpened stake stuck up out of the neck stump.

Throughout those Cook Islands with *makatea* rings, you will find a spook-fest of burial caves. *Tiringa ivi*—"the throwing away of the bones"—is an ancient Polynesian tradition, for the body is but a mere bundle of bones once the spirit exits. When and why the bones were buried in each cave is an unsolved mystery, for they all date from the prehistoric period before the tall ships arrived. The bones in some of the burial caves are revered as those of the great-great-ancestors of the nearest village. Other bones just rot. But whatever their origin, one thing is for sure. It remains *tapu* to touch or move the cave bones. Do so and, at the very least, you'll be cursed.

This, Zinc discovered, was one of those catacombs.

The vault he found himself in was circular in shape, with several shadowy entrances to offshoot tunnels. Picking one would be like playing Russian roulette. Since the trail of blood drips stopped here with the discarded head, how would the Mountie know which one to choose? It struck him that it had been a while since he had last heard Bret's unhinged laugh. Sweeping the beam around the floor where it met the circular walls, the Mountie saw dozens of skeletons ringed on the crushed coral, the bones of each, orange from age, gathered into a neat pile crowned by its skull.

Were these the remains of cannibal kings?

As if lying in wait for the unwary, a sinkhole sank in the center of the bone chamber. Water had washed away the underlying rock, causing the floor to cave in on itself. The yawning pit looked as if it had been ripped apart. The stake with the head spiked on top was wedged into the cracked seam on the far side of the opening, as if to warn the Mountie of the peril below. Only when he let the torchlight sink into the hole did he see Petra crumpled at the bottom of the rift.

Her face was bloody.

Was she dead?

To find out, Zinc would have to climb down and check. Footholds and handholds indented the walls of the twelve-foot drop. Petra lay on a rocky shelf that surrounded a deep pool seething with a nest of snakelike eels. It was obvious from watermarks on the walls that the level of water in the sinkhole rose and fell with the tide, not an uncommon occurrence in the Cooks.

However, if Zinc were to descend into the narrow pit and Bret was hiding in one of the offshoot tunnels, it would be like shooting fish in a barrel—literally—for him to emerge with the speargun and shoot down at the trapped Mountie.

Was that the plan?

Was Petra bleeding bait?

Suddenly, the threat wasn't to Zinc or her, for echoing down the chain of caverns and tunnels from back where the wormhole entered the *makatea,* a bout of madcap laughter burst from Bret. The psychotic had used a parallel path to double back to the beach, and there he had found another quarry.

"Help!"

A single cry.

"Help, Zinc!"

Repeated.

The Mountie knew the voice. "Christ, no," he muttered.

Yvette was in trouble.

BIBLE BELT

Mission

As DeClercq drove over the Stave River bridge to enter Mission, it began to pour. From the Ripper's home on Colony Farm, he had followed the Lougheed Highway inland for twenty-five miles, up the north bank of the Fraser River as the sky above the valley glowered darker by the minute. On the edge of Coquitlam, he had crossed the Pitt River just south of Minnekhada Lodge, the site of last week's red serge dinner, and north of the junction where the Pitt joined the muddy Fraser. From town to town, he traveled along the historical Bible Belt, traversing Pitt Meadows and winding his way eastward through Maple Ridge towns with hayseed names like Haney, Albion, Whonnock and Ruskin. Then, just before the Plumper Reach part of the Fraser, the black sky was split asunder by a lightning bolt, a fizzing flash that filled the valley, followed seconds later by a deafening *boom* of thunder and, as the Mountie crested the bridge that spanned the Stave River tributary, this downpour of rain.

Ah, yes.

The wet West Coast.

The Fraser River has always been the aorta of this province, pumping its lifeblood from the Rocky Mountains to the sea. In the beginning, before there was written history, these banks were home to Sto:lo Natives of the Salish Nation for about ten thousand years. The Sto:lo were a peaceful people—the Eloi of that time—who were prey to Kwakiutl cannibals living by the sea,

Morlocks who ventured upriver on slave-taking raids for food to feed the Hamatsas, their cannibal cult, and Baxbakualanuxsiwae—He-Who-Is-First-to-Eat-Man-at-the-Mouth-of-the-River—their flesh-eating cannibal god.

In 1824, the fur trade lured the Hudson's Bay Company upriver to build Fort Langley on the south bank. The smallpox and T.B. the white men brought cut the Sto:lo population by four-fifths. In 1858, gold was discovered on the Fraser River, and hordes of white miners came rushing in. To keep the mother lode safe from annexation by America, economic honchos at the fort that same year established British Columbia as a Crown colony. When enterprising miners began a lucrative whisky trade to add rampant alcoholism to the Sto:los' escalating problems, the call went out for someone to save those helpless "children of the forest" and "savages in the mission fields" from the moral degradation of white men's vices, and that—Hallelujah, Jesus!—brought the missionaries to Mission.

The man who had answered that call to serve in the mission fields of the Lord was Father Leon Fouquet of the Roman Catholic Church. Here on the north side of the Fraser in 1862, Father Fouquet founded St. Mary's Mission, named not after the Virgin Mary, as you might suppose, but after an Egyptian prostitute who did penance for fifty years to atone for her sins. The mission, after all, was established to eradicate immorality.

Within a year, the Catholics had built a church and a gristmill to foster farming. But if the "children of the forest" were to be permanently weaned from their primitive, heathen culture, what the priests had to do was grab hold of their *actual* children. Consequently, St. Mary's Mission also built the first residential school for aboriginal kids in the Crown colony.

In 1885, the Canadian Pacific Railway came chugging in. Among the pioneer settlers who stepped off the trains to populate the town of Mission around St. Mary's and the railroad station were—to use the Catholics' term—the Devil's servants. The Protestant churches they founded sought to save heathen souls too, and soon Mission had Protestant residential schools for Native kids as well.

"Suffer the little children to come unto me . . ."

The downpour pummeled the roof of the Benz and washed across the windshield like a biblical flood as DeClercq forded the gushing streets of this riverside town of thirty thousand souls forty-four miles east of Vancouver. He was hunting for the address that matched the name of the person who had visited the Ripper shortly before and after the Hanged Man murder in North Vancouver a year and a half ago. His quest conveyed him to the far side of Mission, on the edge of what is now the Fraser River Heritage Park, site of the old St. Mary's Mission. He found the number on a sign that had been staked by the curb at the mouth of a driveway that ran along one side of a spacious wooded lot, with what seemed to be an old church buried back in the trees.

"Private Property."

"Keep Out."

Those were the words on the sign.

The chief superintendent parked his car against the curb and climbed out into the deluge. By the time his umbrella popped open, he was soaking wet. Ignoring the warning to "Keep Out" that had been posted at the mouth of the drive, he sloshed toward the old Gothic Revival church that lurked in the trees. Only when he got close enough to survey the entire building did he conclude that the church was now a house. What clinched it was the fact that the church was painted black.

The desecrated house of God was characterized by pointed arches and vertical lines. The layout was simple and followed the common east–west axis of most chapels. The driveway—more a river than a road today—led DeClercq to the ominous front doors. Crafted from planks interlocked in a herringbone pattern, the door had the heavy hinges of a jail cell, and the knocker was something out of the Satanic Bible.

What was that Lovecraft text?

The *Necronomicon.*

DeClercq rapped the demonic knob on the knocker plate.

Rap . . .

Rap . . .

Rap . . .

Not a sound from within.

Was no one home?

He stepped back from the black door and squinted up into the rain. The facade was fronted with beveled clapboards. Painted black on black above the Gothic arch of the door were three words composed of letters cut with a fretsaw: "TRUE GOSPEL MISSION." Above the name that had graced the church in bygone times, a bull's-eye window of red glass was set into the facade so those inside could look out on the world through its bloodshot Cyclopean stare.

DeClercq wondered if he was being watched now.

Soaring above the peak of the steep gabled roof was a stiletto of a steeple that stabbed at the clouds above. Its base was an octagonal tower with vertical slits for the pealing of the bell in the belfry to ring out. Spiked on top was a slender spire that rose to a point crowned with a warped Christian cross.

Fishing out his cellphone, the chief called Special X.

"Inspector George," Ghost Keeper answered.

"Bob, it's Robert. I'm out in Mission. Standing in Noah's flood in front of what used to be an Indian mission church. The steeple has a damaged cross. Ring a bell?"

"True Gospel Mission?"

"That's the one."

"If you see an old priest hanging around, arrest him," said the inspector. "The task force wants him for a string of sex crimes."

"Against girls or boys?"

"Both," said the Cree.

As was all too common in the news these days, B.C.'s network of church-run residential schools had been exposed as hunting grounds for pedophiles. The 1980s witnessed the closing of Native dorms. A royal commission likened the schools to Nazi internment camps. In 1994, the Mounties had launched a huge investigation aimed at ninety identified suspects. Until his promotion to inspector at Special X, Ghost Keeper was second in command of the task force.

"The cross atop the steeple piqued my memory," said DeClercq. "I recall you mentioning it during a red serge dinner."

"The cross was struck by lightning. The blast twisted the metal. It could have burned down the entire church."

"When was that?"

"The early nineties. Around the time the old reverend vanished. A week later, the mission school burned down."

"Arson?"

"No doubt. Perhaps a former student."

"An open case?"

"Yep. Both the fire *and* the priest."

"No idea where he is?"

"He could be anywhere. We think one of the guys from St. Mary's is hiding in Southeast Asia."

"True Gospel Mission," said DeClercq. "That doesn't sound like a mainstream church."

"It wasn't. They were the cannibal priests."

"*Cannibal* priests?"

"That's what I call them. True Gospel was recruited in London in the early 1800s as one of the missionary societies that went to the South Seas to convert the cannibals discovered by Captain Cook."

"Captain Cook," DeClercq said. "Zinc should be here."

"Yeah, I hear he's following in Cook's footsteps. True Gospel established its church on the island of Tangaroa."

"Year?"

"Can't remember. In the mid-1820s."

"What happened?"

"The mission succeeded. The islanders had no difficulty accepting Jesus and the Last Supper—especially the part where he shared his flesh and blood with his apostles."

"It's a weird concept," DeClercq agreed. "Holy Communion. The rite of the Eucharist."

In Roman Catholic doctrine—they call it transubstantiation—it is not enough that the communicant should *believe* he is eating the flesh and drinking the blood of Christ; at the instant of Holy Communion, when the wafer and the wine are consumed, they are said *literally* to turn into the body of the son of God.

"Cannibalism is inextricably linked to that Christian rite, so that's what True Gospel missionaries used to convert the Cook Islands cannibals to their church."

"What brought them here?" DeClercq asked.

"The Kwakiutls. Having transformed the South Pacific's cannibals into converts, the missionaries set out to accomplish the same result with the North Pacific's man-eaters."

"When was that?"

"The 1850s. Thereabouts. They worked with other missions to get the potlatch banned, and once the Hamatsa cult was under control, True Gospel went upriver to convert the Sto:los."

"What's the connection?"

"The Sto:los were the Kwakiutl cannibals' victims, so Christ was an easy sell. And it was the perfect environment for fire-and-brimstone preachers. In those days, the Fraser Valley was literally full of fire and brimstone. Mount Baker, just across the border in the States, was a fire-spewing, constantly smoking, active volcano."

"Then what?"

"With no more cannibals to convert, True Gospel's missionaries drifted away. Those who remained copied St. Mary's and built a Native residential school. By the latter half of the 1900s, the church had become a family affair."

"How so?" asked DeClercq.

"It passed from father to son. The old missionary saw the crusade through the fifties, sixties and seventies. His son and his son's wife took over in the 1980s. Then tragedy struck two decades ago, when the couple were killed in a flaming car crash on the Lougheed Highway. The church reverted back to the old man, who carried on as its reverend until the day he vanished."

"In the 1990s."

"Uh-huh. Just before the sex scandal broke. By then, of course, the Native residential school had been closed for years. It shut down about the same time as St. Mary's, in the early eighties. The son did that."

"Then he and his wife died in the crash."

"Right, and the old man picked up until he vanished."

"What happened to the property? The church looks like a private house."

"It passed to the grandkid who was orphaned by the fiery crash."

"Grandkid?" said DeClercq.

"Yeah. Raised by the dirty old man. Until his sexual sins from the residential-school period were about to catch up with him. So he put his tail between his legs and ran for the hills."

———

Ten minutes later, DeClercq ended the call.

Using the disappearance of the priest in Mission and the murders in North Vancouver and Seattle as his reasonable and probable grounds, the chief phoned another number to get a telewarrant.

Then he called Mission Detachment on the western edge of town and asked the local Mounties to join him at the church.

A short time later, the handheld Ram-It battering ram smashed in the front door of the Goth's home.

MANA A MANA

Tangaroa

Like a baseball runner who is caught in a hotbox between second and third, Zinc had to make up his mind which way to go, and either way, there was a hindering obstacle in his path.

To get to Petra, who might already be dead, would require a time-consuming climb down the razor-sharp wall of the sinkhole pit. Then he would somehow have to hoist her back up. To abandon Petra, if she was alive, meant she would drown in the rising waters of a well full of eels.

To get to Yvette, who might already be dead if her second cry for help was her final act in life, would require a life-or-death scramble back the way he'd come, guided by the precarious beam of a single flashlight bulb. Slip or trip, and it would be game over.

In the end, however, it was no contest. Since the death of Alex, the Mountie had been eating himself up with grief, guilt and depression, and all of a sudden, from out of nowhere, he had a new lease on happiness in Yvette. If he were to lose this manna from heaven because he didn't give rescuing Yvette his all, there was no question in his mind that he would fall apart.

Was Petra a killer who ran afoul of her partner? Or had she merely provided Bret with a false alibi? In either case, Petra's index of guilt was dirtier than Yvette's, so her rescue was going to have to wait.

Time and tide wait for no man?

Well, they'd have to.

The journey back through the tract of grottos to the beach beside the lagoon was less harrowing than it might have been, thanks to those fix-taking glances over his shoulder on the venture in, plus the trail of shoeprints impressed by his own feet and still preserved in the carpet of crushed coral and dripstone mud on the floor of the cave. The naked bulb held up until Zinc exited through the mouth in the *makatea* and staggered onto the sand, shielding his eyes from the dazzling glare of the sun.

"Yvette!" he yelled.

No reply.

"Bret!" he yelled.

No reply.

Not even a laugh.

"Wes!" he yelled.

No reply.

Zinc was alone on the beach.

The first thing he saw once his eyes adjusted was some thrashing out in the bloody water of the lagoon. A shiver of sharks, having swum in from beyond the reef, were tearing a man to bits. Miles Yeager was no longer stretched out on the beach of the *motu,* nor was there any sign out there of Yvette or Wes. Had they tried to haul the wounded man in for better first aid, relying on the fact that as a general rule throughout the islands, reef sharks stay clear of the shallows within lagoons? But every rule has its exceptions, and this was one of them. Was the meat out there just Miles Yeager's? Or had Wes joined him on the menu?

Zinc noted that only *one* set of fresh prints dotted the sand.

The Mountie studied this trail that ran parallel to his emergence from the lagoon. Obviously Yvette. The feet of a woman, for sure. She had followed his route across the water from the *motu* and waded ashore on the same sandbar as he had done. Passing the headless body on the crest of the bloody tongue, Yvette had tracked Zinc's prints to the gear piled in the shade near the *marae*. As she was rummaging in her bag for something—probably shoes—Bret had exited stealthily from the other Eye of Tangaroa. Catching Yvette by surprise, he had struggled with her and subdued her—

God, no, did he kill her?—then he must have picked her up and carried her off, for only a single set of shoeprints vanished back into the left Eye of Tangaroa.

Reading the marks in the sand, the Mountie pictured what had happened in his mind's eye. That Bret was the attacker was apparent from the evidence. Not only had Zinc heard him laugh from back at the mouth of the cave, but these shoeprints were the same as the ones that he had tracked into the right Eye of Tangaroa. So somewhere in the bowels of the *makatea,* the caves beyond the pair of wormholes that burrowed in from the lagoon must interconnect.

What was that?

He cocked an ear.

Was that Yvette he heard?

Nothing . . .

Nothing . . .

There it was again!

It *was* Yvette!

Crying out in pain!

Frantically, the inspector tore into the pile of gear, heaving things aside until he found another flashlight. With no time to hunt for a backup torch, he cut across Marae O Rongo to reach the other Eye, skirting past the idol of Tangaroa. A moment later, Zinc was swallowed up by the black hole of the alternative route back in.

Damned if you don't.

And damned if you do.

———•◦•———

This cave was unlike the cave next door. Where that network was a festoon of caverns strung in a straight line like a highway—or low way—to hell, this complex was a sponge-work resembling Swiss cheese, with a selection of mouths, tubes and interconnecting cavities. Choosing a route to reach Yvette was like playing the lottery: chances were the one he picked would hit a dead end.

This entrance zone was another cavern fanged with stalactites and stalagmites the size of a giant's teeth. No tongue of flowstone stretched across the rough floor—instead, walking through it was akin to a cross-country hike with hillocks to climb and boulders to scramble over. At the rear, there wasn't a single throat beyond a uvula. Instead, the Mountie was faced with three similar holes into the dark unknown.

Eenie, meenie, miney, moe.

Catch a psycho by the toe.

If he hollers . . .

Another cry from Yvette!

But which hole did it come from?

This cave seemed to be an echo chamber.

Another desperate scream.

No time to dither.

Figuring that the central tunnel had *two* flanks that might interconnect with the parallel passageways, the Mountie chose the middle entry hole.

With the flashlight in one hand and the speargun in the other, Zinc had to mind his step within the confines of the tube. He had learned a painful lesson on his first quest into the razorblade realm of the deadly *makatea,* and the edge of his palm still bled from the multiple lacerations of his brush against the coral. Ideally, a skilled caver will maintain three points of contact with the encasing rock—hands, feet, stomach, buttocks, back, arms, legs or head—until he secures a new hold as a fourth. In the *makatea* of the Cooks, that was wishful thinking, so with only two points—his feet—that Zinc could count on, he had to plan ahead by shining the beam two or three steps in advance before testing the placement of each foot and applying his full weight. As with the sinkhole that had claimed Petra, a thin crust of calcite might overlay a deep hollow where the underlying dirt and gravel had washed away, leaving a false floor above the real floor below.

A pit in which jutting rocks might lurk like punji stakes.

One misstep, and it would all be over.

So despite the precious time that it wasted, Zinc had to watch each footfall.

To add to his growing unease, this tunnel was gradually shrinking in diameter. Since entering, he hadn't seen a sign of human traffic: blood spots or shoeprints on the hard rock floor. Nor had he heard another wail out of Yvette. What loomed before him at the outer limits of the probing beam was a void as dark and as silent as a tomb, and with each step Zinc took toward that constricted nothingness, the ring of razors closed tighter and tighter on him. What had begun as a normal walk had turned into a stoop; the Mountie had to duck-walk to keep from cracking his head. He suddenly realized that he had lost his hat—so absorbed was he in the mounting crisis that he had failed to notice when it had slipped off. A bare head and a low ceiling combined to add yet another peril. Strike the *makatea* and he would scalp himself.

A rush of panic seized him.

It welled up into his throat like a bubble of black bile, and quelling the jitters took a titanic effort.

Bad was sinking to worse.

One of our most deeply rooted fears is the dread of being buried alive. Fear of walls closing in on you can snap the human mind. For those who share the abject terror of claustrophobia, the thought of being encased in stone until the end of consciousness foments a level of panic that rattles every bone. It was cramped in here already, and getting smaller and smaller. Zinc was down on his haunches, and he would soon be on his hands and his knees. And it wasn't just the tunnel that had him in a squeeze, for now the flashlight beam was dimming too, the failing batteries causing the light to flicker.

Smaller and smaller waned the pool of dying light.

Within a couple of minutes, Zinc would be in the dark.

The tunnel Zinc was in pinched out to a dead end. Well, not quite dead—there was a straitjacket crawlway down near the floor, a cubbyhole barely large enough for a man to slither in, and definitely cramped enough for him to get stuck. It was probably a runoff spout from whenever this tunnel was last full of water, and maybe it connected with a parallel passage.

No way was Zinc going in.

The thought of it made him shudder.

He was already turning back when he heard the scream.

Yvette's screech echoed in through the crawlway at Zinc's feet, a shriek that loudly informed him that she was in torment on the other side of the right-hand wall. He stifled the urge to call out to her, for fear of prompting Bret to finish her off. Dropping onto his knees, he bent over to shine the beam into the claustrophobic hole as—*wink . . . wink . . . wink*—the flashlight died.

It seemed to the Mountie as if time had stopped. Plunged into this cocoon of darkness, what options did he have? Abandon Yvette and claw his way back through a tunnel of razors as a blind man or squeeze into this straitjacket of a black hole and pray the elder gods would let him through.

Another scream.

"Nooooo . . ."

Echoing in and away.

"Nooooo . . .

"Nooooo . . .

"Nooooo . . ."

Into the hellhole Zinc squirmed.

At six-foot-two and 190 pounds—his broad-shouldered physique muscled from all that hard labor on the family farm through his developing years, then kept up by regular workouts during his adulthood—Zinc Chandler was too big a man for such a Hobbit hole. With no suitable pocket to store it in, he had to relinquish the flashlight, even though he knew it might be needed later as a club. Only by twisting himself into a Houdini-like contortion was he able to crawl into the bone-hugging hole. So narrow was the sphincter that seemed to tighten around his body that there was no space for his arms except stretched out in front of his head. With one hand gripping the speargun while the other scrabbled at the rock to pull him forward, the Mountie gradually wormed into the crawlway by wriggling his torso and pushing with the toes of his runners. His belly bore the brunt of the squirm along the shaft, and it was scratched by the unforgiving nubs of coral that had been dulled down from razor sharpness by flooding in the past.

Then Zinc got stuck.

The spookiest part of spelunking is the nasty squeeze, and this was a nasty squeeze that caught the Mountie around his chest just back of his shoulder bones. Instinctively, Zinc knew now was not the time to panic, since the only way out of this bind was to be as pliable as could be, and a tense, muscle-bunched body won't "pour" through a nasty hole. Luckily, fear lubricated his skin with sweat. Luckier still, the constriction was cinched around his lungs, so by exhaling all the breath from his diaphragm, Zinc was able to shrink his chest size by an inch. Luckiest, when his free hand felt around for an effective grip, he found he could lock his fingers around the rim of the crawlway. So, shoving the speargun out into the passage ahead, he gripped both hands around the hole's outer edge and, pulling as hard as he could, yanked himself to freedom.

To freedom *and* light.

The tunnel into which Zinc emerged from the grim crawl of death appeared to deliver him into the fire and smoke of eternal damnation. At the far end of this passage, bronze flickers lit up whatever lurked beyond. The glow burnished the ceiling from the anus of this black bowel to the point where Zinc crouched panting and shivering in the clammy chill of the dark. What absorbed the color was moon milk gunked on the rock overhead, a whitish, putty-like flowstone that forms on an organic matrix. Smoke from whatever was burning churned toward the Mountie as the tunnel sucked it away from the bronze cavern like a chimney flue.

Bret's laugh and Yvette's whimper echoed from that chamber.

Leveling the spear-loaded gun at waist height in the same manner he would a sawed-off shotgun, Zinc closed the gap between himself and the realm full of subterranean secrets ahead. What he burst into was beyond his wildest imagination, for this cavern buried deep in the dead coral of the *makatea* housed an ossuary hoarding tens of thousands of bones. The bones must have been sacrificed over several centuries, for they were locked into the drip-stone formations by calcite deposits that had relentlessly creeped around the skeletal sculptures over time. There were stalactites and stalagmites that leered with stacks of skulls. There were columns sheathed with the same kinds of bones: a pillar of scapulas and a pillar caged in ribs. Whether by nature, man-made glue or a combination of both, the cavern was plastered from the floor up the walls and over the ceiling with a ghastly mosaic of disjointed skeletons. The flowstone underfoot was also inlaid with bones and laid out like Marae O Rongo back on shore. Skulls, arranged to face in, delineated the four sides of this religious rectangle. Piled-up long bones—humerus, radius, femur, tibia—humped from the calcite concrete to form the two rows of lesser seats. The throne of the cannibal king at the head of this underground *marae* was a mound of skulls packed in between two stalagmites, both of which were encrusted with jawless braincases. Flanking the royal throne were a pair of torches, and the bronze glow cast off by the wavering tongues of fire seemed to bring the dead back to life.

No bones about it, this hellhole was cursed. A cult of Morlocks had gathered in here to desecrate the bones of the Eloi they had slaughtered. If cannibalism was their religion, this cave was their cathedral. The Christian repression imposed by the idol-burners of True Gospel Mission on their South Seas crusade had hidden the man-eaters' ossuary away from curious eyes behind the quarantine curtain of the lepers' colony. Thanks to dengue fever, those Japanese archeologists had also succumbed to the curse, but somehow Bret Lister had chanced upon this Kingdom of Bones during his Cook Islands convalescence after that stint on Colony Farm with the Ripper.

"Freeze," Zinc ordered. The speargun was aimed at Lister's spine.

The psycho froze.

"Drop the knife."

The blade that had beheaded Pigeon clattered to the ground.

"*Both* knives," Zinc said.

The diver's knife from the sheath on Yvette's calf dropped too.

"You okay?" Zinc asked Yvette.

She nodded, quivering in her bonds.

"Turn around, Bret."

Lister turned. And Zinc found himself facing a triumphant smirk.

"I've been waiting for you."

"You have?" the Mountie said.

Bret licked his lips. "I'm hungry. Let's eat."

The psycho had sat Yvette down on the throne of bones, then lashed her wrists to the stalagmites on both sides. If rape was the motive, Zinc had arrived in time, for though her ankles weren't tied, Yvette still filled her blue bikini. Having witnessed Bret swallow gouged-out eyeballs on the sandbar, the Mountie had feared that a similar mutilation was causing her screams. But now it appeared that whatever Lister ultimately had in mind, the prelude to it was a drawn-out overture of psychological torture.

Thank God, Zinc thought. Just in the nick of time.

"Aren't you going to ask me?"

"Ask you what, Bret?"

"What I did with the speargun I used to spike Yeager and Pigeon, then took into the cave."

Good question.

"What did you do with the gun?"

"I've got it," said a voice behind the Mountie.

The tunnel Zinc had used to enter the grotto had delivered him at the bottom corner of the *marae.* A ninety-degree turn to the left had lined him up with the throne. Another tunnel entered near the other bottom corner, and judging from its angle into the *makatea,* it probably intersected with the parallel cave at about the point where Zinc had found Petra down the sinkhole. It was from the mouth of that tunnel that the answer to Zinc's query about the speargun came.

Whirling, the Mountie found himself confronting Wes Grimmer.

Mano a mano.

Both armed.

It was a Mexican standoff.

With a flash of insight, the inspector understood. Petra hadn't lied. On the night she spent with Bret Lister, Wes had killed and

360

dumped his victim in two parts: the head outside Ted Bundy's house and the body at the foot of the Thirteen Steps to Hell. Then on the night she spent with Wes Grimmer, Bret had killed the Cthulhu sculptor at the convention hotel. And the reason no one suspected they were a killing team was that egotistical rivalry supposedly had them gnawing at each other's throats.

Lawyers, thought Zinc.

A lawyer argues white is black or black is white, according to how he is paid. A good lawyer can argue both sides of a case with the same sincerity. Grimmer was an Olivier who switched on and off as his role dictated. Lister was a Hoffman, a method actor so immersed in his role that it took control of him. And in the end, it didn't matter who acted how, as long as it convinced the onlookers.

Sneaky. Clever.

As for *why* they did it, Zinc had little inkling. Was it some sort of Nietzschean motive? The will to wield power? To become Supermen? Leopold and Loeb? Was it the thrill a pair of big-balled lawyers got from standing above the law? Or was it sex along the lines of what the pathologist Gill Macbeth had suggested while examining the body in North Vancouver?

"Two killers would be my bet. The base of his penis and his anus are both chafed raw."

"A two-on-one?"

"That's how I see it."

"A female in front and a male behind?"

"Or two males, front and back, to form a daisy chain."

Which explained why the crime scene was cleaned up thoroughly. Both lawyers knew the forensic pitfalls.

The flash of insight sparked through Zinc's mind in a second as he and Wes aimed pneumatic spearguns at each other.

"Hobble him, Bret," said Grimmer.

"Shoot, Zinc!" Yvette pleaded.

The Mountie—caught in the middle again—was sandwiched between two psychos. He stood at the foot of the *marae* with his back to the throne of bones. The four of them were in a line that stretched across the cavern: Yvette lashed to the seat of skulls, Brett in the space between her and Zinc's back, Wes in the gloomy mouth of the tunnel burrowed in front of the cop. The torches flanking the throne of bones threw shadows onto the skeleton wall over the black hole; a pair of dark Zinc Chandlers were cast by the dual flames, and above each, a third arm with a knife grasped in its raised hand.

The hobbler.

Bret Lister.

Coming to cripple Zinc.

So first things first—take out the immediate threat—the Mountie pulled the trigger of the air gun to hurl the spear in its barrel at Grimmer before he could fire, and . . .

. . . nothing happened.

"That's *my* gun," Wes said, "and it's out of gas. A pneumatic gun won't fire unless you pump it up. I'm sorry to have to say it, pal, but we played you for a sucker."

Zinc didn't have a usable gun, but he still had the spear. A spear in the grip of two powerful arms muscled from years of heaving sheaves of wheat and bales of hay. Lightning fast on the ball of one foot, the Mountie swiveled 180 degrees around from Wes to confront Bret instead. Having retrieved one of the knives he had dropped onto the *marae,* the backstabber was about to plunge the blade deep into Zinc. With one palm on the butt end of the airless speargun, the cop jerked the barrel up with his other hand, then spiked the barbed shaft up under Bret's chin.

"*Uuugh!*"

The long and lanky lawyer was a lightweight compared with the cop. The pike rammed in by the upward thrust of the subterranean spearman ripped through the soft spot in the center of Bret's lower jaw and spiked up through his gaping mouth until the Tahitian barb struck the hard bone of his cranium. The gaffing jerked the lawyer up off his feet, and like a fisherman swinging around to land his catch in the boat, the Mountie let centrifugal force carry him around another 180 degrees, a full circle that swiveled Bret into the stretch between Zinc and Wes as the other lawyer fired his spear.

Thunk!

The shaft hit Bret somewhere in the back. Zinc let go of the gun so the whirling dervish of a lawyer could spin out across the cavern. Bret's back slammed up against the skeletal wall, driving the barb from Wes's fired spear out through his heart.

One down.

One to go.

With no need to recharge his gun—one pumping of air fueled a lot of shots—Wes was already loading another spear into the piston barrel. The weapon would be rearmed before Zinc could get to him, and if Wes retreated into the darkness of the tunnel, the Mountie would be a backlit target entering a confined space.

How could Grimmer miss?

An errant spear fired in the cavern might hit Yvette. Protecting her as well as himself would be twice as hard, so all Zinc could do to level the odds was lure Wes out of the grotto, and the only way to do that was to flee himself.

Turning, Zinc scooped up the diver's knife that Bret had dropped when he was gaffed off the floor. This cavern was the junction room of a subterranean hub, and like the spokes of a level wheel, a ring of tunnels radiated out from the *marae*. As he dashed past the throne of bones for one of the far tunnels, Zinc grabbed the nearest flaming torch from its socket to light his way back into the *makatea*.

Into the tunnel of razors.

With Wes hot on his ass.

Mana a mana.

And may the best *mana* win.

TABOO

Mission

The shrill shriek of the burglar alarm that was set off when the Ram-It smashed in the plank door of the Gothic church filled the gloomy guts of the mission with what could have been the screams of banshees, warning those partaking in a black mass that Christian infidels were storming the gates of hell. As the Mounties of Mission Detachment rushed in to secure the premises, DeClercq took in those details caught for a second by the sweeps of flashlight beams.

Flit . . .

Flit . . .

Flit . . .

The font just inside the door at the rear of the nave, traditionally filled with holy water, was stocked with a pool of coagulated blood and beset by a swarm of flies.

Flit . . .

Flit . . .

Flit . . .

Gargoyles by the dozen glared down into the nave from the scissor-trussed arrangement of crisscrossed rafters that held the high barrel-vaulted ceiling aloft.

The stained-glass window in the south wall of the nave was a dull rendering of the Last Supper. Surrounded by his twelve disciples—all except Judas Iscariot with halos around their heads—Jesus held a round wafer up in his right hand. The table was set with a goblet of wine beside what was originally an empty plate. Recently, someone had reworked the window through a little creative glazing to add joints of human meat to Christ's plate.

Flit . . .

Flit . . .

Then suddenly the church exploded with light.

A cop had flicked a switch.

What the chief's vision adjusted to was a charnel house of graphic images. The pews and kneelers on both sides of the aisle up the middle of the nave had been removed to accommodate a workshop of Gothic artists. As with the outside of the mission, the inside board-and-batten walls—vertical boards with joints covered by narrow vertical strips—were stained black. A series of moveable full-length mirrors set up like a Stonehenge circle reflected demonic details that had been captured on the canvas of paintings that turned like mobiles from strings strung up to the rafters. At the epicenter of the nave, radiating the visual horrors, stood an artist's easel surrounded by the paints, palettes, brushes and other tools of vivid creation. Next to that was some sort of computer for composing hologram mirages projected by a laser. There was also a sculptor's station for working in clay and resins, with miniature monster models to use as guides. What seemed to be an alchemist's table was off to one side, and closer inspection revealed that it was stocked with a pharmacopoeia of psychotropic drugs. Ecstasy. LSD. MDA. Crystal meth. Special K. GHB. Evidently, the goths liked to work zonked out of their skulls.

Then the chief noticed the pills near the mortar and pestle. Ecstasy and Viagra ground up together. Evidently, the goths liked to *play* zonked out of their skulls, too.

The security alarm kept shrilling.

"Can someone shut that racket off?" DeClercq hollered.

"I'm on it, Chief," said a constable.

Dividing the nave from the altar sanctuary was the chancel arch, symbolizing the sacrifice of Christ. DeClercq noticed a large desk sitting in the throat of the arch, flanked by two railings that had been carved from cedar logs in the shape of Christ's outstretched arms. Nails by the thousands were hammered along the wood, and squatting on each open palm was a statue of squid-faced Cthulhu.

The huge desk was actually two desks fused together like a pair of Siamese twins, so a pair of authors could write face to face and edit one another. On each half of the dual black onyx surfaces sat a laptop computer. Multiple copies of two novels lined the divider that halved the partners' desk. *Crown of Thorns* by Bret Lister, backed by *Halo of Flies* by Wes Grimmer.

The pulpit loomed up from the left front corner of the nave. Rounding the desk on its pulpit flank, DeClercq stepped into the sanctuary beyond the chancel arch.

It, too, had been defiled.

Instead of the three short steps that usually climb to the altar at the east end of a sanctuary, the headboard of a king-size bed abutted this holy of holies. On its reredos, the decorated wall backing the altar, the icon of Jesus on the cross had been inverted to resemble the Hanged Man, its nailed feet suspended from the rafters overhead. The rose window, with its tracery pattern of red glass the color of blood, framed Christ's head, already bloodied from the crown of thorns, like the nimbus on a Hanged Man tarot card.

The space below, which the cruciform icon had previously graced, flaunted a raunchy painting. A graphic depiction of a male and a female having sex, the legs of the male arched like those of a spider, the female spread below, her clitoris bearing a grinning death's head.

The altar itself was lined with bondage equipment: lots of leather, lots of studs, and lots of probes and prods that plumbed the darker depths of the sexual psyche. A CD player was flanked by piles of goth compact disks, labeled with the names of artists such as Alice Cooper, Alien Sex Fiend, Bauhaus, Black Sabbath, Joy Division, Marilyn Manson, Nine Inch Nails, Siouxsie and the Banshees, and the Cure.

There were quad speakers at the four corners of the bed, the sheets and pillows of which were black satin. Satan only knows what went on in this bed. But whatever it was, there were *three* partakers, for three indented pillows lined the bed's headboard.

Abruptly, the alarm stopped trilling and the lights were doused. The constable, it would seem, was no whiz kid. Careful not to ruin any latent fingerprints, DeClercq flicked a switch by the bed with his pen, hoping it would activate a separate circuit.

It did.

The effect was so dramatic that he quite literally jumped in the air. Out of the speakers came blasting Alice Cooper's "Bed of Nails." Lights of the weirdest kind exploded within the church. Infrared, ultraviolet and laser holograms. The mission was converted into a Gothic hell on earth, populated by the most obscene monsters imaginable. The black-lights hit the suspended paintings to bring them to life. If this was a glimpse of the reality of the occult realm, none but a damned psychotic would ever dare set eyes upon it. And as for the holograms, all were horrific mirages of bestial rape, with the same woman being ravaged by the horniest of hell's legions.

So why was her demeanor ecstatic?

Because *she* was the sexual predator?

It sure as hell looked that way.

The woman—whoever she was—was ravaging the monsters.

And if the woman in the holograms was the artist as well, the name she'd used to sign her self-portraits was the Goth.

DeClercq had noticed something when he jumped in the air out of shock. His feet thumping on the landing had caused a trapdoor set into the floor of the sanctuary to bounce. With his pen, he flicked off the switch to kill the music and lights, then, dropping down on his hands and knees, he called for a torch and pried open the lid.

What yawned below was a black well with a ladder of rungs down its wall.

A cop handed the chief a flashlight.

Down the well went DeClercq.

RAZOR BLADES

Tangaroa

Zinc was trapped in the nightmare of a thousand horror films. Someone is fleeing down the hall in a deserted or abandoned building, or someone is scrambling through a sludgy sewer underground, or someone is down on his hands and knees for a frantic crawl along the air ducts of a space station, while back there, hard on the heels of the fugitive lunch-meat, is a chainsaw-wielding hillbilly, or a toxic-waste-slobbering genetic freak, or a creature from another galaxy. With every roadblock encountered by its prey, the relentless monster draws inexorably closer. So how in hell does someone get out of this?

In Zinc's predicament, he was literally caught between a rock and a hard place. Having fled into this hole behind the throne of bones, the Mountie found himself dodging as fast as was feasible—and that wasn't nearly fast enough to gain headway—along a narrow tunnel that twisted and turned through the razor-sharp edges of the honeycombed coral in the bowels of the *makatea*. One slip, one trip, one stagger and stumble because of the uneven floor, and he would be sliced to ribbons by the limestone shredder.

Sort of like catching your thumb while grating cheese.

Except a shredder this big would strip him to the bone.

The torch was a blessing, and the torch was a hindrance. Lose the light and he would have to run this gauntlet blind, reducing his flesh to a skeleton with every flail in the dark. But to be the Olympic torch runner in this hell-bound tube was to light the tunnel for both Grimmer and himself.

Here I am.

All lit up.

Take your best shot.

All that kept the Mountie from taking a spear in the back were the twists and turns that had both men dodging. Hit a straightaway and Zinc might as well have a bull's-eye pinned to his spine.

Occasionally, a dark nook indented one of the walls. A cubby-hole, however, offered no sanctuary. Duck into one of the dents and he would be a dead duck, for sure. The torch would give him away.

Think! he thought.

Think . . .

Think . . .

Shit!

His internal compass had told him that they were in a loop. Just as Halley's comet has a string-of-pearls orbit around the sun, flying out into deep space before returning to our central light source about once every seventy-five years, so this tunnel had taken them out and away from the Kingdom of Bones, only to arc them back gradually to the other side of the cavern from which the chase had begun. Stretching ahead was the straightaway that Zinc feared, and it led to a bend at the far end with torchlight smudged on its curve.

Back to the cavern.

Back to Yvette.

Putting her back in danger.

Think! Zinc thought. Use what you have at hand.

A torch.

A knife.

A dent in the wall.

Hurling the torch as hard as he could toward the bend ahead, Zinc sidestepped into the nearest nook. Seconds later, the beam of Grimmer's flashlight swept around the final curve before the straightaway; it was followed by the spearman, hot on the Mountie's tail. Kicking his foot out from the dark hiding place into Wes's path, Zinc tripped his pursuer and sent him sprawling along the tunnel. The flashlight and the speargun clattered to the floor as Grimmer threw out both hands to bear the brunt of his fall. The lawyer hit the ground within reach of the weapon, and as Zinc came out of hiding to engage him, Wes pawed at the trigger grip with his bloody palms.

His palms, but not his fingers, for they were either dangling from the razor-blade walls or lying like cocktail sausages on the floor to either side.

Zinc gripped Grimmer by his shaved head and stabbed the blade into his back. The lawyer bellowed as the stainless steel sank deep, a snarl magnified by the cramped tube and echoing out in both directions up and down the tunnel. Again and again, the knife rose and fell, until there was no fight left in Zinc's adversary.

Two down.

None to go.

Time to free Yvette.

Gathering up the flashlight and the still-armed speargun, Zinc ventured on to the bend, which was illuminated by light flickering in from the remaining torch flanking the throne of bones. As he exited from the tunnel into the cavern, he caught a hint of something at the corner of his eye, a moment before he was clubbed unconscious by someone who had been waiting for the Mountie to emerge.

Lights out.

MISSIONARY POSITION

Mission

Down the rungs of the ladder, DeClercq sank into a perverse pit of someone's deviant sexuality. At one time, this had been a secret darkroom where that unholy degenerate had developed, printed and pinned up pornographic photos of naked Native kids being abused in the residential school's dormitories. It became obvious to DeClercq that the hand that took these pictures was also the hand that had once gripped the pulpit above as the priest preached his true gospel. The same hand had wielded the strap and a yardstick in the missionary school that the Native kids in these photos had attended. That hand had gripped the terrified hearts and minds of children who were forced to submit to rape and sodomy. The hand of the old missionary, who apparently used this dark hole to carry out his darkest ritualistic desires. Girls or boys, it didn't matter to the lecherous man of God, as long as he could fuck them with his staff and his rod, then pin these yellow, curling photos up on the wall as his masturbatory stimulant for in-between times.

As the Mountie focused his flashlight on this pitiful gallery, the beam picked out the picture of a pale-skinned little girl. She was the only Caucasoid kid among the Mongoloid faces, and DeClercq had no doubt who she was. At about the same time as the closing of Mission's residential schools had deprived the dirty old priest of his dormitory hunting ground, the deaths of his son and his daughter-in-law—the new blood in charge of the mission—in that highway crash had delivered their orphaned child into his perverted hands.

371

A pedophile is a pedophile for life, and without another channel for his lust, he had probably first raped her at a very tender age.

"Jesus Christ!" swore DeClercq as his foot hit bottom.

Caught in the pool of the flashlight beam as he swept it around the black hole to get his bearings was a figurative bed of nails upon which lay the decomposed remains of the lecherous old debaucher. Half-skeleton, half-mummy, the missionary was stretched out, faceup, in his tattered Bible-black suit on a foul mattress crusted with dried juice that had seeped from his desiccated flesh. The pants were torn open at the crotch to get at his groin, and what had been removed from between his legs with the vicious slice of a knife now hung on a crucifix that had been turned upside down on the wall over the head of the bed.

Approaching the corpse, the chief focused the beam on details.

The bony wrists of the missionary were lashed behind his back in the manner of the Hanged Man.

From his emasculated groin jutted a stiff black dildo instead of his penis, the artificial phallus fastened to the bed frame as if erect.

The lower jaw of the fleshless face hung open in a silent scream at whatever had immediately preceded his death. The scalp and its hair, however, still clung to the skull.

That the old priest had rotted away down here in a hellhole of his own making was obvious. But DeClercq grasped that he had descended into the hidden depths of another psyche as well—that of the old priest's granddaughter.

When God turned a blind eye to her repeated rapes at the hands of his pious servant, the child had turned to the elder gods of a faith antithetical to the one in which she was baptized. Years later, the Goth had wreaked revenge down here on her tormentor, and then blasphemed the church up above by conjuring the occult realm.

Down this well of her warped psyche, the Goth would sink every so often with her hammer and nails to assume the missionary position of psychosexual release. Here, with her legs spread wide and straddling the dildo, the Goth would fuck herself as frantically as her tormented soul demanded, and having recreated the ritual of abuse, she would hammer nail after nail into the old man's dead head.

The crown of his cracked skull had been replaced God knows how many times with a substitute of wood that had been covered with the scalp torn off the original bone.

Was she hammering in Christ's crown of thorns?

Was she hammering in the nimbus of the Hanged Man?

Perhaps it was both.

DeClercq couldn't tell.

But one thing was certain in his mind.

The Goth was out there, swimming with her own deep-seated monsters *way* beyond the reef.

BEYOND THE REEF

Tangaroa

Zinc has time-traveled back to 1779 in Kealakekua Bay, and here he sits in his red serge, among a squad of Royal Marines sporting the same color, in a rowboat that bobs in the surf just offshore as Captain Cook shoots a Hawaiian dead on the beach. What a change in the natives' attitude since Cook was first here earlier on the voyage, when he discovered this group of islands in the North Pacific while on his way to America to search for the elusive Northwest Passage. He called them the Sandwich Islands, for the Earl of Sandwich, first lord of the Admiralty, and when he landed on the beach of this Polynesian paradise, the Hawaiians fell flat at his feet as if he were a god.

The Arctic thwarted Cook as it had all others before him, so to loll away the winter in pleasanter climes before venturing to the West Coast for another attempt at the passage, the *Resolution* and the *Discovery* returned to the Sandwich Islands. What a spectacular sight it was for those tall ships to sail into Kealakekua Bay. They were met by nine thousand Hawaiians in fifteen hundred canoes, with hundreds more on surfboards or swimming in the sea like a school of fish, backed by thousands more lining the beaches. The return of Cook had lured the king himself out to greet him, and when the captain was escorted ashore by Koa, the high priest, Hawaiians by the thousands fell prostrate before him.

With the benefit of hindsight, Zinc grasps the undertones. Legend has it that Lono, the god of peace, happiness and agriculture, sailed away from these islands long ago, with a promise that one day he would return to Hawaii. News of the white man's landing a year ago had spread, so all the islanders were here to welcome their god home. What Cook failed to grasp at the ritualistic ceremony that followed his return was that he was being deified.

Unfortunately, the whites overstayed their welcome. The crews of the two ships ate a lot of food, while the continuing presence of this god in their midst diminished the power of the king and his priest. The island returned to normal once the ships sailed away, but now a damaged mast brought them back, and what was once worship of Cook turned to hatred.

A stolen rowboat was the catalyst for this clash. Cook reacted with the same tactic he'd used with good results in the South Pacific when some of his crewmen deserted on the first voyage. He went ashore with armed marines and seized the Hawaiian king to hold him hostage until the boat was returned.

At the moment, as Zinc sits bobbing in the surf offshore, Cook has managed to abduct the king as far as the beach, where he is currently surrounded by two to three thousand Hawaiians intent on stopping him. In a show of force meant to keep the mob at bay, the captain shoots one of the islanders dead with his pistol. Such is the awe in which Cook is still held by the natives that none will touch him face to face. But when he turns to summon this rowboat into shore, Cook is clubbed from behind by Koa, the high priest. That blow exposes the false god for the mortal he really is, and now the enraged islanders fall upon Cook in droves, stabbing him repeatedly with their knives as he flounders in the shallows.

The marines in the boat with Zinc open fire.

The fighting onshore is hand-to-hand.

The surf around them reddens from the bloodbath.

Zinc must have time-warped forward to escape from the battle, for suddenly he is standing on the deck of the *Resolution* six days later. Hoping to save the island from shelling by the ships' cannons, Koa has delivered all that can be found of Cook's remains. The Hawaiians' belief that some of his bones might hold magical power resulted in the dismemberment of the captain's body, so what the

British have for burial at sea is Cook's skull, some leg and arm bones, and his hands. That the remains are genuine is proved by one of the hands, which was disfigured way back in 1764 by a powder horn explosion off Newfoundland.

It occurs to Zinc as he stares at Cook's bones that there is a moral here: when true believers believe they have encountered the supernatural in the real world, that break with reality can get you killed . . .

Too many bones.

For with each echo of that moral in his mind, Zinc sees the bones in front of his eyes double in number, until he's engulfed by them. . . .

———◆———

Throbbing pain at the back of his head kept blurring the Mountie's vision, but eventually it focused on the scads of skulls around him—each one lit up like a jack-o'-lantern, with candles in its eye sockets and slack-jawed mouth—covering the walls, lining the pillars and molded into a throne.

This nightmare that was the Kingdom of Bones turned darker when Zinc tried to move. His wrists were tied together in the small of his back. He had been dragged from the mouth of the tunnel, where the blow to his head had occurred, across the floor of the skeletal cavern to the center of the *marae*. Here he lay, faceup, like some impending blood sacrifice to the elder gods. And once he realized that one of his legs had been tied across the other to mimic the Hanged Man, Zinc grasped that a sacrifice was exactly what he had become.

But a sacrifice for whom?

Still dazed, he looked around.

And that's when he glimpsed her, lurking like a trapdoor spider in the darkness of one of the tunnels. Only as she skulked out of the wormhole and into the flickering glow cast by the skulls did he spot the hammer in one hand, the fistful of nails in the other and the diver's knife gripped in her teeth like a pirate's cutlass.

The Goth glared down hungrily at her next meal. Did the man meat see her grin behind the horizontal blade? *Clang!* She dropped the hammer to one side of his head. *Clink, clink, clink, clink, clink . . .* She let the fistful of nails rain down to the other. Then, crouching, she withdrew the blade from between her teeth, letting it *squeeeak* like fingernails scraping on a blackboard as she tugged it sideways across her enamel. The cop winced from the nerve-shredding noise and tried to cower farther away as she slit the side of his trunks. A firm yank whipped his swimsuit off like a diaper from a baby.

"There," she said. "That's better."

A few strokes and the Mountie was rock hard in her hand. As hard as her grandfather used to get in his living years, and as hard as the dildo that now jutted up from his ghastly remains.

"It's no use trying to fight it. You're no match for Viagra. That's a powerful cocktail coursing through your veins. Viagra is formulated for limp dicks. It works by boosting the blood supply to flaccid flesh. Give it to a virile stud in the overdose that I jabbed into you, and the result is that your cock will still be stiff long after you're gone."

The Goth bent down and bit into the Mountie's chest. She ripped a morsel of flesh away from one of the lacerations he had gained during his grim squeeze through the *makatea* crawlway.

"You taste good."

Blood dribbled down the chin of the cannibal queen.

"You're trying to piece it together. I see it in your eyes. You fear you're going to die without knowing why. Don't fret. That's not going to happen. Why? Because the reason you're here *is* you. I promised to tell you. That was the deal.

"The only way it all makes sense is by lateral thinking. Don't look for logic in anything we did other than creating a setup that would lure you here.

"Why kill Romeo Cardoza at the Lions Gate? Sure, the film *Bed of Nails* created a convenient smokescreen to buy time for the rest of my plan to unfold. And yes, the bar full of hookers and pushers offered us an ideal hunting ground—not to mention the fact that you took off after that other pair all because they sold him the blow the three of us snorted upstairs. No, the real reason for snuffing a Hollywood producer was to bring in the Special External Section of the RCMP. And because *you* were the cop who had dealt with the Tarot back in the days of the Ripper's reign of terror on Deadman's Island, the Cardoza killing was sure to attract *you*.

"There, the hook was baited."

The Goth, still stroking Zinc's engorged penis, turned and blew a gory kiss from her sanguine lips at the skewered remains of Bret Lister, who was slumped against the wall.

"We killed Cardoza, Bret and I. Which gave him the inspiration to write *Crown of Thorns* and *Halo of Flies* jointly with Wes, and gave me the inspiration for the paintings you saw—signed by the Goth—in the gallery at the convention.

"Get the picture?" she asked.

"It took a year and a half to put that together. Then, last Friday in Seattle, Wes and I waylaid a man we chose at random, spiking his head upside down on a stake outside Ted Bundy's house and hanging the rest of him like the Hanged Man at the bottom of the Thirteen Steps to Hell in Maltby Cemetery. Why, you wonder? For two reasons. The similarity with the Cardoza hanging was sure to bring you to Seattle. And with Ted Bundy's house on the ghost tour and Maltby Cemetery pinpointed in the program, you were bound to end up at the horror convention, where we were waiting for you.

"There, the hook was in.

"*Crown of Thorns* and his previous psych remand were certain to make Bret your prime suspect. But he had an alibi for Friday night. So that was sure to shift your suspicion to Wes and his *Halo of Flies*. But when Bret nailed the Cthulhu artist during the masquerade, Wes had an alibi. They couldn't be in it together. They hated each other too much, as everyone—including you—witnessed in their bitter rivalry at the convention. No way would Bret allow himself to be so humiliated in public unless their literary animosity was real. So the only avenue left for you to smoke out the Tarot killer was to join the Odyssey, which was about to fly off to the Cook Islands.

"We knew you'd go, of course. How could you not? It was already in the papers—if you read between the lines—that you were taking a trip to the South Pacific on forced medical leave. The Cook Islands offered you a chance to kill three birds with one stone. Coming here would keep your boss happy, would allow you to investigate Bret and Wes together in a closed environment, and would let you play the protecting hero in a South Seas romance.

"So here you are. Exactly where I planned. The whole affair, from start to finish, was a trap for *you*."

Like all psychotics in a borderline state, the Goth was teetering on the brink. Her words seemed rational, but she struggled to get them out, and the stink oozing out of her betrayed the chemical changes taking place beneath her skin. There was a battle going on inside between Jekyll and Hyde, her latent psychosis threatening to turn florid at any moment, and the outcome of that was bound to be the eating-up of the Eloi surface she wore for the masquerade of so-called reality by the Morlock that was lusting for blood deep in the pit of her brain.

Her crazed eyes locked on Zinc's drug-swollen penis, and her bloodred lips pulled back from her teeth.

"My, my, Grandpa, what a big cock you have.

"All the better to nail you, Little Red Riding Hood.

"No, no, Grandpa. I'm the one with the nails."

And then it was gone, that ominous shadow that had passed behind the dilated pupils of her wild, glittering eyes.

"*Ssssex,*" sibilated the Goth, hissing like that sexual serpent did in biblical Eden. "What won't a man do if given the opportunity to indulge in his wildest fantasies with the wanton woman of his darkest, deepest desires?

"I met Bret years ago, when he was a lawyer crusading for Native victims of sex abuse at missionary schools. My grandfather was guilty of that when he ran True Gospel Mission. My family had been missionaries among the cannibals on Tangaroa in the 1800s— that's our first mission church out on the lagoon—so I had heard tales of the Kingdom of Bones for as long as I can remember. After

Bret's breakdown from overwork and his lockup in the psych ward on Colony Farm, we got together and fucked our brains out for mutual therapy. I told him I wished to see this cave, so he brought me here, and that's when he told me about meeting the Ripper on Colony Farm, and that Jack knew how to open the door to the occult realm."

The Goth swept her knife hand around to encompass the Kingdom of Bones.

"Have you ever wondered what it's like to swim beyond the reef? To relinquish the safety of the lagoon that lulls little people to sleep in favor of a journey into the occult realm of the elder gods, a dimension so wondrous in the power it holds over us that reality is but a weak reflection of what it casts away? The Tarot holds its secret. The Magick is in the cards. The Bible is nothing but a shield to protect those who are afraid to look from what they're afraid to see. Imagine the freedom to be lived if you could cast aside all taboos.

"What would you do for that?

"I'd do *anything*.

"So back we went to Atiu to head home, and that's when Bret got struck by lightning, just like in the Tower, the Broken House, card sixteen in a tarot deck. The card denotes sudden change, and that's what came about. Bret was in the hospital, unable to move. After Bret's breakdown, Wes had taken over his law practice. Bret had referred the Ripper to Wes as a client, so I phoned Wes from the hospital and he flew to the Cooks. We made arrangements to get Bret home. Then we stayed on, and for the next two weeks, Wes discovered sex. What it took with him was finding the right combination of drugs. All I asked in return was a favor. Get me in to meet the Ripper.

"That, of course, was easy. Wes made me a paralegal. The Ripper has yet to be tried for the carnage on Deadman's Island, and periodically he comes up for a fitness review. The psych ward can't deny him access to his lawyer, or to his lawyer's paralegal. So I went in under the pretext of working on his case. Since then, there's been the danger that you might find my name on the Ripper's visitors' list. But if so, I figured that would only yank the hook in deeper. When I fed you clues at the horror convention, you didn't rise to that bait.

"There's not much more to tell you. The Ripper gave me the key to the occult realm, and Bret and I unlocked the door by killing Cardoza in the right way to sign the symbols in the Hanged Man in blood. Open the wormhole to those wonders and you are 'born again' a thousand times more profoundly than any Bible-thumper can grasp. Lovecraft got it onto paper in 'Pickman's Model.' In order to capture the occult realm in your art, you must reflect the experience of witnessing it yourself. I did—and do, whenever I want—and you saw what I see in my painting *Morlocks,* on display in the Morbid Maze at the Seattle convention. Bret did too. Read his books. Both *Crown of Thorns* and *Halo of Flies* come from the other side.

"It was Bret's idea to bring Wes into our unholy bed. Bret got off on the three-way sex we had with Cardoza, and Wes was searching for a father figure to fill the void created by the real one who hanged himself. Any man I fuck stays fucked forever. Once in, Wes wanted in all the way, so we wrote him into the plot we had hatched to lure you here.

"It was my idea that they split up Bret's novels, then have a falling-out. Publishing thrives on publicity hooks. You saw the effect the rivalry had at the convention. People flocked to see if Bret would try to punch out Wes. Eventually, the last laugh would be Bret's, when it was revealed that he was the author of *both* books. It's like the guy who sent *War and Peace* around to several publishers under a different title and got back a slew of rejections. The same with Faulkner's *The Reivers.* Or *A Confederacy of Dunces.* The author killed himself when he couldn't get into print, and it went on to win the Pulitzer Prize. The Hitler diaries? The 'autobiography' of Howard Hughes? A dupe or a hoax gets attention.

"Poor Bret."

The Goth glanced back at him.

"You ruined his master plan.

"You seem to make a habit of ruining master plans. The hatred the Ripper has for you goes beyond the wrath of God. I grew up on sermons about the fire and brimstone of hell. But that's nothing compared with what the Ripper wants done to you, and that's what I owe him for giving me the key. Revenge is a dish best served cold, he says, so I was free to take my time in luring you here.

"Why here?

"Look around. You're in the charnel house of the elder gods. How many souls in torment abandoned these bones? How much *mana* did the cannibals who created this *marae* consume in here? Is this not a Magick place, like Jack the Ripper's Room 13 in Miller's Court? The symbols in the Hanged Man needn't be signed in blood at a Magick place to conjure a complete cycle of occult manifestation, but how much more powerful will the experience be if they *are*? We're going to find out, you and me, by sacrificing you to the Tarot. For every nail hammered into the nimbus around your head—and they're short enough to just pierce your brain—we're going to eat a piece of raw meat cut out of you.

"All they're going to find of you is your skeleton. As for me, not a trace will remain in the here and now. I was born out of time in a banal and mundane age, and now that I have all the time in the world, I'm off to live it, and I'm not coming back. Your bones will make the news, and the news will reach the Ripper. And if you concentrate real hard, I'll bet you can hear his laughter."

The Goth began to chuckle.

The stench of goat cheese permeated the grotto.

She let go of Zinc's petrified cock and cast aside the knife. Then she stood up and shucked off the top of her blue bikini.

"I said that if you played your cards right, you'd get to see my tattoo. Well, here it is."

The Goth stripped off the bottoms.

———— ·•·•· ————

The lashings that tied Zinc's hands and feet were those that had appeared to tie Yvette to the throne of skulls. In a bid to buy time so he could free himself from the biting ropes, the Mountie had kept his mouth shut while Yvette played the Ripper's mouthpiece.

But it was of no use. He was bound too tightly. His wrists were cinched together beneath him in the small of his back, and the ankle of his straight leg was fastened to some sort of natural cleat on the floor.

He couldn't get loose.

This nightmare had turned Freudian with the baring of her tattoo. Not a mark marred the rest of Yvette's flawless body, but her vulva was shaved as hairless as that of a virginal little girl, and etched into the skin around the maw of her vagina was the wormhole mouth of Great Cthulhu—Lovecraft's elder god—whose tattooed tentacle face seemed to writhe like Medusa's snakes in place of her pubic hair.

And now the Freudian monster was going for Zinc's cock.

Straddling his groin with her legs spread, Yvette squatted down to within an inch of him. She hovered over his Viagra-induced erection like the sexual image in Petra's *Jaws of Death* turned upside down. One hand reached out to fetch the hammer that was waiting beside his head, while the other hand selected one of the short nails. The point pricked into his forehead above the center of his eyes, and aiming its trajectory to slam the head of the nail, Yvette raised the hammer.

"Never judge a book by its cover," she said. "Didn't you learn that at the WHC convention? All those normal-looking fans who transformed into the *outré* for the masquerade. Petra might not remember meeting me at Bible camp, but I remember her. Chilliwack and Mission are cheek by jowl in the Bible Belt. She fit the goth stereotype, so you thought she *was* a goth. But what's on the surface isn't always what's inside. I used Petra to blind you concerning me. To be a goth isn't a fashion statement. It's a state of mind."

Her eyes went dead.

The shadow within was back.

"Take this, Grandpa!"

And in went the spike.

So powerful was the pneumatic force of the speargun that it drove the shaft through Yvette's head and spiked the barb out between her blue eyes. The force propelled her forward as she crashed down dead on Zinc, so she failed to spike herself on his penis as planned, and the barb jutting out of her plunging face missed spiking his own head by inches. The hammer clanged down to spray chips of the *marae* at his cheek, and the nail rolled safely off his temple.

The speargun gripped in Petra's shaking hands was the same one Zinc had seized from Wes's corpse and dropped at the exit from the tunnel when Yvette knocked him unconscious. She loomed above the Mountie like a catatonic female William Tell, her heart racing in the cage beneath her heaving breasts and her muscles twitching from tension pent up by what she had done.

"I killed her," Petra said, as if doubting the fact. Her tone was flat. Her stare was blank. Her face jerked from side to side.

"Good," Zinc soothed. "Now get her off me."

Breathing raggedly and moving like a zombie, Petra grabbed hold of Yvette's hair and hauled her from his body.

"Untie me," Zinc said.

The goth queen didn't move. Still shuddering, she stood staring at his drug-engorged erection.

"Easy, Petra. Easy. Let the tension go."

"I can't."

"Yes, you can. Let it out."

Her eyes were still locked on his penis. She nodded her head. Sex and death were her fantasy. Now they were hers in real life.

"Let's work it out," she said.

And untied her bikini bottoms.

"You may not want me," she said, straddling him. "But I want you," she added. "And the way I see it, lover. You *owe* me."

EPILOGUE

STACKED DECK

He was called the Congo Man by staff who worked at the Forensic Psychiatric Hospital on Colony Farm because he was a refugee from war-torn Africa. In fact, the Congo Man wasn't from the Congo Basin or one of the countries that takes its name from that African river. He was from Liberia—at least as near as immigration authorities could tell, since he had fled to Canada with just the clothes on his back—but Rudi Lucke had experienced Carnival in the Caribbean a few years ago, where he had heard that calypso tune by Mighty Sparrow, and because the lyrics about never eating white meat yet seemed to fit the crime that had brought the landed refugee to FPH, Congo Man was a sobriquet that seemed to sum him up.

The Congo Man was a King Kong of muscular power. Politically correct that metaphor wasn't, but in the fantasies that ruled Rudi's secret life, he saw himself as Fay Wray in the giant's massive grip. The Congo Man had arms as big as most men's legs. The Congo Man had a chest that would fit shirts from Jones's Tent and Awning. The Congo Man had a head that made a bowling ball look the size of a pea.

The charge against the Congo Man was that he had cooked a child in a canning pot. The trial had become a *cause célèbre* fueled by the lurid details of the murder: the girl, being white, conjured up countless cartoons from the last century depicting pale explorers bubbling in black cannibal pots.

From 1989 to 1997, Liberia had drowned in the blood of a vicious civil war. Backed by a culture based on warrior initiation, secret Leopard Societies and human sacrifice, seven warlords had used every weapon at their disposal—including sorcery, blood-drinking and cannibalism—to slaughter opponents in merciless bids to seize control of the country. Young fighters, stoned on drugs and alcohol, were encouraged to assimilate the power of the slain by eating parts of them. As for the Leopard Societies, who knows what went down in their secret rites, but the allegation is that after Charles Taylor clawed his way to the top in 1997, he oversaw the torture, dismemberment and cannibalization of enemy soldiers within the presidential palace.

The Congo Man, the prosecution had submitted, was not a refugee who left such horrors behind. Instead, because he suffered from a disease of the mind, he came to Canada and cooked up a recipe for disaster that involved a boiled child in a pot.

So incensed had been the trial judge by the inflammatory facts that she had flouted the law to put the Congo Man away. British Columbia's courts have a nasty habit of assigning judges with no criminal experience to high-profile cases. The case was a minefield of evidentiary problems. The Congo Man had been one of the homeless living on the streets. The pot in which the girl was cooking was found under a bridge. A dearth of credible testimony linked the Congo Man to the pot. The little there was came from a camp of drunken bums. Not only had the accused refused to confess to police, but he had refused to speak to pretrial psychiatrists as well. The shrinks were left to psych him from the details of the crime, a crime that the Crown could barely pin on him.

None of that had concerned the trial judge in the least. She'd been a whiz at real-estate transactions in her day, so she knew how to close a tricky deal. In the end—she *was* the judge—she had shipped the Congo Man to FPH to get his head shrunk.

All of that, however, had concerned the court of appeal. Less than two hours ago, in a stinging judgment, their lordships had overturned the shaky verdict against the Congo Man and ordered the mental hospital to turn him loose.

The Congo Man was about to fly over the cuckoo's nest.

"You look relaxed," DeClercq said.

"I am," replied Chandler.

"So tell me, what did you do after that mess on Tangaroa?"

"Went to Aitutaki. You should see the lagoon. It's unarguably the most beautiful in the world."

"Sandbars?"

"You bet. As far as your eye can see. And not a Friday footprint to crowd you off."

"Blue water?"

"Turquoise. Aquamarine. *Blue*'s too mundane a word for what we snorkeled."

"*We?*"

"Uh-huh."

"We as in *she?*"

The inspector winked.

"Ah, Tantric yoga. No wonder you're so relaxed. It's amazing what five weeks of sexual healing in the sun will do."

"I'm a new man."

"Does she have a name?"

"Yes. But you'd recognize it."

"Is there a future?"

"I doubt it. We have only one thing in common."

"So that's it?"

"Not quite. There'll be a sequel. Same time next year."

"In the Cook Islands?"

"Or somewhere hot. We're going to meet once a year—and only once a year—until the fun burns out."

"So tell me how it happened."

"I took someone else's advice."

"What advice?"

"'Don't judge a book by its cover.'"

"And?"

"I didn't. Once she took the cover off."

This conversation took place as both Mounties drove from Special X to Colony Farm in the chief's aging Benz on Chandler's first day back at work from his South Seas odyssey. It was a glorious spring day of hot sunshine that piqued erotic memories in Zinc's mind of canoeing out to a pristine sandbar surrounded by dazzling fish to make tropical love under coconut palms that might drop a nut on your head.

Live dangerously, he thought.

At the end of the eeriest mile on the West Coast, DeClercq parked his car in the hospital lot. As they climbed out of the vehicle to approach the modern gates, a raven like those that once haunted the Gothic eaves of the old Riverside asylum landed on the fence.

"'"Take thy beak from out of my heart, and take thy form from off my door!" Quoth the Raven, "Nevermore,"'" Chandler quoted from Edgar Allan Poe.

"He may not agree to see us."

"As long as he sees me. I want him to know I'm alive and kicking, despite his puppetry."

"It's no use charging him. He's not fit to stand trial. The Ripper is about as mad as any man can be. Even if he stood trial, he would have an ironclad defense of insanity. The result is that he'd end up exactly where he is. It's a dead end, Zinc."

"And *I'm* the end he wants dead. It's as if the sword of Damocles is poised over my head. There it hangs by a thread, and any day it could fall, depending on the string-pulling by the Ripper."

"We can't deny him a lawyer. He has a right to counsel. FPH is a hospital, not a jail. So we can't cut him off from access to other patients. And as for that occult tarot deck of his, the Charter of Rights protects his freedom of religion."

"We're thwarted."

"The Ripper holds all the cards."

"How long do you think till he comes after me again?"

"Only time will tell."

Having cleared security at Central Control in the Birch Unit, they waited for a nurse to come from Ash 2. The nurse who fetched them was Rudi Lucke, but the message he brought from the Ripper was a negative one.

"He won't see you."

"Where is he now?" Zinc asked.

"Outside, in the airing court that opens off Ash 2."

"Can we get a look at him?"

"Follow me."

They tailed the nurse along a hallway and through a security door, then angled into a corridor with Lexan windows down one side. Beyond that see-through barrier lay a sunny exercise yard, with basketball hoops and a volleyball net for the athletically inclined. For those who wished simply to hang out, there were benches and sun umbrellas.

"Who's the black guy?" Zinc asked.

"We call him the Congo Man. The court of appeal overturned his verdict. He gets out today."

"Christ, get in a fight with him and you might as well have Tyson going for your ear."

The Congo Man straddled a bench facing the Ripper. If that bench were a teeter-totter, the gravity of the black man would launch the white man into outer space.

The Ripper turned.

Had he read Zinc's mind?

Or was it their movements in the hall that caught his attention?

For a moment, the Mountie and the psychotic locked eyes.

Then the Ripper grinned and ran a finger meaningfully across his throat.

The Congo Man and the Ripper shared an interest in Magick. That's why the African had come out to bid farewell to the psycho. Their conversation yesterday had revolved around the *borfimor* of the Leopard Men, the "medicine" bag of each Liberian secret society that spiked a man's virility if it was anointed with human fat boiled down in a pot. They were soldiers of misfortune, that ragtag army of teenage killers who fought a war with red scarves, dark glasses and AK-47s. The Poro was the "bush school" where elders taught them the ancient ways, like how to use a leopard knife—a two-pronged weapon with double-edged blades set at an angle into the handle—to rip out an enemy's throat. The "bush devil" had to be fed, so they ate human meat from the same pot that had boiled and annointed the *borfimor*.

The Ripper had listened.

This morning, it was his turn to confide secrets. The Congo Man's imminent release meant there was much to tell, so as the African's eyes grew wide with lust for the power to time-travel through the occult realm and beyond, the Ripper told the cannibal about the key that was hidden in one of the cards of the Major Arcana.

"What card?" the man-eater asked.

"The Hanged Man."

"Give me the key?"

"Only if you're chosen."

"How?" asked the cannibal.

"The Magick is in the cards. If you deserve the power, the Hanged Man will choose you."

On the bench between their groins, the Ripper stacked the twenty-two cards of his tarot deck. His fingers fanned the facedown spread with the deftness of a gambler on a Mississippi steamboat.

"Pick a card," he said.

The Congo Man picked a card.

"Turn it over."

The cannibal flipped the card.

The card was the Hanged Man.

"You are chosen."

"Give me the key."

"If you'll do something for me."

"What?" asked the African.

The Ripper leaned over to whisper in the larger man's ear.

The Congo Man wore a black patch over the socket that had lost its eye during the Liberian civil war. His other eye, however, was able to take in Zinc.

"Is that a deal?" the Ripper asked.

The Congo Man nodded. He listened intently while the psychotic showed him the Magick key in the Hanged Man card, then he got up from the bench and lumbered off toward the two FPH guards who would soon release him from the psych ward's walls.

Watching him depart, the Ripper scooped his tarot deck from the bench and fanned the cards out, facing him, like a poker hand. Of the twenty-two different cards that should make up the Major Arcana, all twenty-two in the Ripper's deck were the Hanged Man.

Pocketing the stacked deck, he stood up and glanced blankly in Zinc's direction as he walked across the exercise yard to return to his room. The wicked grin still curled his lips, but his eyes now lacked the spark of consciousness.

The Ripper wasn't here.

The Ripper was gone.

His mind was time-traveling back to London in 1888 so that— for the umpteenth time since he had been locked away on Colony Farm—the Ripper could relive that delicious night of Jack the Ripper's "double event."

———— ·+·— ————

As I draw the knife across her neck, the clock strikes one, a single *bong* from St. Mary's Whitechapel, here in the East End. . . .

AUTHOR'S NOTE

This is a work of fiction. The plot and characters are a product of
the author's imagination. Where real persons, places or institutions
are incorporated to create the illusion of authenticity, they are used
fictitiously. Inspiration was drawn from the following non-fiction
sources:

Askenasy, Hans. *Cannibalism from Sacrifice to Survival.* New York:
  Prometheus, 1994.

Barker, Francis, Peter Hulme and Margaret Iversen, eds.
  Cannibalism and the Colonial World. Cambridge: Cambridge
  University Press, 1998.

Beaglehole, J. C. *The Life of Captain James Cook.* London: Black,
  1974.

Begg, Paul, Martin Fido and Keith Skinner. *The Jack the Ripper A
  to Z.* London: Headline, 1991.

Boga, Steven. *Caving.* Mechanicsberg, PA: Stackpole Books, 1997.

Charlton, James, and Lisbeth Mark. *The Writer's Home Companion.*
  New York: Penguin, 1989.

Cherrington, John. *Mission on the Fraser.* Vancouver: Mitchell Press,
  1974.

Cullen, Tom. *Autumn of Terror: The Crimes and Times of Jack the
  Ripper.* London: Bodley Head, 1965.

Daily Telegraph (Sydney). *Captain Cook: His Artists, His Voyages.*
  Sydney: Australian Consolidated Press, 1970.

Davenport-Hines, Richard. *Gothic: 400 Years of Excess, Horror, Evil
  and Ruin.* London: Fourth Estate, 1998.

Davies, Paul. *How to Build a Time Machine*. London: Allen Lane, 2001.

Davis, Richard, ed. *The Encyclopedia of Horror*. London: Octopus, 1981.

Editors of Consumer Guide. *The Best, Worst, and Most Unusual: Horror Films*. New York: Beekman House, 1983.

Evans, Stewart P., and Keith Skinner. *The Ultimate Jack the Ripper Companion: An Illustrated Encyclopedia*. New York: Carroll and Graf, 2000.

Gaute, J. H. H., and Robin Odell. *Murder "Whatdunit": An Illustrated Account of the Methods of Murder*. London: Pan, 1984.

———. *The Murderers' Who's Who*. Montreal: Optimum, 1979.

Gill, William Wyatt. *Cook Islands Custom*. Suva: University of the South Pacific, 1979.

Gilson, Richard. *The Cook Islands 1820–1950*. Wellington, NZ: Victoria University Press, 1980.

Gonzales, Henry. "Spooky Guide to the Seattle Area." *World Horror Convention—Seattle 2001 Program Guide*.

Haining, Peter. *The Flesh Eaters: True Stories of Cannibals and Blood Drinkers*. London: Boxtree, 1994.

———. *A Pictorial History of Horror Stories: Two Hundred Years of Spine-Chilling Illustrations from the Pulp Magazines*. London: Treasure Press, 1985.

Haining, Peter, ed. *The H. G. Wells Scrapbook*. London: New English Library, 1978.

Harris, Melvin. *The True Face of Jack the Ripper*. London: O'Mara, 1994.

Hawking, Stephen. *A Brief History of Time*. New York: Bantam, 1998.

Hogg, Garry. *Cannibalism and Human Sacrifice*. London: Pan, 1961.

Honeycombe, Gordon. *The Murders of the Black Museum*. London: Hutchinson, 1982.

Ivanovic, Vane. *Modern Spearfishing*. Chicago: Henry Regnery, 1975.

Kaplan, Stuart R. *The Encyclopedia of Tarot*. New York: U.S. Games Systems, 1978.

Kautai, Ngatupuna, et al. *Atiu: An Island Community*. Suva: University of the South Pacific, 1984.

Keller, Nancy, and Tony Wheeler. *Rarotonga and the Cook Islands*. Hawthorne: Lonely Planet, 1998.

Kendall, Elizabeth. *The Phantom Prince: My Life with Ted Bundy*. Seattle: Madrona, 1981.

King, Stephen. *Danse Macabre*. New York: Everest House, 1981.

Knight, Stephen. *Jack the Ripper: The Final Solution*. St. Albans, UK: Panther, 1977.

Korn, Daniel, Mark Radice and Charlie Hawes. *Cannibal: The History of the People-Eaters*. London: Channel 4 Books, 2001.

Lestringant, Frank. *Cannibals: The Discovery and Representation of the Cannibals from Columbus to Jules Verne*. Cambridge: Polity Press, 1997.

MacLean, Alistair. *Captain Cook*. London: Collins, 1972.

Maretu. *Cannibals and Converts*. Suva: University of the South Pacific, 1983.

Marriner, Brian. *Cannibalism: The Last Taboo!* London: Random House, 1997.

Martingale, Moira. *Cannibal Killers: The History of Impossible Murderers*. New York: Carroll and Graf, 1994.

Odell, Robin. *Jack the Ripper in Fact and Fiction*. London: Harrap, 1965.

Pollack, Rachel. *The Complete Illustrated Guide to Tarot*. Boston: Element, 1999.

Publications International, Ltd. *Crimes of the 20th Century: A Chronology*. Lincolnwood, IL: Publications International, Ltd., 1991.

Rienits, Rex, and Thea Rienits. *The Voyages of Captain Cook*. London: Hamlyn, 1968.

Rule, Ann. *The Stranger Beside Me: Updated Twentieth Anniversary Edition*. New York: Norton, 2000.

Rumbelow, Donald. *The Complete Jack the Ripper*. London: W. H. Allen, 1975.

Ryan, Paddy. *The Snorkeller's Guide to the Coral Reef: From the Red Sea to the Pacific Ocean.* Honolulu: University of Hawaii Press, 1994.

Sagan, Eli. *Cannibalism: Human Aggression and Cultural Form.* Santa Fe: Fishdrum, 1994.

Salmi, Brian. "Hooker History." *The Georgia Straight* (Nov. 2–9, 2000).

Sartore, Richard L. *Humans Eating Humans: The Dark Shadow of Cannibalism.* Notre Dame, IN: Cross Roads Books, 1994.

Schechter, Harold, and David Everitt. *The A to Z Encyclopedia of Serial Killers.* New York: Pocket Books, 1996.

Schiff, Gert. *Images of Horror and Fantasy.* New York: Abrams, 1978.

Schroeder, Andreas. *Carved from Wood: Mission, B.C. 1861–1992.* Mission, B.C.: Mission Foundation, 1991.

Simpson, A. W. Brian. *Cannibalism and the Common Law.* Chicago: University of Chicago Press, 1984.

Skal, David J. *The Monster Show: A Cultural History of Horror.* New York: Faber and Faber, 2001.

Stonehouse, David. "Traveling through Time." *The Vancouver Sun* (Mar. 2, 2002).

Sullivan, Jack, ed. *The Penguin Encyclopedia of Horror and the Supernatural.* New York: Viking, 1996.

Suthren, Victor. *To Go upon Discovery: James Cook and Canada from 1758–1779.* Toronto: Dundurn Press, 2000.

Tannahill, Reay. *Flesh and Blood: A History of the Cannibal Complex.* London: Abacus, 1996.

Taylor, Michael Ray. *Caves: Exploring Hidden Realms.* Washington, D.C.: National Geographic, 2000.

Trow, M. J. *The Many Faces of Jack the Ripper.* Chichester, UK: Summersdale, 1997.

Veillette, John, and Gary White. *Early Indian Village Churches: Wooden Frontier Architecture in British Columbia.* Vancouver: University of British Columbia, 1977.

Waite, Arthur Edward. *The Pictorial Key to the Tarot.* New York: Harper and Row, 1971.

Weinberg, Robert. *Horror of the 20th Century: An Illustrated History.* Portland, OR: Collectors Press, 2000.

Whittington-Egan, Richard. *A Casebook on Jack the Ripper.* London: Wildly, 1976.

Wilson, Colin. *Mysteries: An Investigation into the Occult, the Paranormal and the Supernatural.* London: Granada, 1979.

————. *The Occult.* New York: Vintage, 1973.

Wilson, Colin, and Robin Odell. *Jack the Ripper: Summing Up and Verdict.* London: Corgi, 1988.

Wilson, Colin, and Patricia Pitman. *Encyclopedia of Murder.* London: Pan, 1964.

Wilson, Colin, and Donald Seaman. *Encyclopedia of Modern Murder 1962–1983.* London: Pan, 1986.

Wolf, Leonard. *Horror: A Connoisseur's Guide to Literature and Film.* New York: Facts on File, 1989.

Slade was a guest of honor at the real-life World Horror Convention in Seattle. During a panel discussion on "How to Write a Horror Best-seller: Is There a Demon You Can Sell Your Soul To?" I accepted the challenge of a gentlemen's bet to construct a novel around three words: "Ted Bundy's house." You have just read the result. The WHC is Slade's kind of group. To my knowledge, there has never been a killer in our midst.

Though inspired by an underground crawl through one of the burial caves on Atiu (in the course of which my palm got pierced by an ancient rib bone), the Kingdom of Bones and the island of Tangaroa don't exist. Cook Islanders make no bones about their cannibal past, but—and I've done a lot of traveling—they won my vote as the friendliest people on earth.

Slade
Vancouver, B.C.